THE ENEMY WITHIN

ROB SINCLAIR

Boldwood

First published in Great Britain in 2025 by Boldwood Books Ltd.

Copyright © Rob Sinclair, 2025

Cover Design by Head Design Ltd

Cover Images: FigureStock and iStock

A CIP catalogue record for this book is available from the British Library.

Paperback ISBN 978-1-83561-833-2

Large Print ISBN 978-1-83561-834-9

Hardback ISBN 978-1-83561-832-5

Ebook ISBN 978-1-83561-835-6

Kindle ISBN 978-1-83561-836-3

Audio CD ISBN 978-1-83561-827-1

MP3 CD ISBN 978-1-83561-828-8

Digital audio download ISBN 978-1-83561-830-1

This book is printed on certified sustainable paper. Boldwood Books is dedicated to putting sustainability at the heart of our business. For more information please visit https://www.boldwoodbooks.com/about-us/sustainability/

Boldwood Books Ltd, 23 Bowerdean Street, London, SW6 3TN

www.boldwoodbooks.com

PROLOGUE

The vibrating phone roused him from his restful sleep. The continued blackness in the room was the first clue that something wasn't right. There weren't many reasons for a late-night call. He reached out to the nightstand and grasped for the phone.

But the screen was black and the vibrating continued.

Not that phone. The other one.

A shot of clarity spun through his mind, pulling him further from sleep and into reality. He put the idle phone down and turned to his side to reach down and open the bottom drawer of the nightstand. He fumbled around at the back until his hand found the thrumming device.

He pulled the phone out and for a couple of seconds the flashing screen lit up the room in ugly green light.

'What?'

No introductions necessary. Only two people had this number.

'I got your message.'

'OK?'

'It's over. Clean up tonight.'

He sighed and worked the words over in his head for a couple of beats.

'Clean up... everything?'

'We have no choice. I'll explain after. But you don't have much time. Get it done now. Clean the whole house. Everything. Make it look... convincing. You know where to meet.'

'OK.'

The line went dead. He didn't move for several seconds.

Clean the whole house.

The instruction was simple enough really, even if he didn't understand why.

He got dressed, washed his face – as though it were a necessary step before he moved on. He dried his skin with the fluffy white hand towel his hosts had left for him in the tasteful en suite. Luxury all around him, inside and out.

They'd been good to him here, really.

Clean the whole house. Everything.

Everything. Which meant everyone.

He took the Beretta pistol and checked it over and kept it in hand as he moved to the door. He wouldn't take any other belongings with him. He wouldn't need them, and they'd only slow him down.

He opened the door and stared into the dark corridor. No lights, no sounds.

He crept outside, his shoes landing softly on the thick, patterned carpet. Not that he could see the intricate weaves right now, although he imagined his feet fitting neatly around the familiar patterns as he walked.

He reached the next bedroom. His heart gently pulsed in his chest. He took a deep, silent breath and pushed the door open a few inches. Not completely dark in there. A little plug-in night-light shone in the corner, creating a colorful array of stars and planets across the back wall. He heard the gentle sounds of sleep from the single bed. Noticed the ruffled hair beneath the covers.

Clean the whole house. Everything.

He'd come back to this one. Perhaps easier that way.

He moved further along the corridor to the next door. The master bedroom. Master and missus. Both were inside. He could hear them even before he'd opened the door: the deep guttural breathing of him, and the softer, quite blunt exhales of her. He imagined them in the oversized bed. Him on his back, mouth wide open. Her pulled close to the very edge of the bed, facing away from her husband, cuddling the silky sheets to her neck for comfort that he didn't give her.

But thinking of her under the sheets only sent a very different image – memories – of her flashing through his mind.

He shook it away. No time for thinking about anything like that now.

Clean the whole house. Everything.

Gun at the ready, he stepped inside.

1

He wanted to sleep but couldn't. His body was exhausted, every muscle, tendon, bone ached, screamed for respite, willed for recovery before the toil of tomorrow.

If he even made tomorrow...

He tossed and turned, trying to find a comfortable position but within minutes an arm or a leg was numbing up, and even if he could get past that unease he couldn't clear his mind of the whirring thoughts. And then there were the sounds. Not noises – they were too quiet – but even as he tried his best to think of absolutely nothing, he inevitably honed in on the sounds. The light clacking of the branch against the window. Not quite rhythmic enough to provide a focus to help him reach slumber. Then there were the breaths of his brothers in the room with him. Not snoring, because he knew none of them were in deep sleep either. Just their breaths. Slow, shallow. In. Out. The occasional grunt.

All annoying as hell.

Gregor turned over again. From his back to his side and he

had to roll his shoulder and shake his arm to get feeling back in it.

'Would you quit moving around!' came a hiss from the nearest bed to him. Vasily.

Gregor didn't respond to his eldest brother. Not his real brother. None of the other boys here were, even if they knew little else but this place, each other.

'I can't sleep either,' came a quieter, softer voice. Andre.

No one said anything to that. Andre was often overlooked by his older, more able brothers. Would his younger age, his weaker body make him the most likely one taken tonight?

Gregor concentrated on the sound now coming from somewhere outside the door. Footsteps. Quiet to start with but getting louder and more distinct with each step.

Clop, clop, clop. A steady rhythm up the stairs.

Clop, clop, clop. A steady, albeit slightly slower, calmer thud along the corridor.

Gregor tensed up. His eyes were wide open, but he could see nothing in the dark room. No light came in through the blackout curtains, no light seeped in through the edges around the door – the corridor outside remained in darkness too. He didn't need the light. A ghoul of the night could see just fine in blackness.

The room fell horribly silent, not even the sound of a breath anymore. Gregor was holding his tight, imagined his brothers were too. As though doing so would protect them.

Was it possible to hold a breath so long that you simply died? He really didn't know. Perhaps he was about to find out because he wasn't letting go.

A creak broke through the ghastly silence. Metal twisting, scraping, crying out. Pleading almost. Only the doorknob turning, but in the quiet room, in Gregor's addled mind it sounded deafening and beastly.

A whimper from across the room greeted the sound. Andre.

'Shut the fuck up!' Vasily hissed.

But what difference did it really make if he heard them? He knew the three of them were in there. Where else would they be?

Gregor waited. Staring to where he knew the door stood...

But nothing happened.

Moments later the footsteps sounded out again. Moving away. To the next door along.

Vasily heaved a sigh of relief. Gregor slowly expelled the air from his lungs, feeling light-headed as he did so, he'd held on to the breath so long. As he sucked air – oxygen – back in, it quickly surged to his brain, matched in equal measure with adrenaline. A delayed response really as he'd have needed the fight or flight chemical powering him moments before.

Now he didn't need it at all.

The boys in the next room did.

Or at least, one of them did.

Above the relieved sighs and gasps from his room, Gregor heard the door to the next room opening. Heard the booming voice. Shuffling. Banging. Cries of anguish. A scream. A thud. The door slammed closed again. Footsteps moved away. Two sets. One set much heavier, harder than the other.

'Just be pleased it wasn't one of us,' Vasily whispered a few moments later when the footsteps had faded away, his voice breaking through Andre's soft sobbing.

'No,' Gregor said. 'There's nothing to be pleased about.'

'You get to sleep tonight. You get to wake up in the morning. Be thankful for that.'

'You think waking up here is a blessing?'

'Better than being dead.'

Gregor wasn't sure about that. But one thing he did know for sure... he'd have one less brother come morning.

* * *

Present day
Buryatia, Russia

He'd never get used to the cold. This cold. There would never be anything normal about such an extreme. Human beings – warm-blooded creatures with no fur – simply weren't made to withstand it. Of course, humans had learned to adapt to the cold, but that wasn't the same thing as belonging. And having to live day after day, week after week, month after month out here didn't make it any easier, any more normal, any more pleasant.

He pulled his knees a few inches higher, closer to his chest, wriggled his fingers a few times to make sure he could still feel them. Just about. Hector, huddled next to him on the mattress, shuffled but said nothing – his movement enough to tell Gregor that his sleep had been disturbed.

Gregor pushed his head closer to his chest, into Hector's shoulder, their bodies curled around each other under the musty old cover. There was nothing sensual about their closeness; having their bodies pushed against the other was simple survival. Gregor closed his eyes and tried to get some more sleep but the memories of him and his brothers and that place came back stronger and faster this time.

He really didn't know which place of confinement was worse. Then or now?

Just like all those years ago he found no more sleep before the sun's rays poked up over the concrete sill of the cell, casting light over the men's bunk in the otherwise unlit space.

Gregor sat up and pushed himself away from Hector who grumbled and curled up into a ball on the mattress. Mattresses, actually. Two of them, one each for the top and bottom bunk, although a couple of months ago, as winter took hold, they'd moved both mattresses to the bottom bunk and had slept together every night since. The two mattresses together approached something like comfort – if you could ignore the horribly cramped conditions for two six foot-plus men, and the inhumane cold.

Other inmates here had taken a different tactic, and had simply torn the mattresses apart, taken the innards out and used the cheap fabric to stuff into their clothing. It made them look like Michelin Men as they walked around the cell block. It probably kept them warmer, but it also meant they had to sleep on nothing but the bare bed, or even worse, the cold concrete floor.

Gregor stood up, stretched, the shivers worsening now his body was unfurled and he was on his own. He walked to the barred window, the early morning sunlight not enough to protect from the chilly air that seeped in through the single-pane window and its draughty surround. No, more than seeped in – the cold air came through in non-stop gusts.

He looked outside. Same as always. Beyond the nine-foot-high concrete wall he saw nothing but white stretching into the distance. Nothing living out there at this time of year that he could see. Even the animals built for this climate were sheltering.

He reached out to the radiator below him, his icy fingers poking through the many holes in his woolen mittens. The metal wasn't even lukewarm. Warmer than the ambient air, sure, but nowhere near enough to adequately heat the room. Only enough to make sure the inmates didn't freeze to death in their sleep. Well, not every night, anyway.

Gregor heard the guards approaching outside. Heard the flaps on the doors of neighboring cells open and bang shut again. Soon it was their turn.

'Breakfast, lunch, and dinner,' the gruff voice said as a tray was pushed through the hole. Gregor moved over and took the tray and peeked out at the two uniformed men standing the other side. He held the eye of the taller, more brutish of the two a moment. Yuri. Gregor received a slight nod, but no more words were said before Yuri slapped shut the flap.

'What have we got?' Hector said, sitting up on the bunk.

Gregor took the tray over.

'Big Mac. Fries. Chocolate milkshake.'

Hector tutted. 'Bastards. It's supposed to be pizza Tuesday.'

Tuesday? Was it Tuesday? Gregor couldn't remember.

Both men chuckled before their more usual moroseness took over once more. Gregor hated laughing. Hated smiling even. They were primitive responses that the mind mistook for something approaching pleasure, releasing endorphins into the bloodstream subconsciously. He didn't want that. He didn't want anything to gloss over the reality of the situation out here.

Both men moved the paltry food about with their fingers as though deciding whether they would dive straight in or not.

Hector slumped back against the wall empty-handed and closed his eyes.

'You don't want any?' Gregor asked.

'Frozen, stale bread and moldy cheese? For the fiftieth day in a row?'

Fiftieth? Was that how long it'd been since the last food shipment? Gregor hadn't been counting, but there was no doubting the food was getting worse and worse, the portions smaller and smaller. The guards had said new supplies were coming any day. As soon as they could mend the railway tracks which had been destroyed in a landslide a hundred miles away. The only route into and out of the gulag. The only sane route, anyway.

'It's not completely frozen yet,' Gregor said, pushing his

thumb into the hard bread. But it would be if it was left out much longer. He'd eaten frozen bread before. Didn't want to again.

'You just have it. I'm not hungry.'

'You could keep it on you,' Gregor said. 'For later.'

'I'm not stuffing bread under my armpit and carrying it around all day.'

'Alex says it helps,' Gregor said. 'The warm moisture actually takes the staleness away after a while, he says.'

Hector chuckled. 'Oven-fresh flavor, apparently.'

Gregor stifled a laugh too. 'Shit, I smelled the stuff he took out yesterday. If that's oven-fresh...'

'Yeast infection, more like,' Hector added.

Gregor bit down hard on the bread and by the time he'd chewed it enough that he could actually swallow the dry morsel, his jaw ached. It took him several more minutes to finish the two pieces. The two cubes of cheese went down a little more easily even if he didn't bother to remove the blue and green spots of mold. Fuck it. Mold was edible, wasn't it?

By the time he got to the cup of water the liquid inside was already turning slushy. He downed it, sending a renewed, more vigorous shiver across his body as the horribly cold liquid traveled through him.

Not long after and the shouting of the guards told them that the doors were about to be unlocked. Hector and Gregor both got ready. As soon as the locks released, they headed on out into the large open space, the other inmates pouring out of their cells too, nearly a hundred men in total in this block, all of them housed on the ground level. Two other levels rose above them, but the cells up there were empty, had been for some time as far as Gregor knew. Now the upper levels were only used for the patrolling guards, looking down on the prisoners as if they were observing dogs in a fighting pit. Although most recently – a few weeks, anyway – there'd been no trouble here between the inmates, or with the inmates and guards. The only concern on most minds now was survival. Which explained why the men came out of their cells with smiles on their faces, greeting each other gladly, almost with surprise, as though they'd not expected to make it through another night.

But then...

After the initial pleasantries were over and done with, Gregor noticed a hush taking over in the far corner. A group of men stood in a circle, heads bowed, a muted conversation taking place.

Gregor edged toward them. Other men were taking notice too. Gregor looked up to the next level as he moved. Six guards patrolled, rifles dangling lazily. None of them were paying the group any attention.

Hector peeled from the group and strode up to Gregor.

'Move away,' Hector said, grabbing Gregor's arm, but he resisted and stood his ground.

'What's happened?'

'They're pissed off and they're about to get themselves shot, the fucking idiots.'

And just looking at the group Gregor could see, feel, their anger now. Creased faces. Bunched fists. Nods and backslaps here and there as they psyched themselves up. They were planning, plotting.

'What happened?' Gregor asked more forcibly.

'Vlad didn't make it.'

'Old Vlad?'

Because there were actually four Vlads here. Young Vlad, Idiot Vlad, Handsome Vlad and Old Vlad.

'Frozen in his fucking sleep,' Hector said. 'Broz woke up next to a damn corpse.'

Gregor opened his mouth to respond but then a ruckus from behind him caused him to sink down and spin around.

Shouting. Banging. Four men rushed about, slamming their metal bedpans against walls, doors. One swiped his bedpan across the back of another inmate's head. A sucker punch. The poor chump – who was that? – didn't see it coming and plummeted to the floor.

Other men started shouting too, huddling into groups, some retreated to their cells. The guards yelled warnings...

Gregor spun back the other way. It was all a distraction. Back at the far end the group of angry men rushed up the stairs. Ten, twelve of them, bounding up. The guards didn't see them until the first of the men raced along the gangway. The frontrunner launched a fist at the trailing guard before he could twist his rifle that way. The inmate carried on past to take on the next, allowing the rest of the rioters to join the melee. Which didn't work out so well for the first, already unsteady, guard when someone grabbed him, lifted him from his feet and tossed him over the railing.

The guard yelled in panic as he flip-flopped toward the concrete. Gregor winced as the guy landed headfirst. His neck snapped, his body collapsed on top of him.

That was when the gunfire started. Booming, echoing rapid fire. Gregor hunched down, covered his head and ran for cover beneath the overhang. He slid up against the wall and cowered. Bullets zinged all around. Men shouted, yelled, screamed.

But it didn't take long for the armed guards to retake control, and soon the guards' yells became the dominant sound.

'Hands on heads! Flat on the floor! Faces down! All of you!'

Gregor did so without waiting to be forced. He placed himself on his belly, hands up, but kept his head skewed to the side so he could look out across the atrium.

Most men had complied, only a few stragglers deciding to

take a rifle butt to the head first. Gregor's eyes found Hector's. His cellmate glared at him with a defiance, an anger he'd not seen before.

Gregor looked away. To the fallen bodies. Just the one guard that he could see. Several inmates, though, lay in pools of their own blood. Pools of blood of their own making, really. Their fight had been rushed. Stupid. Little more than suicide. Perhaps they'd known that but had decided it was worth it. Two fingers up to the system rather than 'living' like this.

Gregor's gaze finally rested inside the cell nearest to him. To the bunk and the unmoving figure there. Glassy eyes stared back at him on a face that was blue from the cold and lack of still-coursing blood.

Old Vlad. Frozen in his sleep.

Gregor bunched his fists, doing everything he could to hold in his anger. To not let it show.

He fully understood the madcap stand those men had just made, even if he didn't agree with their foolhardy method. But he'd never been resigned to his fate here. He simply knew it'd take more than rushing the guards in a fit of rage to get him out.

He kept his eyes on Old Vlad's corpse. No way Gregor would suffer that fate. He'd gone through too much to let his life end like that.

So the question for him wasn't if he'd try to break from this hellhole. It was simply when, and perhaps most importantly, who he could trust enough to help him.

2

ANTIBES, FRANCE

James Ryker opened the balcony door and stepped out into the fresh morning air. The clear sky meant the temperature had dropped from its pleasant high yesterday afternoon and Ryker's bare torso prickled with goose bumps despite the rays of the rising sun on his skin. He didn't mind the cold edge, though. The weather here in winter was far from the summer highs but it was a damn sight better than many other places, and the azure sky made him feel relaxed, rejuvenated, anytime of year.

'Close the door, you're letting all the heat out!' Charlotte shouted from the bed.

Ryker stretched up, his hands nearly touching the concrete of the balcony above. He spent a couple more seconds looking out across the view. Not the most impressive from here, really. Charlotte's modest salary meant she lived well off the most prestigious streets that crammed the coastline not far away in trendy Juan-les-Pins and Cap d'Antibes. The Mediterranean lay around the far edges of those wealthy neighborhoods and if he stood on tiptoes he had just the smallest glimpse of the glistening deep blue water.

But his eyes didn't rest there but on one of the larger, and more prominent buildings on the peninsula. Le Provencal. A derelict art deco hotel, once visited by the world's rich and famous. Soon to be again, should the new owners get their wish.

Ryker would be taking a visit down there himself very soon. Even if his time on the southern tip of France had brought him the pleasure of meeting and getting to know Charlotte, getting to know her very intimately, his primary purpose here remained business.

'James! I said—'

'I heard.'

He turned and walked back inside and closed the door behind him. He looked over to the bed where Charlotte remained snuggled under the covers, her long, dark hair a mess around her face.

'Why do you always do that?' she said, still sounding grumpy though he let it slide. She wasn't a morning person, that was all.

'I love the view,' he said.

'It's a shit view. Probably about the worst view in Antibes.'

'Not from where I'm standing,' he said to her as he gently pulled on the bottom of the covers. The top end slipped free from her shoulders, momentarily exposing her breasts.

'Hey!' she shouted out, yanking the covers back up. 'Damn, just go and stand out there again or something, will you! Just shut the door this time!' But even though she'd tried to shout angrily, she couldn't stop the wide smile from spreading.

He jumped back onto the bed next to her and her body jolted on the mattress, causing her to fall toward him. He put his arm around her shoulder and kissed the top of her head.

'Why do you always have so much energy?' she said. 'You're supposed to be old.'

'Ouch,' he said, even though her words didn't really sting him at all. Actually, he was only seven years older than she was, but he sat the wrong end of forty now. Nearer to half a century.

She snuggled into him a little and after a couple of minutes he could tell she'd closed her eyes again and was drifting by the increasing calmness to her breaths.

'Sleepyhead. It's nearly eight thirty.'

'Shit!'

The reaction was almost instantaneous, and she jumped up out of the bed. Ryker stifled a laugh as she zoomed around the room. Into the bathroom. Less than a minute in the shower. Too quick for him to even think about joining her in there. No, he did think about it, but he was still too busy enjoying the thoughts when she rushed out again, skin glistening.

'I'm supposed to be at the station at nine,' she said, dropping the towel.

She paused a second and turned and looked at him, and she grew in confidence when she noted the look in his eyes as he took in her nakedness.

'You could have had all this if you'd woken me earlier,' she said before she pulled on her underwear.

'Then I'll let the cold air in at seven tomorrow, if you like?'

'Do that and I'll shoot you,' she said as she momentarily glanced to her holstered gun on the dressing table. She finished dressing before she picked the weapon up and clasped the belt around her waist, the holster and the gun soon out of sight beneath her neatly pressed suit jacket. All in all, considering she'd taken less than three minutes to get ready, she looked great.

'What are you doing today?' she asked him as she ran a brush through her hair.

'This and that.'

She paused as she looked at him in the mirror. 'That sounds ominous.'

He shrugged.

'James. Please just tell me it's not something that's going to cause me any more problems?'

He stood up from the bed, moved over to her and put his arms around her waist and gently kissed her neck. 'Why would I do anything to get you in trouble?'

She pulled away from his grip.

'Because... even though I haven't known you very long, I think I do know you.'

She left it at that, and he spent a few moments working the words over in his mind, though he still wasn't sure exactly how he was supposed to take the comment.

Not long after and he was in the kitchen pouring some orange juice and she was at the front door right across in the small open-plan space. She glanced back at him, still standing there in his boxers as he checked his phone.

'I guess you're staying then,' she said to him.

'If I tried to get ready that quickly it'd probably give me a heart attack. I'm old, remember.'

He tapped his heart for effect.

'Will you be here later?' she asked.

'Do you want me to be?'

'I'll call you,' she said. She pulled the door open a few inches. 'But please... remember what I said. Try not to do anything stupid today. Anything else stupid, I should say.'

She walked out and closed the door without waiting for a response.

* * *

By mid-morning the sun had taken away the early morning chill and Ryker walked the twisting, leafy streets of Juan-les-Pins in only his jeans and a light shirt. The cars crammed together along the sides of the tree-lined narrow road and the tall walls of the properties gave little clues as to the wealth and luxury that lay beyond. Much of the area had an understated, old-world vibe. Ryker could see why those with money to spend – from all over the globe – came here.

He took a left at a crossroads to head to a small cluster of shops. Today's recce was, initially, a bit hit and miss. He had a time and place for this afternoon, but this morning he was simply scoping out, and hoping to get a bit lucky. He hadn't been so far today, as he'd already spent time inside and outside two other cafes that he knew his target frequented, but he remained undeterred. The peninsula wasn't that big. He'd make inroads soon enough, whatever happened this morning.

The Cafe des Artisans took up a corner spot and had several outdoor tables all sitting in sunshine at this time of day. Behind the tables, vines grew up and all around a small pergola at the front of the handsome stone building. All but one of the outdoor tables was taken and Ryker really would have liked to sit in the sun, but he knew he'd get to see more from the much larger inside, where his target could most usually be found, he'd heard.

He headed on in and ordered a sparkling water before taking a seat at a table for two in the corner of the far from bustling interior. Quaint and quirky art hung on walls that were poorly plastered, perhaps deliberately so. The smell of fresh coffee hung in the air and the ever-present whir of the bean grinder echoed around the space.

Tempted, Ryker eventually had not one but two coffees in the forty minutes he sat there before he saw the man he was looking for.

Luc Pichon arrived in his glitzy BMW convertible which he squeezed into a spot directly on the road outside. He had his phone to his ear, wore smart designer clothes, big aviator sunglasses over his face as he strode purposefully, confidently for the cafe. His style, his arrogance, made him look more like a wannabe movie star than a man of the law.

But Pichon's job didn't tell the full story of the man at all. One very big reason why Ryker had the guy in his sights.

Pichon put his phone away as he headed in and up to the counter where the young server greeted him warmly. He ordered something before going to his usual spot by the window. Ryker kept a close eye on him through the next fifteen minutes or so, not overly worried about being conspicuous. If anything, he was happy for this guy to know he had some pressure on him.

Pichon took another call on his phone. Then a man Ryker didn't recognize entered and made a beeline for Pichon's table. He was older than Pichon, probably late fifties, decked out in business casual and with wispy gray hair. Ryker hadn't seen him arrive in a car, although his vehicle could have been parked somewhere out of sight. The man sat with his back to Ryker, who readied his phone, intent on getting a picture of the man's face when he eventually stood up and turned back for the door.

That happened less than five minutes later. Except Pichon got up too, so Ryker followed suit. He hadn't tracked Pichon down today only to spy on him. The older man spotted Ryker moving toward them first.

'Bonjour,' Ryker said, loud enough to get the attention of both men. Pichon stopped and sent a sullen glare Ryker's way.

'Hey, you!' came a voice from the door.

Not the older man who'd carried on that way, but someone else who'd just walked in. Younger. Taller. Angrier.

He marched up to Ryker.

'It's you, isn't it?' he said, his English carrying a heavy French slant. 'You're the one who's been with Charlotte.'

The man stopped only a few inches from Ryker's face.

'I guess so,' Ryker said with a sigh. He took a half step back to give him some space. He noted that the older man was outside already. Pichon wasn't. He was still staring at Ryker though now had a self-satisfied grin plastered on his face.

'I know about you. You've got a lot of people talking.'

'Saying what?' Ryker said.

'She's my sister,' the man said. Thierry, Ryker now realized.

'I think Charlotte's old enough to—'

Thierry grabbed Ryker's arm and squeezed hard. The guy was strong, even if it was stupid of him to be putting his hands on people he didn't know. 'She's been hurt before. Badly. If you hurt her...'

'I'm not going to hurt her,' Ryker said, shaking from Thierry's grip. He glanced over the guy's shoulder again and spotted Pichon on the outside now, by his car, still in an exchange with the older man.

'You know what happened, don't you?' Thierry said. 'To her son?'

Yes, he did know. She'd told him. Her son, Patrice, only five years old, had been shot dead in Paris not quite two years ago. Charlotte had worked for an anti-drug task force there. Had got way too close to bringing down some very bad people. The drive-by hit had been intended for her. Unluckily, Patrice had been in the back of her car at the time and of the fifteen shots fired, four bullets had inadvertently hit his little body. Two had hit Charlotte although she was far luckier than her son.

The shooter was later found dead too, though the investigation into his death was still pending. From what Ryker had since seen from records he'd been able to access, it wasn't clear if the gang the shooter worked for had killed him for his mistake or if someone from within police ranks had overseen the revenge.

Either way, Charlotte remained broken from the ordeal and had left Paris not long after, moving all the way down to the south of the country, where she was originally from, to try and rebuild her life. Although despite her trauma, she'd only stayed out of law enforcement for six months before the bug had bitten her again.

Once more she was on the tip of something big, which also explained why Ryker was in town, even if she didn't know the full story to that just yet.

'Yes,' Ryker said. 'I know what happened to Patrice.'

Thierry looked disgusted by the comment. 'Did she actually tell you, or did you find out by sticking your nose in where it doesn't belong?'

Ryker sighed. The truth was Charlotte had confided in Ryker about the horrific incident first, although he had since done his own digging too. Habit. He decided to not admit that to her brother. Ryker didn't think he'd appreciate it.

'Seriously, if you do anything to cause her pain...' Thierry jabbed Ryker in the chest.

'Then you'll come after me. I get it.'

Outside, the old man was walking away. Pichon was about to get into his car but then caught Ryker's eye and winked. Ryker went to move past, but Thierry grabbed his arm again.

'I'm serious. You be careful... or you'll be sorry.'

Once again Ryker pulled from the guy's grip.

'You be careful too, Thierry,' Ryker said with just enough menace to get the guy to think twice. Ryker didn't really mean him any harm, but he also wasn't about to let a man he'd never met before intimidate him like that.

Ryker pushed into Thierry's shoulder as he moved past. He headed out of the door. Pichon's BMW fired up and before Ryker had taken another step the engine revved and the car shot off down the street. Ryker carried on to the footpath and looked along the road in both directions. The BMW was out of sight already. No sign of the old guy now either.

Damn it.

Although Ryker did have a picture of him.

He glanced back at the cafe. Thierry had made his point and was now waiting in line.

Ryker checked his watch.

Not quite how he'd intended things to go with Pichon, but he had somewhere else to be soon enough anyway.

3

There was something melancholic about the abandoned Le Provencal. The looming building took up a prestigious spot among the natural pine forest of Juan-les-Pins, rising several stories on a rocky outcrop that gave unobstructed views out across the Mediterranean. Yet even on a beautiful, sunny day the shell of a building looked lost and forlorn. A grand rotunda sat at the back of the property. Previously landscaped gardens spread outward from the building to where Ryker stood in an area that was now a mess of weeds and rubble from previous failed attempts at bringing the structure a new life.

Soon another attempt would be on the way, nearly fifty years after the once world-renowned art deco hotel, frequented by A-listers, had first closed down. Few iconic buildings could have survived half a century of neglect, and it was a testament to the status of Le Provencal that it had. Its new life, if successful this time around, would be as luxury apartments. Multi-million-euro luxury homes, only for the wealthiest. A new construction fence had already been laid around the perimeter signaling the possibility of the commencement of work in the near future.

Ryker wasn't so sure the old lady would be lucky after all. Not with what he knew of some of the partners behind the scheme.

He heard the engine noise of the arriving party and headed back around to the front of the property. A pickup truck was now parked inside the open gates, 'Kyril Construction' emblazoned on the side. He didn't know who was driving though, didn't care about being discreet or getting caught out roaming around the property when he shouldn't have been. So he walked right up to the truck. The man behind the wheel only clocked him when he was a few yards away and wound down his window.

'Hey!' the guy shouted over before carrying on in French. Private property. What are you doing here, that sort of thing.

'Sorry, I don't speak French,' Ryker lied as he came to a stop, happy to play at least a little dumb for now.

'Private property,' the man said, now in English. 'There's a sign.'

He pointed to said sign on the gate. One of many signs.

'Sorry, I don't read French either.'

'But...' The guy glanced at the sign – propriété privée – and opened his mouth to try once again to respond to Ryker but then didn't bother, as though he'd figured out Ryker was toying with him.

'You shouldn't be in here,' the man said.

'You're meeting with Pierre Bennette?' Ryker asked.

The guy didn't answer but his eyes narrowed in suspicion.

'Let me ask you a question,' Ryker said. 'Have you, or your company, actually signed a contract to work on this place yet?'

No answer.

'It's important. From your perspective. Because if you haven't already signed anything, then my advice to you is to keep it that way. Leave. Now. And don't come back here. But if you have already signed a contract... maybe get yourself a good lawyer.'

'What are you talking about?' He wasn't just suspicious now, he was angry.

'I'm talking about your new customer. Pierre Bennette. And the fact that he works hand-in-hand with Valeri Litvinov. Russian oligarch. Drug baron. You know him?'

No answer, although both the anger and suspicion were replaced in a few heartbeats with a much more wary and nervy look.

'Who are you?' the man asked.

'Doesn't matter. Just take my advice and get out of here.'

Except the guy didn't move.

'I'm not a cop, and you're not in trouble,' Ryker said. 'Yet, at least. I guess you didn't know about Litvinov, right?'

No answer once again.

'I'll take that as a no. But you do know of Litvinov?' No answer. But the sour look on his face suggested he did. 'Your business is based around Antibes so you must do. The guy gets his grubby fingers into every big project around here these days. You really should have done your homework on Bennette.'

The man still didn't say a word but the next moment his window glided up and his engine turned back on. He backed out toward the road. Just as he was turning another car came up behind him. White Range Rover, slick-looking on huge wheels. Bennette. But truck guy didn't seem to care. He reached the road and floored it and sped off out of sight.

Bennette seemed to take pause for a moment as though he couldn't understand what was happening, but then he looked over and spotted Ryker and carried on in. He parked, got out. Bennette was in his forties and looked as slick as his car with cream linen trousers, an open-necked shirt, brown leather shoes, no socks. He had perpetual four-day stubble to give an otherwise youthful face a bit of a harder edge. But even if he was as tall as

Ryker and filled out his clothes with gym muscle, this guy was no physical threat to Ryker. And he wasn't that important either, nothing but a moneyman.

'Who are you?' he said to Ryker. Apparently it was obvious that Ryker was English given Bennette had gone straight for that language rather than his own, even though they'd never met before.

'James Ryker. From Kyril Construction. My buddy had to shoot off somewhere.'

Ryker indicated to the road and Bennette glanced over his shoulder as if to confirm in fact that the truck was nowhere in sight now. Ryker could also tell that Bennette didn't really believe him, but he didn't care much about that. He was interested to see how this would play out.

'Why don't we go take a look inside?' Ryker suggested. 'I've got a few concerns about viability.'

'Yeah? What concerns?'

'Probably easier to show you.'

Bennette obviously didn't like the idea given the sneer on his face, but Ryker turned and headed toward the building nonetheless. He'd already taken a look inside earlier. Was as impressed with the vast grandeur of the interior as he was awed by the amount of work required to turn the decrepit shell into luxury living once more. In places the upper floors had crumbled. In other places ceilings were jacked to keep them in place. Window glazing and frames had all been ripped out many years ago, so Ryker walked straight in through the open entrance into what used to be a grand atrium. Now it was a festering mess with discarded litter, graffiti on the walls from rebellious youths – even Cap d'Antibes had them – and the smell of stale urine mixed with damp concrete.

'You know, you really should think about getting this place—'

Ryker turned and paused when he saw the gun pointed at his face '—secured.'

'Is that so, Mr. Ryker?' Bennette said, looking all the more confident now he had his little toy in his hand.

'Do you even know how to use that thing?' Ryker asked.

'You want to find out?'

Ryker shrugged. 'It's not even real, is it?' He craned his neck as though inspecting the gun.

'Yes. It's real. And I won't hesitate to shoot you if you don't tell me why you're here.'

'You won't?'

Bennette didn't respond.

'Thought you said you wouldn't hesitate?'

Bennette scoffed, looked a bit puzzled, as though he'd thought the gun might have made this part of the meeting between them a bit more straightforward from his point of view.

'So?' Ryker said.

'Why are you here?'

'You won't shoot me,' Ryker said. 'Because if you do someone's going to hear and then the police will descend within minutes. And I noticed the security cameras around the site. It wouldn't take long for the police to see me and you walking in here right before the gun goes off. And I know your friends probably have some of the police paid off around here, but do you really think they can get you off a murder charge when the evidence is so obvious?'

'Why. Are You. Here?' Bennette asked.

'To ask you some questions. Mainly about your relationship with Valeri Litvinov.'

No tell on the man's face now. But he also didn't question who Ryker was talking about, which showed he did know the name at the very least.

'Litvinov is a crook,' Ryker said. 'An old-school gangster, in many ways. One who's very rich and pretty damn influential around here.'

'Sounds like a man you should be careful of.'

Ryker shook his head. 'No. It's the opposite. I'm the one you should be careful of. I've been taking down scum like you and him my whole life.'

Bennette's hand twitched a little, his edginess increasing.

'Ask me again,' Ryker said.

'What?'

'Ask me why I'm here?'

Bennette hesitated, but then, 'Why are you here?'

Ryker didn't answer. Instead, he darted forward. Bennette didn't get the shot off before Ryker swiped the gun from his grip and then swiped his feet. Bennette landed on the pockmarked concrete with a thud. Ryker turned the gun on him.

'I'm here to find out everything you know about Litvinov. Associates. Businesses. Locations. Whatever you have that will help me bring him down.'

Bennette didn't say a word as he glared, panting.

'You can start now,' Ryker said.

'Why the hell would I tell you anything?'

'For starters because you have a gun pointed at you.'

'A gun you won't shoot for the very same reason that you said I wouldn't.'

Ryker pulled the trigger and the gunshot echoed around the concrete shell. The bullet smacked into the ground a couple of inches from Bennette's face, covering him in dusty fragments.

'Perhaps I mis-sold that theory to you,' Ryker said. 'Sounds pretty loud in here, but how many people are even walking by right now outside to hear that one shot? How many of those people would even recognize it as a gunshot and not a car back-

firing or someone dropping a pallet or something on a construction site?'

Bennette pursed his lips and glowered as though pissed off
that Ryker had got into his head so easily before.

'Next time I won't miss,' Ryker said. He lowered the gun to
point it at Bennette's knee. 'I think we'll start here.'

'OK, OK!' Bennette said. Ryker relaxed a little. Which meant
he was slightly off-guard when Bennette made a move on him.

Honestly, he hadn't expected the guy to have the balls for it.

Bennette leapt up and launched his knee into Ryker's groin
and Ryker was only able to pull back from the hit at the last
moment to at least take away some of the force of the blow. He
grunted in pain and shock and his finger twitched on the trigger,
but he held back. He didn't want to shoot this guy. So for now he
wouldn't.

As Ryker recovered from the blow Bennette didn't stick
around to fight it out. He turned on his heel and sprinted for the
outside. So Ryker followed.

He grabbed a plank of wood from the ground and launched it
forward. The wood spun through the air and Bennette must have
heard it coming because he glanced behind him and ducked, and
the wood somersaulted past him and crashed into the edge of the
doorway in front.

The clamor, or something else, caused Bennette to divert,
away from the exit. Toward the grand spiral staircase.

Ryker chased him up.

'Bennette! There's nowhere for you to go!'

But Bennette took no notice and bounded up to the next
floor. He ran for a corridor, stumbled a couple of times which
allowed Ryker to close the distance. He thought again about
shooting. It'd bring the guy down, at least... But Ryker didn't.

It looked like Bennette was about to head down the stairs on the other side but then he diverted left instead, underneath a small scaffold tower which he yanked as he passed through. The metal and boards wobbled and gave way just as Ryker reached them and then collapsed down, bouncing and clanking to the floor.

Ryker cowered and lifted his arms up above his head and took several blows from the falling debris before he could continue on. Bennette had pulled away. Nearly ten yards in front now as he raced along a gloomy corridor. The floor creaked. Felt like it was bouncing from their weight. The end of the corridor opened out to another balcony overlooking the inside of the rotunda at the back of the building. Once a grand ballroom perhaps.

Now it was... a death trap.

As Bennette found out when the floor beneath him gave way and he screamed as he plummeted down. Ryker winced at the sound of the impact. He slowed up. The moaning and groaning from below told him that Bennette had survived the fall. Ryker continued to the edge of the hole.

'You OK down there, buddy?' Ryker said, peering below.

'Fuck! You!' Bennette yelled through gritted teeth.

Ryker dodged around the hole, keeping to the remaining portion of floor closest to the supporting wall which would be more stable than the barely supported overhang.

He casually moved down the stairs, stashing the gun in his waistband as he moved. He walked across the broken tiles of the rotunda and to the pile of rubble where Bennette lay twisted. He was covered in gray dust, cuts and scrapes all over him and his nice clothes were dirtied, bloody and torn.

'That was a bit dramatic, wasn't it?' Ryker said.

Bennette roared at him, like an injured animal might to try and scare off a predator.

Ryker focused in on Bennette's left leg. The tibia and fibula were snapped about halfway to the knee, the white of bone protruding up toward the ceiling.

'That looks pretty nasty,' Ryker said, crouching down.

Bennette whimpered.

'Ask me again,' Ryker said. 'Ask me why I'm here?'

Bennette didn't.

'I'm here to make you talk,' Ryker said. He took hold of the twisted leg and applied just enough pressure to cause Bennette to scream in agony. He understood. 'So now you talk.'

4

'You know why you're here, don't you?' Father asked.

'This is my home,' Gregor responded, lifting his gaze from the knife he was sharpening and to the ramshackle building in front of him, the tower of the church rising above behind it.

Father laughed. 'Yes, this is your home, but that's not what I meant.'

'Then what did you mean?'

'What are we doing here? What is our purpose?'

Gregor swooshed the knife's blade across the granite block a couple of times as he thought. The smell of fresh meat stuck in his nose from the two dead rabbits by his feet. The rabbits he'd be skinning and butchering just as soon as this conversation was over.

'I don't know,' Gregor said, feeling as pathetic as the answer sounded. As much as he was petrified of this man, he wanted to please Father still.

'It's OK,' Father said. 'You're still young. You've a lot to learn. But the most important thing is that you do learn. From me.'

'So what is our purpose?'

'To protect our people.'

'From who?'

'From everyone.'

They both went silent. Gregor continued to sharpen the knife. Delaying, really, as he hated touching dead animals. Really hated having to tear the skin from the rabbits.

He felt Father's eyes on him.

'Do you remember your real parents?' Father asked.

'No,' Gregor lied, the answer slipping out without thought. But those memories were personal. His alone.

'It's a shame. Your real father was a good man. Honorable. And very important, to our people. The most critical thing, is that you get to carry on his work one day.'

Gregor looked up at Father, unsure what to say. This felt like a good conversation, like a compliment almost, but... as ever something else – something more sinister – lay underneath it all.

'What did you do to Max?' Gregor asked.

'You don't need to worry about Max. You won't see him again.'

'You killed him?'

Father glared but said nothing.

'Did he suffer?'

'You shouldn't ask about it. All you need to know is that I made good on my promise. If you all follow my lead, do what I tell you, then you'll have everything you ever need from me. If you disobey me, if you betray me, then... it's the end for you.'

Gregor gulped. Even though Father spoke softly, almost affectionately, there was no mistaking the intent behind his words.

'You trust me, don't you?' Father asked.

'Yes.'

'And I trust you, Gregor. More than any of the others. That's why it's so important that you tell me everything. Always. Whenever there's dissent, whenever there are whispers behind my back, I need to know that you'll bring it all to me. Just like you have done in the past. It doesn't change just because Max has now left us.'

Gregor didn't say anything as he carried on sliding the knife across the block.

Until Father grasped his wrist. Firmly. So hard it made Gregor wince, and his eyes welled.

'Gregor. You'll tell me everything, won't you?'

'Y-Yes... Father.'

Father smiled and released Gregor's wrist.

'Good boy.'

* * *

Present day
Buryatia, Russia

'Do we have a problem?' Yuri asked as he and Gregor stood on the stairs, looking out toward the huddles of convicts, most of them standing in groups around improvised fires. They used wood gathered from the surrounding forest, and set it alight in garbage cans to provide some warmth. Yuri and the other guards allowed it. Even allowed certain inmates outside the walls to gather the wood. A signal of humanity from the guards. One of very few privileges.

But there was no doubt the atmosphere had worsened in the gulag over the last three days since Old Vlad's death, the death of the guard, plus the five other convicts gunned down.

'They're not happy,' Gregor responded, and had noted several sullen glares in his direction in the few seconds he'd been talking to Yuri.

'They're not happy? You people are fucking criminals. You deserve to be here. We're just trying to do our jobs, and what do we get in return? Thrown off the balcony. Our necks snapped.'

'Five of us were killed.'

Yuri didn't respond this time as he took a long drag on his cigarette. The food rations were severely depleted, but apparently the gulag remained well-stocked on cigarettes. Most of the inmates had stashes too. Gregor didn't smoke. He especially didn't smoke in prison where he knew cigarettes were a kind of currency, but also a way for certain people to wield power. He'd stay away from that as much as he could. He didn't care about being a boss in here. He just wanted out.

'Any news on the supplies?' Gregor asked.

'A few more days, I heard,' Yuri said, before he dropped his cigarette butt and stamped it out with the heel of his boot, staring over at a group of inmates as he did so, as though imagining crushing a skull. 'You know it's just as bad for us, as it is for you.'

'I know,' Gregor said. Although he didn't really agree.

Yeah, the guards were stuck here too, but he was damn sure their living conditions, their meals, remained several steps up from that of the inmates. In theory the guards were supposed to work shift patterns. No one lived out here in the middle of nowhere, so the guards were shipped in with supplies. Six weeks on, four weeks off. Except this crew had only been on their third week when the railway line had been cut-off more than seven weeks ago. Since then, nothing. No food. No rotation. Just non-stop hellish cold for all.

Which partly explained why the guards, in many ways, had become relaxed around the inmates. Why they allowed them the privileges they did.

But there was still no getting away from the fact that it was a hundred prisoners – many of them violent men – against twelve guards.

Eleven guards now.

'I'm sorry about what happened to Old Vlad,' Yuri said.

Gregor nodded in response.

'If we had the choice, we'd make it warmer in here for you. We'd give you better food. We're just doing what we can to survive. To make sure you all survive too.'

'Yeah,' Gregor said. He went to walk away but Yuri grabbed his sleeve.

'If they're plotting another attack... you tell me. Another of ours gets killed and I might just hold you responsible.'

Gregor yanked his arm free. 'I don't want anyone else hurt.'

'You don't want yourself hurt, you mean.'

'Which is why you can trust me.'

Gregor walked down the stairs and over toward the second of the groups of men. The one where Hector was. Even if Hector wasn't the biggest, most brutish, most likable, most charismatic even, he'd become something of a leader among the majority of the inmates.

Hector had been locked up in the gulag for nearly ten years, far longer than Gregor's four months. With Old Vlad dead he was now the longest-serving inmate. His crime? He'd been a prominent critic of the Kremlin. A journalist who'd tried not to challenge in a political sense, but simply to expose corruption and nefarious actions of those in governance. He'd been jailed on multiple charges, ranging from fraud to money laundering to espionage. He didn't talk about it much directly, but others had suggested there was no evidence to support any of the charges.

Not a big surprise as it was clear Hector had been screwed over, and he remained hugely bitter toward the government, critical of the prison system. Given his natural intelligence he was able to articulate that in a way that some of the more brutish inmates couldn't. Quite simply, he was just a normal guy, but in many ways it was his averageness that made him a natural leader in this place. He was someone everyone felt comfortable around and they listened to him when he talked.

Hector gave Gregor a sly eye a couple of times as he approached.

'You should be careful,' Hector said to him, his eyes now focused on the fire. All of the other men kept their eyes off Gregor too.

'Excuse me?'

'You and him. Like comrades. People don't like it.'

'If we keep a good relationship with the guards, it's better for us. They're keeping us alive.'

'Only until they let rip with their AKs.'

That comment drew a few disgruntled murmurs.

'He says it should only be a few more days before—'

'Bullshit,' Hector said.

'What is?'

'A few more days? They've been saying that for weeks. And if the powers really wanted to help they could have sent helicopters with food, the new rotation. Who's even the one communicating with the outside world? Perhaps none of them is. We've all been left here to die.'

'If that were the case, the guards wouldn't still be guarding us. We'd all be in it together.'

Alex, standing next to Hector, humphed. He was one of the newer arrivals, but Gregor already sensed he'd had enough of this place and not a day went by when he didn't talk of mutiny of some sort. But then he was one of the men with little to lose. He'd been convicted of three gangland murders and even though he claimed to have been set up, Gregor didn't doubt at all that the man was capable of violence. 'There's more of us than them. A lot more. Why are we still living like this?'

'What do you suggest?' Hector said. 'That we overrun them? Sacrifice a few more of our own in the process and then break out and run hundreds of miles across wilderness?'

'Why not? Look around you,' Alex said. 'This isn't a hotel. The conditions outside are barely worse and at least out there we're free.'

Hector nodded, as though he actually saw some sense in the proposition.

'Out there you're dead within days,' Gregor said. 'Even if you survived to the next town you'd be killed or recaptured.'

'You don't know that.'

Gregor sighed, thought. 'I'm not saying I want to stay here either. What I'm saying is we need to be smarter about it.'

'So what?' Alex asked.

'So let's not be foolish. Like Pavel.'

Hector rolled his eyes. 'Pavel was an idiot.'

An idiot who'd been allowed out to collect firewood. Except he'd tackled his chaperones and run off into the forest. Unarmed. With nothing but his prison garb. The guards had come back inside relaxed as anything. Had even made grim jokes to the inmates about the escape.

Three days later the prisoners woke up to find Pavel's frozen-solid corpse in the atrium. Apparently, he hadn't even made it half a mile.

Actually, the basic idea hadn't been that bad. He'd seen an opportunity and taken it. His mistake had been his poor planning. He hadn't taken anything from the guards. Not their weapons or their clothes. Had he done so he would have given himself a fighting chance.

Hector opened his mouth to say something, but Gregor lifted his hand to stop him. His cellmate shot him a scathing look.

'You hear that?'

For the first time everyone around the fire had their eyes on Gregor. Some looked confused. Others worried.

'Train,' Hector said.

'Train,' Gregor said, his face breaking out into a smile.

5

Rain pelted down on the group of boys. Gregor shivered and coughed as water cascaded onto his skin. Their underwear – their only clothing – was soaked through and the ground beneath their feet had turned into a lake of muddy water. Father stood in front of them, under a corrugated metal overhang that kept him mostly dry, although Gregor noticed his pants legs glistened with water that had bounced off the puddles on the ground.

Strangely, Father didn't look as angry as he'd expected. Which only made him all the more nervous. In the ten minutes the boys had been outside – since Father had woken them and ordered them out of their beds – he'd not said a word at all. Neither had the boys even though it was plainly evident why they were standing there. The writing was quite literally on the wall.

'Fuck. This. Place,' Father said, his eyes on the boys rather than on the two-foot-high, ten-foot-wide scrawl. 'After everything I do for you cretins every single day, this is the thanks I get?'

The boys didn't utter a word. Father stepped out from under

the metal and into the rain, his form even more sinister as the deluge soaked him.

'You have a choice. Tell me who did this. Or... Remember what happened to Max?'

Gregor gulped. Of course they remembered what had happened to Max. All the boys were terrified now. Except... Strangely, their brother 'disappearing' in the night hadn't crushed their rebelliousness, as Father had likely intended, but fired it up further. Particularly in Sergei, the eldest, tallest, strongest of them. Sergei, who'd stolen a bottle of brandy from the main house two nights ago. Who'd encouraged his brothers to drink it last night, but who'd drank most of it himself. Before stumbling outside to leave his mark, and his brothers in shock.

Gregor stepped forward from the line. 'It was Sergei.'

Father glared but said nothing. He moved two steps along the line, away from Gregor, until he was face-to-face with Sergei who rose a couple of inches higher than the older man.

'You did it?' Father asked.

'Yes,' Sergei said.

'Why?'

Sergei paused before answering. 'I was drunk. It was a mistake.'

Gregor cringed. He hadn't expected Sergei to just blurt it out like that. Like he didn't even care.

Gregor shuffled back into the line, the others around him all sent daggers his way as he did so.

'I'm very pleased you admitted that to me,' Father said. 'Honesty is one of the most important qualities a man can possess. In the morning, while your brothers are at breakfast, you'll come down here and you'll get rid of it. Every last spot of paint. Do you understand me?'

'Yes, Father,' Sergei said.

'Good. Now back to your rooms, all of you.'

Father stepped aside, turned to face the door to beckon the boys that way. Gregor didn't move straight away. He was too shocked. Had Sergei really just been almost entirely let off for not one but two indiscretions?

'You're dead,' Sergei whispered as he moved past, only cementing the fact that Gregor had likely just made a huge mistake.

* * *

'This isn't right,' Hector said, staring out between the bars of their cell as though he might be able to see anything out there, even though the railroad was out of sight, running in from the opposite direction in the west.

'Why not?' Gregor said.

'It's been, what? Three, four hours already?'

They had no watches, no clocks, so had no way of knowing for sure. But it certainly felt about that long since they'd heard the train approaching, since the guards had hurriedly corralled the inmates back into their cells. The movement of the sun from the east to up behind the building behind their cell only confirmed the passage of time. And that dusk wasn't far off. With it an extra chill – if that was even possible – had taken over inside.

The warmth of the early morning sunshine felt like a lifetime ago.

Hector put his hand to the radiator and grimaced.

'The water's not far off freezing in there.'

Gregor humphed. The creaking and cracking of the pipes had started almost as soon as the prisoners had returned to their cells – an indication that the paltry heating had been turned off. It hadn't been off for weeks. Gregor had falsely thought the meagre warmth from the radiator was pointless. Now, after only a few hours without it, he realized he was wrong and wished for the chance to cuddle up to the barely warm metal.

'Are they punishing us?' Hector said. 'For the dead guard?'

Gregor didn't think so. This was because of the train, and whoever had arrived on that thing. At first he'd hoped – as had every guard and inmate – that the arrival meant fresh food, new guards, maybe even a new directive that would somehow see the conditions here become more hospitable.

So far it felt like the opposite.

'Will you fucking say something!' Hector shouted.

'Yeah. I agree with you. This isn't right.'

Although the response only seemed to add to Hector's agitation and he paced the cell a couple of times before moving to the door which he pounded with his fist.

'Hey! What the hell are we waiting for!'

He pounded some more and soon enough Gregor heard murmurs of discontent rising from other cells too.

But everyone went silent when they heard the thumping boots of the guards moving into the atrium. A lot of guards.

Hector, fist midair, slowly brought his hand down as he turned to Gregor. He looked worried. Gregor felt the same, though tried not to show it.

The noise died down for a few seconds before shouted instructions were barked out.

Come out of your cells. Hands on heads. Straight line facing the guards.

'They're gonna shoot us down?' Hector whispered to Gregor.

And Gregor didn't answer because he really didn't know, and really hoped it wasn't that. Yet an image spun through his mind, nonetheless. A TV show he'd seen as a child. A dramatic retelling of the execution of the last tzar, Nicolas II, and his family during the Red Terror campaign of the Russian Civil War. He'd watched the scene in horror as the tzar, his wife and five children were taken from their beds in the night and lined up against a wall. He'd gasped in shock when the firing squad had let rip on the seven, bullet holes tearing into them all, the little children included, before they were bayoneted just to make sure...

The doors to the cells unlocked. Hector pulled theirs open and tentatively stepped out. Gregor followed. The inmates moved in near silence, only a few nervous murmurs between them and a lot of confused and apprehensive faces. In the middle of the atrium stood two long lines of soldiers – not guards. They were back-to-back, one line facing each of the strips of cells, their rifles raised and at the ready.

Gregor and Hector stood side by side as the line of prisoners grew. Gregor glanced up. The regular guards were up there, looking down.

The images of Nicolas II and his family burned even more fiercely.

'If we rush them, we can take them,' Hector whispered. 'We have more.'

Gregor said nothing.

'I said everyone out!' yelled a soldier. A high-ranking soldier. His uniform – the two red stripes and the single star on his shoulder – showed he was a major. He wasn't armed but as he marched behind the line of inmates across from Gregor, two corporals rushed behind him. The major stuck his head into a cell.

'I said out!' he boomed.

The next moment the two corporals rushed in as the major stood at the ready, hands clasped behind his back. The sound of a fight rippled through the cell block – thuds, whacks, groans of pain before the two inmates who'd been intent on... – what exactly? – were dragged out of the cell. The corporals pulled them to their position in the line and hauled them to their feet. Only for the soldiers to then launch their fists into the prisoners' stomachs causing them to collapse back down again.

'Get up,' the major said, sounding calm, collected. 'Get up or you get a bullet in the head right here.'

The inmates slowly pulled themselves into position.

'Are we ready?' the major shouted over to someone Gregor couldn't quite see.

'Let me do a final check.'

Yuri. Gregor recognized the voice. He clenched his fists a little harder and the next moment saw Yuri scuttling along the lines, counting the inmates. He glared as Yuri finally passed by him, but Yuri wouldn't meet Gregor's eye at all.

'Everyone's here,' Yuri called out.

'Good. Then let me get started. My name is Aleksandrovich Potemkin. And I'm here today to change your lives.' He let the comment hang as he slowly paced between the two lines of inmates, his hands still clasped behind his back, his gaze switching left and right as though trying to meet the eye of every man. 'As you know, the conditions here have been hard. And, unfortunately, they're only going to get harder. You might have thought the train arriving today, finally, would be bringing fresh supplies. But distribution problems mean that isn't the case.'

'Bullshit,' Hector said quietly with a mock cough, bringing his hand up to his mouth to further stifle the word.

Potemkin whipped his head around and Gregor tensed, worried for his friend. But then Potemkin simply turned and carried on his spiel. Which Gregor too believed to be bullshit already.

'And those problems, I'm afraid, are set to continue into the near future. The truth is, I'm not sure when full, normal service will be possible here. And to compound issues, you probably noticed the heating went out a few hours ago. The maintenance team here has since worked tirelessly trying to make it good but it's beyond their abilities, given the lack of available parts. Honestly, they don't know when we can get that system back working for you.'

Potemkin stopped walking and cupped his hands to his mouth and blew into them, then shivered theatrically.

'And it really is cold here,' he said with a big, wide grin. The indignity of it, of this piece of shit trying to make light of the hell they'd been living through here... Gregor wanted to stride over there and stomp on the guy's head. 'So let me get to my point. I'm here with an offer. An offer to get you out of this place for good. An offer of freedom.' He reached into his jacket and pulled out a piece of paper and wafted it in the air. 'Each of you will receive one of these, if you agree. It's a legal document. Ratified by the Ministry of Justice. It confirms the end of your incarceration here, or anywhere. It doesn't matter what you did, how long your sentence. Today, you can walk out of here free men.'

'OK then, let's go,' said one smart-ass, taking a step forward until Potemkin turned to him.

'Did I say you could move out of line?'

He quickly stepped back and shrank down as Potemkin walked toward him, right up into his face. Gregor was a little surprised when the major didn't smack him or shoot him right there.

Potemkin held the paper up again. 'In exchange for your freedom, you will join the military forces of Brightstar – the most sophisticated private army on this earth. You'll be clothed, fed, paid. Two years of service and then you get to go home. See your families again. Live again. You get to go home free men.' He turned and paced again. 'No. Actually, you get to go home as heroes.'

'Do we have to fight?' someone else shouted out.

'Of course!' Potemkin answered, smiling again, as though the answer made everything so much nicer and more appealing. 'You will be taken from here today to a training camp. Within weeks you will be deployed to Eastern Ukraine to continue the fight against Naziism and injustice there.'

'Fuck that shit,' said Handsome Vlad. He spat on the ground in front of him then turned and walked back to his cell.

Gregor inwardly groaned. Several other inmates shuffled on their feet – a combination of sympathy for their friend but also others perhaps contemplating making a similar stand. Gregor knew that Handsome Vlad's parents came from Donbas. Several of his family members had been killed by the Russian-backed rebel forces there. And he was far from the only one here to have suffered from the war. He was simply the only one stupid enough to bring his emotions out there and then.

Smile gone, Potemkin looked like he'd swallowed a mouthful of cocaine-crazed wasps. He barked at his two corporals and the underlings marched into the cell and everyone else stood still and listened to the fight – the beating – that followed. Potemkin headed into the cell too and moments later Vlad's screams echoed around the frozen atrium.

'This is insane,' Hector whispered. 'What are we going to do?'

'We take the offer,' Gregor said.

'Are you fucking crazy?' Hector hissed. 'I'm not going to war. I'm no soldier.'

'I'm not staying here, and you shouldn't either.'

They ended their hushed conversation when Potemkin came back out, dragging Handsome Vlad by his neck. His face was a pulpy mess. It looked like at least one of his eyes had been gouged. Potemkin, blood streaking his uniform and dripping from his knuckles, pulled Handsome Vlad back to his place in the line.

'Stand up,' Potemkin said, eerily calm, even as his chest heaved from exertion. 'I said stand up!' he boomed and most inmates, even the guards and soldiers, jolted from the severity of the bark.

But Handsome Vlad didn't stand up. Most likely he couldn't.

Potemkin sighed. 'Unfortunately we can only take able-bodied, willing fighters. So this man will have to stay here. Except all the guards are leaving today. They're overdue their break. But I'm not sure when the next rotation arrives. Do you know?'

Potemkin turned to Yuri who shook his head.

'So anyone left behind here... You'll be confined to your cells, awaiting the next train, and hopefully some good fortune. If that's what you want?'

He looked over the group. Was he actually waiting for a response?

'The choice you're giving us then,' Hector said, and Gregor really wished his friend would have just kept his mouth shut for once, 'is we either give two years of military service to Brightstar, or we starve to death here, if the cold doesn't kill us first?'

Potemkin nodded, as though finally satisfied that someone got it. 'Almost, but not quite. Not two years of service and then free men. You will be free men today. The papers I hand out will confirm it! Now make your choice. All of you. If you're coming with me, stay right where you are and we'll bring out your uniforms. If you want to take your chances and stay here, simply walk back to your cells. And good luck.'

Not a single person moved. Potemkin's smile returned.

'Very good. Then let's get you all out of here.'

6

ANTIBES, FRANCE

It was dark as he approached Charlotte's apartment building. He hadn't seen her since the previous morning when she'd left early to go to the police station. Yesterday they'd communicated through texts several times but today he got the distinct impression she was giving him the cold shoulder.

He stepped out of the car, approached the intercom and pressed her number, but got no response. A niggle at the back of his mind told him not to worry. Whatever he'd uncovered over the last thirty-six hours, he was sure it wouldn't bring harm directly to her.

Yet that niggle continued to grow as he stood out there in the cold, the stars above him bright in the clear night sky.

He pressed the intercom again but still no answer. He spotted a young woman the other side of the glass security door, coming toward the exit with her phone out, talking and giggling as she moved. Ryker stepped back from the door and waited for her to open up and head out before he moved in. He took the stairs to the fifth floor and knocked on Charlotte's door. He heard her padding across the carpet inside and when the soft sound stopped, he knew she was staring at him through the peephole.

'I know you're in there,' he said. 'I'm not sure what you think I've done wrong—'

The door opened and then caught on the chain and Charlotte's face poked out between the gap.

'You don't know what you've done wrong? Are you kidding me?'

'Maybe open up, then you can tell me all about it.'

'I don't want to see you.'

'Charlotte—'

'I told you, James. Don't go getting into more trouble. Don't go doing anything stupid that will come back to harm me. My work.'

'Let me explain—'

'Thierry was right. I should have never got involved with you.'

'What the hell has he got to do with this?'

'He's my brother,' Charlotte said. 'He's got everything to do with my life.'

'Oh, then next time we're getting cozy together let's invite him over.'

'Get lost, James.'

She went to close the door but he put his shoe in the way and she banged the wood against it a couple of times. In his thin sneakers it actually hurt pretty bad, but he didn't move his foot.

'We need to talk,' Ryker said. 'Whether or not you think I've done something wrong, we need to talk. I need to tell you what I found. About...' He looked over his shoulder as though someone might be listening. 'You know who.'

'Move your foot,' she said, her anger still clear in the demand. Ryker didn't. 'I said—'

Ryker peeled his foot back and the door slammed shut. And

stayed that way. He was about to head off when he heard the latch release.

'Come in,' she said after she'd opened the door and stood to the side. 'But you better make this good. And quick.'

Ryker moved on in. She slammed the door shut and brushed past him to the sofa where she slumped down. She was already in her PJs. He could smell food. A stew perhaps. Two dirty plates and two empty wine glasses sat by the sink.

'Yeah. I had company,' Charlotte said. 'You want to know who?'

Ryker shrugged. 'So here's what I have,' he started, but Charlotte raised a hand to cut him off.

'Wait up. Maybe I should get this recorded. Because I'm pretty sure if you're going to tell me what you've been up to the last two days that you're about to implicate yourself in a series of crimes.'

'I am?' Ryker said.

'Kidnap, torture for starters?'

'And who did I kidnap and torture?'

'Oh, you know, only one of the key persons of interest in my investigation.'

'Bennette?'

'Yes, James! Pierre Bennette! Who was checked in to a hospital last night with a horrific leg fracture and cuts and bruises all over him.'

'I didn't do any of that.'

'I'm sure you didn't. So it wasn't you who attacked him at that old hotel?'

'No, I didn't. He pulled a gun on me first.'

'And you went all Rambo on him and fought back, and then what? Threw him off a balcony before you interrogated him under duress?'

Ryker sighed. This was clearly going nowhere.

'Do you want me to tell you what I know or not?' he asked.

She folded her arms in defiance. 'You're here, so why not. But I haven't yet decided against putting you in handcuffs and turning you in myself.'

'OK. Let me know if you do decide. Yeah, I interrogated Bennette. But I didn't torture him. He broke his leg trying to run away from me. After pulling a gun on me.'

'He pulled a gun on you, and then ran away?'

'I mean, I disarmed him first...' Ryker pulled the weapon from his jeans. Charlotte winced when she saw it then relaxed – but only a little – when Ryker placed it on the dining table. 'Maybe you should check it. Fingerprints would confirm it's his. No idea if it's registered or not. Maybe it's been used in a crime before.'

'It certainly has now.'

'OK, let's move on from Bennette. Charlotte, let me cut through the bullshit. I've found enough evidence for you to make a move on Litvinov. It's that simple. I have names of associates, I have businesses which I know he's laundering money through. I've been to scope out three separate locations today on the Côte d'Azur where I know he's carrying out his crimes. Drug stores for his stashes coming over from North Africa. Warehouses where he processes illegal immigrants before they're sent off to whatever sham of a life he's got planned for them. Women, children, men, all ready to be exploited. And it's not just hearsay, I've got photos and—'

He went to take out his phone but again Charlotte halted him.

'OK. You've said enough.'

'But—'

'James, you need to go.'

'Charlotte, I know this isn't how you normally do things here, but you can use what I have at least. Take it to your superiors. Discuss it. Use it to build your case.'

'How can I?' she shouted. 'Every single piece of evidence you've just mentioned, everything you know or you've got on your computer or your phone or wherever else has been obtained illegally! We can't use it! If anything, you've made it even harder for us to crack down on him now.'

'You're wrong,' Ryker said. 'I—'

'It doesn't matter what you think. I don't want any of it. Why are you even doing this? Who the hell are you to come into my life like this and—'

'I'm here to help.'

'I never asked for your help!'

'But you'll need it,' Ryker said. 'Especially with the blockages you've got in your own team.'

She looked really pissed off now. They'd never discussed that subject openly before, but he kind of knew that she suspected there was an informant in the police ranks. Top criminals like Litvinov always needed leverage like that.

'Charlotte, it's Pichon. I know it is.'

'You need to go.'

'Are you listening to me? Pichon is on the take—'

She shot up from her seat. 'Get out! Get out, now!'

Ryker really didn't want to, but she wasn't giving him much choice.

He left the gun where it was and headed for the door where he turned back to her.

'If you change your mind—'

'Just go. And please don't come back.'

So he left.

He got back into his car and decided to make the call there and then.

'Ryker, how'd it go?' Peter Winter asked. An old friend. His old boss, kind of. Currently one of the most senior personnel with the Secret Intelligence Service, more commonly known as MI6. One of the most senior? Head of Ethics was his new title. A strange job title for anyone who operated in the clandestine world.

'I'm not sure I've won myself much goodwill just now,' Ryker said.

'So she doesn't want it? None of it?'

'We didn't even get to discussing the details. She's scared. And I don't think it's because of how I got the intel, even if that's what she claims. I think she's scared because if I rip open the wasp's nest, she's the one standing right there on the outside.'

'You think Pichon would go after her?'

'Undoubtedly. And he'd know she was getting help from somewhere. We pushed her too far too soon.'

Winter sighed and Ryker could practically hear the cogs turning.

'We need to keep on top of Litvinov before he gets wind and clears out.'

'You have a plan B?' Winter asked.

'Of course.'

'Does it involve a mess?'

'It involves getting to the end goal in the quickest way possible.'

'A big, old mess then.'

'For Litvinov and his cronies, yes.'

A further silence.

'Do you need help for it?' Winter asked after a while.

'No.'

'Then get it done. I'll wait to hear the fallout from this end.'

'Got it.'

'Good luck.'

The call went dead.

7

Ryker had spotted the BMW convertible driving around the streets and decided to follow. A slice of luck, although he'd been determined to 'bump' into Luc Pichon one way or another today. As it turned out, Pichon was headed for a mid-morning snack once again. At the same cafe as the last time the two men had met. A creature of habit.

Although this time Ryker didn't bother to order anything for himself. Instead he simply followed Pichon into the cafe, waited while the guy had a flirty chat with the server before he headed off to his seat. Then Ryker went straight up to him. He pulled back the chair opposite Pichon and sat down.

'Excusez-moi?' Pichon said, his face not betraying his distaste at the interruption.

Ryker reached across the table and grabbed Pichon's wrist and dragged the man toward him. He turned the wrist over and Pichon grimaced and writhed.

'I'll snap it if you make me,' Ryker said.

Pichon threw a couple of expletives and the other three patrons on the inside took notice.

'Don't worry,' Ryker said, looking them over. 'We're police.'

Pichon went for his gun with his free hand but the weapon was across his body and before he'd even touched the grip Ryker twisted his wrist further.

'Ah, ah. You wouldn't get it before I snap your bones. And you wouldn't get a shot off before I jammed that fork through your eyeball.'

Ryker nodded at the cutlery.

'You can't do this! I'm—'

Ryker twisted again.

'I am doing this. Let's make this quick, if you like. So I don't embarrass you in front of these people.'

Pichon said nothing but Ryker could see the shame on his face at the indignity. He thought he ruled this little town. Not anymore. Though Ryker did want to make this quick before any of the other patrons tried to intervene or called 117.

'I'm taking your gun now,' Ryker said. 'It's better for both of us that way.' Pichon barely resisted as Ryker reached around the table and carefully pulled the gun free. He stashed it in his waistband.

'You're protecting Litvinov. Tell me about that.'

'Who?'

'Valeri Litvinov.'

'I don't know what you're talking about!'

Ryker sighed. 'This isn't a situation where you get a choice to come clean or not. You either do it here, now, or we do this another way. The other way ends up much worse for you. Just trust me on that.'

Pichon gritted his teeth but said nothing.

'Tell me about Litvinov. What's he got on you? Is he threatening you or are you just doing it for the payoff?'

Pichon whimpered and shook his head.

'Not much of an answer. It could make a difference. I might go easy on you if you're being forced to help him.'

Pichon shook his head. Ryker wasn't sure if it was an admission of something or not.

'The investigation into Litvinov has been stalled over and over. Is it only you blocking it or is there someone else higher up too?'

'You'll pay for this!'

Ryker pulled on the wrist further and Pichon shouted out in pain and his whole body twisted in the chair.

'This is getting boring now,' Ryker said. 'The second option for how we do this is looking more and more likely. So let me try one more thing. I have three locations for Litvinov's... other businesses. You know, not the real estate business. Not the tax-free investment funds. I'm talking about the seedy stuff he tries to pretend he's not into anymore. Drugs. Prostitution. Human trafficking—'

'You're insane!'

'Possibly. So you probably shouldn't disappoint me. Now, I sent details of all three of those locations to your colleagues. Evidence of what happens there. You know what happened? Absolutely nothing. I doubt anyone even performed a drive-by. Why is that?'

But Pichon still didn't say a word. And honestly, Ryker hadn't really expected him to. Men like Pichon thought they operated above the law – because most often they did. And the confidence and superiority complex that came with that life often meant they were too stubborn for their own good, and too slow to recognize when their world was about to come crashing down around them.

'OK. We'll do this the other way. Let's go.'

Ryker stood up and dragged Pichon up with him.

'You're driving,' Ryker said, before pulling Pichon toward the door. He only resisted a little. Not because he was truly scared, but most likely because he just wanted to get out of there where other people were seeing his weakness. And probably because he still thought he could turn this situation around so that he was on top.

Ryker only let go of Pichon's wrist when they were right by his car, and he kicked him forward to propel him onto the shiny bodywork. Pichon groaned when he hit the metal, and the impact left an ugly dent.

'Oops,' Ryker said, before he opened the door and then pushed Pichon into the driver's seat.

Ryker took the gun out as he moved around to the passenger side and slid in, and already knew Pichon had reached for the backup gun in the glove box. Ryker took hold of Pichon's wrist again and slammed his hand against the dashboard. The second time he did it the gun clattered free. Then he smacked Pichon's head into the steering wheel to hopefully act as a further deterrent. The blow caused a gash on Pichon's nose and blood oozed down his nice shirt and onto the expensive cream leather seat.

'Are you done now?' Ryker asked.

A few more French expletives followed but Pichon didn't try anything else stupid. Ryker picked up the second gun and stuffed it under his seat.

'We're going to the warehouse off Avenue de la Roubine, the other side of Cannes. You know which one I'm talking about so just drive.'

The engine remained off.

'Pichon, stop Pichonning me off. You know the place. Take me there.'

Pichon grumbled under his breath but then started the engine and soon they were on their way.

The drive would take over half an hour. Plenty of time to talk. Except Ryker already realized Pichon was going to offer him little willingly.

Still, he wasn't interested in sitting in silence.

'Tell me how you got involved with Litvinov,' Ryker said, his fingers still wrapped around the grip of Pichon's service handgun which rested on his lap.

Pichon said nothing as he kept his eyes on the road.

'This isn't me trying to wear you down, trying to find snippets of information or inconsistencies that I can throw back at you as gotchas. I already know you're in cahoots. Just tell me about it. You're my way in, but it's Litvinov I want.'

'You're not with the police, or... anything like that, are you?' Pichon said.

'No shit, Sherlock.'

'Then what are you? Just some crazy guy out for revenge?'

Ryker didn't answer the question straight away. He was quite pleased that Pichon had decided to try and figure Ryker out, and to express that out loud too. It meant the guy wasn't about to zip his lips for the next forty minutes. But he was also really, really far off the mark. And Ryker was happy for him to stay there.

'You don't need to know about me,' Ryker said. 'So let's stay concentrated on you, and how you came to the position of being paid off by a corrupt Russian billionaire.'

Now Pichon decided to go all quiet again.

'Do you even know much about Litvinov and his past? Or do you only care about the money he gives you for favors, and the promotions you have your greedy eyes on knowing that you're so well-protected for not doing your job.'

Nothing.

'Come on, even if you want to pretend with me that you're a legit cop, I know your department is investigating Litvinov. Officially at least. So tell me what you know. Start me with where he comes from.'

Pichon sighed. 'Litvinov was born in the former Ukraine SSR.'

Nothing more.

'OK? That was a good start, but do you think you could add to it? Perhaps ten times over?'

Pichon looked more and more riled by Ryker's continued mocking.

'Litvinov was an accountant,' Pichon said. 'He made a lot of money when the Soviet Union fell as he bought up huge pieces of land across Ukraine and Chechnya for next to nothing. Land which was eventually sold or leased back to the government for oil and gas pipelines. Pipelines which his own companies won the rights to build and maintain.'

'Yeah, yeah, that's the part from Wikipedia. Thanks. So he got horribly, stinking rich because he had a few buddies in high places who sold him stuff on the cheap. Every oligarch has the same story. Tell me the part about the fun stuff. The drugs. The trafficking. The murders.'

Pichon took another pause before carrying on. 'We believe Litvinov was probably always involved with the mafia in Chechnya. He was well-educated and had a degree in finance and used his skills to help them launder their money. Then he became rich himself because of the political connections he gathered in keeping the mafia's money off the books, away from regulators.'

'What you're saying is he paid off people in government, made friends that way, and then when the Soviet Union fell and everything was privatized, he used those same connections to make himself rich.'

'And he made some enemies in the mafia because of it. They didn't like that he was profiteering.'

'And rather than give them any kind of a share, he instead decided to take over their business too.'

'He tried. And a lot of blood was spilled. If he ever went back to Chechnya he'd be arrested and put on trial for several murders, if he wasn't simply assassinated by the remnants of the gang he left behind.'

'Instead he came to France to live the life.'

Pichon gave nothing else. So Ryker decided to add some extra flavor himself.

'Except he didn't just bring his money here. He brought the business that he'd taken over too. Moved it all several hundred miles west. He started sourcing drugs from North Africa to add to what he'd already established coming out of the Middle East, opium from Afghanistan in particular. And over the last three decades he's benefitted from a long line of wars and conflicts where he's been able to make serious money from trafficking refugees. Because a few billion simply isn't enough, is it? Or maybe it's not even the money and he's just a narcissist who enjoys holding power over other people. What do you think?'

Pichon didn't answer.

'So tell me, if you know all that about Litvinov, why is he still a free man?'

'You want me to say something to implicate myself, don't you? Except I've done nothing wrong.'

'Call him.'

'Excuse me?'

'On your phone. Call him. I'd like him to be at the warehouse too. A little meeting between us all.'

Pichon made no attempt to do so. So Ryker reached over and into Pichon's pocket for his phone and Pichon did the stupid thing of trying to resist. An elbow to his nose got him to realize it was best to acquiesce.

'And now you've made even more of a mess of your nice shirt,' Ryker said, indicating the growing patch of red. 'Unlock it.' He held the phone out in front of Pichon's face and the screen unlocked. Ryker scrolled through the contacts list. 'Which one is Litvinov?'

'Why would I have Valeri Litvinov's phone number? He's someone I'm investigating.'

Ryker resisted laughing out loud at that. 'Ah, here it is. Uncle Eric. That's Litvinov. I know because I know the number myself. But why the fuck do you call him Uncle Eric?'

Once more Pichon decided not to answer.

'I'm calling him now. So you'd better get your happy, chatty side ready.'

Ryker hit the green button and the call rang through on the BMW's dashboard. Pichon went all fidgety as though he couldn't believe Ryker was doing this and he had no idea what to say.

'Just tell him the truth,' Ryker said. 'And tell him to meet us there.'

'What is it?' came Litvinov's gritty voice through the boomy speakers. Each word made Pichon wince.

'I've got...' Pichon looked over at Ryker. 'I've got some guy who wants to meet you.'

'What are you talking about?'

'Seriously. I'm... He's got a gun. He's pointing it at me right now. We're going to the old bread warehouse. He wants you to go there too.'

'Is this a joke?'

'No! It's not. He's—'

'Pichon, you stupid... Get rid of him.'

'I don't think that's going to happen,' Ryker said.

Silence. Except for the sound of the tires on the tarmac and Pichon's heavy breathing.

Then the call ended.

'Do you think we got his agreement?' Ryker asked, quite obviously tongue-in-cheek, he thought, although the doubtful gaze he received from Pichon suggested the cop hadn't understood.

Little more was said. Pichon didn't need any help finding the place. Of course he didn't. He knew exactly what the warehouse was and how to get there. The old bread warehouse, he'd said to Litvinov. Ryker didn't know what he'd meant by that. Perhaps just a code name, or perhaps something else. Ryker might follow up on it.

Pichon pulled the car off the main road and through the open chain-link fence to the property. The warehouse was large, a single-story with corrugated steel walls and roof and a small brick office block attached in one corner. There was no signage on the outside of the building at all. No vehicles either, Ryker noticed. Not many signs of life at all, as the forecourt was empty of... anything. Just a large, open, tarmac space. Clean, though. No litter or debris or weeds or anything like that, suggesting the place was used and kept neat rather than abandoned.

'First to arrive,' Ryker said as Pichon parked up. 'Or maybe you didn't do a good enough job of persuading him.'

'I did what—'

'It's fine. We'll work around it. Let's go inside.'

Pichon turned the engine off but then didn't move, as though he was in two minds.

'I said let's go,' Ryker said as he opened his door. He stepped out, and kept the gun held out toward Pichon as he moved around to the driver's side. Pichon pulled himself out slowly, awkwardly, like an old man would. Ryker prodded him in the back with the gun. 'Move.'

They headed toward the office block, Pichon edgy as they

walked, looking this way and that. Ryker mainly kept his focus on the cop, aware for any sudden, stupid move he might make.

'What exactly is your plan here?' Pichon said. Ryker didn't answer. 'This is crazy.'

'You let me worry about that.'

They reached the door which had a PIN-code lock on it. Pichon paused there, glanced at Ryker as though to question what they were going to do about it.

'You know it, though, don't you?' Ryker said. 'Because you're the one who gets the area ready for some of the shipments. I know that because I've seen you here. And you know why Litvinov has people like you do those jobs, don't you?'

Pichon held his tongue.

'So he's got evidence, you idiot. Direct evidence linking you to his crimes. What? Did you think he just trusted you or liked you or something?'

Pichon still didn't say a word but turned back to the door and pressed in the six-digit code before he opened the door.

The small foyer inside was dark and chilly and quiet. Ryker let the door close behind him as he looked around.

'Let's make ourselves comfortable,' Ryker said. He nudged Pichon forward, aiming for the double doors straight ahead of them that led to the main warehouse floor.

They didn't make it there.

The door to Ryker's left burst open. So too the one in front, to his right. The first gunshot grazed his fingertip and caused Pichon's sidearm to fall from his grip. The second gunshot whizzed past his ear and caused both him and Pichon to duck and cower.

Then came pressure to the back Ryker's skull.

'Any sudden moves and you're dead,' the man behind him said, and within a couple of seconds there were men all around, like cockroaches who'd crawled out of the cracks in the walls. 'Hands in front.'

Ryker did as he was told. Cold metal wrapped around his wrists as the handcuffs were clicked into place.

'Walk.'

So Ryker did, aided by the gun pressed at the back of his head. He moved between the gathering men. In through the now open double doors.

Into the very heart of the wasp's nest.

8

Ryker grimaced, tried to ignore the growing pain in his wrists, the metal digging deep. They'd hung him from a hook in the ceiling, the cuffs on his wrists attached to a locked carabiner. His ankles were roped together, and his feet dangled a foot from the floor.

Eight men in total crowded around him in the big and near-empty space of the warehouse. Near empty because old racking remained in place across one of the walls, and two large propane tanks stood in a corner, but other than that there was little indication of what took place here. It was simply a stop-off point. Goods – both drugs and people – came in, and those goods were quickly taken back out again. They weren't the kind of goods that anyone wanted stored in one place for any amount of time, so for the most part the place stood empty.

Not today though.

Eight men. They ranged in physique and looks from the small and scrawny to the big and the brutish. All had the glint of no-good in their eyes. All except for one man. Valeri Litvinov. He didn't look much like a billionaire, nor like a mafioso. Just an average guy. He wore cheap-looking business casual, unpolished brown shoes. His hair was a mess of gray and mucky brown, a choppy style that was popular with teens in the nineties but looked odd on a guy pushing sixty. He had a potbelly from too much food and wine and too little rigorous exercise, and his skin was heavily tanned and lined from too much of the Côte d'Azur's sunshine. His eyes were hollow, but his face wasn't hard. Plain, really. Like his mood which Ryker couldn't read at all.

'So you decided against a bullet to the brain,' Ryker said. He glanced from Litvinov to Pichon who stood a couple of steps behind the boss. He looked more confident again now, a contrast to his bloodied shirt and the dried stuff around his horribly swollen nostrils.

'I haven't decided against anything,' Litvinov said. 'But I have the benefit of time here. A chance to think things through before I make that decision.'

'If you say so.'

Ryker again glanced at each of the men in his view, trying to figure the dynamic. Who the underlings were. Who the second-in-command was. No particular indication from how they were positioned. There was no one by Litvinov's side, in his ear. Although he did recognize the meaty guy next to Pichon from some of the surveillance pictures the police had – which he'd helped himself to. The guy was an enforcer from the motherland who'd followed his boss across the continent. But as mean as the guy looked, he was nearly as old as the boss himself.

'Why don't we start with who you are?' Litvinov said. 'And why you put a gun to the head of my... associate, in order to get in front of me.'

'Associate. You mean the crooked cop?'

Pichon's face twitched. Anger. But he held back a response.

'My name's James Ryker.'

No reaction to that from anyone in the room.

'Do I know you?' Litvinov said.

'I feel I know more about you than the other way around. And that's the way it's going to stay.'

'I wouldn't be so sure,' Litvinov said.

'What? You're going to torture me?' Ryker said. 'But which one of these guys is the torturer? I'm guessing it's not you.'

'No,' Litvinov said. 'It's not me. That'd be my friend here.'

Ryker had spotted him before when he'd been counting but hadn't paid much attention to him. But he came closer now, lugging a holdall with him. He was tall, slim, with glasses on a Roman nose. He had a resting sneer that showed off big teeth which up close made him look like a mad surgeon from a low-budget slasher movie.

He knelt down in front of Ryker and opened up the bag to reveal the grim looking tools inside. He took out some fabric scissors and snipped away at Ryker's jeans, working up from his ankles. Ryker initially resisted, swinging his feet, but the reality was that any movement like that only caused the metal of the cuffs to dig further into the skin on his wrists and if he did too much it'd tear right through his flesh.

'You don't think you should ask before you take my clothes off?' Ryker said, still sounding unfazed and confident although it was becoming harder and harder.

'OK,' Litvinov said with a sigh as though growing weary. 'Let me put it for you like this. I don't yet know what we'll be able to get out of you. How far you're willing to go here before you talk. But let me tell you one thing, James Ryker: I won't be finished with you until at the very least I've eradicated that grating confidence of yours.'

'Is this what you did to Mehdi Hakim before you killed him?' Ryker asked. 'And Oscar Petterson?'

The surgeon paused a moment as though waiting to see what

the boss would say to the two names, but then carried on snipping.

'You know who I'm talking about,' Ryker said. 'Hakim was a drug smuggler from Morocco. You two were working together until he tried to take his goods elsewhere. So you tortured and killed him so that... Well, I don't know. Perhaps just because. His mutilated body washed up on the coast of Corsica. No hands, no feet, no head. Although there was some speculation as to whether the parts were taken while he was alive or after death.'

'I can assure you, Mr. Ryker, they found him exactly as he left here.'

'This warehouse?' Ryker asked looking around. 'You killed him here?'

'After he'd given me what I needed from him. And after I'd... got even.'

'But you didn't actually do any of that, did you? You just have your goons doing the blood work.'

'I wouldn't want the blood of scum like you on my hands.'

'Literally. Because metaphorically your hands are covered.'

Litvinov laughed. An unnecessarily hearty laugh. The surgeon had finished cutting through Ryker's jeans and shirt, had removed his socks, leaving Ryker dangling in his boxers. Litvinov moved a little closer, his eyes flitting across Ryker's body. Perhaps taking in the network of scars.

'De-gloving,' Litvinov said. 'We'll start with de-gloving.'

The surgeon rummaged and pulled out a basic scalpel.

'You know what I'm talking about?' Litvinov said.

Ryker did, but he didn't answer.

Litvinov raised a hand and mimicked pulling off a glove. 'Literally, like taking off a glove. Except not a glove, but your skin. We'll start with your feet given your hands are... you know.'

Four of the men came forward and with the gun still pressed

to Ryker's skull the extra muscle took hold of him, pinning him in place. Ryker bucked against the restraints but there really was no point. Blood dribbled down his wrist as the cuffs cut deeper. De-gloving his feet? If he twisted too much, he'd de-glove his hands too.

'We'll do this first, and then we'll talk some more,' Litvinov said. 'But I'll tell you now what I need to know. I need to know why you are here. Why you targeted me. Who sent you. Who else knows what you know. You understand?'

Ryker said nothing. The surgeon moved the scalpel toward Ryker's right ankle. The tip of the blade pressed into his skin. Pierced the skin. Blood dribbled out along the metal. The surgeon looked up at Ryker and smiled.

'Wait!' Ryker shouted out. 'Wait!'

The surgeon paused with the scalpel. A smile spread across Litvinov's face. 'I already explained,' he said. 'We'll talk after this.'

The surgeon drew the scalpel across, the small blade easily slicing across an inch or so of flesh.

'I said wait!' Ryker shouted out, panting now. 'There's... there's something you forgot to ask me first.'

Litvinov's smile faltered. 'I did?'

'You forgot to ask me why I chose this warehouse.'

The smile faded altogether. The surgeon pulled the scalpel away from Ryker's skin.

'You have several locations like this one,' Ryker said. 'But I chose here. Pichon drove me over from Cap d'Antibes. What was it, forty minutes?' He looked over at Pichon who just looked confused. 'And we only called you about halfway into that drive. He asked you to meet us here. You didn't exactly agree, did you?'

Litvinov didn't respond but Ryker had his attention at least.

'Then we get here and there's not a car in sight outside,' Ryker said. 'But you were all in here, waiting.'

'I think I'm missing your point.' He looked down at the surgeon. 'Please, continue.'

'No! Wait!' Ryker said. Relieved that the surgeon bothered to listen. 'You had a few minutes to hide the cars, so you could fool me into thinking this place was empty. So you could ambush me. But my point is... you were already here.'

'That's your point? I'm not sure—'

'I knew you were already here. That's why I chose this place!'

Litvinov opened his mouth to say something then thought better of it, then a deep frown spread as though admonishing himself that he didn't know what to say. That he didn't yet fully understand the implication of Ryker's revelation. So Ryker would help him.

'I knew you were already here because I hacked your phone three days ago, so I've been able to follow you on GPS since then. And I was in this warehouse two days ago. I broke in at night and installed eleven cameras around the place.'

Ryker looked out across the warehouse now, up into the corners of the room. The men were doing the same. Most of them, anyway. Not Litvinov though. He continued to glare at Ryker.

'It's not true,' Pichon said. 'He's bluffing. There's nothing here.'

'There is,' Ryker said. 'I promise you there is. Some are hidden in the light fittings. Some in the grilles for the air ducts. But there's one right there too.' He nodded to the right. 'Attached to the underside of the racking. Third shelf.'

One of the goons strode over there. He looked and felt under the metal. Then paused when he found the little wireless lens stuck there with double-sided tape. He pulled it out and held it aloft.

'Like I said. Eleven cameras. Wireless. Connected for live stream.'

The goon walked over to Litvinov and whispered something in his ear.

'This has worked out even better than I imagined,' Ryker said. 'You've just implicated yourself in the murder of that Moroccan smuggler. You've confirmed you're in cahoots with Pichon. You've made very clear what you intend to do to me.'

Litvinov barked out an instruction and the goon and two others – two who were previously helping to hold Ryker in place – moved off around the room, searching.

'And do you know who's been watching the feed this whole time?' Ryker said. 'Pichon's colleagues back in Antibes. Some pretty influential people from further afield too. The SWAT team is probably en route right now.' Ryker craned his neck a little. 'Can you hear the sirens?'

Litvinov shook his head but said nothing. He waited for one of the goons to come back to him. Just like his friend before, the guy whispered in the boss's ear.

'I call bullshit,' Litvinov said. 'There are no other devices. Just that one. And it's not even equipped for wireless transmission.'

Ryker laughed. 'OK then. So your boy there is a comms expert? Great. Let's go with that. Have your surgeon de-glove me in front of the world. Your face will be everywhere on the internet within hours. You'll be more famous than you ever dreamed.'

'Nothing I do is for fame. It's—'

He didn't finish. Because Ryker was finally ready. It was stupid of them to not check his pockets where he'd stashed a paperclip to pick the cuffs he thought they might use to secure him. A paperclip he'd managed to get into his hand before they'd strung him up. And stupid of all of them to give him so much time. And perhaps even more stupid of them to take away two of the men who'd been holding him in place for his torture.

So with all of the men preoccupied with their doubts about the cameras that may or may not have been planted, that may or may not have been recording, live streaming, Ryker made his move.

He unclasped the unlocked cuffs and fell down to the floor. It was hard to land properly with his feet roped together but he just about managed it and he bounced back up, swung around and jabbed the pointed end of the open handcuffs into the neck of the man behind him. The one with the gun. Ryker pulled the cuffs forward, tearing a three-inch hole in the man's neck. Blood gushed. He fired his weapon. Knee-jerk reaction. The bullet hit one of his own men. Ryker prized the gun free and fell down onto his backside. He shot off at anything he could see moving. Three, four, five quick pulls of the trigger. At least three hits.

He swiveled, legs outstretched, and his still-bound feet swiped the surgeon off the floor. The guy flopped down and the scalpel dropped free. Ryker reached forward and started to cut through the rope, but a gunshot pinged into the floor right by his side, sending a chunk of concrete shrapnel into his hip. He fired back without looking and tried cutting again. He yanked his legs apart to snap through the remaining rope before he jumped back to his feet.

He had no idea where Pichon had gone. Litvinov...

At the far end of the warehouse. Scurrying away like the weasel he was.

But another gunshot caused Ryker to scuttle back before he could get another shot off.

Except he didn't shoot at the gunman. Nor at the escaping boss, but at the propane tank just beyond him.

The explosion sent a wave of fire and superheated air out across the warehouse floor. Two men screamed and ran liked crazed animals as flames consumed them. Ryker raced forward to Litvinov who'd been a little luckier. No flames on him but he was on the floor, the shock wave having felled him. His last remaining enforcer tried to haul him up, but Ryker reached them before he'd managed the feat. He launched his foot up under the guy's chin and sent him flying toward the leaping flames. Ryker grabbed Litvinov by the scruff of his neck and dragged him back. Litvinov tried to resist so Ryker stomped on the guy's knee. The crack didn't sound too pleasant. Litvinov wouldn't be walking for a while. The boss screamed in agony, and his resistance disappeared as Ryker dragged him further away. Back toward the office block.

Above the din of the growing fire Ryker heard sirens.

'Told you I wasn't bluffing,' Ryker said.

He pulled Litvinov to the outside just as the first of the police vans arrived. Ryker let go and looked across the forecourt. Pichon was there, at his car door. A coward to the end. His plan had been to simply run. With the sirens and the lights of half a dozen vehicles fast approaching, he seemed to have a change of heart and pushed his car door shut as though pretending he'd just arrived on the scene.

So Ryker let go of Litvinov and raised his gun and fired off one final round. The bullet hit Pichon in his leg and he fell to the ground clutching his stricken limb. Ryker dropped the gun as the police piled out, shouting instructions at him and the others. Still, Ryker strode across to Pichon and pulled him up to his feet, even as the police, guns held out, crowded around him.

'Make sure you take him in too,' Ryker said. He tossed Pichon forward and he stumbled and rolled into a heap by the feet of his colleagues. One final indignity for him.

Before he could say or do anything else, Ryker was forced to his knees, then pushed face down to the floor as the police surrounded and subdued him.

9

One of the biggest surprises was that he'd fallen asleep at all. He'd tried to stay awake as long as he could, certain that Sergei and possibly the others too would attack him for speaking out to Father. But he'd lain there for hours as his brothers snored, as confused as he was scared.

And he had fallen asleep. For how long? He had no idea. But when he felt pressure on his chest his eyes sprang open and he bucked and tried to shoot up only to find Sergei on top of him, pinning him down.

His brothers crowded around too, taking hold of his arms and legs.

'You shouldn't have done that,' Sergei said. Even though his words were spoken with hatred, he had a smile on his face. A wicked smile.

Until he pursed his lips and sniffed forcibly a few times, collecting phlegm at the back of his throat. Gregor winced and writhed but his brothers had him pinned in place. The wad of spittle pushed through Sergei's lips, dangling above Gregor's face as it stretched down, down.

'Hold his head!' Andre shouted excitedly as though this was a show for them all.

They let go of Gregor's legs to hold his head and it gave him a chance to buck more and try to kick Sergei off him. But Sergei just grunted and sent a fist onto Gregor's nose which crunched under the pressure. Blood poured, heading back into his throat. Heading from his nostrils to his lips. He gagged and opened his mouth to cough and splutter and the spit-wad finally came loose and plopped onto Gregor's face, right between his top lip and his nose. It mingled with the blood and dribbled into his mouth and he wretched and spat and...

He found a surge of strength and he smacked Sergei in the back. Sergei pulled to the side, giving Gregor even more leverage with his legs, and he turned his body and kicked out again. Hit one of his brothers. Kicked out more as he bucked and tried to get them all off. Sergei, as big as he was, went flying.

Smack.

Gregor jumped up off the bed. He turned to face the four-some, expecting them to come at him. But his brothers stared down at Sergei who lay crumpled on the floor. He moved a hand to the back of his head. He'd cracked it on the side of the nightstand?

Blood.

'I'm sorry!' Gregor shouted.

Sergei rose to his feet like a demon pulling itself from the depths of hell.

Gregor cowered back. 'Father!' he squealed. He stepped back again. Wall. He had nowhere to go.

Sergei raced forward and Gregor was caught in two minds and lifted his hands to protect his face. But Sergei wasn't going for his face. Instead he lifted his foot and crashed it down onto the side of Gregor's knee which cracked. His leg caved and he collapsed to the floor, screaming.

'Ever hit me again. Ever hit any of us, ever betray any of us... and next time I'll kill you,' Sergei said.

Gregor said nothing, just continued to scream as the pain in his broken, twisted leg consumed him.

* * *

Present day
Buryatia, Russia

The train was old, rickety and not exactly fast, but perhaps the tentative speed was more to do with the horrendous conditions outside. For the last half hour they'd seen nothing out there but a wall of white, the blizzard snow falling near horizontally. At least it seemed that way with the train heading straight into the wind.

'Gregor, that's the best food you've had for weeks,' Hector said, nodding at the half-eaten meat sandwich on Gregor's lap. 'If you're not having it, I will.'

Gregor responded by finishing it off in three bites. He hadn't intended to leave it but had been busy thinking. In fact, he'd hardly said a word in the more than two hours they'd been on the train. Most of the others were boisterous, rowdy, relieved.

Most. But not all.

'It stinks,' Gregor said.

'I know,' Hector agreed.

'There are murderers here. Rapists. Scum who would have spent their entire lives behind bars. Who should spend their entire lives behind bars.'

A few others took notice of Gregor's words and he received a couple of scathing looks and the hubbub in the carriage died down a little.

'What's your problem?' said Broz, a meaty airhead sitting across the way. 'You think you're better than us?'

'It won't make much difference anyway,' said Young Vlad who was squashed next to Broz. 'How many of us do you even think will make it to the end of two years?'

A few murmurs but no one fully responded.

'I'm serious,' Young Vlad said, getting to his feet. 'You all know of Brightstar?'

'Yeah,' Hector said. 'A private army run by an oligarch. It's the Russian army in all but name except this way someone gets to make money out of it, and the Kremlin get to pretend the actions taken are nothing to do with them.'

'And they get to use guys like us in the ranks,' Young Vlad said. 'Cheap, expendable labor. You saw that guy, Potemkin. He hates us. We're not going to be his heroes anytime soon. We're cannon fodder. We'll be sent on suicide missions.'

'The best of us will survive,' Broz said, sounding confident and up for the challenge.

'You think?' Young Vlad said. 'Have you ever been a soldier? Ever stood on the front line?'

'No. Have you?'

'Young Vlad was a private,' Gregor said. 'And yeah, he was on the front line.'

'Until he ran away,' Hector added with a devious chuckle.

'What?' Broz said, eyes pinched with distaste now. 'You're a deserter?'

'If you'd been there, you'd know why,' Young Vlad said. 'Come on, Gregor, tell them.'

'You as well?' Broz said, looking more and more sullen.

'I wasn't a deserter,' Gregor said.

'Then what?'

'It's irrelevant to you.'

'You sure about that?'

'Yeah. I am. But I agree with Young Vlad. It might feel right now like we got a good thing, getting out of the gulag. But they're giving us two weeks' training before sending us to the front line. You really think that's how an elite army works?'

Broz said nothing in response.

'And at this time of year, if the bullets and the bombs don't kill us the conditions will. Most of us won't survive a few months, let alone two years.'

'Why do you think they're using convicts at all?' Young Vlad said. 'Because there aren't enough sane young men back home to sign up for this shit. Which is why we weren't exactly given a choice. It was this or die in the gulag.'

Like Handsome Vlad who'd been left there, beaten and locked in his cell.

By now the train carriage had quietened down, everyone listening to the conversation. Which likely meant most others had already had some doubts about what lay ahead, but back in the gulag with the choice of freezing to death or getting out... everyone had chosen getting out.

'Look,' Young Vlad said, pulling up the fabric on the sleeve of his green overcoat. 'What do you think this is?'

No one answered although Gregor assumed everyone realized even before Young Vlad told them. 'A bullet hole. How many of you have just been given a uniform with bullet holes? You don't need to be a genius to figure that one out. And if we carry on along this path, it won't be long before your uniform is on the back of some other loser.'

'And you can be sure they'll give us the absolute worst equipment,' Hector said, and his voice had even more people eagerly listening in.

'I heard Brightstar were arming some regiments with World War II rifles,' Young Vlad said. 'Most soldiers get left out in the middle of nowhere with a single magazine each. Told to hold a position for days, weeks at a time.'

'So what are we going to do about it?' Broz said.

Now everyone turned to Hector. The voice of reason. The one who needed to make this call.

'We already got out of the gulag,' Hector said. 'That was the hard part. There's nearly a hundred of us on this train, versus the guards, plus the twenty soldiers that came to the gulag.'

'All of them have weapons,' Broz said.

'For now.'

'So what?' Gregor said. 'You think we should just storm the soldiers' carriage and take over? We'd sacrifice tens of us.'

'May as well take our chances on the front line,' Broz added.

Hector sighed and Gregor could tell he was deep in thought. 'I know where we are,' he said after a few seconds looking outside, where the sky had cleared some. Although all Gregor could see was white – fields and hills and trees all covered in snow. No life. 'We're not far from Lake Baikal now. There're towns dotted all around it. At most we'd have fifty, a hundred miles of trekking to the nearest place.'

'With soldiers after us.'

'No,' Hector said. 'Because we'll kill them all. We'll take their clothes, their equipment.'

A few murmurs of disquiet. The conversation had taken a dark turn very quickly and Gregor could tell not everyone was fully on board.

'And how exactly do we do that?' Gregor asked.

'Like you said before, Gregor. We need to be cleverer than Pavel. Give ourselves the best chance of making it.' He leaned forward and others did too before he spoke in a more hushed tone. 'So this is what we'll do.'

* * *

Conversation had been minimal ever since Hector had laid out his plan. A few men had directly agreed. Others had stayed silent, but that was simply indirect agreement as far as Gregor could tell.

No one had challenged him. No one had told him not to do it. Likely because even if the plan was far from flawless, everyone knew the reality was that two years of service for Brightstar brought with it an equally large risk of death.

'I need a shit,' Gregor said, rising to his feet. Hector grabbed his arm and Broz looked over too. 'I said I need a shit. Nerves. You know?'

Hector let go. 'Be quick.'

Gregor moved off to the end of the carriage. The two sentries the other side of the door noticed him coming and stood glaring as he approached the door. He knocked and pointed to the toilet door behind them. They glanced at one another before one opened the door and Gregor stepped through.

'Be quick.'

'Yeah. I know.'

Except Gregor didn't go into the toilet. He carried on past. Toward the door for the next carriage.

'Hey! Wait!'

Gregor paid them no attention and kept going. He pulled open the door. Heads spun his way. Within a beat half a dozen soldiers in the carriage bounced to their feet, guns at the ready.

'It's OK, it's OK!' Gregor said, empty hands aloft. He relaxed a little in his stance. 'What's all the fuss? I thought we were comrades now.'

'What are you doing here?' one grumpy soldier asked him.

'I need to speak to Yuri.' Nonplussed looks from all. 'He's one of the guards. Go get him now.'

They didn't. But they didn't need to, because at the far end of the carriage Yuri got to his feet. He strode along the gangway, grabbed Gregor by the arm and took him out into the vestibule. The carriage door slammed shut behind them.

'What the hell are you doing? They could have shot you!'

'Why would they do that?'

'Because... Because...'

'Whatever. Save it. There's something you need to know.'

Yuri's eyes pinched with intrigue. Or possibly just suspicion. Gregor looked over his shoulder. Making sure he was out of eyesight of the prisoners in the next carriage.

'In about twenty minutes the prisoners are going to fight back.'

Yuri scoffed. 'You're serious?'

'Yes.'

'Those lousy motherfuckers. Even after they've been given their freedom?'

Gregor decided not to go into that one.

'Why are you telling me?' Yuri asked.

'Why do you think?'

'You want me to save you?'

'You always asked me to tell you if there's any trouble coming. This is it.'

Yuri contemplated that. As though he wasn't really sure he wanted to stick to whatever his end of the bargain was anymore.

'OK. First of all, you tell me everything. And then... I'll decide what help I'll give you.'

Which was about as good as Gregor could hope for. So he started talking.

10

He hobbled across the lawn to the bench where Father had beckoned him. The old man stared at him the whole way and he couldn't read the look as he watched Gregor struggle with the huge cast on his leg. Amusement? Pity?

Probably both.

'How is it?' Father asked as Gregor awkwardly sat down, grimacing as he did so.

'It hurts. All the time.'

'It will get better.'

'What if it doesn't? Sergei said maybe I'll never walk properly again.'

As if on cue, Sergei glanced over from farther across the garden where he and the other boys were digging the foundation for the new outbuilding. He smirked before looking back at the hole.

'I think you will.'

Gregor said nothing as he continued to watch his eldest brother a few moments. In a few days they'd be pouring concrete in there. How he'd love to bury Sergei in it.

'I know you're not happy about what happened,' Father said.

'Not happy? Sergei broke my leg! But that's not even the worst part. The worst part is that you did nothing to punish him. Actually no, even that's not the worst part. The worst part is that it only happened at all because I was trying to help you!'

This time it was Father's turn to not respond. It only made Gregor all the more angry although he did try to rein it in as he knew he couldn't blow so hard right next to Father. It'd only end badly for him.

'You don't see the error in your actions?' Father said after a few moments of silence.

'No!' Gregor said. 'You've always told me about being trustworthy. You asked me to tell you if there were ever any problems with my brothers. I thought I was doing the right thing.'

'I understand why you were confused,' Father said.

Gregor opened his mouth but then lost the thought.

'But you're right about this being about trust. The point is, Gregor, out in the rain, you destroyed all the trust your brothers had in you.'

'By telling you the truth.'

'Sometimes telling the truth isn't the right thing to do. For you. For others.'

'I don't understand.'

'I know. Because you're young. But this is how you learn, from your mistakes. Now you need to find a way to build trust with your brothers again because our plans don't work if you're not a unit.'

'So if I do hear bad things, you don't want me to tell you anymore?'

'Now, that's not what I said at all, is it? A successful man needs many different faces, Gregor.'

Father sighed, showing his disappointment. He stood up,

groaning a little as he did so. 'You'll look back on this as being a good thing. For you.'

Father walked away toward the others.

Gregor watched them all, working together, harmonious.

He was angry. He was jealous. As much as he despised Sergei right now, he wanted to be back with them all. Even with his cast on he had something to offer, but Father had forbidden it, as if further punishing him.

But Father was also right. Gregor would learn from this. He'd come back stronger.

A successful man needs many different faces.

He'd win his brothers' trust back. He'd win Father's favor too.

And then he would get his revenge.

* * *

No one in the carriage had said a word for several minutes, although every few seconds anticipative glances were sent Hector's way. He was the man in charge now. The one everyone was looking to, waiting on, for the signal.

Crucially there'd been no ambush from the soldiers. Yuri had kept to his word, as Gregor had hoped. He'd suggested that there was more glory for him if he and the guards were part of the defense force that thwarted and overcame the inmates. Sure, a small number of soldiers would die in the initial fight, but Yuri wasn't a soldier so what did he care?

Perhaps he was even jealous of the inmates now, with them getting a chance to see action with Brightstar while he was sent off to some other crumbling gulag.

Hector shuffled in his seat and a flurry of heads turned his way.

He didn't say anything, just looked outside.

'OK,' he said, his tone calm, matter of fact. 'Let's go.'

There was no sudden surge. No battle cry. But everyone moved.

Gregor pushed and shoved his way up to the front of the carriage. His job, along with two others, was to rush the guards on the other side. The first line of attack. They'd disarm the guards in the vestibule, take the guns and provide covering fire into the soldiers' carriage while another dozen or so prisoners swarmed in. Others would do the same at the carriage behind them where a smaller group of soldiers traveled. Everyone else would wait for the fight to spill out onto the snow.

Gregor slung open the carriage and was greeted with a momentary glare from the guards there, who'd already seen him, interacted with him not long before. Had Yuri spoken to these two about the plans?

Apparently not, because their looks changed in a flash from hostility to panic.

They simply hadn't expected the onslaught. Probably thought they were all on the same side, or something.

Gregor smashed the heel of his hand into the nose of the first guard he got to. Then he grabbed the guy by the shoulders and tossed him into the path of the other onrushing inmates behind him. The guard clattered into them like they were skittles and three of them went down in a heap and the confusion and the chaos gave the other guard in the vestibule enough time to pull up his rifle. He swung it a few inches toward Gregor who was moving quickly forward still, before realizing the threat to him lay beyond. Still, Gregor ducked when the guard opened fire – nothing more than an instinctive reaction.

He barreled into the next carriage, hands aloft.

'In there!' he screamed. 'The prisoners are attacking!'

Soldiers bounced up and rushed forward. From the carriage

behind, Young Vlad pulled the emergency cord and the train jolted. Gregor nearly lost his footing as boots rushed past him. He grabbed a handrail to keep upright and swung around. Carnage behind him already in the inmates' carriage. Several soldiers fired through the narrow space and received a volley of fire in return.

A bullet whizzed past Gregor's ear, and he ducked down behind the seat.

'Gregor, get up!' came a voice above him before a strong hand took him by the arm. Yuri. And he didn't look happy. 'What the hell is this?'

'I'm sorry... they... they changed the plan.'

Yuri growled rather than answer back. Another wayward bullet caused them both to duck down again before Yuri dragged Gregor up and into the aisle.

'This way!' he yelled, shoving Gregor forward, who didn't hesitate before rushing that way, squeezing past more soldiers who were ready and willing to join the fight but unable to make much forward progress in the cramped carriage.

In a few seconds the train would come to a complete stop and they'd get their turn.

Gregor and Yuri made it to the next vestibule. In the carriage beyond, the remaining guards and soldiers stood at the ready. Potemkin there too. He caught Gregor's eye a moment.

'Did you tell him?' Gregor asked Yuri.

'Of course not! But you told me they weren't attacking for another hour. I was still discussing with the others what we would do.'

The train's wheels scraped and hissed as the hulking beast continued to slow on the iced-up tracks. Gregor cowered when Yuri suddenly grabbed him by the scruff of his jacket. Yuri pushed him up against the train door.

'If you lied to me...'

'Wh... what! Why would I lie?'

They both shunted again when the train came to a stop and Gregor pulled away from Yuri's grip. The shouting, screaming, gunfire spilled out onto the snow. All on the north side of the train. Lake Baikal lay in that direction. All those little towns dotted around it. The ones Hector and the others thought they were running to for safety. Gregor edged back the other way, to the door on the south side as near everyone else piled into the snow.

'No, Yuri...' Gregor said, taking the guard gently by the shoulder when it looked like he was about to join the ruckus. 'Stay here.'

'What?' Yuri said. 'This is what you suggested. That I—'

'It's too soon. Wait.'

Gregor looked both ways along the train. No one in sight now. Everyone else was outside or in the midst of a fight for survival inside.

So Gregor made his move. He yanked Yuri closer to him and hauled his knee up into his groin. Yuri groaned in pain and threw his fists up to attack, but Gregor hit him in the balls a second time then sprang up as he sent a devastating uppercut onto Yuri's chin. His head snapped back and smacked onto the wall and Gregor launched a fist into his gut which caused him to double over and then collapse down to the floor. As soon as he hit the deck Gregor lifted his boot and crashed it down onto Yuri's face. His nose erupted. Gregor hit him again. Again.

He was out cold.

Gregor took the guard's rifle then quickly swapped uniforms too. He had no interest in wearing the shoddy, bullet-ridden seconds.

He stayed crouched as he checked the rifle over. All good. He turned the handle and pushed the creaky door open a few inches. The snow beneath him lay untouched. It looked so serene out there in the cold, even if shouting and gunfire continued to drift over from the other side of the train.

He dropped down into the snow. Was about to rise up when he realized he wasn't alone.

'You think you're pretty clever, don't you?' came the sullen voice to his right. A voice that was accompanied by a cold barrel of a handgun pressed up against Gregor's temple.

Despite the predicament, Gregor turned his head a couple of inches so he could better see the major.

'Please,' Gregor said, quivering, shaking. 'I'm... helping.'

'You might have fooled your guard friend. You don't fool me.'

'What? I'm begging you!'

He didn't wait for a response to that lie. Gregor sank down, swiveled and swiped Potemkin's feet from him and the major collapsed down as an arc of snow swept up into the air around them. Gregor kicked out and knocked the handgun from the major's grip. He pointed the rifle at Potemkin's face.

The major didn't look undeterred. Just very, very angry.

'You'll burn in hell,' Potemkin said.

'Maybe. But not yet.'

Gregor pulled the trigger and the bullet tore into Potemkin's face just below his left eye, sending ugly blood spatters out across the white snow.

He ducked down a little to look under the train to the other side. The fight was dying down. The soldiers were nearly in control. Bloody bodies littered the ground.

The inmates' fight had been rushed and chaotic. Just like Gregor knew it would be. Yet he'd only had to help a little to persuade them otherwise. The truth was they'd wanted the fight.

Had any inmates successfully made a run for it?

It didn't matter to Gregor.

He quickly peeled off Potemkin's overcoat. A very nice overcoat. A very welcome extra layer for what he knew would be a torturous journey ahead.

A journey he'd be completing alone.

He turned and rushed off across the snow.

11

CANNES, FRANCE

No one had come to speak to him in the time he'd been locked up in the cell in the police station in Cannes. Two nights so far. He knew the police wouldn't be able to hold him without charge much longer. So the key question was whether or not a charge was coming his way.

Yeah, he'd committed some crimes. Breaking and entering. He'd attacked and kidnapped a policeman. Assaulted some people. Shot a few others. But those last couple at least had been justifiable self-defense. And the rest of it had been gathering evidence of more serious crimes. Vigilantism in the extreme, but still.

Well, vigilantism in the sense that the French authorities had no idea about Ryker's tenuous ties to the British intelligence services.

He hadn't been the given the chance of calling Peter Winter back in London. Not that Ryker's work here was anything like official. Still, sometimes the guy stuck his neck out for Ryker and made things happen.

Would he today?

The cell door opened. A uniformed police officer stood next to Charlotte. She looked... great. And he was really pleased to see her for all sorts of reasons, even if she looked mad as hell.

'You're free to go,' she said to him.

Ryker didn't care to ask how or why that had come about. He walked out of there, along the corridor, through into the reception area of the police station. It took a couple of minutes to sign out and gather his belongings. Charlotte was waiting for him in the sunshine when he stepped outside.

'You're a piece of shit,' she said to him, folding her arms in defiance.

Ryker didn't say anything in return. He felt she wasn't quite finished.

'Who even are you, really?'

'I haven't lied to you about anything.'

'No? But I think you've told me so little of the truth.'

'I told you I wanted to help you with your investigation.'

'Yeah. After we'd already been seeing each other for weeks. And I thought you just meant because you wanted to help me! I confided in you that I was struggling with my work but really you only ever came to me in the first place because of it. Am I right?'

'That's not... strictly true.'

'So what are you?'

'It's complicated.'

'Yeah? All I know is I got a call from some woman at the DGSI telling me we had to let you go.' The DGSI was France's main internal security agency, so perhaps Winter had helped after all. But perhaps something else.

'It didn't have to go down like this,' Ryker said. 'I had the evidence for you.'

She walked up to him and he thought she was about to slap him in the face so was caught off-guard when she launched her knee into his groin. He doubled over and took a few seconds to work through the pain.

'I... probably deserved that.'

'No. What you deserve is to be locked up.'

'You must see this is a good result,' he said as he straightened up. 'However rich and connected he is, Litvinov will hopefully never get out of prison. And I've dealt with Pichon too. The blockage. You can break open everything now.'

'But this isn't how I wanted it done! I wanted it done the right way.'

'This was the only way, and deep down you know it.'

'You know what I think? You're a selfish, self-centered—'

'I put my life on the line here,' Ryker said. He held up his hands, showing off the ugly cuts on his wrists which were a mess of red and black and purple. 'This isn't about me and you. It's about taking a dangerous criminal off the streets.'

'Not about me and you? Yeah. You're right about that. There is no me and you.'

She went to walk away but Ryker moved over and blocked her path. 'Charlotte, please—'

'You need to leave. Leave this whole area and don't come back.'

Ryker would have said something in response but he could tell by the force in her words that she wasn't going to change her mind.

'I'm giving you a chance here,' she said. 'Because I recognize that having Litvinov behind bars is good. But that doesn't mean I'll ever think what you did was the right thing. And even if the DGSI want you to be a free man, I'm not sure I do. So you need to go now. If you stay here, I'll do everything I can to get you back in there.'

She nodded back at the police station. Then brushed past him and strode away.

* * *

Ryker was distracted as he sat in the back of the taxi on the way to Antibes. He hated how things had ended with Charlotte. He'd never intended to hurt her, to cause her any emotional pain, to cause her any problems at work either. And the intimacy they'd shared over nearly three months was real, even if he didn't believe either of them had ever intended for it to become anything long term or serious.

Still, the way it had ended left a sour taste and he wasn't against the idea of lying low in the area for a couple of days before trying to go and see her again. He had nothing else to get to immediately.

Those thoughts swirled in his mind along the drive. Distracted, yes, but not so distracted that he didn't notice the car following behind them. A Volkswagen Golf. White, a few years old. It'd first appeared not long after Ryker had sat in the taxi and now, twenty minutes later as they approached Antibes, it remained a safe distance behind.

A few minutes later the taxi driver came off the main road to enter the narrower twisting streets of the town. Ryker had given the driver the address for his apartment but now he wasn't so sure he wanted to head back there.

'Take the next right,' Ryker said. The driver did so. Ryker glanced behind. The Golf appeared again. 'Then this left.'

Again, the driver followed. As did the Golf.

'OK, pull over here.'

'But—'

'Here's fine.'

The taxi driver stopped. There was nowhere to actually pull over on the cramped one-way street with cars tightly packed along the right-hand side. Ryker pushed forty euros out to the driver, let him keep the hefty tip, and stood out of the car.

He fixed his gaze on the Golf which was now at a stop about thirty yards behind. He couldn't see who was sat beyond the glass but apparently whoever it was didn't mind too much about being conspicuous.

The taxi sped off. Ryker remained rooted. He went to turn but then the passenger door of the Golf opened and a woman he didn't recognize stepped out. She opened her mouth to say something but before she could Ryker turned and ran.

'Stop!' the woman shouted out.

Ryker didn't. He heard the revs of the engine behind him. The car would close in on him in seconds.

Would they mow him down?

Who the hell were they?

DGSI most likely. The very same people who'd had a hand in having Ryker released from jail, according to Charlotte. Although he knew well from past experience in this country – and many others – that just because someone helped him out, it didn't mean they were an ally. Perhaps they'd only let him out so they could haul him to somewhere more... suited to their methods of interrogation.

Ryker took a left into a narrower alley. Too narrow for the Golf which pulled to a stop at the entrance. Ryker continued to sprint. When he looked back a second time the car was gone.

He took a right, then a left which opened out onto a two-way road once more. Not ideal, even if he couldn't see the Golf now. A park lay ahead. Not a big park. Just a small green space sandwiched between houses and low-rise apartment buildings. It had a few trees, benches, a playground. No roads for the Golf. So Ryker aimed for it.

Except the Golf came blasting into view ahead of him.

'Shit.'

He ducked left, between parked cars and out into the road. The Golf gunned for him, but Ryker reached the other side just in time. Tires screeched as Ryker darted down another narrow and secluded alley, lined with stinking industrial bins. An intersection sat at the far end. Ryker initially headed right but then the Golf appeared at the entrance twenty yards ahead. He spun on his heel to go back the other way but before he reached the junction again the woman burst into view on foot.

She slammed to a stop, the gun in her hand pointed toward Ryker.

He stopped too. He half turned so he had both the woman and the Golf in view. A man stepped out of the car and edged forward. Like the woman, Ryker didn't recognize him. Like her, he had a gun pointed at Ryker.

'Please, Ryker, we're not here to hurt you,' the woman said.

Ryker said nothing as he went over the options for his escape. The biggest question was whether to use lethal force or not.

'We only want to talk,' the man added.

Only at that point did Ryker take pause. Not because of what they'd said, but because of their accents. They spoke in English but they weren't English; they didn't have the same Latin lilt as French speakers.

They were Russian. Or something else similarly Slavic. Which was not what he'd expected initially. But then he had just had a big hand in bringing Litvinov down. Perhaps these were with him.

Except they hadn't shot him on sight.

'Who are you?' Ryker asked, looking them both over.

The man and the woman both stopped walking. Not quite within Ryker's reach. But close enough that they couldn't miss if they opened fire.

The woman seemed to be in charge because she was the one who lifted the barrel of her gun first, into the air. A signal that Ryker wasn't about to be gunned down.

'We only want to talk to you,' she said. 'So are we good?'

Ryker wasn't so sure. The man dropped his aim. If Ryker wanted to make a move, now was the time.

'Please,' the woman said. 'I know what you're thinking. You're thinking how you can attack us and get out of here.'

'Damn right.'

'Please don't.'

'I asked who you are.'

'Take a guess?' the man said.

'You're not with the French authorities. I can tell by the accents. You're not with Litvinov because you haven't shot me. And you look... drab. Agents. I'd say Russian SVR?'

SVR being the rebranded KGB.

The man smirked.

'Close enough,' the woman said.

'This is to do with Litvinov, though, right?' Ryker asked.

'Actually no,' the woman said.

'Then what?'

'We need your help,' the man said.

'We're here because there's someone we need you to find,' the woman added.

'Excuse me?'

'Gregor Rebrov.'

'I've no idea who that is,' Ryker said.

'Except you do,' the man responded. 'Gregor Rebrov is the son of Natasha and Roman Minko.'

Those names he did know. And hearing them turned his brain to mush. He couldn't find a word in response.

'You remember them, don't you?'

'Yes,' he said.

'He's got a new surname, but Gregor Rebrov is their son. And he's missing. We think he's in danger.'

'And you think this is relevant to me why?'

'Because we know about what happened back then.'

Both the man and the woman slipped their guns away now.

'Like we said, we only want to talk to you,' the woman said. 'Because we think you can help. We thought... you'd want to help.'

Ryker mulled it over for a few seconds.

'OK,' he said. 'Let's talk.'

12

TWENTY YEARS AGO

Limassol, Cyprus

They were driving away from the coast. Away from the glistening blue waters of the Med and the white-sand beaches and the high-end – and low-end – resorts. Heading inland the scenery took on a very different and more secluded feel to the sun-drenched tourist hotspots, with only a few small villages dotted around the barren landscape. Here the land was rugged and rocky around the foothills of Mount Olympus which rose to prominence in front of them. Perhaps not as high as its namesake mountain in nearby mainland Greece, but the mountain dominated the island, like a sleeping giant looking down on its dominion. The peak retained a dusting of white, the last of the season's snow, although with the current warm spring weather it'd likely be gone within days.

'Remember what I told you,' Wiley said, snapping Ryker from his thoughts. 'Let me do the talking.'

'Whatever you say,' Ryker said, his hands tight on the wheel, his eyes focused ahead, although he could tell Wiley, in the passenger seat of the van, was glaring at him.

'You don't like that I'm in charge here,' Wiley said.

'It is what it is.'

'But you don't like it.'

'I can deal with it. I'm not in this for ego.'

'Except yours is as big as they come.'

'Said the pot to the kettle.'

'Anyone ever tell you you have a bad attitude?'

Where'd that come from? Ryker wondered.

'No, never,' he responded. 'Can you believe it?'

Wiley chuckled. 'No, I don't believe it. You've been in a pissy mood since we left. Just because the boss told you to back down on the—'

'I was trying to give him some advice. Trying to help him understand that this really isn't the best way to do things. Too risky. For us.'

'You don't think we can handle these guys?'

'It's not about us handling them. It's about us getting the money.'

'Yeah. You got that right. So no macho shit from you. Let me do the talking. You can stand behind looking mean or something.'

'You got it.' Ryker gave a mock salute.

They carried on in silence for several minutes before Ryker took them off the winding country road and onto a much more twisty and bumpy unpaved track. At times rocky, at times sandy, the path caused a dust cloud to billow from the back end of the weighed-down van.

'No chance of a stealthy approach then,' Ryker said, looking at the cloud through his wing mirrors.

'Good. Because if we surprise them, they'll probably just shoot us dead.'

Ryker didn't respond to that. Wiley had made several comments now about how edgy this meeting could turn out to be. The fact was, Ryker was feeling a lot more confident, and he felt Wiley's nerves were getting the better of him. The guy wanted Ryker to take a back seat to make sure everything went smoothly but actually it was this guy who might cause the situation to turn south very quickly.

'This is it,' Wiley said as they came over a small hill and into a big open clearing in a yellow dust bowl. There was little life out here, certainly no towns, villages, or even isolated farms. And with the land rising all around them the place was entirely concealed. And empty, except for a few trees dotted around the perimeter, Wiley and Ryker's van, the four cars already parked up, and the eight men out of the vehicles and all facing toward them as they approached.

'Shit, we are seriously outnumbered,' Wiley said.

'But this isn't a fight,' Ryker said. 'It's an exchange.'

'I know what the fuck it is. And I know how to do this. Just remember your part.'

Ryker shrugged and pulled the van to a stop twenty yards from the much larger group.

'He's not here,' Ryker said looking over the eight men.

'Minko?'

'Yeah.'

'Why the hell would he show his face to us here? He's not that careless.'

Still, Ryker had hoped the top dog might have made an appearance today. Given he was shelling out fifty million euros of his own money in this deal.

Ryker turned the engine off. Neither man moved.

'After you,' Ryker said.

Wiley finally built up the courage and stepped out into the sunshine. Ryker followed him to the front of the van and hung on the edge of the hood. Both of them were armed. Ryker had a Glock pistol in his hand which he let hang down by his side. Wiley had the same, in his waistband. The eight guys in front were altogether more heavily equipped, though. Shotguns, AKs. One man wasn't armed but held on to a cell phone which he had up toward his face, pointed toward Wiley and Ryker. A video phone? Ryker hadn't seen one before – the new tech was hellishly pricey and who the hell else would he be able to video call anyway?

'You think Minko's watching us on that thing?' Ryker said to Wiley, who only turned and shot him a look in response.

Then Wiley carried on to the middle where two of the men had moved to greet him. Ryker knew them both by now although he'd not met either face to face. Niko Kovac and Artur Zubarev. Kovac was Cypriot, but his father was from the former Yugoslavia and the younger had fought for the Bosnian Serb army during the Siege of Sarajevo. Zubarev was from Ukraine, like his boss Roman Minko. He was a former SVR operative. Apparently.

The three men began a conversation that Ryker could only glean snippets of given the distance and the whistling wind which shot sideways across the plain, coming down off the mountain. With it plumes of sand were sent spiraling around the bowl causing the men to intermittently cower and rub at their faces.

After a couple of minutes, even picking up only scraps, Ryker could tell the conversation wasn't going well. Kovac and Zubarev had wanted all of the goods here, he'd gleaned. Not just the sample that Ryker and Wiley had brought with them in the van.

Soon, Ryker had had enough. He moved forward. Minko's

guys took notice first before Wiley eventually turned and gave an imploring look, but Ryker didn't stop.

'What's the problem?' Ryker asked.

'Who the fuck are you?' Kovac asked.

'James Ryker.' He held out his hand. Kovac looked at it like it was a piece of steaming dog crap.

'I told you to—' Wiley started but Ryker cut him off.

'You really thought we would just lug fifty million euros worth of arms across the island to here?' Ryker said. 'It's two shipping containers of equipment.'

'And yet that was the damn deal, asshole,' Zubarev said.

'No. The deal was we source the goods, you pay us the money,' Ryker said. 'The goods are in place. Wiley's got the full list, pictures, serial numbers. We've got samples here. Once the money is transferred, we tell you the location of the containers. We can even take you there, if you want. But I assure you, the goods are ready and waiting in Limassol.'

'You assure us?' Zubarev said. 'Interesting.'

'Why don't we go and show you what we've got,' Wiley said.

Kovac and Zubarev didn't look impressed but the four of them headed to the van. And Ryker was glad to have Wiley for this part because the guy certainly knew his munitions. He spent a few minutes going over the various small arms that Minko would get for his money although it was the big stuff that everyone was more interested in.

'Gentlemen, the Starstreak surface-to-air missile system,' Wiley said, before groaning with effort as he lugged the huge container toward the back of the van and undid the clasps. He pulled the lid up and stood aside with a beaming smile on his face. Kovac and Zubarev were practically drooling. Guns were one thing, but they were hardly that difficult to get hold of for a man with resources and connections like Roman Minko. But cutting-edge equipment like this?

'There are three launch platforms,' Wiley started, with a well-oiled spiel. 'A self-propelled launcher. A three-round, lightweight launcher and a man-portable launcher. You'll get the equipment for all three.'

'How many missiles?' Kovac asked.

'One hundred.'

Kovac whistled, clearly impressed.

'The laser guiding on these is as good as any army is using right now. It can't be jammed by infrared countermeasures, and not by radar or radio countermeasures. And you can take out anything in the skies with these things.'

'And this is the man-portable launcher,' Ryker added. 'You can see the size of the thing. Now perhaps you get why we haven't brought everything out to you today.'

Wiley gave him another dirty look for having the audacity to talk, but Ryker took no notice.

'It's very impressive,' Kovac said as he placed the launcher carefully back into its case. He took a step back and folded his arms across his broad chest. 'But you can see our predicament. You want us to transfer fifty million euros to you for... this. And for your word that we'll get the rest.'

'The rest is ready and waiting for you,' Wiley said. 'Just not here.'

Zubarev moved away and Kovac followed.

'Keep your fucking mouth shut,' Wiley hissed to Ryker before he scuttled off after the other two. 'Gentlemen. We're good here, aren't we?'

The three stopped again in the middle. Ryker tentatively moved up to them.

'I don't know,' Zubarev said. 'Are we good?'

He looked to Kovac who didn't answer. Ryker glanced beyond at the other men. To the guy who still had the video phone held aloft. If Minko was watching this, was he getting all of the conversation from that distance?

'This is how we'll do it,' Kovac said. 'You brought us a sample. We give you a sample. Five million. Then we all go to the containers. If we're satisfied, you get the rest there.'

'No deal,' Wiley said, shaking his head. 'You really want this entire party to rock up to the port? How's that going to look? You just need to send a couple of trucks.'

'You're not getting the full amount until we have control of the goods,' Zubarev said.

Wiley looked at Ryker as though seeking his advice. 'You're in charge,' Ryker said to him. 'Your call.'

Zubarev beckoned several of the men over and they began unloading the van. Another man, carrying a small, rugged-looking briefcase, came over to the middle. He opened up the briefcase which had a built-in laptop, most likely with a satellite connection.

'Five million now,' Zubarev said as the guy with the laptop started to input the details for the transfer. 'I'll ride with you back to Limassol if you want. Stay with you until it's done. I can be your collateral.'

He said that with a certain snideness as though he saw absolutely no threat from Ryker or Wiley.

Wiley sighed a couple of times before caving. 'You got it,' he said.

'Please confirm the details for the transfer,' the laptop guy said, turning the screen so Wiley and Ryker could see it.

'All good,' Wiley said.

The guy's finger hovered over the enter key.

'Wait!' Ryker said, and everyone looked at him.

Wiley really should have reacted more quickly, but apparently he hadn't seen this part coming up at all.

Ryker lifted his gun and fired, and the bullet tore through Wiley's cheek and exploded out the back of his skull.

Blood and bone and brain sprayed out over the laptop and the man holding it. Wiley's body caved in on itself as every other gun in the vicinity was turned to Ryker.

He dropped his Glock and lifted his hands in the air.

'We're good!' he shouted out.

Thankfully nobody got trigger happy.

'What the fuck was that?' Kovac asked.

'Tell your man not to press that button.'

Laptop guy moved his finger away from the bloodied key.

'This better be good—'

'Wiley was screwing you,' Ryker said, cutting Kovac off. The dust bowl went deathly silent. Even the wind died down in that moment as though shocked by the revelation. Or just waiting to hear the juicy explanation that followed. 'He set you up,' Ryker added.

'You're telling us there's nothing but what you brought out here?'

'Actually, no,' Ryker said. 'It really is all ready for you. But if you'd paid the money... When you went to collect the equipment, you'd have had a big party waiting for you. He was working undercover, paid off by British intelligence.'

'No way,' Kovac said.

'It's true. And it's why I already arranged to move those containers somewhere else.'

Kovac and Zubarev both looked dubious.

'You don't believe me? His real name was Carl Logan.'

'How'd you know?'

'Because I make sure I get to know who I'm working with.'

Kovac moved forward and placed the barrel of his handgun on Ryker's eye socket.

'And how do we know it's not you that's screwing us here?'

'You decide. Do whatever checks you want. I am who I say I am.'

'And what?' Zubarev said. 'You want us to give you the fifty million? Is that it?'

'If you want the goods, you still need to pay. Just not to the account you were about to transfer to, which is being monitored by the British government.'

'Or we could kill you out here right now and save us the money.'

'Good luck finding your munitions.'

'Oh, it wouldn't take long for us to make you talk first.'

Ryker shrugged. 'Try it, if you like. Or we could get out of here right now before Wiley's people realize what's happened and descend here.'

Zubarev looked at the corpse then kneeled down and ripped open Wiley's shirt. 'He's not wearing a wire.'

'He doesn't need a wire. The whole thing was a setup. His people know we're here. Take his phone. Check his calls, messages.'

Zubarev fished out Wiley's phone and spent a few seconds tapping through, though he didn't reveal if he'd seen anything incriminating or not.

'OK. So you take us to the goods,' he said, after pocketing the phone. 'Then what do you get from this?'

'I was hoping you'd still pay me.'

'Fifty million? Except you've just screwed over our supply line.' Zubarev kicked Wiley as though to further emphasize the point.

'He was never a legit supply line for you,' Ryker said.

'Still, now we have to work on finding a new one.'

'I'm not greedy,' Ryker said. 'You've got more heat on you here than you wanted. I'll take only what my cut should have been. Times two. Given I won't be getting any more work out of that guy either.'

'And your cut is?'

'Let's call my payday a straight five million.'

Kovac cackled and pushed the barrel further against Ryker's eye. 'You're lucky we're even having this conversation with you in one piece.'

'I get it,' Ryker said. 'How about four?'

'Two million, when we get the equipment,' Zubarev said. 'And we never see you again.'

'Deal,' Ryker said.

Kovac pulled the gun down. 'And you get to take your buddy home too.'

'We'll follow you,' Zubarev added.

Laptop guy snapped his case shut and the three of them walked back to their vehicles.

After taking a moment to inwardly compose himself, glad to still be breathing, Ryker grabbed Wiley's lifeless body by the ankles and dragged him toward the van.

13

The drive back to Limassol felt much longer and more nervy than on the way out to the exchange. Partly because Ryker was traveling back to the resort town with a dead body in the back of the van, partly because the exchange still hadn't taken place and there remained plenty to do to make sure he got the outcome from the situation that he wanted. Needed.

For all the glitz of the high-end hotels that lined the coast, the Port of Limassol was an ugly industrial behemoth – not just the largest port in Cyprus but one of the busiest points of sea trade across the Mediterranean, handling millions of tons of cargo every year.

The cranes of the port loomed large off to Ryker's right, beyond the seemingly endless stacks of colorful shipping containers. Ryker carried on driving right past it all, onward to a small cluster of warehouses. He parked on the road outside and waited for the traveling convoy to do the same. He looked all around – no one in sight here – before he got out and headed over to the first of the trailing vehicles. Only three vehicles had followed down here. Perhaps the one with the 'samples' had disappeared with the goods.

No one got out but the passenger window of the black Mercedes wound down and Kovac poked his ugly mug out.

'This is it?' Kovac asked, indicating the warehouse behind Ryker which had two long rows of shipping containers stacked outside of it.

'No,' Ryker said. 'We're nearby but it's not here.'

'Then why are we stopped here?'

'Because I'm nervous. I told you back at the exchange that I don't think it's a good idea us all arriving in convoy like this. Given who Wiley was—'

'Given who you say he was.'

'Yeah. And it wouldn't surprise me if this isn't just a simple sting. In my mind it might be better to quietly move the containers first. Use a couple of low-level guys. You can check the goods once you get them to a more... private location.'

'Ryker, you show us where the containers are now. You prove to us you even have the goods. Or I'll take you somewhere more private and I'll cut off your damn privates. And that'll just be the start.'

'OK,' Ryker said, holding his hands up. 'I think we're clear that this is the approach you want.'

'Just get in the fucking van and take us where we need to be.'

Ryker said nothing more as he retreated. He swung a U-turn and sped off back toward the port but then took a right, through a broken security fence and onto a piece of abandoned wasteland. Perhaps once a factory or warehouse had stood here but whatever it had been was now just several piles of rubble which had six-foot-high weeds growing out of them in places. The concrete and tarmac on the ground was riddled with huge potholes and the van jolted and bounced over them. More than once Wiley's bloody corpse jumped into the air before splatting back down, the mess in the back of the van worsening all the time. Ryker wished he'd had the chance to torch this thing already. A fire so hot it'd turn the dead guy to dust.

He drove the van to a stack of mostly rusting shipping containers a hundred yards from the entrance. Beyond the containers rose a huge mound of rubble nearly twenty feet high. Ryker swung the van around to point back toward the exit then shut the engine off and stepped out.

He gazed all around as the three cars pulled up next to him and the gaggle of men emerged. The guy with the camera phone remained; obviously Minko was still keen to observe from afar.

'This is it?' Zubarev asked, looking as dubious as he sounded as he and Kovac came over. 'Which containers?'

'On the far side there. The ones from Yelda LLC.'

Those two looked just as old and decrepit as the rest of them in this scrapyard.

'Show us,' Kovac said. He pulled out his handgun again which he pointed at Ryker's face. 'But give me your weapon first.'

Ryker did so without question and Kovac handed the Glock over to Zubarev while one of the other guys came over to pat Ryker down.

'He's clean,' the guy said before retreating to his friends.

'You know I still don't trust you. At all,' Kovac said. 'We have someone looking into your background right now. Your dead friend too. If we find anything that's not how you said it was... I'll bury you.'

Ryker shrugged. 'Do you want to see what's here or not?'

Kovac answered with a wave of the handgun, and Ryker turned and walked toward the two containers. He walked slowly. A little tentatively, but mostly it was because he was focusing on two of his senses in particular as he moved. Sight. Hearing. His eyes darted about. This place wasn't that isolated, not like the dust bowl from earlier. Behind them the port was large, open, prominent. Cranes and trucks whirred and clanked. Men and women on foot in bright orange and yellow jackets moved about, but in their surroundings they looked like ants. In front of him the rubble piles shielded the waste ground from whatever lay beyond. Nothing overlooking them in that direction.

No sense that they were under surveillance of any kind.

Except when Ryker was only a couple of yards from the containers, a faint and rhythmic mechanical sound rose above the chugging of heavy machinery at the port.

Whoop. Whoop. Whoop.

Getting louder and more distinct all the time.

Ryker paused and turned to look at Kovac and Zubarev. They'd heard it too. Then, as if from nowhere, the sound amplified to an almost unbearable din and the helicopter shot into view above them, from beyond the rubble pile, the rotors blasting air down toward them. The helicopter circled above, revealing the combat-ready SWAT officers, legs dangling out of the open back, semi-automatic rifles in their hands. As it hovered all of fifteen yards above them, a further, more high-pitched sound filled Ryker's ears. Sirens. All around. Then the high revs of engines. Finally the cascade of blue lights and the swathe of police cars and armored response vehicles piled along the port access road toward them.

A voice, amplified from a loudspeaker on the helicopter, told them to drop their weapons. Told them to drop to their knees, hands behind heads.

Not a single person on the ground listened to the instruction.

'Get the fuck out of here!' Ryker shouted.

Kovac shouted to his crew as he fired off his handgun at the helicopter. The exposed SWAT guys hunkered as the bullets thwacked somewhere on the bodywork. The pilot jerked the control stick, causing the helicopter to tilt wildly. But the next second shots were coming back toward the men on the ground who raced for their vehicles.

'No!' Ryker shouted as he grabbed Zubarev by the shoulder to haul him back. 'This way!'

Two of their vehicles were already moving, retreating toward the exit, but they'd never make it past the police who were piling in.

Ryker, Kovac, Zubarev and one other remained on foot and Ryker beckoned them toward the containers as he set off at pace.

He sped past the Yelda LLC containers, hearing Kovac grumble under his breath as though he was reluctant to run away from his treasures.

Bullets pinged into the metal of the containers, sending sparks flying. Ryker wasn't armed now but Kovac and Zubarev and their friend intermittently fired off their weapons as they moved. Although, in doing so they fell behind as Ryker launched himself up the rubble pile behind the containers, the stacked metal giving them some sort of cover from the police on the ground.

Broken bricks and crumbling concrete gave way under Ryker's weight and caused him to intermittently slip as he scrambled up the hill. He heard a roar of pain behind him and glanced to see Kovac and Zubarev's friend collapse to the ground with a hole through his back. Further afield one of their cars ploughed head-on into a police truck. Perhaps not the driver's intention but the car was mangled in an instant, no chance for anyone in the front to make it out of there alive. The second car skidded and slid to a stop and two men jumped out, guns at the ready. They wouldn't survive. But hopefully their last-ditch attempt at survival would provide some cover.

'Come on!' Ryker encouraged Kovac and Zubarev and Ryker soon made it to the top of the pile – the most exposed point. But beyond it he knew there was cover. Once they dropped down, they'd be out of sight of the ground vehicles. With any luck the helicopter wouldn't follow. A security fence lay at the bottom. A row of large retail shops sat on the other side of the fence. A big open parking lot. A vehicle Ryker had ready and waiting.

Before he descended Ryker looked back again. As their friend lay bleeding out, Kovac and Zubarev scrambled up behind Ryker.

'Get down!' Ryker shouted just before a barrage of bullets came their way from the helicopter.

Zubarev was hit in the back. Kovac fired off the rest of his ammo. Ryker thought about leaving them both.

He growled in frustration as he retreated a couple of steps. Kovac continued on past him. Ryker reached Zubarev who lay sprawled, panting heavy breaths.

Ryker pulled the gun from his grip and fired off at the helicopter.

'Help me,' Zubarev said as blood gurgled from his mouth.

'Sorry, buddy,' Ryker said, before racing after Kovac.

The two of them practically bounced down the rubble pile to the security fence. Ryker launched himself at the chain-link metal and hauled himself to the top. The barbed wire there cut and tore into his skin but the wounds he received were nothing compared to getting gunned down by the SWAT team. He rolled into the landing on the other side. Kovac was a little more cautious, trying to move carefully over the barbs.

'You don't have time!' Ryker shouted to him. He lifted his gun and for a moment it looked like Kovac thought he was the target, but Ryker fired off the remaining bullets at the helicopter. The pilot ducked the craft out of sight below the rubble. Perhaps Ryker had even forced them to land this time.

Kovac finally jumped down.

'You better have a good plan,' he said to Ryker with a snarl.

Ryker said nothing but sprinted across the forecourt to the waiting car. A plain car. A silver Fiat 500 that'd blend here with the other mainly small European vehicles.

'You chose this for a fucking getaway vehicle?' Kovac said as he squeezed his large frame into the small passenger seat.

'You're welcome to find something better on your own,' Ryker said. He turned on the engine and raced for the road.

Kovac said nothing more as Ryker took a right, taking them north and away from the port. No cars on their tail but Kovac opened his window and looked out and up a few times, searching for the helicopter.

'We actually fucking did it,' he said after they'd traveled nearly three miles, deep into the busier streets of the city.

Ryker decided not to question the use of the word we.

'You have any other vehicles ready?' Kovac asked. 'Because we're better changing soon if we can.'

'No. But we should get out on foot. Get someone else to come pick us up.'

'Us,' Kovac said before snorting. 'You're not with us.'

'I'm with you right now.'

'And there is no one else. You saw. They're all dead.'

'Zubarev wasn't.'

Kovac glared at him. Perhaps because Ryker had used Zubarev's name. A mistake. The adrenaline coursing through him had led to the momentary lapse, but Ryker had no reason to know their names.

'I thought you were going back for him,' Kovac said, Ryker glad that the guy didn't question the slip. Perhaps he hadn't understood the implication.

'I did. But he was too far gone. He would have slowed us down too much.'

Kovac scoffed. 'Stop the damn car,' he said.

Ryker didn't straight away. Not because he was ignoring the instruction but because he was looking to not draw attention to them. So instead he carried on steadily and waited until he found a parking spot on the road. He slid the small car into the space, right outside a Turkish kebab shop where several diners gorged.

Kovac pulled his gun up to Ryker's temple.

'Give me the weapon,' Kovac said.

Ryker obliged. 'We're both out of bullets,' Ryker reminded him.

'I'll beat you with this thing until your head's mush.'

'Out here?' Ryker said, nodding at the variety of restaurants, shops, and cafes that lined the street. Pedestrians walked by, blissfully unaware. 'Subtle.'

'I'm gonna ask you this one time. Did you set us up?'

'You think I wanted to be shot at?'

'Except you didn't get shot, did you? And why's no one followed us?'

'You didn't get shot either,' Ryker said.

Kovac only humphed in response.

'I warned you about turning up like that,' Ryker said. 'It was your choice, not mine.'

'Yeah. How convenient for you.' Kovac pulled the gun down and opened his door. 'Wait there.'

Ryker did so as Kovac stepped out and made the call to his boss. It didn't take long. Less than a minute before he poked his head back inside.

'Get out, we're walking.'

They walked away along the street, Ryker doing a better job than Kovac of keeping the jitters under wraps. But there were no cops here. They were in the clear. After walking less than half a mile they turned a corner, and Ryker spotted the pristine white Mercedes S-Class parked in front of them. The back window glided down as they approached. Roman Minko stared out as Ryker and Kovac came to a stop.

Roman Minko. Not just a hugely wealthy arms dealer, but a hugely wealthy arms dealer with a reputation for ghastly violence. An arms dealer who had growing political clout to match his resources.

Which was the very reason why Ryker was pleased to finally be in front of the man, despite the bloodshed and chaos that had preceded it.

'James Ryker?' Minko said.

'Yeah.'

'Get in the car.'

Ryker probably would have done so anyway. But the gun barrel pushed into the small of his back – not by Kovac but by another man who'd appeared from nowhere – was enough to persuade him.

He ended up wedged between Kovac and Minko in the plush cream interior at the back of the Mercedes which smelled of... something expensive. Jasmine and spring blossom or some other such shit. Expensiveness. Serenity too, that went against the almost overbearing disquiet.

The driver floored it and they were on their way.

14

PRESENT DAY

Antibes, France

An open, relatively busy area was Ryker's preferred choice for the subsequent conversation with the as yet unidentified man and woman. He didn't think there was a serious threat of a sniper trying to take him out or anything like that and he had no concerns over people eavesdropping or seeing him out here with these two agents. Supposed agents.

The three of them sat at a picnic table in a long and narrow tree-lined park that ran directly alongside a twisting paved promenade, busy with cyclists and joggers and walkers.

'When did you last—' the man started, but Ryker cut him off with a wave of his hand.

'No. First off, you two need to prove to me you are who you say you are.'

'My name is Irina Kakabadze.'

'And I'm Giorgi Mekvabishvili.'

Ryker rolled the names around his tongue before replying, 'I'll stick with Irina and Giorgi if you don't mind.'

Giorgi shrugged. Irina showed no reaction.

'Now prove it.'

Another shared look before both reached into their pockets and drew out wallets. Giorgi showed Ryker a Russian driving license bearing his name and photo. Irina had a driving license too, but hers was from Georgia.

'Interesting,' Ryker said.

'What is?' Irina asked.

'I thought you were both Russian.'

'You assumed.'

'It doesn't matter where we're from,' Giorgi said.

'Correct,' Ryker said. 'It matters who you work for and why you came to me.'

'We won't tell you who we work for,' Irina said. 'And it's not like we carry around ID cards from our employer. Do you?'

'That's because I don't have an employer.'

'And who says we do? Officially at least.'

'OK, fine,' Ryker said. 'Point made. How'd you track me down?'

'You really can't figure that one out?' Irina asked.

'Litvinov? So the Russians, SVR, were keeping tabs on him. As an ally or as a threat?'

'Who says this has anything to do with the SVR?'

'OK. Let's keep playing that game. But my interest in Litvinov drew you to me.'

'Yes.'

'But you're not here about Litvinov, but to talk to me about Gregor... Rebrov, is it?'

'That's the surname he's taken now. His mother's family name. But you knew him as the son of Roman Minko.'

Ryker let the conversation pause there as old memories resurfaced once more from that mission many, many years ago. In truth he'd not thought about it, about the people involved, for a long time. Better that way. Because he didn't like what was coming back to the fore now.

'I haven't seen or heard from Gregor for a long time. I only ever knew him as a little boy.'

'But you knew his parents very well,' Irina said.

'Yes. I did.'

'In your capacity as an agent for the British intelligence services.'

'Not quite. But not far off. Kind of like me thinking you're SVR perhaps.'

'Look,' Giorgi said, leaning across the table a little as though to show what he said next would have more purpose than the conversation that had preceded it. 'We can talk in vague terms all day about what we do, what we did in the past, who we work for, but let's not waste our time. OK? We have a problem, and we think you could help.'

'And your problem is Gregor Rebrov.'

'Our problem is that he's missing, and we want to find him.'

'To help him or to kill him?' Ryker asked.

'We have no orders to kill him.'

'Not an entirely clear answer.'

'What do you know about Gregor's life?' Irina asked.

'Absolutely nothing. I told you, I haven't seen him since he was six years old.'

A flicker in Irina's eyes suggested she didn't believe the answer. The truth.

'So why don't you two tell me what he's been up to. It might help me make more sense of why you're here.'

Giorgi sighed. 'Gregor Rebrov grew up in an orphanage near Donetsk,' he said. Then he paused there, as if to study Ryker's reaction. Ryker hadn't known about the orphanage, although the location did create a lot of questions in his mind. Questions he probably wouldn't get answers to from these two. 'He lived there until he was sixteen years old.'

'Which takes us to around ten years ago,' Irina added. 'By which point the Donbas area of Ukraine was already controlled by Russian-backed separatists.'

'OK. Thanks for the history lesson.'

'We have a period of time where we don't know much about Rebrov's life, or even where he was. But he came back onto our radars after the Russian... special operation started in Ukraine.'

'Invasion,' Ryker said. 'It was a full-scale invasion. A war. And as we sit here today, it's far from over.'

Neither seemed particularly moved by his clarification. Which told him a lot about their likely allegiances. Unless they were just really good at hiding their emotions. Which was probably true too.

'However you look at it, Rebrov fought against the Russian army,' Giorgi said. 'But not in an official capacity. He became aligned with a terrorist group who we believe were responsible for several bomb attacks in Russian territory. People died. Civilians. Rebrov was arrested in Volgograd and sent to a prison in Buryatia.'

'Siberia?'

'Yes. I understand you've been—'

'Kept prisoner in one of those old, decaying gulags? You're right. And you also know way too much about my past for my liking.'

And which was making him seriously consider how to deal with these two from here. In the past he wouldn't have hesitated in simply assassinating them to help eliminate the direct risk to him. But Irina and Giorgi only knew what they did because a higher power had told them. It was the higher powers Ryker needed to be concerned of here, whoever the hell they were.

'A few weeks ago, Rebrov was set to be transported out of the prison, along with many others,' Irina said. 'They were being taken west but... there was an incident on the train.'

'An incident?'

'We don't know full details.' Probably a lie. 'But the prisoners fought against the guards. Attempted to flee. Many were shot but... Rebrov escaped.'

Ryker turned that over in his head before he burst out laughing.

'You think this is funny?' Giorgi said.

'The story of people being killed? No. I'm not a sadist. But what I do find funny is you two coming to me for help. The war in Ukraine is a disgrace. A show of power from a madman. The fact Gregor and whoever else are doing what they can to fight back—'

'Fight back? A car bomb attack at a market in Rostov killed eighteen innocent people.'

'Yeah. I feel sorry for those people,' Ryker said, and he really did. 'But the story you've just explained tells me everything I need to know. Gregor is your enemy. He's—'

'Except we never told you who we work for,' Irina said.

'You didn't. But if you were somehow affiliated with him and his cause, you would have come right out and told me, and painted him as an ally, maybe even a hero. In fact, I'm surprised you didn't just try to convince me of that in the first place as it would have been more likely to work. As it is, I won't be helping you find him.'

Ryker stood up and went to walk away but Irina took hold of his arm.

'Do you know where he is?' she asked.

'I've had no contact with Gregor since he was six years old.'

Ryker pulled his arm free.

'I don't like how this has played out,' Ryker said. 'And I really don't like how you two know so much about me. I might follow up on it, do what I can to make sure there aren't any threats to me out there. And... you know so much about my past, right? So you know what I'm capable of.'

'We do,' Giorgi said. 'And yet we were more than comfortable to sit and talk openly with you, and to reveal our hand. So perhaps think about what we're capable of.'

Except they hadn't revealed their hand. Not fully, at least. Although Ryker did at least take note of the poorly veiled threat.

He turned and walked off along the promenade and only looked back after a couple of hundred yards. In the far distance Irina and Giorgi remained near the same spot, now on their feet, leaning against the promenade railing, talking.

Ryker took out his phone. Winter answered almost straight away.

'How soon can you get to Antibes?' Ryker asked. But then an idea struck him as Winter bumbled with his thoughts and words at the unexpected question. 'Scratch that. Not Antibes. Let's meet up somewhere else. Italy's not far. The north. I'm sure you can catch a flight to Milan easy enough.'

'Milan? Ryker, what on earth are you talking about?'

'Gregor Rebrov. That's who. Or maybe you remember him as Gregor Minko.'

Silence from Winter for a few moments. 'Ryker, what's going on?'

'It's a good question. Come out to Milan, I'll tell you all about it. And make sure you brush up on your history. Because I want to know everything you know, and everything you can find out, about Gregor Rebrov. And I mean absolutely everything.'

* * *

Bergamo, Italy

Ryker arrived in Milan by train, spending the night near the station in the center of the city. Having initially agreed to meet Winter the following day in the ever-busy tourist hotspot of Piazza del Duomo, Ryker changed plans on the fly the following morning and took a train a few miles north to the smaller and quieter, and quainter city of Bergamo.

The hilly surroundings of the city provided it with an unmatched vantage point over the surrounding area, which explained why the upper town, on a prominent outcrop, had come to be encircled by hefty stone walls and centuries-old Venetian defense systems. Those defense systems had long fallen into disuse and the modern city now stretched away on the plains below Città Alta, but Ryker found solace in the idea of gaining an advantage from a high perch. As such, he'd checked into a room on the sixth floor of a basic hotel that overlooked an old square full of charm, with citrus trees dotted around a central fountain and a small church taking up a prominent position on the far side.

More than an hour before Winter was due to arrive, Ryker had already headed to the rooftop of the hotel which sat two stories taller than any other building around the square. He remained there until five minutes before the planned meeting, watching every person that came and went to the square through the three narrow pedestrianized entryways that provided access.

Not many people, really. With no shops or cafes or restaurants, the pretty square was quiet. And Ryker saw no threats.

He arrived by the fountain thirty seconds before Winter was due and had to wait less than five minutes before he spotted his old ally walking across to him from the northeast corner – the most obvious entryway if coming from the funicular railway which connected the lower and upper towns.

'Well, isn't this pleasant?' Winter said, looking around as he came to a stop. 'I didn't realize you'd asked me to Italy for some sightseeing.'

'You're late,' Ryker said.

Winter checked his watch. 'A few minutes.'

Ryker continued to scan around.

'You think we're being watched?' Winter said.

'Actually, I don't think we are,' Ryker answered. 'Which is the problem.'

'I assumed it's why you changed the meet at the last moment.'

'It was a test. To see if either of us were followed.'

'But... you were hoping we would be?'

'I was sure we would be.'

'By the two Russians?'

'One of them is Russian. One of them is Georgian. Unless you're going to tell me otherwise.'

'No, I'm not. I ran the names. Both seem to be who they say they are. Both have very full but quite plain backgrounds. Neither is on our lists as being part of any Russian or other intelligence agency.'

'What does that make you think?'

'That perhaps they're part of an outfit that's as secretive as some of those that we've worked with. Or... they're straight-out liars and they're something entirely different.'

'I'm not sure that's a very good explanation.'

'What did you want the answer to be?'

'I don't know. But I felt for sure this was bait. Them coming to me, bringing up Gregor Rebrov. Bringing up the past. The idea was to get me hooked and to go looking for him. So they could follow me to him.'

'Except they didn't follow you here, you're saying.'

'I don't think so.'

'So what does that tell you about your deduction?'

'That I still can't figure out why they came to me. What they want from me. What they want from Gregor.'

'If you ask my opinion—'

'Winter, sorry, but opinions right now aren't really what I'm looking for. What facts do you have for me.'

Winter sighed and rubbed at the stubble on his chin for a few seconds. It wasn't like him to be unshaved. Perhaps the last-minute travel had caught him out. 'Litvinov, as far as we know, was not a protected asset for the Russians. So us helping the authorities in France bring him down, bring him to justice, doesn't cause any problems on that front.'

'And yet this Giorgi and Irina still knew about what we were doing in France. So they were at least keeping tabs on Litvinov.'

'Except we don't know who they work for.'

'I should have tied them up and found the answers the old-fashioned way.'

'Old-fashioned? I don't think that technique will ever go out of fashion, unfortunately.'

'But they didn't just know about Litvinov, they knew about me, my past, and the fact that I'd worked for Roman Minko.'

'You're worried?' Winter said. 'I don't like it when you're worried.'

'I'm not worried. I'm confused. And now here we are in Bergamo and there's no one in sight who's followed us here.'

'Which apparently is a bad thing.'

'Why don't you just tell me what you know about Gregor.'

'After your... mission ended, Gregor grew up in an orphanage near Donetsk. It's called Saint Josaphat, run by the local Orthodox Church.'

Ryker ground his teeth, helping to keep the bubbling anger in his gut from breaking.

'You're angry,' Winter said.

'Yes. I am.'

'Why?'

'I think you know why.'

'What happened to his family was a long time ago. And there really was no other way. You knew that then—'

'I'm not the same man now that I was then.' He truly believed that. In fact, he felt shame remembering how he'd been in the past, a man who carried out often grim orders without feeling, without question. But that wasn't him, it was simply how he'd been trained to be, how he had to be to survive. They'd turned him into a killing machine, and it was only through trauma that he'd peeled out of that skin.

'I think that version of you is still in there,' Winter said. 'Just like the new you, this revamped tough guy, but with a heart... He was in the old you too. Very hidden mostly, but definitely in there. It was that part of you – your conscience – that used to drive me and Mackie up the wall.'

Mackie was Ryker's old – his original – boss back in the day. Until the Russians had executed him to try and set Ryker up. A nasty ending to one of the most defining relationships in Ryker's life. Which made it all the more grating that Winter had the audacity to chuckle at his own words, at least until Ryker sent him a death glare.

'I know one thing,' Ryker said. 'The orders I followed for you, Mackie, back then? I'd never follow now.'

'I know that. And don't forget I know how we've both come to this point in our lives. What we've both suffered and lost.'

Ryker humphed; he really didn't want to dwell on any of that.

'No one ever kept tabs on Gregor?' Ryker asked. 'My mission ended and a six-year-old boy was simply abandoned and left to it?'

'I didn't keep tabs on him. Did you?'

'No,' Ryker said. 'Because I followed orders and went on to my next assignment, then another and another. But like I told you, I'm not that man anymore.'

Winter paused as though weighing up whether to challenge the repeated assertion. He didn't. 'Gregor left the orphanage at sixteen. Then there's a gap in his timeline.'

'This is pretty much the same story I heard already.'

'Yeah? So what next?'

'He wound up working with the resistance in Donbas,' Ryker said. 'Fighting against the Russians and the Russian separatists. Then he was arrested in Russia on charges of terrorism. Taken to Siberia. Held without trial. Except when a bunch of prisoners were being moved, there was an... incident. A train crash or, I don't know what. But Gregor escaped and hasn't been seen since.'

'It sounds like you know about as much as I do. The Russians have Gregor on a most-wanted list. He's a terrorist in their eyes, linked to several attacks on civilians, although we haven't been able to determine the strength of those claims.'

Ryker mulled that but didn't say anything.

'There is one part I can add some flavor too, though,' Winter added.

'Which part?'

'The prisoners from the gulag in Buryatia weren't just being moved. We've had multiple reports recently of long-serving convicts in Russian prisons being offered a second chance. Freedom, in exchange for signing up to head to the front lines in

Ukraine. Not as part of the official Russian army, but as part of their many private mercenary groups.'

'Which are controlled by the Kremlin in all but name.'

'They are. But it's a worrying trend. From what I know the state of the prison in Buryatia was beyond inhumane. Freezing temperatures, lack of heating, food, filthy conditions, brutal guards.'

'You don't need to talk to me about how harsh the gulags still are.'

'I know. I'm just giving context. There are thousands of inmates in these places, many of whom have never even been to trial, and probably never will. The fact is, that prison is now empty, as far as we know. It was too isolated, too expensive to run, and so every man there was given the chance to sign up—'

'Forced, really. Given the hell they were living in.'

'It probably wasn't too hard to persuade them. Except it looks like someone, somewhere, didn't do full diligence on who these men were, what their crimes were, what their allegiances were. They just wanted the whole place cleared out.'

'You're saying they should have known Gregor was one of them? An anti-Russian rebel?'

'Perhaps those in charge didn't care so much, but whatever they did or didn't know, Gregor didn't get away by accident. The prisoners launched an audacious escape. I hear that tens of soldiers were killed, including a highly decorated major. And nearly every prisoner was killed in the resulting melee, or executed in the snow after the soldiers had regained control. Only three of them were brought back. Probably so they could be used as pawns one way or another, scapegoats, whatever.'

'But Gregor escaped?'

'He did. And he was the only one. So how about that?'

'You think he had help?'

'I have no idea.'

'And you don't know where he's gone?'

'No. This happened south of Lake Baikal. The whole area is a frozen wilderness right now. And it's more than three thousand miles from Moscow.'

'Gregor wouldn't go to Moscow.'

'I'm just giving you a sense of the scale here. You think he went back to Ukraine? It's even further.'

Ryker said nothing and Winter became agitated, shuffling and sighing as though trying to say something but not sure how to.

'You actually want to find him now, don't you?' Winter asked.

Ryker didn't answer.

'I can understand why.'

'I'm not sure you can.'

'OK. But I think I do. And I know no amount of dissuasion from me will get you to change your mind. So I won't try. But how long will it even take you to get out to Lake Baikal without alerting every Russian authority? And then what? Go on a weeks-long expedition through the snow and ice?'

'No,' Ryker said. 'Because this guy isn't hiding out there.'

'You don't know him.'

'I knew both of his parents. A lot better than you did. If he's got even half the wits of those two...'

'So what are you thinking?'

'I need to start from the beginning, rather than the end.'

'Ukraine?'

'Donbas, specifically.'

'You want to travel to an active war zone?'

'Winter, if I was afraid of fighting, do you really think we'd be standing here talking at all? All I need from you is some help getting me there.'

'I can do that.'

Ryker really hadn't expected that at all, at least not without some persuasion, bargaining. But then that reflected their relationship now. Not as one-sided as it used to be. Ryker wasn't just a tool to be used anymore, as he had been back in the old days. They weren't equals exactly, but at least there was a reasonable amount of reciprocity now. Winter had his position of official authority, but he still relied on Ryker for the very reason he was on the outside, looking in. 'But... what will you even do when you find him?'

'I'm not sure yet. Can I ask one more thing too?'

'You can ask.'

'Keep a look out for those two agents. And just an ear to the airwaves or whatever it is those nerds in those windowless offices do these days. I want to know who else is out there looking for Gregor, and who else is out there looking for me.'

'I'll do what I can.'

Ryker offered his hand to Winter who was too surprised to take it for a few seconds, as though he hadn't expected the show of camaraderie.

'Keep in touch,' Ryker said.

After a momentary awkwardness, Winter turned and headed off. Ryker waited for several more minutes, eyes ever busy. He still saw no threats, no watchers. Nothing.

And he didn't like it one bit.

15

TWENTY YEARS AGO

Paphos, Cyprus

No one in Roman Minko's S-Class talked on the journey. Not a single word. Ryker really wanted to open up the conversation and ask what was happening because the longer the silence went on the more doubts crept into his mind as to exactly how this situation was about to play out. But he didn't. He kept his mouth shut and waited.

They'd left Limassol and headed west toward the capital, Paphos, eventually ending up north of the city on a hilly and rocky coastline. The driver pulled the Mercedes to a set of solid metal gates, set between a tall, white-painted rendered wall. No sign from here of what lay beyond but as the gates opened Ryker caught a glimpse of the huge villa. On three stories, the building was modern with smooth white walls, hard angular lines, huge windows. A large turning circle at the front included a giant abstract sculpture in the center, several metallic cuboids melted into one another.

'You like it?' Minko asked, nodding to the sculpture as the vehicle came to a stop.

'It looks... expensive.'

'It was. Custom made. Like everything here on the inside and out. Do you know what it is?'

'No idea.'

Minko tutted as though Ryker were an idiot before he stepped out of the car.

'This way,' he said, and Ryker, Kovac and the driver headed toward the oak door of the villa. A monstrous thing, six feet wide, nine feet tall. Before they arrived there a well-dressed man opened from the inside to beckon everyone in.

Ryker followed Minko through the lofty, airy interior. The space was too large to feel lived in even if every wall had fancy art and every surface had smatterings of delicate and intricate ornaments.

They moved through to a—

Ryker never got a chance to see because without warning something hard crashed into the back of his trailing leg. He stumbled forward before a second even more powerful strike sent him to the deck, groaning in agony.

He flipped onto his back to see three men – Kovac among them – crowded around him. Kovac had a gun in his hand once more. One of the other men held a baseball bat – a bat which had felled Ryker. His leg throbbed. No broken bones but it'd leave a horrible bruise and he'd be limping for a few days at least.

Probably about as good an outcome as Ryker could hope for, as to finish off the trio, the third man held a nearly two-foot-long machete, the blade held aloft as though he was ready to swipe down.

'Probably best if you stay down,' Kovac said.

'Welcome to my home,' Minko said from the other side of

Ryker, and he turned his head to see the guy a few yards away casually propped against the back of a giant cream leather sofa that overlooked floor-to-ceiling windows, the ocean rippling silently beyond the glass.

A living room. They were in some sort of a living room. Not that it mattered to Ryker's predicament what this room was. He already realized Minko had no qualms about doing violence whether this was a cherished living space or not.

'Thanks for having me,' Ryker replied, and he received a boot to the gut for doing so.

'We'll start with you telling me where my weapons are,' Minko said. 'Because those two containers you took my men to were empty.'

Ryker said nothing. Not because Minko had revealed anything he didn't already know but because he wanted Minko to explain how he knew. And Ryker knew that wouldn't happen from him asking.

'I was watching the police as they opened up those containers.' He pointed up to the ceiling. 'A drone. You know what that is?'

Ryker nodded.

'Of course you do. You know a lot about military weaponry. It's something we'll get to the bottom of soon. But drones, unmanned aerial vehicles, they're the future. The US already has UAVs capable of traveling long distance, high altitude, near silent, and equipped with hellfire missiles! All of it controlled by a spotty geek with a joystick hundreds of miles away. My drone? It's not even in the same ballpark. Much smaller, no weapons in sight. But it's also even more discreet. So discreet the police had no idea it was there, hovering above the port as that firefight unfolded. And it's also equipped with a high-quality video camera capable of live transmission. Which is how I watched the police open those containers even after they'd gunned down several of my men and you two had somehow escaped.'

Once more Ryker didn't say anything when Minko's little monologue came to an end.

'So where are my weapons?' Minko added.

'They're somewhere safe.' Ryker again received a kick to the gut.

'No one told you to speak,' the guy with the bat said.

'It's OK, Eric,' Minko responded. 'He can speak. He can explain.'

'I told your guys there was a chance you were being set up,' Ryker said, his voice strained as the stabbing in his abdomen subsided. 'It's why I killed Wiley. But I'd already moved the goods myself before the exchange this morning. A failsafe if things didn't go to plan.'

'That, or he was trying to steal it all for himself,' Kovac said.

'No. What the hell would I do with that stuff? The containers are in the parking lot of the building site on the corner of Limassol Marina Street and Kioproulouzate. Ready and waiting.'

No one said a word for a few moments but then Minko beckoned over the guy with the bat and whispered into his ear. A moment later he disappeared.

Good for Ryker. One fewer man to fight off if it came to that.

'So why the lie?' Minko asked. 'Why didn't you take my men there?'

'Like I said, I was worried about a setup. An ambush. Which is exactly what happened. I wanted to do things more discreetly. I even stopped right by the port and again tried to convince your guys to not do it like we did. At that point I could have given them the correct address and you could have planned to pick up the containers in the middle of the night. Instead I took them where Wiley had always intended us to be. A setup, just like I thought.'

'And you shot your accomplice in the head?' Minko said.

'Wiley... His real name is Carl Logan. He's got ties to British intelligence.' And the last part wasn't even a lie. Carl Logan really did have ties to British intelligence. The only thing Minko didn't know – and hopefully wouldn't ever – was that the man on the floor in his living room was Carl Logan. Although... perhaps not from now on. Perhaps it wouldn't be so hard to get used to being James Ryker.

'Why would British intelligence be interested in me?'

'You mean apart from you buying fifty million euros of UK-manufactured military equipment on the black market?'

Minko smirked at that as though amused by Ryker's retort, or perhaps just pleased about his own wealth and power.

'And how did you find out about him?' Minko asked.

'I said to your guys already, if you don't believe what I'm telling you then do whatever checks you want on him, and me.'

'We are,' Kovac said. 'As we speak.'

'Good. Then you'll find I'm telling you the truth. Didn't you wonder why it was so easy for Wiley to get hold of those weapons?'

'Who said it was easy?' Minko asked.

'I do,' Ryker responded, and the big boss clearly didn't like the abrupt tone as his face soured. 'I helped him organize it all. Those weapons were originally on a ship bound for India. The goods were manufactured in the UK for the Indian army. Except that ship was attacked by pirates off the Somali coast. An explosion on board during the raid caused the whole thing to sink, cargo included.'

Minko smiled now, looking pleased with himself again, as though the whole thing was his doing. It wasn't.

'Except the containers with the weapons for India never made it out of Europe,' Ryker continued. 'The ship was forced to make a stop at Gibraltar to resolve a fuel leak. Your containers were taken off there and brought to Cyprus. The hit in Somali was planned. So too the explosion. C4, to be precise, not a gas leak or anything else like what's been reported.'

Minko said nothing but nodded his head.

'You think I'd go through organizing all that without knowing who I'm working with?' Ryker said. 'Wiley... Logan was ex-military. But as you'll find out if you look, his official record is as bland as they come. Which I think means he was special forces.'

'Says you,' Kovac said.

'Yeah, says me. Except he left the army more than ten years ago and since then, what? He's now a private security consultant? Bullshit. You find me one company he's worked for? Because I couldn't. I bugged his phone and for the past three weeks I've been intercepting his calls, messages. I even followed him to a meeting with his handler. Right here in Cyprus. I haven't found anything out about that guy. His identity is even more scrubbed clean than Logan's.'

'And you didn't think to inform Mr. Minko of any of this beforehand?' Kovac said.

'I don't work for Mr. Minko, or you, or anybody else. I'm in this for the paydays. Only I was concerned that if this was a setup, the money I was promised would never come to me. That's why we've ended up here like this.'

'So you killed your friend in cold blood?' Minko said. 'You thought that would impress me?'

'And then he demanded five million euros for telling us where the goods were,' Kovac added.

'There was no demand,' Ryker said. 'But I still haven't been paid a thing for any of this. So yeah, about that?'

Minko laughed. 'And you, James Ryker? What about you?'

'What about me?'

'You're ex-military too.'

At least according to the newly created identity, which had some elements of truth to it. Easier to remember and be tested on the details that way.

'Yes. But not special forces like Wiley. I have no high-up connections to see me through life. I spent three years in the deserts in the Middle East, fighting insurgents, trying to stop their hate spreading to the West. The thanks I got for that was a dishonorable discharge.'

'Because you executed two unarmed men, I was told.'

The guy really was quick at finding information.

'They were wanted terrorists,' Ryker said. 'And I was never court-martialed or charged with any crime. Everyone who cared knew I did the right thing, but I was scapegoated. I don't know why. I was given the boot. Since then I've worked where I can.'

'You worked for Wagner Corporation,' Minko said.

'Among other outfits. I was with Wagner for more than two years. Mostly in Chechnya but also Syria.'

'Ty govorish' po russki?' Minko asked. Do you speak Russian?

'Yes,' Ryker answered. 'If I have to.'

Minko snorted and Ryker couldn't tell what that meant. Perhaps he was impressed, or perhaps a bit aggrieved that Ryker had chosen to answer the question in English still.

Another man came striding across the shiny tiles and over to the boss. Ryker hadn't seen this one before. He spoke quietly with Minko for a few moments; Ryker eagle-eyed the boss looking for any tells on his face. Then the man disappeared again. To where, Ryker had no idea.

'The goods are where you said they'd be,' Minko said. 'And they're now in my possession.'

'You're welcome,' Ryker said to Minko.

'And you are James Ryker, disgraced soldier. And your dead

friend... Carl Logan. Although I haven't been able to verify exactly who he worked for, even if you claim he was a spy.'

'And you won't be able to easily,' Ryker said. 'That's the whole point.'

Minko kind of sneered at that as though not impressed by Ryker's response.

'I only have two questions,' Minko said. 'Before I decide what to do with you from here.'

'OK?'

'I was promised a supply line of weapons. But the man who made that promise is dead because you shot him in the head.'

'But he also lied to you.'

'I'm not so sure it was all a lie. Intelligence services fund rebel groups all over the world.'

'Believe me, this isn't MI6 wanting to help your cause.'

'And you'd know that how?' Kovac asked.

'The police raid which saw your friends killed, for starters.'

Kovac gritted his teeth and growled.

'My question is, with your friend dead, do you have the ability to get me any more weapons?'

'Honestly? No. Not directly.'

'You're not much use then, are you?' Kovac said, although Ryker kept his focus on the boss because he knew it was that man he needed to persuade here.

'But I helped set up this shipment,' Ryker said. 'You don't need someone like Logan for that. I can do it again. I'm resourceful. You've all seen so.'

'You definitely are resourceful,' Minko said. 'Which brings me to my second question. Are you prepared to work to pay off your debt to me?'

'Debt?'

'What, did you think you were still getting your five million?' Kovac said, a snide smirk stretched across his face.

'Yes, debt,' Minko said. 'I'm down several men and a weapons supply line.'

You also just got fifty million euros of brand-new military equipment for free, Ryker thought, but decided not to add.

'So you owe me. Given how short-handed I've become over the course of today, I'm willing to give you a chance to work off your debt. Or... our relationship can finish here today.' He nodded to Kovac and the machete guy who swung the blade above his head, practically drooling at the idea that he might get to use the thing.

'I'm not dying today,' Ryker said.

'Good,' Minko said. 'You can be Niko's new right-hand man. You're in his hands now.'

And with that Minko walked out of the room.

16

'I really appreciate the ride home,' Ryker said – as sarcastically as he could – to Kovac who was driving the Jeep Wrangler at speed along the highway back toward Paphos. The vehicle was one of several that Ryker had seen parked in and around the quadruple garage block adjacent to Minko's villa. By that block also stood a pool house that was bigger than most millionaire's mansions on the island. Four bedrooms in there, apparently, the space often used by Kovac and others who were on Minko's payroll.

Ryker at some point, perhaps.

Although for now he was being driven back to his apartment in Paphos, no clues given yet as to what work he'd be carrying out for Minko, under Kovac's guidance, in order to pay off his 'debt'.

'Take this next left,' Ryker said once they were off the highway and into the narrow streets of the historical old town. 'You can stop here.'

Kovac did so. Although he also turned the engine off and followed Ryker onto the footpath.

'Are you going to come and tuck me into bed too?' Ryker asked.

Kovac didn't answer as he looked up at the narrow apartment building that was sandwiched between two larger and more ornate brothers.

Ryker turned and walked to the door. Kovac followed. Ryker opened up and headed for the stairs, Kovac a couple of steps behind. They reached the fifth floor. Only a couple of apartments here, same as on every floor. Ryker's looked out over the back of the building – the cheaper apartment as the view of the brick wall only a few yards away really wasn't anything special at all.

Ryker moved to his door. He had the key in his hand, but he realized he didn't need it because the lock was obliterated and the door hung open an inch.

He glanced back at Kovac.

'You should be more careful,' he said.

'You did this?' Ryker asked.

'Me? I've been with you most of the day.'

'OK, but you knew about this?'

'What? Did you think we would just take you on your word?'

Ryker pushed the door open and stepped inside. The place was completely trashed. Ryker didn't have much here. Just the basic furniture that the apartment had come with and a few personal possessions – clothes, mostly. But everything was smashed or torn open.

A statement, because they hadn't needed to make the mess to find whatever they thought they were looking for.

'So not only am I down my five million, I owe the landlord a few thousand for all this?'

'Sucks to be you,' Kovac said, barely able to hide his amusement. 'How long do you have on this place?'

'It's week by week. I wasn't planning on staying here that long.'

'Yeah. Neither would I. It's a shithole. Probably better if you get something closer to the boss anyway.'

Ryker picked up one of his shirts from the floor. It'd been shredded.

'Is that a new style or something?' Kovac asked before adding an unnecessarily hearty laugh. Then he slapped Ryker hard on the back. 'I'll call you when I need you.'

He turned and carried on to the door before pausing.

'By the way,' he said. 'How'd you know Artur's name?'

So the guy had noticed. And he hadn't forgotten.

'Logan told me.'

Kovac snorted. 'Yeah. Course he did.' He carried on out, slamming the door behind him which bounced against the door frame. 'See you soon, Ryker.'

* * *

Given he had no view to the street he had no way of looking out to make sure Kovac had actually left, but Ryker stayed by the front door – which he'd held closed with a chair – for more than ten minutes before he felt sure enough that Kovac had truly gone. He'd been on edge the whole time, one question on his mind in particular.

What had they found?

He really wanted to believe that the trashed apartment was little more than a message to him. That they didn't really trust him. That they were watching him. But the fact was, if they'd looked hard enough, they'd have found out that near everything he'd just told Minko was a lie.

Ryker moved back through to the tiny kitchen of the apartment. Cupboard doors hung off their hinges. The little food he had in the place had been spilled all over. Ryker crouched down by the oven – a greasy, rusty old thing that took about half an hour to heat up to a usable temperature. Strangely it looked untouched by the intruders. They really should have pulled this thing apart. Firstly, because it was way beyond safe use, and secondly, because if they'd taken away the loose panel at the very bottom, they might have found something.

Ryker got onto his knees and pulled the panel free and reached his hand into the space underneath. He arced his arm around so he was feeling up beneath the far corner of the appliance where he'd taped the box. He pulled the box free and took it out and slumped against the kitchen unit. He lifted the lid. Two passports. One bundle of cash. Not a lot really, but plenty enough for Minko to have buried him if it'd been found.

He flipped open the first passport, for the United Kingdom, which bore the name of Carl Logan. He looked at the picture a few moments. A picture of him. A couple of years old now, although undeniably him. The only difference he could really see was in the eyes. Something about the eyes of that man from two years ago didn't match what he saw in the mirror anymore. There was more life in the younger man. More naivety too, perhaps.

Ryker pocketed the passports and put the cash back. He took out his phone. The call was answered on the second ring.

'Logan, where the fuck have you been?'

Mackie. Charles McCabe was his full name. Logan's boss. Ryker's boss. He was James Ryker. For now, at least.

'We need to meet up,' Ryker said.

Silence for a few moments. 'I didn't even know if you were alive or if one of the bodies they carted away from the port was you.'

'I was tied up.'

'Literally?'

'No. I think I'm in.'

'Meet me in two hours. You know where.'

The call ended.

* * *

Nowhere public. That wouldn't have been sensible under the circumstances. Any cafe, bar or whatever that they chose ran the risk of them being seen and overheard. Nothing outdoors either. Even if it gave them better opportunity to watch for people spying, and better opportunities to run, it was simply too open and ran the risk of them being seen by someone from afar. And Minko had already made it clear he had the technology for surveillance from the sky.

So they met at the safe house. A safe house that wasn't far removed in size, layout and quality to the apartment Ryker had been staying at for the last few weeks. A few noticeable differences though. This apartment was empty of furniture. No one stayed here. But it wasn't empty of equipment. Windows were locked and boarded over. It didn't make the place conspicuous from the outside because every other unit in the building was abandoned anyway. The front door had a steel panel on the inside and enough robust locks to mean that if anyone was trying to break in, they'd be better off just trying to smash through the wall. There were also weapons here. Cash. Radio equipment and cell phones to contact the outside world. A supply of bottled water and tinned food that'd last anyone hiding here a few weeks.

This was a safe house in the true sense of the word. A place for an agent to escape to and hide if they needed to lay low and await help.

Or a place for a clandestine meeting because it was regularly swept for bugs, and radio jammers were used to make it even harder to eavesdrop here.

Ryker arrived first and did a once over. Nothing looked out of place. He heard the locks on the door release and stood watching as it opened.

Mackie wasn't alone and Ryker's first instinct was to ready himself to flee. Actually to attack and then flee.

'It's OK,' Mackie said, as ever adept at reading Ryker's mood. He held his hands up to further show Ryker there was nothing untoward here. 'He's with me.'

Mackie and the much younger guy walked in and shut and bolted the door. Ryker walked through to what would be a living room, were there any furniture, and waited for the other two to come in. When they did, an awkward silence followed as Ryker took in the two men, waiting to see what they would say.

Mackie was as ever dressed in office gear. In his late forties and with thinning silver hair and a pudgy body, he looked more like a self-loathing career accountant rather than a commander for the Joint Intelligence Agency. A good disguise perhaps. He'd brought Ryker into the fold at the JIA when the agency had been set up only a few years ago. Jointly funded by the US and UK governments, the JIA's original and continued primary purpose was in combatting terror groups that posed a threat to the West. The JIA and its operatives were a step further removed from government, from laws and regulations, than the CIA and MI6.

As for the guy with Mackie, Ryker had never seen him before.

'You get him straight out of school or something?' Ryker said, nodding to the younger guy who was nearly as tall as Ryker but scrawny and fresh-faced. 'Does his mom know he's out late?'

'Believe it or not, you two are a similar age,' Mackie said.

'I just don't have the battle scars to show for it,' the man said, sliding his hands down his blemish free cheeks.

'That's what happens when you sit behind a desk all day,' Ryker said.

'Desk? What desk?'

The guy looked around, pleased with himself at his quip.

'This is Peter Winter,' Mackie said. 'He's my new assistant. You'll be seeing a lot more of him. Winter, this is Carl Logan.'

'I was Carl Logan,' Ryker said.

'Sorry, yes, where are my manners,' Mackie said, looking all pleased with himself. 'Nice to meet you, James Ryker.'

'So they bought it, then?' Winter asked Ryker.

'The identity switch? For now, yeah. But it depends how far they dig and how good a job you've done of backfilling our histories.'

'I did everything possible,' Winter said. 'I've got you a new passport.' He held it up. 'And anything else with picture ID has been amended in official records. It's down to you now to be convincing. To make sure you know everything about James Ryker's life should anyone ask.'

James Ryker's life. Essentially Wiley's life, but with the name and face changed.

Ryker took out the two passports of Carl Logan from his pocket and tossed them to Winter. He tried to catch both at the same time and ended up with neither in his hands and looked more than a little embarrassed as he scooped them off the floor. Winter tossed over the passport in the name of James Ryker, but it didn't even reach Ryker's feet. Deliberate?

'Why don't you give me the lowdown of what happened?' Mackie said as Ryker picked the passport up. Same picture as the one he'd just given away with his real name. 'It's been nearly two days since last contact.'

'The exchange was this morning,' Ryker said. 'It went exactly as I planned it. Wiley had no clue at all.'

'You killed him?' Winter asked.

'Yeah,' Ryker said. He lifted his hand and made a gun shape and pretended to shoot Winter. 'Just like that. Bullet to the head.'

'You seem really torn up about taking a man's life.'

'I thought you were an assistant, not a psychotherapist.'

'Actually he's a man of many talents,' Mackie said, looking at Winter with a certain pride in his eyes, and oddly Ryker actually did feel jealous. Usually he didn't feel at all.

'Fair enough,' Ryker said. 'But no, I don't care that the guy is dead, or that I killed him, or that I killed him only so I could cement the bogus story of how the dead guy was a spy to keep Minko and his men off my back.'

'Just be content that he wasn't a good guy,' Mackie said. 'You know about his history in Afghanistan. Karma, you could say.'

'I couldn't give a crap if he was good or not,' Ryker said. 'His death—'

'Execution,' Winter chimed in.

'His death was necessary. And his history in Afghanistan? The dishonorable discharge? That's me now.'

'The point is,' Mackie said, 'you're sure they bought it?'

'I'm alive. So yeah, I think they did. The police raid went ahead just as planned through your tip-off, although I'm not doing that again without better protection. They had no clue who I was and—'

'We couldn't take the risk,' Mackie said.

'Yeah, sure. But I had to take the risk, not you. But I got out of there, alive, so I guess it worked out.'

'And it would have been obvious if the police were trying to protect you,' Winter said. 'We couldn't risk your new friends noticing.'

'Thanks so much for your kind consideration of my life.'

'You met Minko?' Mackie asked, apparently not at all bothered that Ryker could very easily have been killed out there earlier. At several points over the day, really.

'I did. At his villa outside Paphos. A whole bunch of his crew too.'

'And from here?'

'I'm on the inside. But only just. He said he wants me to work for him. To pay off my debt.'

'What debt?' Winter asked.

'His dead men. The fact he hasn't got a weapons supply line from Wiley, aka Carl Logan, going forward.'

'He'll find another,' Mackie said.

'I'm sure he will. Are we going to help with that?'

'For now? No. You play it easy. Do what he asks of you. Get as close as you can to him.'

'For what purpose?'

'How do you mean?'

'I don't even know what the endgame is here. Because you haven't told me.'

'Because it's still undecided,' Mackie said. 'We know Minko's building up arms as fast as he's building up political support back in Eastern Ukraine. The election is next year. We all know his goal.'

'Independence for Donbas,' Winter said as though it needed explaining to Ryker.

'And even if he wins the popular vote in the region, he's never going to become president of Ukraine. Most likely, he'll have to fight for independence. And we're sure he's up for it.'

'And which side of that fight will we be on?' Ryker asked.

'And therein lies the problem,' Winter said. 'Because for now, we're on neither side. The current president of Ukraine is in bed with the Russian president. Minko isn't friendly with either man. As it stands, both Ukraine and Russia would fiercely object to any move for independence for Donbas. But both countries have elections next year. A change in either ruling party could change the playing field dramatically for Minko.'

'And for us,' Mackie said.

'So for now I simply continue to live a lie until you decide whether Minko is an enemy or an ally?'

'For now you find out absolutely everything you can about Minko, his crew, his friends, associates, enemies,' Mackie said. 'Find out who's funding him, where he's keeping his money. As much detail as possible on those finances so we can move to close it all down if we have to. And I want to know where those weapons are going. What his plans are for getting more.'

'Not much then.'

'Not much, no,' Mackie said. 'Because until things change, this is your whole life now, James Ryker. Go live it. And don't get caught out.'

'You mean there isn't a rescue crew ready and waiting to airlift me out?' Ryker asked, quite clearly tongue-in-cheek given his tone and the smile on his face, but Winter and Mackie both remained deadpan. Ryker's smile faded.

'Just don't get caught out,' Mackie repeated.

Ryker's phone chimed in his pocket. He lifted it and hesitated a moment.

'That them?'

'My new minder,' Ryker said. 'Niko Kovac.'

Mackie whistled. 'The Slavic Slaughterer. Rather you than me, Carl... I mean James.'

'Yeah?' Ryker said as he answered.

The call didn't take long. Not a conversation. Just a demand from Kovac.

'I'm needed back at the villa,' Ryker said to Mackie and

Winter as he put the phone away. Neither of them responded. Ryker made his way to the door.

'Good luck,' Winter called.

'Don't go doing anything reckless,' Mackie added a moment before Ryker stepped out.

* * *

He pressed the button for the intercom outside Minko's villa and waited. No voice sounded out but after a few moments the gates opened up and Ryker drove through. The villa looked just as imposing at nighttime as it had during the day. A series of lights lit up the vast property, making some of the lines look even more harsh and more foreboding.

Ryker parked his rented car next to the group of others by the garage and made his way to the front door. Just like earlier in the day the door opened before he even got there. A woman stood there this time. Ryker hadn't seen her before but her formal clothing suggested she was another of Minko's security crew.

'You're Ryker?' she asked.

'Yeah.'

'I'm Lina.' She offered her hand which Ryker took. A more pleasant welcome than he'd expected, which at least took away a little bit of the dread that had filled Ryker's thoughts on the way over. 'They're through there.' She nodded to the right. The same direction Ryker had been earlier.

He headed that way and into the oversized living room where several people were already seated. Minko. Kovac. A woman. And a little boy, maybe five or six, who was carrying a helicopter which he whooshed through the air as he raced around the glass coffee table. He screeched out the noise of the rotors too. The woman looked at him gleefully while Kovac and Minko chatted.

Until they realized Ryker was there and all eyes turned to him.

'Gregor, come here,' the woman said as she got to her feet. She beckoned the child over and wrapped him up in her arms.

'Ryker, welcome back,' Minko said with unexpected pleasantness in his voice. Kovac, on the other hand, retained his resting bitch face. Ryker wasn't sure which response concerned him the most.

Minko strode over and shook Ryker's hand with vigor.

'Please, come and meet my family.' He turned to the woman and boy. 'My son, Gregor. And my wife, Natasha.'

Natasha let go of the boy and moved toward Ryker. He held her eye the whole way. Held her eye as she reached forward to peck his cheeks. He pecked back. It was courteous after all.

Even if one thing rumbled in his mind the whole time.

Don't go doing anything reckless.

Mackie's words to him all of an hour ago.

'A pleasure to meet you, James,' Natasha said, the twinkle in her eye saying a whole lot more.

'You too, Natasha.'

17

PRESENT DAY

Donetsk, Ukraine

Ryker had been to war zones before. He'd lived in them, fought in them, he'd hidden in them. Every one he'd been to revealed the same two things: the barbaric nature of humans, and the hardy survivalist nature of humans.

Downtown Donetsk where Ryker had arrived a few hours ago was a world away from some of the destroyed and abandoned smaller towns around the larger Donbas region in Eastern Ukraine. Cars trudged by in the streets, people on foot headed to work, went shopping, but the scars of war were never far away with bullet holes riddled in brickwork and stonework of buildings. Other structures were burned-out shells and military patrols could be spotted here and there. Donetsk and nearby Luhansk too had been in the grip of fighting for more than a decade, and although the city and its people were weary, life simply ground on, any which way.

Ryker hadn't stayed in the city long, instead traveling outwards to a smaller satellite town. Here the scars of war were several times more severe. Entire streets of basic single and two story homes had been pulverized by artillery and air raids. No home lay untouched. Many who'd survived and stayed had hurriedly and shoddily erected extensions – makeshift shelters, really – to make up for the lost space from collapsed or burned-out sections. Roads which had likely once been tarmac had been torn apart by exploding munitions and were now pits of mud, riddled with ridges and craters and debris. At least at this time of year the mud had hardened. A thin layer of new snow covered it all, giving the already quiet area an even more bleak and eerie feel.

And yet this town wasn't abandoned. People here were still surviving through it all. Helping others to survive, to live through their new reality.

Ryker's boots crunched on the fresh snow as he walked. He huddled down into his thick overcoat trying to stop the cold from seeping down his neck. The warm winter sun of the Côte d'Azur felt a long way away now. But he wasn't bothered by the cold. He'd seen much worse, had to endure much worse.

He momentarily thought about Gregor and his position. How it must have been for him in the hell of a frozen gulag. How it would have been for him escaping through the wilds of Siberia in winter. Ryker had done the same once after being captured by the Russians on an undercover mission. Although a different, but similar, memory surfaced now of a time he'd had to drag himself through the snowy Scottish Highlands over tens of miles, for several days, with a badly broken leg. He'd only been a young man at the time, coming toward the end of his grueling training for the JIA where they bombarded him with drill after drill, exercise after exercise, assignment after assignment that would eventually turn him into the man they needed.

Even if it was one of many, he'd always seen that particular experience as a turning point for him, perhaps the first clear example of just how much pain and suffering Ryker was able to endure.

Was Gregor up to such rigors?

He parked the thought. Dwelling wouldn't help him right now. And he needed to keep alert. Few people roamed the streets here, but Ryker noticed more than one pair of suspicious eyes watching his movements from behind the glass of the gloomy homes. He'd had little time to fully scope out this particular place, this area, to determine the political landscape here, but he knew a lot of the basics. Donetsk and Luhansk, which made up the Donbas region in Eastern Ukraine, had seen a huge influx of native Russians from across the border after the World Wars. On the breakup of the Soviet Union, Ukraine gained independence, but the large Russian-speaking population of the Donbas area had seen it keep close ties with the old country. Those ties had been tested many times over the years, but particularly as Ukraine as a whole shifted further and further toward Western Europe, and further and further from Moscow, politically and socially.

Donbas had first come under siege from Russian-backed separatists in 2014. Had unofficially broken from Kyiv not long after with both Donetsk and Luhansk declaring themselves independent republics. The full-scale Russian invasion starting in 2022 had only further cemented the stranglehold of the separatists, but Kyiv and the Ukraine army hadn't given up on Donbas and the fighting continued. The shelling continued. Despite elections across Donbas, proclaiming victories for the separatist groups and seeking to garner officiality to their independence, there remained large numbers of the civilian population loyal to Kyiv. Gregor, apparently, was one such person.

Ryker knew where his own feelings on the subject lay, but

he'd keep that to himself and for now, as an outsider, he could claim a certain ignorance and would keep his head low and out of the political mess.

In theory, at least, although that was easier said than done, given he was about to start asking questions about Gregor...

The church of Saint Josaphat was small and unassuming with a single spire rising into the sky. The outside was covered in a dull gray render, one corner of which had a series of pockmarks from heavy gunfire. The roof, the windows, the doors looked intact though and it was clear the place was still in use, perhaps a refuge even for those who'd lost everything.

The orphanage immediately next door to the church looked quite different. The plain-looking redbrick structure that stretched fifty yards along the road had a foreboding to it, reminding Ryker of World War II concentration camps he'd seen across Eastern Europe. Many of the windows were boarded over although the big arched wooden doors at the center of the structure looked in good condition.

No buzzer, so Ryker knocked on the door and waited.

'Who is it?' came a gruff male voice not long after. Russian, rather than Ukrainian, which was interesting, but not necessarily full confirmation of anything. Perhaps the people here were in favor of Russian intervention in their lives, or perhaps they were simply wanting to appear that way to protect themselves.

'I'm here to speak to whoever is in charge,' Ryker replied in Russian. His command of the language was strong although he knew it carried an ever so slight Moscovian edge to it, from his teacher, and a perhaps more detectible foreignness to it from his own native language.

'No visitors,' the man said.

'I'm not a visitor. I'm looking for my brother. My biological brother. He lived here. It's really important I find him. Please.'

No response and Ryker wondered for a moment whether the man was still there on the other side.

'What's your name?'

'James Ryker,' he said. The name would at least help him explain the accent and the bogus story of him having been brought up in a Western family, should the need arise.

'And your brother?'

'Artur Zubarev,' Ryker said, pulling out a name from back in the day under Roman Minko's command. Of course, the now dead Zubarev wouldn't be listed as a past resident here, but he had no idea how this man would react if he'd said Gregor Rebrov, who he might well have known.

'I'll be back.'

Silence followed and Ryker turned to the street and watched the nothingness happening out there for a while. No one in sight. No sounds of life even, not even a bird call. Whatever the politics that had led to this town being turned into this, he felt immensely sorry for the folk who'd simply wanted to live.

He faced the building again when he heard hefty locks release and then the thick wood door opened with a scrape and a creak. He set eyes on the man first. Presumably the man he'd already spoken to. He was older than Ryker had expected, probably in his early sixties, and more weary-looking than his gruff voice had suggested. A battered old Kalashnikov hung from a leather strap on his shoulder, tatty but functional clothes beneath. The man reminded Ryker of the so-called Dad's Army from World War II-era Britain. Men who were too old to fight on the front lines but volunteered to keep watch over townsfolk, and to act as the last desperate line of defense if needed.

'James Ryker?' the woman standing behind the man said. She was perhaps in her seventies with light brown hair speckled with gray that was wrapped around her face, and drab but warm clothing – long corduroy skirt, roll-neck sweater.

'Da.'

'You can finish with the Russian. I speak good English.'

The man grumbled something at that, as though unimpressed with the use of the foreign language, but he then stepped aside to let Ryker into the gloomy interior.

'Thank you, Dmytro,' the woman said to the man. 'I'll take our guest from here.'

Ryker followed the woman along a plain corridor and into an office that looked like it'd gotten stuck in the 1930s, with a mishmash of old teak-stained wooden furniture and fittings. The only office effect that placed the room in the twenty-first century was a desktop computer, although that was itself way past its best use with an aging and yellowing plastic shell.

'Please, take a seat.'

Ryker did so in one of the two basic chairs across the desk from where the woman sat down.

'You're in charge here?' Ryker asked.

'I'm the matron. I think that's the right word. I don't own the orphanage. The Church does. They fund us. My name is Tetyana Petryk. You told Dmytro you're looking for your brother.'

'Correct.'

'And his name is?'

'Artur Zubarev.'

'And you believe your brother lived here?'

'That's what I've found out.'

'Do you mind me asking how you found that information?'

'I'd rather not go into the details of what happened to us, our parents. But I know he was here. From the age of six, probably for about ten years, up to around ten years ago.'

She clasped her hands together on the table and held his eye a moment, as though testing him to see if he would offer anything else. He knew she didn't believe a word he was saying. That was fine. What interested him most so far was the obvious suspiciousness, not to mention the armed guard. He was happy to test them, see where it led.

'You still have children here now?' Ryker asked, looking around the room as though they were hiding there. But he certainly couldn't hear any sounds of kids anywhere.

'We do, but we're much smaller now than before. This orphanage has been open since 1934—' it still looked like that year inside '—and at our peak we had more than fifty boys here. Today we have only nine. But you can probably appreciate recent years have been hard on this area.'

'I can definitely appreciate that.'

'And you believe your brother was here until... ten years ago?'

'Yes.'

'Because I've been here for more than thirty years, so would have been here the whole time your brother was. And I know the name of every boy who's been here in that time. But I don't know that name.'

'You don't even want to check your computer just to make sure?' Ryker said, indicating the machine right next to her.

'I don't need to check. No Artur Zubarev has ever been here under my watch. I'm sorry if you wasted your time traveling here. From England? That must be very hard to do right now?'

Ryker shrugged. 'I'm very well-traveled. Actually... The thing is, Zubarev is our family name. Artur is the name our parents gave him. Like him, my name was changed. I also believe he came to be known as Gregor Rebrov? Or Gregor Minko, even. Do those names sound more familiar?'

He tried to speak so calmly, innocently. The sudden change in color on her face, the sudden hardened edge to her features and the whitened knuckles as she clasped her hands together more firmly told him that the names not only meant something to her, they meant a lot.

But she didn't say a word.

'Gregor Rebrov,' Ryker said. 'You do know him, don't you?'

'I think you should leave.'

'I will. When you help me. I'm only trying to find him. That's it.'

'You won't find him here.'

'Do you know where he went?'

'No.'

She kept looking over Ryker's shoulder, as though she was hoping someone – Dmytro – would come to her aid. She'd been suspicious of Ryker from the start but now she was downright scared.

'You're not his brother,' she said. 'He's a young man. You're... you know.'

'Old enough to be his father?' Ryker said. 'Thanks. It doesn't change the situation. I know Gregor. From a long time ago. And I don't mean him or you or anyone else here any harm. I came here for information, nothing more.'

'I can't help you.'

'Is that normal?' Ryker asked. 'For a boy in your care, a kid who spent ten years of his life here, to just up and leave one day and you have no idea where he goes and you never hear from him again?'

'It sounds to me as though you have no experience of living in an orphanage.'

'Actually, I do,' Ryker said. 'You get all sorts in these places. And I know when a kid disappears like that, there's normally a story behind it. So why don't you tell me it.'

'I'd really like for you to leave now.'

She stood up from her chair. Ryker remained rooted.

'This is how it is,' Ryker said. 'I'm not here for trouble. But I'm not leaving until I have the information I came for. It's up to you whether you give it to me, or whether I have to find another way.'

She looked across at the door a couple more times. He knew she wanted to shout out to Dmytro. Were there more armed guards here too?

'And your friend with the AK?' Ryker said. 'It's nice for the boys that you have someone like that here to help protect you and them, just in case. But honestly... you don't want him to get hurt. Do you? Because he would. Very quickly.'

She said nothing but her fear continued to rise. Perhaps because Ryker had dispensed with his calm, innocent tone.

'I can be gone from here in a few minutes,' Ryker said. 'And if you tell me the truth, you'll never see me again. I only want to know what caused him to leave here, and where he went, because you've already given me enough to tell me that something happened.'

'Very well,' she said, looking as unsure about the prospect as she sounded. 'Follow me.'

Ryker stood and moved to the door with her. She hesitated before opening it and Ryker tensed a little, readying himself. Prepared for her to do something stupid like call out for help or make a run for it. He took a tentative step out into the corridor and spotted Dmytro a few yards away, idling.

'You're done?' he asked Ryker.

'Not yet,' Tetyana answered for him. 'But we will be very soon.'

She went to set off in the opposite direction and the guy teetered.

'It's OK, you can stay there,' Tetyana reassured him, although he looked put out by her instruction.

Still, he nodded and stayed where he was and Ryker and Tetyana set off. They took a right turn and finally Ryker saw signs of life. The windows to the left side of the corridor looked out over a quadrangle. Aging kids' toys sat in mishmash piles on a frozen lawn. No kids playing in the cold today though.

They went through a set of double doors, then another and beyond the windows to the left sat another courtyard. Different to the last one though. No kids' toys on the frozen ground here. Piles of rubble instead. Tetyana stopped and Ryker's eyes were drawn to the far corner of the square where the low-rise building was in ruins, what remained of the structure charred and blackened from smoke.

'What happened?' Ryker asked.

'Not from the war, which is what we tell a lot of people,' Tetyana said. 'That a shell hit us in the night.'

'You're going to tell me Gregor did this?'

'I knew him the whole time he was here. He was a sweet boy. To start with. But I always sensed there was something behind his sparkling brown eyes. A sadness, but also torment.'

Just then a door further afield opened and two boys – perhaps ten or eleven – jumped out giggling and laughing. They abruptly stopped when they saw Ryker and Tetyana and then quietened down and walked off sensibly in the other direction.

'They respect you,' Ryker said.

'I hope so.'

'Did Gregor?'

'As he got older, he became more and more combative. I never knew the story of what happened to him before he came here.'

She paused. Ryker wasn't sure whether it was because she was seeking his guidance on that story. He certainly wouldn't give it.

'But he was a troubled young boy. Young man, by the time he

hit his teens. He didn't like authority. And he didn't like some of the other boys.'

'That sounds like the majority of teenagers to me.'

'No. It wasn't. It was different to that. We used to have a teacher here called Olek. He was wise, experienced. He was a father figure to the boys. In fact they called him Father. But Gregor battled with him relentlessly. It got to the point where... we knew the two couldn't carry on together. We tried to find another place for Gregor. A foster home. We never managed it before... that.'

She indicated to the destroyed structure.

'What happened?' Ryker asked.

'A fire. In one of the dorms. We don't know for sure how it started. Some of the boys said Gregor was smoking and it was an accident. Others said they thought he started the fire deliberately, simply to cause us trouble.'

Her emotions were getting the better of her as she spoke, her words increasingly jittery.

'Someone was hurt?' Ryker asked.

'One of our boys became trapped. Olek went through the flames to help him. There's no fire service here within thirty miles. We did what we could to douse the flames, but...'

'They both died,' Ryker said.

Tetyana nodded.

'I'm sorry.'

'I'm sorry,' she said. 'I'm sorry that I persevered with Gregor for so long. I should have seen the warning signs sooner. It's been years since he left this place, but the black cloud still lingers.'

'What happened after the fire?'

'The police investigated. If you call it an investigation. It's not quite as sophisticated here as perhaps you're used to. They decided it was an accident. Although Gregor had already disappeared by then, so it didn't make much difference. The morning after the fire, he was gone.'

'But he was sixteen. A child still, technically? So don't you have to—'

'He ran away.'

'You didn't alert the authorities?'

'Yes, I did. But we haven't seen Gregor since.'

Although Ryker didn't sense that she was particularly bothered by that. Had they ever even tried to look for him, really?

'You don't have any idea where he went?'

She hesitated.

'Please, just tell me,' Ryker said. 'Then I'll go.'

'I don't know exactly where he went. But I heard he ended up with a group in Donetsk.'

'A group?'

'Rebels. A militia group. They called themselves the Panthers but I don't think they even exist now.'

'Why not?'

'Because they were nothing more than terrorists and they were rightly wiped out.'

She spoke those words with real venom.

'Was he political when he was here?'

'He was a boy.'

'So that's a no?'

'It's a no. This is a safe place. A place of peace and religion. Even despite what happens outside these walls.'

'The other boys who were here at the time,' Ryker said. 'Many of them will be men now too. Are there any who Gregor was friends with? Who might have kept in touch without you knowing?'

She hesitated again. She'd make a terrible poker player.

'I haven't seen him for a while, but one of his closest friends was Vasily Dovbyk.'

'He lives near here?'

'Nearer to Donetsk. A couple of towns away.'

'Do you have an address?'

'No. I just know he lives there. But it's not a big place. Head out on the road west. You'll find him.'

Ryker didn't like the way she said those last words. Her face changed as she did so, the fear at his presence gone for a flash, replaced with something a little too assured for his liking.

'I've kept up my end of the deal,' she said. 'I hope you'll do the same.'

'OK,' Ryker said. 'I'll go.'

'And please don't come back. I'd hoped we'd moved this place on from Gregor Rebrov.'

Ryker took one last look at the burned-out shell in the corner, which remained sad and broken ten years on from the fire and the two deaths.

Moved on? To him it didn't seem like they had at all.

18

The short drive less than five miles west didn't give Ryker much time to think. He didn't fully trust the story he'd been told by Tetyana. How she'd gone from being so cagey about Gregor to then taking Ryker through the orphanage and divulging about the fire and the deaths and Gregor's subsequent disappearance. Something about the situation didn't add up. Not to mention the fact that she'd quite readily given Ryker the name of Vasily Dovbyk – an apparent friend of Gregor's from back in the day. There weren't many reasons why she'd do that, but one very obvious reason was as a means of setting a trap for Ryker, even if he didn't know why she'd do that.

But she was at least right about one thing: It wasn't hard for Ryker to find Vasily. He'd realized what she'd meant by her parting comment as he approached the small town on a broken-apart road. Much like where the orphanage was located, a single main road led into and through the town here, a road which might have once been a hub, but now – along with the buildings surrounding it – was a pile of rubble and mess.

Ryker stopped the rental car fifty yards short of the start of the buildings and stepped out and hung on the door a moment as he gazed toward the first building on the left. An old factory or warehouse type structure, judging by its size, plain, functional shape and the concrete-block perimeter wall. The building had two stories and the roof had collapsed in across much of the top floor. At maybe only fifteen yards across it certainly wasn't that big, but far bigger than the tiny houses that led off down the main street from it. But it wasn't the size and style of the building that had told Ryker this was likely the place he'd been sent to find, but the armed sentry who stood beyond the rolled shut metal gate, an assault rifle in his relaxed double-handed grip.

Ryker carried on toward the gate on foot, keeping his eyes busy as he moved although he saw no other people or vehicles about. The guard had taken notice as soon as Ryker had moved from his vehicle and when Ryker was ten yards away, he spoke into a radio attached to the lapel of his thick overcoat.

'Good morning,' Ryker called over in English with a cheery wave.

The man redoubled his grip on the weapon, but the barrel remained pointed to the ground.

'Are you Vasily Dovbyk?' Ryker asked.

No answer but the guard firmed up his stance further.

'I'm looking for Vasily Dovbyk,' Ryker said, in Russian this time.

Now the barrel came up, pointed at Ryker's center mass. He stopped walking and put his hands in the air.

'I need to talk to Vasily,' Ryker said.

'You should leave here, stranger,' the man said.

Ryker kept his hands in the air but took two more steps forward until he was only a further step from the metal gate. The guard beyond wore a thick ushanka which hid a lot of his head and face and only now that Ryker was up close did he realize how young the guy was. Early twenties perhaps. Fighting age. Ryker briefly wondered why he was standing guard here then, rather than being put to good use someplace else.

'You work for Vasily?' Ryker asked, staying in Russian now.

'I told you to leave.'

'I've got five hundred US dollars in my pocket,' Ryker said, nodding down at his side. 'You can have it if you tell Vasily I'm here to see him. I just want to talk. About his old friend Gregor Rebrov.'

No reaction on the man's face to the name.

'A few questions then I'm gone,' Ryker added. 'I don't even need to come inside. We can all stand out here freezing our balls off if that's what you prefer.'

It seemed like the guy was mulling the proposition, but he didn't say a word.

'The money's yours,' Ryker said, taking another half step forward so he was in touching distance of the railings of the gate. 'Take it.'

He swung his hip out a little and the guard's greed or curiosity, or whatever it was, got the better of him and he moved forward and took his left hand from the rifle grip and pushed it through the gaps in the railings. At the same time he tried to keep his rifle barrel pointed at Ryker, but so close to the gate he simply didn't have enough space to achieve both of his aims.

Plus, it was just pretty damn stupid of him.

Ryker reached out with both hands in a quick motion. He took hold of the guy's free hand and dragged it toward him. He took hold of the rifle barrel and pulled the weapon through the railings. The guard's body was dragged forward and his face smacked into the gate. Ryker twisted on his wrist and at the same time pulled on the rifle to angle it away from him and position it adjacent to the railings, the guard unable to drag it back inside.

Which he didn't attempt to do anyway, because he was more concerned about his wrist breaking, so let go of the rifle altogether as his body crumpled sideways to try and save his bones.

Ryker let go of his wrist and took the rifle properly in his grip and pushed the barrel up against the man's forehead.

They both paused a moment, Ryker allowing the guy's predicament to sink in, but also to see if there'd be any response to him taking the weapon, any attackers bursting from the building or its surroundings.

No. Nothing.

'Anyone else inside?' Ryker asked.

'N... No.'

'Vasily's not here?'

A headshake.

'Then who were you speaking to on the radio?'

No answer.

'I won't hurt you if you do what I ask,' Ryker said. 'Now open the gate.'

The young man slowly straightened up, his face all twisted in anger – and perhaps embarrassment. Ryker tracked his movement with the rifle as he moved to the side and took hold of the gate, and with a hefty tug the fixture creaked on its rollers and slid aside a few feet.

Ryker indicated that was enough and moved inside. He patted the guy down. No other weapons. He was about to give the young man a further instruction when he spotted movement by the side of the building. A man rushed out, weapon raised, shouting in Ryker's direction. Perhaps he hoped the speed of movement would take Ryker by surprise, but what he really should have done was just let rip with his rifle before he gave Ryker the chance to do the same. Most likely he didn't want to risk his friend being caught in the crossfire. Ryker had no such worry so fell to his knee and let off two shots of his weapon. One bullet hit concrete, the other hit the gunner in his foot and he caved down, screaming in agony.

Ryker took hold of the guard by the neck and brought him close, and the guy stopped resisting when Ryker launched a fist into his kidney and pushed the rifle barrel up underneath his chin.

'Is anyone else here?' Ryker said through gritted teeth. 'Because if you lie to me again...'

The guy half nodded.

'Vasily?'

Another nod.

'Inside?'

'Yes.'

'Show me.'

Ryker shoved him forward and put the rifle barrel into his back to keep him moving. They headed toward the guy on the ground, who after a few seconds of battling through pain had the stupid idea to try to re-aim with his rifle. So Ryker squeezed off a shot which landed in the dirt, as intended, but close enough to cause the injured man to rethink.

'Next one doesn't miss,' Ryker shouted out, still covering himself behind the first guard. 'Throw the rifle.'

The guy huffed and hesitated but then did as he was told.

'On your feet.' The man cringed in pain as he did so. 'Show me your waistband.'

The guy lifted his coat. Nothing else under there.

'You lead the way. Another stupid move and I'll kill you both. Now take me to Vasily.'

The injured man hobbled toward a side entrance, a trail of red left on the icy ground in his wake.

He banged open the door. Not because he was trying to be

noisy, Ryker didn't think, but because of how he stumbled forward on his bleeding foot after he'd pulled down on the handle.

Ryker pushed his hostage in through the doorway into a dusty and chilly corridor.

'Keep going,' he said to the man in front when he sent a questioning glance Ryker's way.

They took a few more steps but the man in front was hesitating in his movement now, and Ryker didn't think it was because of the injury.

'Call out to Vasily,' Ryker said. 'Explain what's happening.'

'I don't know what's happening,' the man in front shouted back.

'You made a mistake, that's all. I'm only here to talk to Vasily. No more shots fired. No more blood spilled.'

The guy stopped moving, so Ryker and the other guard did too. Then the man in front shouted out. Ukrainian now, rather than Russian. Ryker didn't understand every word, but he got the gist. He was doing as he was told, explaining there was a stranger there to speak to Vasily. A stranger with a gun, but still...

'He'll be at the end,' the man said, pointing further down the corridor. Three other doorways lay to the left and right before that.

'OK. Then keep moving,' Ryker said.

The man passed the first door and carried on, moving with a bit more purpose now.

As Ryker drew adjacent to the first open doorway on his left, he noticed a flicker of a shadow moving on the pockmarked floor beyond. Too obvious.

He hauled his knee up and pushed his foot out to propel the guard forward and then ducked down and sidestepped as a looming figure launched toward him from beyond the threshold.

He tried to adjust the aim of the rifle, but the attacker had the initial advantage and knocked the barrel away and Ryker had to let go when the blade of a katana swooshed through the air toward him.

He lost the rifle but he dodged the sword as the beefy man spilled out into the corridor and smashed into Ryker, slamming him up against the corridor wall. Ryker wormed his way out and grabbed for the sword handle, smothering the big man's grip. Then he swiped at the man's leg. He was hefty, probably over two hundred fifty pounds, but in the melee was easily unbalanced and Ryker managed to kick his front foot from the ground. A tug to his shoulder sent him tumbling. He let go of the sword as he fell, and it clattered along the floor to the young guard. Ryker darted for the rifle and scooped it up but before he'd taken aim he spotted the top of the blade right above him.

Ryker paused. The big man pulled himself back to his feet.

'Perhaps think again about what you're going to do with that,' Ryker said to the guard. 'If you don't kill me with the first swipe...'

The sword shook in his grip. He was scared. Behind him the injured guard looked on, a little lost. From his crouched position Ryker glanced across to the big man again. Then relaxed a little before he straightened up, holding the rifle lazily, one-handed.

'You're Vasily?' Ryker said to the big man.

No answer, but that was answer enough, really.

'I'm not here to fight any of you,' Ryker said.

'You shot me!' the one guard shouted before launching a Ukrainian slur at Ryker, who had no idea what it meant, but it was delivered with belief.

'And, really, you don't look to be in any fit state to fight me,' Ryker said to Vasily.

Yeah, the guy was big, muscled, but Ryker now noticed that his left shoulder was slumped, his arm dangling, and his left leg was caved in awkwardly at the knee, which perhaps explained why it'd been so easy to unbalance him, and also explained the discarded walking stick on the floor in the room beyond.

'Don't underestimate me, comrade,' Vasily said, apparently not yet on board.

The guy with the sword was caught in two minds too, switching his gaze back and forth between Ryker and Vasily as if awaiting an instruction to attack.

'Don't you dare drop that steel,' Vasily shouted at his man. 'If he shoots me, slice him open.'

Ryker let go of the rifle and the weapon dropped down by his side, bouncing on the shoulder strap.

'How about no shooting, no slicing,' Ryker said. 'Just a conversation.'

No one said anything to that.

'I'm here to talk about Gregor Rebrov.'

Vasily was seething but after a few moments he relaxed a little. 'We can talk. But try anything stupid and you're dead,' he said.

Ryker didn't bother to argue with the paradoxical statement, given he was the one with the rifle still.

Vasily retreated into the room behind him, picking up his walking stick before hobbling to a grimy-looking armchair which he slumped down into, groaning as he did so. Ryker looked about the room – a large room rammed with boxes – as he moved in. The two guards came in behind him and fanned out. The guy with the sword still looked at the ready even if Ryker sensed he didn't really want to try and fight. The one with the bloody foot looked jaded. He bent down, pulled off his boot and gasped.

'He shot my fucking toe off!' he yelled, holding up the severed appendage.

Ryker didn't say anything in return as he held Vasily's stare. The big guy looked unfazed.

'War injury?' Ryker asked Vasily.

The guy humphed. Ryker shrugged. He didn't really care if Vasily didn't want to share details.

'A stroke, actually,' Vasily then said. 'But the trauma from the shrapnel in my spine likely caused it.'

A stroke? Even with his rugged features it was obvious the guy was probably late twenties at most. Still, he was clearly in charge of this little outfit, despite his injuries.

'I'm looking for Gregor Rebrov,' Ryker said. 'I've been to the orphanage. Tetyana gave me your name.' Ryker looked around the room again. 'She a good customer of yours?'

No reaction on Vasily's face for a moment but then a wide, toothy grin spread across his face. Well, most of his face because the left side didn't move so much, likely because of the stroke, and made the smile look quite sinister.

'Actually, she's one of the best.'

Vasily pulled himself out of the chair and hobbled toward a stack of boxes. He rummaged before turning to Ryker. 'PG Tips,' he said, holding up the small, branded box. 'Her favorite English tea.' He moved across and rummaged some more and Ryker heard the chink of glass bottles. Then Vasily turned and before Ryker could see what he had in his hand the guy launched the projectile. A bottle, Ryker realized at the last moment, and he caught it one-handed as he backstepped and took hold of the rifle with the other hand and swooshed it toward the guards, just in case. They flinched, but there was no ambush, even if his initial thought had been that was why Vasily had launched the object his way.

He looked down at the bottle.

'Gordon's. Her favorite gin,' Vasily said. 'She's a lover of all things British. She spent several years there as a child.'

Which likely explained her good English.

'So you're a bootlegger,' Ryker said, scanning the boxes once more.

Vasily's features soured. 'Bootlegger? I'm a businessman. I source and sell the luxuries that people around here still crave.'

'I didn't mean to offend you.'

'And yet here you are, in my space, having shot my friend.'

'I'll be gone soon enough. I'm not here for you, or your goods. I'm looking for Gregor. I was told you were friends with him.'

Vasily laughed in such a way as to indicate they weren't friends at all.

'She actually told you that?' Vasily said. Then he sighed.

Ryker didn't know exactly what that meant, though likely thought that Tetyana actually had sent him here to set him up. Perhaps she saw Vasily and his little crew as being more formidable and capable than they actually were.

'You were at the orphanage with him, though?' Ryker asked.

'For a long time. Me and many other boys. Some were like brothers to me. Others... not so much.'

'Which was Gregor?'

'In the end, definitely not my brother.'

'Tetyana told me about the fire. About how Gregor left after that.'

Vasily ground his teeth. 'She told you about that?'

The way he asked the question suggested it was unlikely.

'She said Gregor was a troublemaker. That one night he set a fire. That a boy got trapped. That a teacher died trying to save him.'

'Not a teacher.' Vasily was mad now, his face red with anger.

'We called him Father. I don't need to explain to you why. But it also didn't happen like you said. The fire was only set after.'

'After what?'

'After Gregor killed them both.'

A silence followed. An edgy, nervy silence. Even if Ryker didn't think these three all that intimidating, the conversation was going south. These weren't allies of Gregor. Vasily despised him.

'He murdered Sergei,' Vasily said. 'Because Gregor was insane with jealousy that Father favored his brother over him. So Gregor slit Sergei's throat in his sleep. When Father was alerted, he came to stop Gregor, but Gregor killed him too. He only set the fire to give the distraction he needed to escape.'

It sounded so vicious. Callous. Ryker struggled to connect what he remembered of the boy to the person he'd apparently become.

'Why would Gregor do any of that?' he asked.

'Because he's a snake. And a coward.'

Ryker knew there had to be a lot more to the explanation than that, but he also didn't think he'd get the full unbiased story here.

'You came here searching for Gregor?' Vasily asked.

'Yes.'

'Why? What is he to you?'

'I heard he was working with a rebel group in Donetsk,' Ryker said. 'The Panthers.'

'That didn't answer my question. I can tell you're not Russian, or Ukrainian—'

'I'm British.'

'You're a long way from home. So what do you care about Gregor? Or the Panthers?'

'I'm just looking for him. I don't need to be trouble to you.'

'You already are. You know what the Panthers did, don't you?'

Ryker didn't bother to answer.

'They murdered Russians. Murdered friends of ours.'

Ryker put both hands back around the rifle now.

'Gregor is a parasite,' Vasily said. 'And the Panthers were terrorist scum. And anyone who thinks otherwise... is not welcome here. You made a mistake coming to me.'

'I can see that,' Ryker said. 'So I'll go now.'

As relaxed as he could, he turned the rifle to the two guards.

'Over to Vasily,' he said, waving the barrel at them both. The guy with the sword moved first, edging in an arc toward the boss. The other guy hobbled after him. At least until Ryker burst forward and stomped on his injured foot before coming up behind him. The guy screamed as Ryker snaked his arm around his neck. He pushed the rifle out toward the other two, enough of a threat to keep them in position at the other end of the room.

'You piece of shit,' Vasily said.

'Just protection,' Ryker said. 'The Panthers. Tell me where I can find them. Names. Anything.'

'I said they were in Donetsk. I also made it very clear they're not my people.'

'They're your enemy. Given what's been happening here these last few years, I'm pretty sure you'd know a lot about them. Perhaps even helped to pull them apart. Give me something. Names, locations, whatever. Then I'm gone.'

'You've got a strange way of trying to convince me to help you.'

Ryker said nothing. In fact, everyone in the room was silent a few moments. Surprisingly, the next person to speak, or choke out, was the man Ryker was holding.

'They used to... meet at the old theatre... on Nikolenka Street.'

Vasily looked even more mad, though he didn't counter what his man had said.

'Yeah?' Ryker responded. 'And I can still find them there now?'

'Not anymore,' Vasily said. 'But that's where they made their last stand. Perhaps you'll find some answers there.'

'And Gregor?'

'If I knew where Gregor Rebrov was, I'd have gone there and killed him myself.'

And Ryker truly believed that the man would at least have tried.

'I'm leaving now,' Ryker said. 'So let's do this nice and easy. I said I don't want to hurt any of you.'

'I'm not getting the sense your word means much.'

'I'll walk out of here if you let me.'

No response to that.

'Do you have any more men here?'

Still no response. So Ryker stamped on the man's foot again and he writhed and moaned. Vasily remained stony-faced but the other guard winced at the sight and the sound, still not a lot of fight in him.

'Is there anyone else here!' Ryker shouted.

'No,' Vasily said.

Did Ryker believe him? Not fully. But there was only one way to find out. Ryker shoved the man forward, stepped back and slammed the door shut. Then, rifle in hand, he turned and raced for the exit.

19

TWENTY YEARS AGO

Paphos, Cyprus

Don't go doing anything reckless.

Ryker stared up at the ceiling, listening to the soft sounds of her breathing. She always sounded so peaceful, content when she slept. He knew that wasn't really the case. Her problems and anguish were unbearable at times, yet whenever he'd spent the night with her, and once they'd actually fallen asleep, she would barely stir, barely make a sound even until the morning.

Warm orange rays from the rising sun streamed in through the opaque drapes. Ryker glanced at the clock on the nightstand. Roman Minko's nightstand. His clock. His bed. His wife. But Ryker didn't feel dirty or ashamed or guilty. If anything, he felt more fulfilled waking up here, next to her, than at any other time in recent memory.

Six past seven. Early. But he couldn't stay with her much longer. Sooner or later there'd be others roaming around, even if her husband was miles away.

He shuffled a little in the bed and for a moment he thought she was waking too, but then she simply sighed and edged closer to him, her cheek to his shoulder, her long auburn hair draped across his chest.

He rubbed at his eyes as those same words from Mackie spun.

Reckless. Of course it was reckless to be sleeping with Natasha Minko. And Ryker knew that, and he really did, in theory, know better than to add risk to an already risky op. And he knew Mackie would go crazy if he knew. Would he pull Ryker out of here?

Perhaps he'd even kick him out of the JIA.

Would he even bury Ryker? Mackie certainly had the authority to make a call like that, although Ryker genuinely hoped their relationship would never fall to such a low. Mackie wasn't just his boss, he was a father-like figure, guiding Ryker through life. He'd first brought Ryker under his wing when Ryker was a lost teenager roaming the uglier streets of London. Having initially used Ryker as an asset to target the drugs gangs he found himself hanging around, Mackie had later been recruited to join the newly formed JIA not long after the war on terror had started following the 9/11 attacks.

The JIA was specifically set up to operate more secretively than any other spy agency in modern times. And its agents were expected to work on assignments that were more dangerous and more extreme. Which meant rigorous training, both physical and psychological. Years of training. Years of his body being forced to the limit, years of mental torment.

Torture. Most people would simply describe what they put Ryker through as torture. The whole thing was designed to wear away his humanity until all that was left was a rock-solid robotic operative. One that didn't have morals, feelings, that didn't suffer from guilt or shame or fear. No empathy, no sympathy. A machine who would obey every order, no matter what. Fight to the death if necessary.

And that training had worked. Ryker was that man. The man Mackie needed and had already relied on to great effect. Except... every now and then, a little spark occurred somewhere deep at the back of Ryker's brain. A tiny light flickering, signaling that the old him, the boy from the streets, was still there.

Not that he'd ever admit to that, but he also wouldn't ignore it. And, quite simply, whatever people told themselves, sexual attraction remained a primal instinct in humans just like in any other animal, and that's exactly why Ryker found himself in bed with Natasha Minko. Again.

She took in a long inhale and lifted her head and locked eyes with him. Yeah. Definitely a sparkle of life still in Ryker's brain. Especially in moments like these.

'Hey,' she said.

'Hey.'

He kissed her forehead and she craned her head around him to look at the time.

'It's early,' she said.

'Yeah.'

'Why do you always wake so early?'

'You want to wait for Niko to find us like this?'

He said it in jest, but her face soured. She didn't like to be reminded of their sneakiness. Of her infidelity and the risks they were both taking.

'Mama!' came a faint shout from somewhere outside the room. Not by the door. If the boy was at the door, he would have already tried the handle, like he had before.

Hence why they always locked the door now.

Natasha groaned and got up from the bed and Ryker only caught a fleeting glimpse of her curvy nakedness before she grabbed her silk robe from the floor and slung it over her shoulders.

'Mama!' Gregor called out again.

Natasha turned back to Ryker and gone was the contentedness of her sleep. He could see the turmoil in her eyes. About him, but mostly about other things. Her husband. He wondered if the intimacy she shared with Ryker offered her support. It offered her an escape at least, although whenever he'd tried to get her to open up to him, she pulled away.

He stood from the bed and slipped on his boxers and was surprised when she came up to him and wrapped her arms around him.

'Thank you,' she said.

'For what?' he asked.

She turned for the door, unlocked it, slipped out into the corridor, leaving the door slightly ajar.

Ryker picked up his clothes and heard Gregor and Natasha outside the room. There was nothing wrong with the boy. He'd only been calling because he was awake and hungry. Ryker held back until he heard them both padding down the stairs. Then he quickly dressed and retreated back to his own bedroom – the guest suite, on the same floor as the master bedroom and Gregor's bedroom. Not entirely his, really. The guest suite was used by whichever bodyguard was assigned to stay the night in the main villa. Last night that was Ryker. Lina had stayed in the pool house. Everyone else, Minko, Kovac included, were out of town.

At least they were supposed to be, but as Ryker stood there in his room, he heard cars outside. He moved to the window and pulled back the curtains a little to look out. Beyond the glare of the rising sun he saw two vehicles gunning along the drive for the house.

His first thought was that this was a raid. The police. His second thought was that it was Minko rushing back home because he knew what Ryker had been up to last night. Several men would barrel in, guns at the ready and Ryker would be dragged outside and beaten to death. At best.

The cars came to a stop. Doors opened. He heard Minko's angry voice. The guy blasted into the villa downstairs shouting and swearing, and Ryker pulled open the bottom drawer of the dresser unit. His fingers wrapped around the butt of the handgun and the biggest question in his mind was whether he'd simply make a run for it or whether he'd tackle Minko and anyone else head-on first.

But no one came rushing up the stairs after him. In fact, even as Minko's rant continued, the man had headed through to the far side of the villa downstairs, his voice now more muffled. Ryker uncurled his fingers from the gun and closed the drawer. He moved out and to the stairs, Minko's voice becoming louder and clearer again and more boomy all the time. He was halfway down the stairs when Kovac appeared at the bottom. He stood there and glared up at Ryker.

'What's the problem?' Ryker asked.

'Where's Mrs. Minko and Gregor?'

'I'm not sure.'

'You're their fucking bodyguard. Where are they?'

'I heard them go down for breakfast.'

Ryker glanced across through the open arch to the expansive kitchen. No sign of Natasha or the boy in there.

'But they're not there, are they?' Kovac said. 'Would you even know if they'd left? Would you even know if someone had crept inside in the middle of the night and kidnapped them both?'

How could Ryker answer that one?

So he said nothing. He didn't need to anyway. Because the next moment he heard the patio door in the breakfast room open and then he heard Gregor's giggles and Natasha and the boy walked in, towels wrapped around them.

'Hey, James!' Gregor shouted, rushing up to Ryker and grabbing his legs. Kovac looked like he was chewing on razor blades. Natasha, hair dripping, skin damp, looked embarrassed and pulled Gregor back to her.

'What the hell is all that shouting?' she asked.

Kovac said nothing but turned his glare to her now.

'What?' she said.

'Early morning swim?'

'Yeah.'

Kovac humphed.

'You're back early,' she said.

'Yeah. Because we got a big fucking problem.'

'Hey! Language,' Natasha said and thumped him hard on the arm.

'Boss wants you,' Kovac said to Ryker, before he turned and headed for the living room.

Ryker stayed where he was and tried not to look but he knew Natasha was trying to get his attention.

'Could you try making it a little less obvious,' she whispered to him.

He gave her nothing but a raised eyebrow in response.

'I can practically smell what you were up to last night,' she added, and tried really hard not to smile.

'That explains the early morning swim then,' Ryker said.

She stifled a giggle. 'I had to think on my feet.'

'Will you play in the pool with me?' Gregor asked, tugging on Ryker's shirt.

'Maybe later. If your daddy lets me.'

'Damn. The sheets,' Natasha whispered before bounding up the stairs. 'Gregor, come get changed!'

The boy sped off after her. He was never far from her side. For all the turbulence she lived through every day he knew the boy kept her from breaking. Even if the boy also kept her here, with Minko.

Ryker parked those thoughts as he headed into the living room where several men – basically the entire entourage – were gathered to watch Minko pace up and down, shouting and swearing and gesticulating.

'What's going on?' Ryker said as he stopped by Lina, who was about the calmest and most level-headed of anyone who worked near Minko.

Except Lina didn't get a chance to answer because Minko had taken offense at something. Well, at Ryker, although what specifically triggered him, Ryker didn't know. But the boss's rant stopped and he turned and glared daggers. Then he stomped across the tiles and right up to Ryker's face.

'What's going on? I'll tell you what the fuck is going on. While you were here playing silly games with my son, ogling my wife on the sun lounger in her bikini like you do...' Minko pulled back a little and smiled, although it was the smile only a crazy, unhinged person would give. 'Yeah, you do.' He whipped around to the others. 'You all fucking do. And why not? If you were as important as me, you'd have a wife as good as her. But you're not. None of you is. Which is why you work for me.'

He stopped there and held Ryker's eye once more. Ryker really wanted to grab the guy by the throat and pummel him into the ground. Show him what it felt like to have someone bigger and stronger take out their petty grievances, their insecurities on him for a change.

'What's going on is that the shipment of weapons has been lost,' Kovac said, perhaps because the boss hadn't actually answered the question after all. For his efforts he received the boss's ire.

'Lost?' Minko said. 'The weapons have not been lost. They've been stolen!'

'How?' Ryker asked.

'The ship sank in the Black Sea. Or the ship was made to sink in the Black Sea. Nothing's been recovered, but I'm not an idiot.'

Ryker realized all eyes were on him still. The newest member here. The one everyone still didn't fully trust.

'Kind of a coincidence, don't you think?' Minko said.

'What is?'

'Those weapons came to me through the same play in which they've been taken from me.'

Ryker said nothing.

'Or maybe it's not a coincidence at all. What's your expert opinion here?'

'Are you accusing me of something?' Ryker asked.

'Should he be?' Kovac said and took a couple of steps closer, obviously loving that the boss's anger was directed at Ryker. He'd try and amplify that any way he could.

'I wasn't,' Minko said. 'But your reaction right now is telling me otherwise.'

'Whatever happened to your weapons, it was nothing to do with me,' Ryker said.

'No,' Minko responded. 'Like I already said. You were too busy lazing around here, swimming in my pool. Eating my food, enjoying my wine.'

'For three months all I've done is whatever you've told me to.'

'Is that right?'

Ryker nodded.

'OK then. So this is what I'm telling you to do now.' Minko turned around to the group again. 'This is what I'm telling you all to do. Find. My. Weapons. And find me who took them and bring them to me.' He came up into Ryker's face again. 'You got that?'

'Whatever you say, Mr. Minko.'

'Damn fucking right.'

20

PRESENT DAY

Donetsk, Ukraine

The abandoned theatre looked worse on the inside than it did on the outside. A classical early twentieth century design, the exterior had brown-painted rendered walls that were heavily weathered, the surface missing huge chunks here and there – a combination of age, lack of care, and direct damage from recent conflict. But the inside was a complete mess. Ryker looked out from the stage that had all manner of debris scattered across it, from broken seats to broken lighting, electronic equipment, clothing, trash. The upper circle of seats looked relatively intact, but the lower circle had been torn apart with more than half of the seats ripped out and piled high in one corner and the rest of the space covered in debris much like the stage. The lighting no longer worked, but the whole area was lit up with daylight pouring in through the gaping hole in the ceiling above, wisps of snow falling through and settling below in a neat circle.

Everything looked quiet, almost serene despite the mess. Mess caused from fighting both outside the walls, but also from within. Bullet holes riddled seats and walls, empty casings lay strewn. There were signs of charring too with web-like black soot marks trailing up the walls, likely from small fires, explosives perhaps. Ryker pushed aside a splintered wooden plank with his foot and crouched down and touched the dark, dry patch underneath. Blood. Plenty of that around here too.

A fight had taken place. A big fight. The last stand of the Panthers, according to Vasily. The bodies had been removed but little else had been done to clear this place out since.

No, that wasn't strictly true. Ryker moved across to the far end of the stage where a flagpole protruded out from a fixture on the wall. Tatters of fabric remained hanging. Red, black. Kind of hard to tell exactly what the flag had looked like, except for the unmistakable patterns in the black swirls. Fur. The Panthers. The bodies had been removed from here after the police or whoever had stormed inside and attacked the rebel group, but so too had any evidence of the rebel organization, right down to any insignia or other representation. Which perhaps also explained the splotches of black paint on the walls here and there where murals had been sloppily covered over.

The Panthers had been wiped out; so too had the evidence of their existence.

Ryker sighed. There were no answers left here.

He moved for the exit, coming out on a side alley, and he ducked his head down into his coat to save from the biting wind. Snowflakes fell more heavily now. He moved for the road, his car parked on the near side. He stopped by it but didn't get in. Instead his focus remained on the gray car – a Toyota Corolla – across the street. It hadn't been there when he'd first arrived at the theatre. In fact, there'd been no other cars on this section of the street at all then. Which made sense because every building in the vicinity was abandoned. But he'd first spotted this car ten

minutes earlier out of the dirty window of the theatre as he made
his way down the stairwell from the upper seats.

While his own car now had a dusting of white across its body,
the Toyota had none even though it'd been standing in the snow.
Because the occupants remained inside with the engine idling,
the heating likely on to save them from cold creeping in.

Ryker walked past his car and across the road, making a
beeline for the Toyota. Its windows were tinted and he strained
his eyes to try and see who sat beyond the glass. He had no
weapon on him now. He'd dropped the rifle from Vasily's place
before leaving for Donetsk, because he simply didn't need the
hassle of lugging around such a heavy-duty weapon, or having to
explain why he had such a weapon to the police if he were
stopped for whatever reason. Still, even unarmed, he was undeterred as he strode for the car. If this were a simple attack squad,
they would have made a move already.

He craned his neck as he walked, catching the briefest of
glimpses at the driver behind the glass... A man. That was all he
could tell.

The next moment the engine revved and the car lunged
forward, its wheels initially struggling to find traction, the back
end swinging and nearly catching Ryker before it shot off down
the street.

* * *

Ever since he'd been approached by Irina and Giorgi in Antibes,
Ryker had wondered why there'd been no hint of anyone following, spying on him as he traveled east to track down Gregor.

Why now? was the big question turning in his mind as he sat
in the restaurant on the other side of Donetsk from the theatre
and awaited his food.

He'd made a note of the license plate of the Toyota and earlier sent it to a couple of old 'contacts' but it'd turned up nothing. The plate wasn't registered, a fake.

It was possible the person – people? – inside the car had followed him from Vasily's place, perhaps it was even one of Vasily's guys, or associates at least, but the most interesting aspect was that the watchers had just taken off like that. Which had been the very reason he'd simply walked out toward the car. A test, for them, to see how they'd respond.

They'd definitely not been there to attack him, or they would have. And rather than allowing Ryker to get too close and identify them, they'd simply sped off as he'd approached.

He'd not seen them or anyone else following him in the hours since, but he'd be even more vigilant from now on.

The young waitress brought over his food – a plate of stewed beef with steamed vegetables. A nice, warming meal on a cold winter's night. The glass of red wine would give further warmth and comfort. More than likely he'd have more than one.

He thanked the waitress and took a large sip of his wine before digging in to the meal. The food wasn't bad. Far from the best he'd eaten, but perfectly palatable. Really, it was nice to see a place like this – just a simple, traditional local restaurant – surviving given the chaos around it. Donetsk was far from the front line of the Ukraine-Russia war, but it'd seen its fair share of fighting nonetheless, and the residents who'd remained had to be ever ready for more fighting, barrages of shelling, and the city had been attacked by both sides in the conflict at various times.

But the city folk had no choice but to get on with their lives, and business owners still needed to make a living. Although Ryker wouldn't exactly call the restaurant thriving. At eight thirty only four other patrons – two separate couples – remained. By 9 p.m. Ryker was all alone and the staff looked like they were ready to get things wrapped up for the night, the head waiter coming out with his mop and cleaning around the tables across the other side from Ryker.

Ryker beckoned the young waitress back over.

'Another glass of wine, please?' he said to her in Russian.

She looked over at her boss and then gave Ryker an apologetic look.

'Sorry, sir, I—'

'Don't worry,' Ryker said. 'I see you're closing. But if you're finishing soon, you could join me for a drink somewhere else?'

He could tell she really didn't like that idea by the jittery look on her face. And he could understand why. He was way older than her, not to mention a stranger.

'Sorry, I don't think that's a good idea,' she said.

Still, as she reached for his empty wine glass, he took hold of her hand. Not too hard, just hard enough to let her know he wasn't messing around.

'That's fine,' Ryker said. 'But you and I, we do need to talk.'

She squirmed and looked over at her boss again, but he was walking away to the kitchen.

'About Gregor Rebrov,' Ryker added and then let go of her hand, sensing she was about to shout out in panic.

She didn't shout, but fear spread across her face at the mention of that name.

'It's OK,' Ryker said. 'I'm a friend. You can trust me. I'm only trying to find him. To help him.'

'I don't know who you're talking about. You need to leave before I call the police.'

She held her hand close to her chest, stroked it as though it were injured.

'Your brother is Eduard,' Ryker said. 'He was killed in the

theater over on Nikolenka Street. You know, the place where the Panthers used to meet. He was one of them, wasn't he?'

She kept looking back to the kitchen as though hoping her boss or anyone else would appear to save her.

Ryker stood up from his chair and she flinched. He held his hands up.

'Like I said. I'm a friend. I just need help finding Gregor. Can you help me?'

Before she could answer the head waiter came back out with his mop and a clean bucket of water. He paused and locked eyes with Ryker, as though understanding there was a situation.

'Are you OK?' the waiter asked, though it wasn't clear if the question was directed at Ryker or the young woman.

'Everything's fine,' she said. 'He's leaving now.' Then she lowered her voice. 'I don't know who you're talking about. But please, don't ever come here again.'

She turned and darted for the kitchen before Ryker could respond.

* * *

It'd been a tough call how to approach Inna at the restaurant. Ryker hadn't had much time to research the Panthers. He'd had a brief conversation with Winter before going to the theater, but he'd never heard of the group and confirmed a quick search across key SIS databases didn't reveal a match to that name. The online searches Ryker had performed across local news sites had drawn next to no hits either, at least among noteworthy news outlets.

What Ryker had found, was reference to the firefight at the theater, described by Russian-promoted news agencies as a raid on a terrorist cell. No mention of the Panthers by name, but perhaps that was because the Russians and the Russian-backed separatists didn't want to give prominence to the group for fear of it taking on more significance in the aftermath. As far as they were concerned, the cell had been eliminated.

Still, Ryker had found the name of Eduard Buleza in the news, with two separate reporters claiming he was the leader of the group of rebels, and also that he'd been killed in the theater shoot-out.

The woman in the restaurant, Inna, was his younger sister, who Ryker had tracked through social media. Having tipped her off, he remained close by the restaurant as he waited for her to leave, although not without first having moved his car around the corner to make it look as though he'd disappeared for the night. He hid fifty yards away from the restaurant, in the dark of an unlit alley which gave him a decent view of the restaurant's frontage.

Inna didn't leave until well over an hour later. The head waiter had left only fifteen minutes after Ryker, a couple of kitchen staff a short while after that. He didn't know for sure that she was alone in the restaurant once they'd gone, but he saw her figure wandering around behind the windows in the near-dark interior a few times. More than once she'd stood at a window, parted the blinds to peep out. Looking for Ryker? Possibly, because he'd definitely rattled her by mentioning Gregor.

A car came by. He couldn't determine the make and model in the dark with little street lighting, but it crawled to a stop right outside the restaurant. The car's lights remained on. No one got out. Then Ryker noticed the blinds part again. Inna. She gave a wave to the outside but didn't come out straight away. But the car was for her, he was sure. Perhaps a normal habit, or had Ryker really spooked her so much that she wouldn't leave the restaurant alone?

Not even two minutes later and Ryker spotted movement further along the street from the restaurant. Two figures, on foot. Hard to tell at distance, and with both wearing long coats and hats, but it appeared to be a man and a woman judging by their size and shape. They came to a stop by the restaurant door, no real acknowledgment from them to the waiting car, although they were both watchful, and Ryker caught glimpses of both their faces as they searched the street. A young woman. An older man. He didn't know either.

Moments later the restaurant door opened and Inna stepped out, glancing along the street in both directions before finally acknowledging the new arrivals with a cautious smile. A conversation started, all of them nervy, looking about them the whole time. Inna took out her phone and turned the screen to the twosome. No way at distance for Ryker to see what she was showing them but... it seemed pretty obvious what was happening.

She'd snapped a picture of Ryker. Sneaky. And it did make him wonder when she'd have done that. Most likely it would have been before he'd even mentioned Gregor to her, otherwise it would have been an obvious part of their final conversation. So did she secretly take pictures of everyone who came in? Perhaps it was even taken from CCTV as he had noted a camera inside the restaurant.

The conversation was over. Inna locked the front door of the restaurant and stepped into the passenger seat of the car which moved away and off down the street. It passed the man and woman as they walked back the way they'd come.

Ryker was on foot too, so it'd be much easier to follow them than Inna. Plus, he got the impression they were likely of more interest anyway.

He set off from the alley, keeping in the shadows as much as he could as he headed past the dark and empty restaurant. The man and woman took a right turn and Ryker sped up a little. He made it to the corner and spotted them only thirty yards ahead now. He kept it steady, the cold wind in his face. A strong gust caused him to wince and look down and momentarily close his eyes and when he looked up again... they'd gone.

Ryker stopped. The street was dark, quiet. Not a single car had passed by and none were in sight – at least none that were moving. He also couldn't see any cross streets here.

They'd perhaps gone into one of the dilapidated buildings.

He moved off again, stepping with more caution now. After ten yards he spotted the turning on the left. A narrow and pitch-black alley. Much like the one he'd hidden in moments before.

Ryker moved across the street and came up to the head of the alley. He could see nothing down there. But heard a faint sound. A shuffling footstep. A gasped breath.

He moved into the alley. One step. Two. Three. Four.

'You can stop now,' came the man's gritty voice, speaking in Russian. The instruction was accompanied by a gun barrel pressed into the back of Ryker's head.

Ryker halted his movement and sighed as the young woman came into view in front of him, stepping out of the darkness, her young face barely lit by the faint moonlight.

'Who are you?' she asked.

Ryker didn't answer. Instead, he ducked down, took hold of the man's lower arm and twisted it around, pushing his wrist, elbow and shoulder to bursting as he forced him down to the ground. He didn't fire the weapon before Ryker took it from his grip and, still holding on to the man's arm with his free hand, pointed the gun at the woman.

'Same question to you,' Ryker said to her.

'Let... go!' the man shouted out in pain.

Ryker didn't. But he did turn away from the woman. Toward the sound of vehicles approaching from the road. A dark car burst into view, tires skidding as it slammed to a stop across the street. Other cars were fast approaching and the walls of the buildings lining the road lit up in strobes of blue.

Ryker turned back to the woman. Noted the obvious fear in her eyes.

'They're not with me,' Ryker said as two people jumped out of the unmarked car.

The woman said nothing.

'Go!' the old man shouted.

The woman looked really unsure. Petrified. Ryker let go of the man as the newcomers barked out instructions for them to get on their knees. The old man got to his feet.

'Go!' he yelled again, this time directed at Ryker.

He didn't need to be told another time. He grabbed hold of the woman and dragged her away down the alley into the darkness, not heeding the shouted warnings from the new arrivals. He didn't look back at all until the woman wrestled from his grip and turned and screamed in horror.

'Papa!'

Ryker glanced at the head of the alley where a crowd of figures now stood. He heard the next strike as much as saw it – a baton to the face of the old man whose body crumpled to the hard ground.

'We need to go,' Ryker said, taking hold of the woman's arm again. She shrugged him off but then did the sensible thing of turning and racing further away from her father.

'You know where we're going?' Ryker asked.

She didn't respond, but he could see no way out of here. A dead end, possibly. Except she wasn't letting up and then she made a sharp turn to the right, kicked open a door. Ryker followed her inside. An old apartment building, perhaps. They raced along a corridor, up stairs. The inside was dark, old, musty. No signs of life. They came out onto a rooftop and the woman sped off again. She clambered over a wall which took them onto the roof of the neighboring, slightly taller building. Through a door, down stairs. Through a hole in a wall, jumping down half a story into the next building. A corridor. More stairs down. Down. A basement? They went through a door and up two turns of a staircase to another door. An exit door with a bar across the middle. She paused there. Turned to Ryker. They were both out of breath. Her cheeks were bright red from the exertion, from the stinging cold perhaps too. She looked over his shoulder. Ryker didn't bother. No one had followed them. He already knew that.

'They were tracking you, not me,' he said in Russian.

'I don't think so. We're careful,' she responded, switching to heavily accented English.

'Yeah. Me too.'

'Who are you?' she asked.

'My name's James Ryker.'

She glared at him but didn't say anything.

'Why are we stopping here?' he asked.

'Because I'm trying to decide what the hell I'm doing.'

'That was your dad?'

Her lip quivered. 'I left him. I can't believe... I left him.'

'It was his decision.'

'Who are you?' she asked again, a little more venom in her words now.

'I told you—'

'Not your name. What are you doing here?'

'I'm looking for Gregor Rebrov.'

'Why?'

'You know him?'

'I asked you why you are looking for him.'

'I'm a friend. From a long time ago. I'm trying to find him. Trying to help him.'

She said nothing to that.

'Do you know where Gregor is?' Ryker asked.

She shook her head.

Ryker held the gun out to her, the weapon dangling in his loose grip.

'I'm a friend,' Ryker assured her.

She took the gun and for a moment he thought maybe she'd turn it on him. No. She hid it in her coat.

'Do you know where Gregor is?' Ryker asked again.

'Yes,' she said. 'Yes, I think I do.'

21

TWENTY YEARS AGO

Kerch, Ukraine

Myriad lights twinkled in the distance off to Ryker's left causing an amber glow to hang in the air above the city. In front of him lay the Kerch Strait, black and more than just a little bit eerie. Only a few small lights were dotted out there, individual crafts navigating the water, some entering or leaving the Sea of Azov, some traveling the short distance to Russia only a few miles away.

Ryker leaned back against the metalwork of the hire car and pulled out his phone. He'd left a message for Mackie nearly an hour ago and the guy still hadn't bothered to return the call. They hadn't spoken in weeks. Not since Ryker had left Cyprus, partly because they were limiting communication as far as possible to avoid any fallout, the risk of eavesdroppers, but also simply because Ryker had been too busy. But he'd wanted to speak now because he'd sensed a change in mood with Kovac over the course of the last twenty-four hours and he didn't like it.

All he'd been told was to come to this place at 8 p.m. It was now seven fifty-five.

The phone vibrated in his grip and hadn't even completed a full chirp before he hit the green button to answer.

'Mackie?'

A short pause. 'How is everything?' Mackie asked.

Ryker snorted. 'In about five minutes I'll find out. If you don't hear from me again, I'll be somewhere at the bottom of the Kerch Strait.'

'Are you in trouble?'

'The more I get to know this Kovac guy, the more I realize he is really fucking insane.'

'Ryker, I don't need to know about the man's mental state, I need to know what he's found. What you've found.'

'On Minko's weapons? Next to nothing. And it's not through lack of trying. The boat carrying his haul went down not even a hundred miles from where I'm standing, but no one knows a thing.'

Mackie sighed.

'Just tell me it wasn't you,' Ryker said. 'Tell me this isn't a play by you or MI6.'

'Why would it matter to you if it was? Your job is to get close to Minko. Aren't you doing that?'

Ryker didn't answer.

'But no, I assure you I know nothing about what happened to those weapons.'

'It has to be someone in the know,' Ryker said.

'An inside job?'

'Don't you think?'

'You're telling me there's someone else on Minko's payroll who's playing against him?'

'It's a strong possibility.'

'Do you have any idea who?'

'Other than I know it's not the psycho, Kovac. Do you?'

'No.'

'Is that really true?'

'Yes, Ryker, it's really true. And I don't like how you're talking to me right now. You sound way too... jittery. It's making me question if you were ready for this.'

'Look at it this way,' Ryker said. 'You want me to be as close as possible to Minko, don't you?'

'Yes.'

'Because right now, I'm not. Right now, Minko is hundreds of miles away while I'm out in Russia, Ukraine, Georgia, Armenia, chasing empty leads with Kovac never far away waiting for me to slip up.'

'You're on the inside, that's what counts.'

'Or just under watch still. But that's not my point. My point is I need to be even closer. I need to give him something of worth.'

'Like what?'

'Well, I can't turn up one day telling him I've got another shipment of fifty million euros' worth of military grade weapons for him, given the story I gave him the last time.'

'No, probably not.'

'But if I can find the missing ones and help him recover them?'

'What are you asking me for?'

'We'll get to the bottom of it one way or another. But I'm not sure how many people will have to die to get us there. Like I said, perhaps it's an inside job, or perhaps it's a rival. Or perhaps it's another intelligence agency. But someone in authority knows something. It's the most likely explanation.'

Mackie had a comeback to that, but Ryker's distraction meant he didn't really hear it because as he looked over to the approach road he saw the jostling beams of two vehicles, approaching at speed.

'I gotta go.'

He slipped the phone away and seconds later the SUV and van skidded to a stop right by him. Kovac emerged first.

'Who were you on the phone to?' he asked.

'Pizza delivery. Thought you'd all be hungry.'

'Damn starved,' said Lina as she stepped out. She moved to the back of the van and hauled open the doors.

'Help us get these assholes inside,' Kovac said.

Three bound and gagged men lay crumpled inside the van, nothing on but boxer shorts.

'Who are they?' Ryker asked.

'That's what we're gonna find out,' Kovac said, not bothering to hide his delight at the grim prospect of what was to come.

* * *

Lina, Ryker, Kovac, Klaus, Calhoun. A strange mix of people, from different countries, with different backgrounds. Minko was the glue that brought them all together. Money too, perhaps, as everyone close to Minko benefitted financially. Whatever it was, the five of them had belonging alongside each other. Safety too.

The three men across the empty warehouse floor were not part of this group.

Each of them gently swung, their roped ankles attached to chains hanging from the ceiling. Their wrists were roped together too, their mouths plugged with fabric gags. They'd had their final indignity thrust upon them since being dragged from the van with the removal of their underwear. Not that they likely felt any embarrassment hanging there, only fear and dread.

The man on the right had already pissed himself, much to the amusement of Kovac and Calhoun. Two meatheads. Calhoun, an Irishman, was as big and brutal as Kovac and had the résumé of real-life battles to back up his brutish prowess. Having fought very different wars that Minko likely had no direct interest in, never mind involvement, they'd come to work together for one reason only. They were animals.

Kovac paced up and down in front of the three men but didn't say a word. He had a look of disgust on his face. He paused by the man on the right, looked down at the puddle of urine underneath. He shook his head then turned and walked back to his crew.

He stood in front of Calhoun and just stared at him for a few moments, as though the two men were having a silent conversation. Then he moved to Ryker and did the same. After several seconds of silence – a silence only broken by the heavy breathing and occasional moans of the captives – Kovac finally spoke. To Ryker.

'Find out what they did with the weapons.' Kovac outstretched his hand to Ryker, a hunting knife as vicious looking as the man in his grip. 'Let's see what you've got.'

Ryker took the knife and stepped forward to the captives. The men's moans grew louder, more panicked. The one in the middle bucked causing his body to swing ungainly. Ryker moved to the man on the left first then walked along the line, not quite meeting their eyes with their heads a couple of feet below Ryker's.

He stopped at the man on the right and crouched down so they were at eye level although the man did everything he could to avert Ryker's gaze.

'This is simple,' Ryker said, voice low and calm. 'You give me information and I don't have to cut you into pieces.'

The man whimpered and then tried to shout out. Ryker reached for his gag and loosened it just enough, pulled out just enough fabric for him to speak.

'Tell me about the boat. How it sank. Where. We need the missing containers back.'

The man shouted at Ryker in Russian. He hadn't been told these men were Russian or Ukrainian or whatever else but had chosen to open up to them in English because... why not? A test, in a way. And it was clear the man had understood him because of his answer.

I don't know anything about a boat.

Ryker shuffled to the next man and held the knife up to his throat. He pushed the blade against the skin until he felt resistance and until he saw a line of blood slide across the metal. Once again he pulled the gag out to give the man a chance to speak.

'Where are the weapons?' Ryker asked.

'I don't know!' the man shouted in accented English. 'You have the wrong people! Please!'

'Come on, Ryker, what the fuck is this?' Calhoun shouted over. 'Just because you have their dicks in your face, you're not supposed to be flirting with them.'

'Maybe if you suck them off, that'll get them to talk,' Kovac said, to a round of laughter at Ryker's expense.

'I bet he's a pro,' Calhoun added.

Ryker didn't respond but shoved the gag back into the man's mouth before moving over again.

'I'll give you all one more chance,' Ryker said. 'After that... it gets bad.'

The man in front of him shook with fear and even if Ryker couldn't understand the garbled words, he knew the man was begging. He went to loosen the gag but then paused as their eyes met. Ryker didn't move for a few seconds and the man's moans faded too.

Then Ryker stretched up and he thrust the knife forward and

it dug deep in the man's gut. He roared with effort and quickly drew the blade downward and across. The man's mid-section opened up, the thick flesh and muscles parted to leave a gaping hole. Intestines and entrails and blood gushed out and covered the man's head before splatting to the floor.

'What the hell was that!' Kovac shouted as he stormed over. He took the blood-dripping knife from Ryker and grabbed his arm. 'Outside. Now.'

Ryker shrugged Kovac off him and headed for the exit. Kovac palmed the knife to Calhoun before following Ryker out into the night.

'Are you stupid or something?' Kovac said.

'What? You wanted me to go easy on them?'

'No. We wanted to interrogate them.'

'And they're a lot more likely to give up whatever they have now that they know we're not messing around.'

'Yeah, except that guy can't speak with his fucking guts on the floor, so now we only have two to go at.'

'If they know anything then it's plenty.'

'Unless the one you killed was the only one who knew anything.'

'Then why the hell are the others strung up too? Who the hell even are those three?'

'What? You didn't think to wait to find that out before you sliced one of them open?'

'I just sped this thing up. If they know anything, they'll talk soon enough.'

Kovac clearly didn't agree but simply increased the depth of his sneer rather than bite back anymore.

'You know what I can't work out about you?' he said after a long stare off.

'I'm sure you're about to tell me.'

'Clearly you have no issue with killing people. That's twice now you've ended someone in front of me just like that.' He clicked his fingers for effect. 'But is it coz you're a dumb psycho who likes blood. Or... something else.'

Ryker scoffed. 'Dumb psycho? Coming from you? Interesting.'

Kovac didn't respond because the next moment the door opened. Calhoun. Blood covered his arms and speckled his face. No sign of the knife now. Apparently, he hadn't bothered to wait before going at the other two.

'You're up,' Calhoun said to Kovac.

Ryker made a move to follow them back in.

'No,' Kovac said. 'You wait out here.'

A moment later the door slammed shut.

* * *

Kovac rode with Ryker back into the city. The remains of the three dead men were ablaze back in the warehouse a couple of miles behind them. The fire was the extent of the clean-up. Even if the fire burned all night, most likely bone and teeth would be found in the ashes and perhaps the authorities would soon identify the victims. Kovac didn't care. Minko wouldn't either. There was no direct evidence of Minko's involvement, but even if anyone connected the deaths to him it would simply act as a chilling reminder about what happened when people wronged him.

'So?' Ryker said after the silence had dragged on long enough.

'What?'

'What did you find out from them?'

'We haven't found the weapons yet. But we have a couple of leads.'

'Are you going to tell me those leads? You haven't even yet told me how you came across those three men.'

Kovac didn't answer straight away, as though deciding whether or not to reveal what he knew. 'The guys we had were responsible for sinking that ship. They went out on a dinghy and stuck C4 to the hull in the middle of the night. The idiots didn't even know about the weapons.'

'So why did they do it?'

'Why do you think? They were paid.'

'By who?'

'And that's the lead. Some guy called Cheko or something. But that's all they knew. Because apparently the one you killed was the one in charge who'd met Cheko and got them the money. Ten thousand euros between the three of them. They were bottom feeders.'

'You don't know who this Cheko is?' Ryker asked.

'Not yet. Those guys didn't have a clue about the weapons, so we still don't know if the containers were even onboard when the ship went down or if they'd been taken off before. Kind of like the play you made in Gibraltar.'

Ryker kept his eyes on the road although he knew very well Kovac was accusing him.

'You said a couple of leads. What was the other one?'

'Did I?' Kovac simply shrugged. Perhaps he'd misspoken before. Or more likely he'd now decided not to tell Ryker the full story.

'So what now?' Ryker asked.

'Now we go clean ourselves up. Sleep. Tomorrow, we go searching for Cheko.'

Ryker pulled up outside the apartment complex Kovac was staying at. A friend of his father-in-law. Ryker was in a hotel, all of the men having originally made their own arrangements as they'd traveled around the many towns dotting the Black Sea coast searching for leads. Harder for anyone to link their movements together that way, and it also gave them the space to go in their own direction when needed, do their own thing.

Which was exactly what Ryker needed right now.

'Come pick me up at eight,' Kovac said.

'What for?' Ryker answered.

'You have something else to do out here?'

'No, I...'

'You have a lead you're not telling me about?'

Ryker toyed with a thought. A crazy idea really. But if it worked...

'Yeah. I have a lead to follow.'

'What fucking lead? You're only telling me about this now?'

'You're only asking now. It's a guy from my Wagner days. He's been in Crimea for years. It's not a leap that he may know something.' A lie. A friend from Wagner? Perhaps the now dead Wiley had such a friend, but he certainly didn't.

'Then I'll come with you.'

'It's a long drive, and he doesn't know I'm coming. I don't even know if he's there. It could—'

'I said I'll see you tomorrow. 8 a.m.'

Kovac stepped out of the car and headed inside.

Ryker didn't bother to wait until he'd made it back to the hotel. He went around the block and pulled the car over to the side of the road and took out his phone and made the call.

'I'm in deep shit,' Ryker said when Mackie answered.

'Go on.'

'I just killed a guy. Someone I know.'

'Jesus, Ryker. Who?'

'Kovac pulled three guys into a warehouse to torture them

about the missing goods. I don't even know how he found them, but...'

'But?'

'One of them was this guy I know... He worked for SBU.' Ukraine's security services.

'You're sure?'

'I'm sure. And he knew me. I had no choice.'

Mackie sighed but didn't otherwise respond.

'It means SBU were in on it,' Ryker said. 'They went after Minko's weapons. Maybe they even recovered them all.'

'I didn't know,' Mackie said, likely going back to the conversation they'd had earlier. 'I would have told you otherwise.'

'Fine, I believe you.' Saying so was the quickest way to move on. 'But... this could actually play out for us. If it doesn't get me killed.'

'What are you thinking?'

'SBU helped scupper Minko's plans. This is at least semi-official. You can find out the details through your connections.'

'You think I have SBU on speed dial?'

'The man I killed was called Cheko. Only Kovac thinks that's the guy he's still looking for.'

'So... you want me to give up even more people, SBU agents potentially, for Kovac to go slaughter? For you to slaughter?'

'Hopefully it won't come to that. But Kovac... I really think he's on to me. And the way I killed Cheko... He trusts me less than ever. I need to give them something back.'

He got no response.

'Come on, Mackie. Tell SBU about me if you have to. Get them to realize that we need those weapons. That's all.'

Mackie sighed again. 'Give me a couple of days.'

'I don't have a couple of days. I'm taking Kovac out in the morning to meet with a contact.'

'What contact?'

'An old ally from Wagner.'

'You have an old ally from Wagner?'

'No, I don't.'

'Then who the hell are you meeting?'

'That's the thing.'

'It is?'

'How soon can you get Peter Winter out here?'

'You want Peter Winter to act as a Wagner mercenary?'

'You told me he's talented. And one of the biggest talents of someone who works for the JIA is being able to lie convincingly.'

Silence from Mackie.

'Can you get him out here?' Ryker prompted. 'And armed with some answers about those weapons?'

'If I want to keep you alive, I'm not sure I have much choice.'

22

The ride up the coast of the Sea of Azov was scenic, rocky, rural. Isolated. Ryker and Kovac chatted little, the only talk being questions from Kovac which showed his continued distaste and distrust for Ryker.

'Why the fuck is a Wagner guy living out here?'

'You can ask him.'

Kovac grumbled in response and that was the end of another stilted conversation.

Nearly two hours into the drive and Ryker pulled the car onto a short dirt track road which wound toward a cliffy outcrop of land where an old stone farmhouse stood. The modest building wasn't in the best condition, but it didn't look abandoned either. All its windows were in place, doors too, the roof looked decent. There was no car or other vehicle outside.

'You're sure he's here?' Kovac said as Ryker braked to a stop.

'I'm sure he's been here. Like I said, I didn't tell him I was coming, so I don't know if he's here right now.'

'You better hope he is, otherwise you've just wasted my day.'

Ryker got out and started a slow walk to the house. He

glanced behind him every now and then, ever wary of the man following him. Ryker reached the door and knocked.

No answer.

'Surprise, surprise,' Kovac said. 'So what now?'

'We can call him,' Ryker said.

He put his hand to his phone, but Kovac stopped him.

'No. I want to take a look around first. Inside.'

'He'll be pretty pissed.'

'I couldn't give a shit what he thinks. I don't know him, and he's not here.'

Kovac moved across to the nearest window and slammed his elbow into it. The single pane shattered. Kovac pulled the sleeve of his jacket over his wrist and swept around the edge of the window frame to knock out loose shards. Then he slipped through the window. For a big guy he was remarkably nimble. Moments later the door opened.

'No alarm,' he said. 'Nice and easy.'

'Are you paying for the window?' Ryker asked as he moved inside.

Kovac rolled his eyes and both men paused in the narrow hallway. Kovac stared at the array of pictures on the wall.

'So which one is your friend?' he asked. 'The gray-haired woman who looks like she's a retired farmer or something. Or the little black and white dog?'

And at least one of them was in nearly every picture. A couple of kids too, although the infrequency suggested they were distant relatives rather than the woman's children. Only two photos had a man who looked anything like Ryker and Kovac's age.

'This isn't his place,' Ryker said.

'No shit. So who's the woman?'

'A relative. I don't know the details. I just know this is where to find him.'

'Except it isn't, is it? Because he's not here.'

Ryker moved along the hallway, into the kitchen. He'd rather be in a more open space. And he hoped the slight delay would give him a spark of something.

'Call him,' Kovac said. 'And put it on speaker because I want to hear this guy and what he's got to say.'

Ryker took out his phone. He put in Winter's number. His finger hovered over the call button a couple of seconds until he finally took the plunge. The rings sounded out. Winter answered right before voicemail.

'Who is this?' Winter asked.

'Ryker.'

A pause, then, 'Long time, old friend.'

Ryker tried not to cringe at Winter's bad acting. Talented? Perhaps it was better he wasn't here in person after all.

'Hey, shitheads,' Kovac said, 'I don't need any small talk, and guy-on-the-phone, I don't know who you are but we've just driven more than two hours to come find you and you're not here.'

'Who the fuck is that?' Winter said, and he actually sounded a lot more hard-edged than Ryker imagined the clean-cut guy would be able to muster in the flesh. Yeah, it was definitely better he wasn't here for this.

'You know what?' Ryker said. 'Why don't you two just talk it out.'

He took the phone off speaker and handed it to Kovac.

Kovac glared and grumbled and brought the phone closer to his ear. His hand further from his side where Ryker knew his gun was stashed.

As was Ryker's.

And with Kovac preoccupied, Ryker went for it.

He drew his weapon out of his waistband and really thought he'd get at least a shot off before Kovac realized.

No. The guy was wilier than that. The phone dropped from his hand and he reached across with his left to pull out his gun as he sank down.

Ryker pulled his trigger but the shot missed, and as he tried to adjust his aim Kovac burst back up and clattered into Ryker and sent the two of them flying. Ryker landed on his back with a thud, his gun fell from his grip. Kovac slammed down on top of him, the barrel of his gun an inch from Ryker's eye...

Ryker yanked his head to the side just before Kovac pulled the trigger. The bullet pinged into the stone tiles, the sound right by Ryker's ear deafening and disorientating. But not enough to stop him. He grabbed Kovac's wrist, trying to prevent him from retaking his aim. Ryker held him at bay for a few seconds, but the guy was too strong. So Ryker reached up and sank his teeth into Kovac's arm. He bit down hard until his teeth tore into flesh and Kovac yelled in pain or anger or both. It gave Ryker the distraction he needed to push the gun further away as Kovac squeezed on the trigger and several bullets erupted in quick succession.

Ryker slid out from underneath and grabbed the first thing he could from the side as he jumped back to his feet. A copper pot. He swiped it toward Kovac and the gun went off one final time before the pot smashed into Kovac's hand. His gun fell free. For a moment it looked like he would go for it but then he instead grabbed a vase which he tossed at Ryker as he launched himself forward. Ryker swiped the vase away and it smashed against the worktop, sending glass through the air.

Kovac pulled a chef's knife from a wooden block as he charged. Ryker dodged the first swipe but Kovac moved quickly around the side and Ryker could do nothing as the knife slashed across his bicep.

As Ryker righted himself Kovac came at him again. They both ended up back on the floor. No knife now. No gun, either. Kovac didn't seem to care. He rained punches down onto Ryker's face. Big, meaty fists hammered him again and again and Ryker's vision blurred, his focus faded.

The initial flurry soon died down, Kovac panting heavy breaths from his exertion, Ryker on the brink of unconsciousness or worse. Kovac grabbed Ryker by the scruff of the neck and lifted his head from the floor.

'I knew you were a lying piece of shit,' he said. 'And I don't even want answers from you now. I just want to see your brains spilled out beneath me.'

He slammed Ryker's head back down.

'I'm gonna enjoy this.'

Kovac sent his fist crashing into Ryker's cheek again, putting all of his upper body weight into the shot, causing his torso to slump right down near to Ryker's battered face.

'Come on, tough guy,' Kovac whispered in Ryker's ear as Ryker coughed out blood from between his burst lips. 'What have you got?'

Ryker answered in action rather than words. His left hand, roaming to his side, scrabbling for anything he could find to use as a weapon to try and fight back, wrapped around the telephone cable stretching down from the wall. He yanked the cable free and before Kovac rose back up, Ryker twisted the wire around Kovac's neck.

He pulled hard on both ends and Kovac spluttered and grasped at the wire. Ryker roared with effort as he tightened the cable further. Kovac's face went beet-red, his eyes bulged. He clawed at the plastic, slapped Ryker feebly, all the strength from before dissipated.

Ryker took his chance to flip Kovac off him. It meant letting go of the cable but as he swiveled over he grabbed the fallen copper pot and smashed it against Kovac's skull as he tried to pull the loose cable free. Ryker jumped on top, the roles reversed, and he hit Kovac with the pot again. Again. Again. His nose caved in. His jaw shattered. His cheekbone squashed into his face. Ryker didn't stop. He kept going until Kovac's arms flopped down.

Ryker tossed the bloodied pan across the kitchen. Kovac wasn't dead. Not quite. His chest rose and fell. Air bubbled out of what used to be his nose. His left eye had disappeared behind broken bone and torn flesh, but his right eye remained open, blinking, looking up at Ryker.

'Yeah... you were... right not to trust me,' Ryker said, still getting his breathing back under control. 'You want to know... a little story?'

He got no answer from Kovac. The man was nearly done for. Ryker only hoped he'd hold on long enough for what he was about to say.

'Wiley wasn't the agent. I am. And now I'm taking your place by Minko's side.'

Kovac tried to speak or cough or splutter or something, his body jerking a little, blood spilling out from his mangled lips.

'And the man I killed yesterday? He was Cheko. SBU. I don't know how the wires got crossed. Why those two you tortured led you to believe Cheko was someone else. Maybe they were too beaten up. Maybe they didn't know. Or maybe they were just trying to con you. But... I'm going to find those weapons now. I'm going to be the hero in this.'

Kovac somehow managed to find the strength to lift a hand up. His fingers lightly brushed across Ryker's face. Was he trying to choke Ryker or something? Ryker swatted the hand away.

'You want to know the funny thing?' Ryker asked. 'Today wasn't supposed to go down like this. The guy on the phone? His name's Peter Winter. He's my boss's assistant. I asked him to come out here to pretend to be my contact. He was going to get us the intel on Cheko and lead us to the weapons. You and me? We could have both been heroes. But fate can be as cruel as it can be damn hilarious. Because he's still stuck in Cyprus. His plane had a fuel problem so he's sat in the airport. I only found out when I woke up at 6 a.m. that he couldn't get out here. I should have planned it more in advance.'

Ryker laughed. Kovac didn't react at all. It took Ryker a few moments of checking to confirm the guy was still clinging on to life.

Yeah. He was.

'This place?' Ryker said, looking around. 'Found it on satellite images this morning. One of a few places I thought about coming to. Middle of nowhere. No one around. When I saw it coming up on the road and realized there were no cars here, I took a chance. Nothing more than that.'

He pushed his hands onto Kovac's throat, squeezed hard. The guy's one good eye bulged.

'You didn't have to die today,' Ryker said. 'If you'd just trusted me a little more, I wouldn't have pulled the gun on you. But you know what? I'm glad about this.'

Ryker squeezed even harder, held on tight. It didn't take long. Only a few seconds before the little light behind Kovac's eye went out for good.

'You piece of shit,' Ryker said as he stood up off the corpse.

He went over and picked up his phone, blood smearing over the screen as he did so. The call was still connected.

'Winter?'

'Ryker, what the hell?'

He was breathing heavily, like he was all in a panic. Like he was the one who'd almost been killed.

'Is he dead?' Winter asked.

'Yeah. He's dead.'

'What an absolute mess. I don't know why you couldn't just delay—'

'No. This isn't a mess—'

'Ryker, you've just murdered Minko's highest-ranking soldier!'

Murder? Ryker didn't dwell on the word, nor Winter's agitation.

'This was a good twist,' Ryker said. 'Sometimes the best decisions are made under pressure.'

'Good? You think Mackie—'

'Winter. It's done. I'll clear things at my end. Just find me the damn weapons.'

He ended the call, retrieved both fallen guns, and headed for the door.

23

PRESENT DAY

Voronezh Oblast, Russia

Ryker and the young woman, Nadia, had left Donetsk the same night they'd met, without either stopping to even collect any belongings. A hasty decision, but one that clearly suited them both. They initially traveled in Ryker's rental car toward the Russian border. They dumped that car and journeyed on foot from there, crossing the unmanned border in an area of dense woodland, and carried on toward a small farming town on the Russian side where Ryker found a rusted old Lada which he hot-wired.

As the sun rose on a frigid morning, he was driving while Nadia slept. They'd talked little on the nervy journey so far, her only giving Ryker the basics. Her name, the fact the older man was her father. She was twenty-three, and she'd known Gregor since she was seventeen. Although she hadn't explicitly said so, Ryker took that admission, plus all the other circumstantial evidence, to mean that she knew too of the Panthers, and what had happened to them. What had happened to Gregor.

She stirred when the crappy car bounced over an unseen ridge in the uneven road. After a few minutes of silence she took out her phone and scrolled for a couple of seconds.

'I've heard nothing from him,' Nadia said.

'Your father?'

She nodded.

'Most likely he's in police custody still,' Ryker said.

She scoffed. 'You have no idea, do you? No idea what they do to people like us.'

'Like you?'

She shook her head.

'You're with the Panthers?' Ryker asked.

She didn't answer.

'I was told Gregor was,' he added. 'I've been searching for him. At the orphanage. At the theater. It's why I went to the restaurant to speak to Inna. Because her brother—'

'Eduard. Her brother was Eduard. And he was executed by the police inside that theater. On his knees, hands tied behind his back. I saw it.'

'So you were with the Panthers?' Ryker asked. She shot him a hostile glare, obviously annoyed at his response.

'A lot of my friends were arrested or killed that night.'

'I'm sorry,' he said.

She only shook her head at that.

'Was Gregor arrested then too?' Ryker asked.

'No. He was taken weeks before. But... the way it all fell apart so quickly... The ones who were taken first were interrogated for information. Tortured. Piece by piece, the Panthers were torn down from the inside. Now...'

'Now what?'

'Now there's nothing left.'

'You're left.'

She humphed. 'There's nothing I can do on my own.'

'There must be others.'

'A few girls like me? All the men were killed or taken.'

'Your dad?'

'He's... too old. He protects me, but that's as far as his politics takes him. He doesn't want to fight. The war in Donetsk is as good as over. Every man of fighting age who wanted to rebel is already killed or taken or has run.'

'I'm sorry,' Ryker said, feeling weak that he couldn't come up with anything better.

'You say you're looking for Gregor. But... why?'

'You asked me that already. I heard he was in trouble. I want to help him.'

'And what did you hear?'

'That he was imprisoned in Siberia. That he was going to be signed up to fight for Brightstar, the mercenary group, on the front lines...' An incredulous gasp left her lips. Perhaps she hadn't known that part of the story and knew how crazy it was that Gregor would have been sent to the front lines fighting for the Russians. '...But he escaped from the transport train. Near Lake Baikal. A long, long way from home.'

She nodded but said nothing.

'But that's all I know. I've no idea where he went after that. Or where he is now.'

'Who are you?'

Of course, she'd asked that question several times now, both before and after they'd set off together, but apparently he'd never given her a satisfactory answer.

'A long time ago, I worked for Gregor's father, Roman Minko. His real father. You know that name?'

'Of course. Everyone in our area knows that name. Roman Minko wanted independence for Donbas. He was one of the first prominent people in our lifetime to not just say it, but to try to make it happen.'

'He did,' Ryker said. 'But he wanted true independence. Not to be a puppet state of Russia.'

'It's what Gregor wanted too. Want many of us wanted. But not enough of us. It's why the Panthers found enemies in so many places.'

'But you knew Minko was Gregor's father?'

'He never told me directly. But it only takes one person to know something like that and the whispers spread like wildfire.'

'Your English is good,' Ryker said. 'Where'd you learn it?'

He received a scathing look in return. He hadn't meant to offend her, but it was becoming more and more apparent that she had an excellent grasp of the language, similes, idioms, metaphors and all. Kind of like the matron at the orphanage.

'I thought perhaps you'd lived there at one time,' he said.

She tutted. 'I know we're here together, right now, but... I don't trust you.'

'Thanks. And yet here we are traveling through Russia in a stolen car, looking for an escaped convict who's a good friend of yours.'

She said nothing to that although something about the look on her face caused him to rethink.

'Boyfriend? You were together.'

She nodded. 'But that doesn't change anything. For you.'

'No. It doesn't.'

'But still, I don't trust you. Because even if I believe you've told me the truth about how you know Gregor, how you knew his father, it still doesn't explain to me how you'd know about the prison. Brightstar. His escape. The Panthers.'

'No. Perhaps not. But just trust that I'm not trying to find him to harm him.'

She didn't respond, but did caress the form of the gun under her coat a little, as though emphasizing that she at least had the comfort of the weapon to balance the lack of trust.

After that they both went silent again, and before long she was back to her phone, checking things over before she turned the device off once more. To save battery, but also to stop it being tracked.

'Still nothing?' Ryker asked.

'About my father?'

'Or Gregor.'

'Nothing about either.'

And it'd been two days since the phone that Gregor had 'acquired' on his trek across Siberia and further west had last thrown out its GPS co-ordinates. According to Nadia, Gregor had first contacted her three days after his escape. She had known nothing about those events, and she hadn't even known which prison he'd been held in. She'd assumed she'd never see or even hear from him again, as had happened with other friends of theirs. But he'd called her and given her the basic story, and the phone's details, and she'd had a friend install software that would allow her to track the phone's location from there.

She'd had intermittent contact with Gregor since then as he made the long and perilous journey west across enemy territory to reunite with her in Ukraine.

Except she'd heard nothing at all from him, and the phone hadn't relayed a signal for nearly two days.

And yet he'd got so close. Not even a hundred miles from the Ukrainian border.

'Do you know this area?' Ryker asked.

'I've never been. I only know that we won't find any friends here.'

'Probably not.'

'Are you a spy?' she asked Ryker matter-of-factly, after a few more minutes of silence.

'Not exactly.'

'But there's not many other explanations for someone like you to be here. To know Gregor. His father.'

Ryker shrugged.

'You work for the British government?'

'Not anymore.'

'But you did?'

'At one time.'

'And you were working for the British government when you knew Roman Minko?'

Ryker thought about that one before answering.

'Yes,' he said.

'Did Roman know that?'

'No.'

'So you were working undercover? He was your country's enemy?'

'No. It was more complicated than that. And it was a long time ago. A lot has changed since then, for me, and for your country.'

She looked aggrieved. 'It's not a very good explanation. You're basically admitting to me that you're a liar. That you operate with ulterior motives. And yet you claim I can trust you?'

'I've got a complicated past, and I'm sorry but I'm not going to divulge anything you don't need to know. Which is most of it. But I'm looking for Gregor because I want to help him, because I feel I owe it to him and his family. That's the truth. I mean no harm to him. Or to you. But I do have a question for you?'

'OK?'

'Here we are, traveling through Russia to find Gregor, having known each other only a few hours. But... if I hadn't showed up in Donetsk, asking questions, what would you have done?'

'How do you mean?'

'Would you have done this alone? With your father?'

'I wouldn't have done this with my father because he doesn't even know that I've been in contact with Gregor. I tell him little to protect him. And now... I have no one else to help me, whose life I could bear to put on the line.'

Ryker laughed. She didn't seem to appreciate it. 'So what you're saying is, you don't mind me coming along for this, because it means nothing to you if I get killed.'

'It's not how I would have said it.' The words were delivered deadpan but then the slightest smile took hold.

'No offense taken,' Ryker said, before his phone buzzed in his pocket. He lifted it out and glanced at Nadia before answering, weighing up whether he was happy to talk with her right next to him.

Yes. Because he did want her to trust him.

'Yeah,' Ryker said.

'You made it to Russia?' Winter asked.

'We did.'

'Good. I won't ask for details, but I have something I thought would interest you.'

'Go on.'

'The two people who came to you in France, Irina Kakabadze and Giorgi Mekvabishvili.'

'Yeah?'

'I've been digging to find out who they work for.'

'And?'

'And I haven't found the answers.'

'Not the revelation I was hoping for.'

'Perhaps not. But it's increasingly looking likely that they aren't with the SVR, or any other major agency, otherwise we would have found tracks by now.'

'So what have you found?'

'That since they came to you in Antibes, Mekvabishvili's body washed up on the shore of the Med not far from Nice. A boating accident, it's being reported as. And Kakabadze hasn't been seen or heard from at all.'

Ryker gripped the phone a little more tightly.

'It definitely adds an extra layer of mystery,' Winter added.

'That's one way of putting it.'

'Anyway, that's it. I thought you'd want to know.'

'I did. Thanks.'

Ryker ended the call. He kept his eyes on the road but knew Nadia was staring at him.

'Anything I should know about?' she asked.

'No.'

He glanced over, noting the suspicious look on her face.

'Nothing that affects what we're doing here,' he said, sounding as convincing as he could.

'OK,' she said. 'I believe you. Your secret past, et cetera, et cetera. And anyway... if you take this next turn—' she glanced at her phone screen once more '—I think we're almost there.'

24

Having initially traversed dense forest on entering Russia, the latter part of the journey had been across flat, open farmland – a desolate looking area in the middle of winter. The place where Nadia instructed Ryker to pull over had no towns within at least ten miles, and for a long time they'd seen nothing but sporadic farmhouses and barns.

The farmhouse nearest to them now was modest in size with rendered walls, a tiled roof, the overall weathering and upkeep suggesting the structure was past its best, but then everything out here at this time of year looked forlorn.

Regardless, the building was definitely inhabited. Ryker could tell by the smoke trailing up from one of the two chimneys. Two outbuildings lay to the side of the farmhouse, a Jeep-style vehicle parked there alongside a knackered old compact that looked in worse condition than the Lada that Ryker and Nadia had traveled in.

'How close are we?' Ryker said as she fiddled with the phone.

'The last signal I got was about two hundred yards east of that farmhouse, but there's literally nothing else out here for miles.'

'So it looks like this is the place, then.'

'But... why would he even stop here?'

A good question.

'Let me have a look.'

She initially regarded his outstretched hand with suspicion but then passed the phone over. Ryker looked at the GPS data first, quickly confirming the position was as she'd said, but then moved into her mapping app as he thought.

'He didn't travel from Siberia on foot,' Ryker said, thinking out loud.

Nadia scoffed. 'Obviously.'

'So he had to have used trains, cars.'

'Cars would make more sense, particularly around here.'

'Exactly,' Ryker said. 'But he also would have wanted to travel on more scenic routes, avoiding big towns and cities, so most likely, if Donetsk was his destination—'

'It was. He told me so.'

'Then I can see why he'd have come along this very road. Because north of the river there's too much development, and south of here he'd have to detour to get around the mountains.'

'What's your point?'

'I'm just confirming I think we're in the right place. And why did he stop here? Most likely because he had to. He hadn't stopped anywhere else for maybe ten hours or so according to the data you have here, so he was low on fuel, food, water, energy.'

'That doesn't explain why he didn't move on from here.'

'But we have to conclude that he hasn't. Say he'd lost the phone, or it'd broken, or whatever. He'd have arrived back in Donetsk by now. Or found another way to communicate with you.'

'Maybe.'

'But looking at the map... there really is nothing out here but that farmhouse. He's either still in there, or at least he was. Either way, we need to go take a look.'

He handed the phone back to her. She looked incredibly dubious about his suggestion, scared again. Like she had back in Donetsk. But what else had she expected? They'd traveled out here to find Gregor and they were potentially so close.

Ryker took the car the rest of the way to the house, pulling up only a few yards from the other vehicles.

'You really want us to just walk in there?' Nadia asked.

'Yes.' Ryker said. 'Open your coat. Keep your hand on the gun in case you need it.'

She gulped and nodded.

'What about you?'

'We only have one gun. And I'm hoping we won't even need it. I'll lead the way.'

He got out without waiting for a response and closed his door gently, eyes not leaving the house in front of him. If someone was inside, they likely would have seen or heard the car approaching but no one had come out to greet them.

Nadia stepped out too and they both edged toward the house. But they didn't make it far before Ryker heard noise behind. By the outbuilding.

'Who are you?' came the shout in Russian.

Ryker slowly turned, being careful not to make a sudden move. A good decision because he was soon looking down the barrel of a shotgun. The thickset man, gnarled face, who held it up, stood ten yards away.

Perhaps Ryker should have had the handgun after all.

'Sorry to disturb you,' Ryker said in Russian. 'But we're lost. And we're really low on fuel. We hoped you could help us.'

'You're not from here,' the man responded.

'We're traveling.'

'But your car's from here.'

'A rental.'

'You actually paid to rent that?'

'Maybe they screwed us. Because I'm not from around here.'

Ryker chuckled at his own jibe, but the man wasn't buying it. That was fine. The situation already told Ryker that there was something here. The gun pointed at him could perhaps be explained when trespassing on someone's property, but the manner of the man's questions, the nervousness in his tone... He was hiding something.

Ryker turned to Nadia and whispered, 'Go the other side of the car. It'll shield you. Shoot if you need to.'

'But—'

He faced the man again and took a couple of steps forward, lifted his hands in the air.

'Please, you don't need the gun,' Ryker said. 'We didn't mean to upset you.'

'I'm not upset. You need to get off my property.'

'I'm not sure the car would make it. I have cash.'

Ryker went to put his hand in his pocket. The guy really didn't like that.

'Hands in the air!' he shouted. All jittery now. He flicked the barrel from Ryker to Nadia, not knowing who to focus on now they'd split up.

Which was exactly Ryker's aim.

He burst forward. The man panicked. Nadia fired. She missed. Perhaps she'd intended to. The man fired. Ryker heard the dinks as the buckshot splatted into the bodywork of the Lada. Nadia screamed, but it was more out of shock than pain. He hoped.

Ryker thumped into the man and they crashed down onto the

floor. Ryker prized the shotgun free and jumped to his feet before smacking the hefty butt of the weapon across the man's face. His eyes rolled as Ryker turned the shotgun around and pointed the barrel at the man's chest.

'Do anything other than what I say and this thing'll tear your heart to shreds.'

He grumbled in response, his face not full of defeat just yet, but he was definitely not looking too confident anymore.

'We're looking for a friend,' Ryker said. 'A young man. Ukrainian. Mid-twenties. Tall, dark brown hair. Traveling alone.'

No response at all from the man.

'His name is Gregor Rebrov.'

The man still said nothing.

'Nadia, do you have a picture?'

She scuttled up behind Ryker, one hand on the gun, her phone in the other.

'You OK?' he asked, glancing at her. No signs that she'd been hit by the shotgun pellets and she nodded as she fumbled before turning the phone screen away from her and to the man on the ground.

'Have you seen him?' Ryker asked.

The guy stared blankly at the photo but didn't say a word.

'We know he passed by here. Two days ago. So where is he?'

Still no response. But Ryker heard a clink beyond the open door of the brick outbuilding.

'Who's in there?' Ryker asked.

Still no response. The guy was determined to do things the hard way.

'OK, on your feet.'

He didn't move. So Ryker jabbed his foot into the guy's groin.

'Up.'

This time, he did move. Ryker prodded the shotgun into his back to get him to go forward.

'If this is a trap, I'll kill you and whoever else you have hiding in there,' Ryker said.

The man still didn't say a word. Ryker prodded the barrel into his back again and the man stumbled forward over the threshold into the darkened interior. Ryker took a step inside too then spotted the figure in the corner, crouched down. Another shotgun, this one in the hands of a young man.

'Down!' Ryker shouted to Nadia, and he fired and hunkered behind the older man as his friend opened fire. A poor shot to make because he only hit his buddy in the leg and the guy went down screeching as Ryker charged forward. No chance for him to reload as Ryker launched a spinning kick which took the weapon from his grip. He followed up with a knee to the face and the man – barely a man, actually – crumpled over.

Ryker glanced behind him. Nadia had the older guy tamed on the floor, him clutching at his leg which had several bleeding holes.

'Get up,' Ryker shouted to the younger man. A very young man. Possibly only a teenager, tall but wiry. 'Is this your son?' Ryker shouted to the older guy.

'Please... don't hurt him.'

Finally he sounded concerned.

'That would have been less likely if you hadn't both shot at us,' Ryker said. 'Where's our friend?'

No response from either. The boy pulled himself up to his feet, his busted lip pouring blood down his chin.

'Where's our friend?' Ryker asked him a little more calmly.

'Down there.'

He nodded to the closed hatch in the floor.

'He tried to steal from us!' the older man shouted. 'He had a knife to my boy's throat!'

The boy nodded as though to confirm.

'What would you do?' the old guy added.

'I don't know,' Ryker answered. 'Tie him up in a basement and shoot anyone who came asking questions of him?'

The man grumbled something under his breath.

'It doesn't make sense,' Nadia said. 'He's been here two days.'

Ryker knew what she meant by that. Gregor had been here – held captive? – for two days. Two days in which the police, the SVR, the army hadn't come to take him away. Which likely meant these people hadn't called anyone about the trespasser. Certainly not straight away.

'Open the hatch,' Ryker said to the boy. He moved over and heaved the metal lid open, revealing a concrete staircase leading down. 'Any more surprises?'

The boy shook his head.

'After you.' He turned to Nadia. 'Stay there. Use every last bullet on him if he does anything stupid.'

Ryker followed the boy down, the room below revealed step by step. Not a big space. Concrete walls, floor. An old war bunker, perhaps. A few shelves, tools, provisions.

A bloodied, crumpled heap in the corner.

Gregor Rebrov, bound and gagged. But alive and awake, at least.

The boy reached the bottom and turned to Ryker and gave something like an apologetic look. Almost embarrassed, as though none of it had been his idea, or desire. But then, as Ryker joined him at the bottom of the stairs, the teenager's gaze flicked to the side. Ryker spotted the movement only a beat before he heard the roar of the charging figure, and didn't have enough the time or space to turn the lengthy shotgun that way before the figure grabbed him and heaved him sideways and up against the wall with a clatter. Ryker kept hold of the gun, even as the wind was knocked out of him, but he couldn't recover before the burly man ducked his head and rammed into Ryker a second time, his shoulder slamming into Ryker's ribs with the force of a juggernaut. Pain shot through his abdomen, he gasped for air.

'Papa!' the boy yelled.

Ryker didn't know why. Perhaps to tell his dad upstairs that the fight was still on. Perhaps to ask for his assistance. But the shout only gave Ryker focus somehow. And right after the word had parted his lips, Nadia fired in response. Two shots. Not a full unload, like Ryker had said.

Which perhaps meant she was in trouble...

The beefy man, snarling, spittle flying, took hold of Ryker's arms to stop him swinging the gun and hauled a knee into Ryker's kidney. It wasn't often Ryker was outmatched for size and strength, but this guy was huge. So if Ryker couldn't gain the upper hand through brawn, he needed a different tactic.

Battling against the man's grip, he got just enough movement on the shotgun and fired. The blast hit the boy in the shoulder and he flew backward from the force. The big man had a momentary panic. Ryker used it to his advantage. He let go of the gun and pulled one arm free of the man's grip and hauled up his elbow onto the man's chin. The vicious uppercut would have snapped some people's necks. On this guy it only sent him a half step back and only added to his anger.

He roared again as he came forward. But the roar turned to a yelp when Ryker ducked down at the last moment and the guy's fist slammed into the concrete wall. Definitely smashed bones. To go along with the pain that erupted in his groin when Ryker first drove his fist there, before he grabbed hold of his testicles and squeezed as hard as he could until he felt a pop.

He slid between the man's legs and out the other side as the guy fell against the wall, writhing in agony, holding his destroyed genitals.

'You OK up there?' Ryker shouted.

'I am,' Nadia said. 'He's not.'

Though the man up there was still alive, at least, as Ryker could hear him moaning.

'Can you get him down here?'

No response as Ryker quickly surveyed the scene in front of him. He retrieved the shotgun. All three attackers were out of the fight. The boy was bleeding badly but medical attention would see him recover just fine. The ridiculously big guy – the boy's uncle, perhaps? – would survive too, but he wouldn't have any children of his own, if he hadn't already.

Ryker flinched at a clatter then turned and watched the dad rolling and banging down the stairs. He landed in a heap by Ryker's feet. One of his boots had a neat hole in it. So too his thigh.

Nadia followed down and looked on aghast at the carnage before she locked eyes with—

'Gregor!'

She pushed her gun away inside her coat and rushed over to the corner and pulled him to his feet. He was groggy, his head lolling, but he soon found some strength now that she was by him, most likely short-term strength as adrenaline surged.

Nadia pulled off his gag, untied his ankles then wrists. Gregor held Ryker's eye for just a moment before Nadia wrapped her arms around him and he wrapped his arms around her and sank his head down into her, squeezing his eyes shut as she sobbed.

Ryker gave them a moment. Kept his eyes on the three idiots, just in case any of them had another really stupid idea.

No. They were all done with those for now.

The embrace ended and Gregor took a step toward Ryker then paused, the expression on his face changing from intrigue, to anger, to sadness, to happiness, to... something else.

'Baby,' Nadia started, 'this is—'

'James Ryker,' Gregor said.

'It's been a long time.'

Gregor said nothing more but stormed over and Ryker was initially caught off-guard, ready to defend or attack, before Gregor flung his arms around him.

'Yeah. It's been a long time,' Gregor said. 'A really long time.'

He pulled away, Ryker a little shell-shocked from the affection. Nadia too looked surprised. But Gregor was beaming.

At least for a moment, until he looked over the three men on the floor.

'Are you OK?' Ryker asked.

'Yeah,' Gregor said. 'No. Actually, no, I'm not.'

He had some nasty cuts around his face, and his right shoulder was a little slumped as though he had pain there. He also limped on his left leg a little.

'The way that freak tackled you by surprise?' Gregor said. 'He did exactly the same thing to me. I thought I had the other two under control until then.'

'It's done now,' Ryker said.

'I only wanted some gas. Some food.' Gregor sounded solemn as though reliving the moment he was captured, beaten. 'To start with they didn't even know who I was. But they still tied me up, brought me down here. Beat the shit out of me. They told me I wasn't going anywhere unless I got them money.'

'We can go now,' Ryker said, indicating the stairs.

'But then the kid figured who I was,' Gregor said. 'I don't even know how. Probably because he's the only one of the inbreds who bothers to look to the outside world. Maybe he saw something on the internet. But still they didn't just call the police. You want to know why?'

The question was directed at Ryker, but he didn't answer.

'No one does anything around here if it's not for money. That's what they said. Over and over. They didn't want to just give me up. They wanted to make sure they got paid for it. I was like a prized possession for them.'

'Then we really should go,' Ryker said. 'If they've been talking to—'

Gregor whipped the gun from Nadia and spun. Three shots. Three hits. One bullet into the forehead of each of the men. Not even the blink of an eye between each pull of the trigger.

Gregor straightened up and locked eyes with Ryker. 'What?' he challenged.

Ryker said nothing.

'I thought he was reaching for something,' Gregor said. Though he didn't even bother to say which of the three men he was talking about. A threadbare defense if ever there was one.

'I'm only protecting myself, Nadia,' Gregor added. 'That's what people like me do. We protect those closest to us, at all costs.'

Ryker nodded but still said nothing.

'Someone like you, with your past, should know that better than anyone.' Gregor brushed past him and to the stairs. 'Now let's get the hell out of here.'

25

TWENTY YEARS AGO

Paphos, Cyprus

Ryker and Calhoun rode together back from Paphos airport to Minko's villa. The Irishman had been sullen the whole way. For the last three days actually, since Ryker had broken the news of Kovac's death. And the bogus story of how Ryker and Kovac had been ambushed by Cheko's 'gang', before Ryker saw off Cheko and escaped, badly beaten. Kovac had been less lucky.

But the upshot was that Ryker had identified the location of the weapons – with a bit of undisclosed help from Winter and Mackie since then, obviously.

Ryker pulled up to the gates and pressed the intercom, and moments later the gates rolled open. He took the car through and to the villa.

'Has he ever told you what the story is behind that statue?' Ryker said, indicating the interlocking cubes.

'Why you asking?'

'Just Minko told me there was a story.'

'It's not much of a story. There're seven cubes. It's his lucky number.'

'Lucky how?'

Calhoun shrugged. 'No idea. But he has references to seven all over the place.'

'Like on the license plates of all of his cars.'

'Yeah. Stuff like that. It's embroidered on the cuffs of his shirts too, where some people would have their initials. I don't know. Someone told me in Russian mythology seven is important. Seven gods. Seven parts of heaven? And something about seven... goats, I think.'

'Seven goats? What are you talking about?' Ryker said laughing.

Calhoun's face soured further. 'The fuck do I know?'

'Maybe you're thinking about the Brothers Grimm story.'

'I am?'

'A mother goat leaves her seven kids home alone. Warns them not to open the door as it could be a wolf wanting to eat them.'

'And?'

'And they didn't listen. A wolf knocks and persuades them he's their mother. They open the door. Six of them are eaten.'

'Why only six?'

'I think the wolf got too full. The end of the story is that the mother returns home and she finds the wolf asleep, cuts him open. The six kids jump out, still alive. She fills the wolf with rocks and sews him back up. When he wakes and goes down to the river to drink, he's so heavy he falls in and drowns.'

'What the actual crap is that?' Calhoun said.

Ryker shrugged. 'Just an old story.'

'But what's the point?'

'To listen to your mother, perhaps. Or maybe it's about revenge.'

'Listen to my mother? She's a vicious drunk. She'd definitely be the one cutting open that wolf.'

'Who knows,' Ryker said. Although he always thought it was more a cautionary tale about being wary of newcomers. The wolf at the door.

Except here, Ryker was the wolf.

Hopefully they wouldn't cut him open in his sleep though.

They got out and made their way to the house. Calhoun seemed distracted by the statue as they walked, as though his mind was still deliberating the meaning of the seven cubes, or that he was still contemplating the moral of the story.

Soon they were inside. Ryker spotted Natasha in the kitchen as he made his way across the hall. Gregor came bounding up to him.

'James, you've been gone so long!' Gregor shouted excitedly before Ryker lifted him and swung him around. 'Will you play in the pool with me?'

Ryker put the boy back down. 'As soon as I can.'

'Boss wants you both outside,' Lina said, appearing from the downstairs bathroom and she took Gregor by the hand and led him away to the living room.

'How'd you get the kid to think you're the shit?' Calhoun said. 'He doesn't even know my name.'

Ryker shrugged. 'I'm like the cool uncle. You're like the...'

He couldn't think how to finish the sentence. Calhoun tutted and shook his head, obviously offended, but whether by Ryker's words or more the boy's actions he didn't know.

They walked through to the kitchen. Natasha knew they were there, but she did her best to ignore them, facing away as she pretended to wipe down the surfaces which already looked pretty damn sparkling clean.

'I need a leak first,' Ryker said. 'See you out there.'

Calhoun carried on through the open patio doors and out of sight.

'Nat,' Ryker said quietly, but certainly loud enough for her to hear. But she didn't turn around.

He moved up to her and put his hand to her shoulder.

'Hey...'

He stopped when she turned around and he took in her face. Bulbous. A gash above her swollen left eye had been stitched. Her nose was twice the size it should have been. Her arms were horribly bruised too.

'Shit,' she said, looking at him. 'You look nearly as bad as I do.'

She touched his swollen, blackened cheek for the briefest of moments, then focused on the stitched wound just visible on his bicep beneath the sleeve of his T-shirt.

Ryker didn't care about his wounds, and he had no words in response.

He knew exactly how she'd been hurt.

He wanted to comfort her. He wanted to storm outside and rip Minko's limbs from his body.

'He took the news of Niko pretty badly,' she said. 'You know how it is.'

Yeah. Ryker did. Whenever Minko got angry, she was on the receiving end. Behind Ryker's anger something else tormented him though. Guilt. He wasn't supposed to feel that, yet for a flash it tore at his insides. Minko had beaten her because of Kovac. If Ryker hadn't killed the guy...

'What did you tell Gregor?' he asked.

A bruised eye here or there was one thing, but it looked like she'd gone twelve rounds with a heavyweight with her hands tied behind her back.

She tutted. 'Does it matter? He's barely even letting me see him. My own son. I was only with him just now for five minutes while Lina and Roman talked outside.'

Ryker stood there feeling useless. He couldn't find any words of comfort or encouragement at all.

'You need to get out there,' she said before she walked off.

So Ryker did. Minko was lazing in the sunshine with a cocktail glass in his hand. Calhoun had plonked himself on the edge of a lounger.

'Here he is,' Calhoun said. 'The man of the moment.'

Minko shuffled up in his seat and turned to Ryker.

'Jesus, your face,' Minko said as though he actually cared.

'It's fine,' Ryker said. 'It'll heal.'

'I heard you got knifed too,' Minko added.

Ryker lifted his sleeve to his shoulder to show the stitched gash on his arm. 'It's not a problem.'

Minko got to his feet. The waist of his tight swimming shorts cut into his frame, causing his flabby belly to spill over. His heavily bronzed skin showed he spent way too long out here doing nothing. The life of a rich man who had servants and goons to do everything for him.

'You did a good job,' Minko said. 'I want to thank you. You saved me a lot of money, a lot of hassle getting those weapons back for me.'

'It's what you're paying me for,' Ryker said, although actually he hadn't received any money just yet. He was still paying off his initial 'debt'.

'I'm cut-up about Niko, though,' Minko said.

He didn't sound it. Perhaps he'd worked out all his anguish on his wife already.

'He fought for his life,' Ryker responded. 'He was unlucky.'

'Niko was never unlucky,' Calhoun said. 'I still don't know how they got the better of him.'

'Same,' Minko said. 'So why don't you talk me through it. Again. From when you gutted that guy in the warehouse. Talking on the phone is one thing, but... you know what I mean.'

Ryker composed his thoughts first, aware that this was a test. A chance to see if Ryker's story remained consistent. 'Niko wanted me to go first on those three. I decided a brutal start would yield the best results. And it did.'

'We got the results. Not you,' Calhoun said. 'All you did was gut some guy for no reason then sit outside while we got answers.'

Ryker ignored him. 'They got a name from the other two. Cheko. Turns out the guy was an SBU agent.'

Minko sneered at the mention of SBU, even though he already knew all this.

'I found out where he was. Me and Niko went after him. We found him. We got him to talk. He told us they'd paid three punks to go out and sink that ship. But they'd already taken the containers off that night. Mid-sea.'

'Just like the play you made before.'

'No, not really. Anyway. The point is it was the Ukrainian authorities who did this. They took your weapons probably because they see the rising threat you pose.'

Stroke his ego. It was the best way to keep him sweet.

'Why would SBU make an underhand play like that rather than just have the coast guard raid that ship and impound it all?' Minko asked.

'Who knows why the security services do what they do? Maybe they were going to give the weapons to your enemies.'

Minko raised an eyebrow as though insulted. 'And my enemies are?'

'Anyone who doesn't believe in your aim for independence in Donbas.'

He didn't look convinced. 'And then?'

'We got Cheko to talk and we'd already killed him when we were ambushed. Maybe he'd sent out an alert, I don't know, but a crew of four turned up. We fought them as best we could but they overran us both. Beat us. Tried to get us to tell everything we knew.'

'And did you?'

'We didn't tell them a thing. And eventually we managed to fight back. I got away. Niko didn't.'

'You left him to die?' Calhoun said. 'Isn't that what happened with Zubarev too?'

'No, it wasn't,' Ryker said. 'And Niko was already dead when I ran, otherwise I would have helped him.'

'I guess we'll never know for sure.'

'You do know. Because I just told you so.'

'Only one body was found in that farmhouse,' Minko said. 'Niko's.'

'Is that the official line from the authorities? SBU are hardly going to tell the full story, are they?'

Minko looked even more dubious.

'The biggest question remains how did SBU find out about those weapons in the first place,' Ryker added.

Calhoun scoffed. 'You're right about that.'

'And what do you think?' Minko asked.

'It can only be someone close to you.'

'You think I have a rat here?'

'I think you need to seriously consider it.'

Minko turned to Calhoun. 'Do you agree?'

'All I know is all of this shit only started since this guy came along.'

'Yeah, because before I came along you didn't have the fifty million euros of weapons, dipshit,' Ryker said.

Calhoun flinched as though to go for Ryker but then just shook his head with despondence.

'I agree with you,' Minko said to Ryker, which he could tell only further riled Calhoun. 'The fact SBU were involved shows they see me as a threat. It means I'm succeeding in something. I need to be ready.'

'Ready for war?' Ryker asked.

'Ready for whatever needs to be done,' Minko said. 'Which is why I have another purchase planned. Even bigger than before. These goods are coming from the Middle East this time. But no one outside my close circle knows about this. Do you understand what I'm saying?'

Minko held Ryker's eye.

'You're supposed to answer, dickhead,' Calhoun said.

'Yeah. I understand,' Ryker said.

'Calhoun can fill you in. Now leave me in peace.'

26

FOUR DAYS LATER

The pool area at Minko's villa was quiet. The whole garden, where Ryker roamed, was. The villa itself too. Natasha had taken Gregor on a playdate. The first time she'd left the house in several days as she awaited her cuts and bruises to clear to the point that they were very nearly covered with careful makeup. About the first opportunity she'd been allowed to spend quality time with Gregor during that period too. Lina had taken them but she and Ryker would swap over duties this evening, and Ryker might get the chance to spend an evening with Natasha once Gregor was in bed. The first time in a long time.

Despite no one being around Ryker still made doubly sure he was alone before he made the phone call.

'How is everything?' Mackie asked.

'Calm,' Ryker said.

'That's probably a good thing. After what happened in Crimea.'

'Possibly.' Although it also made him think something big was about to explode. 'Any news from Belarus?'

Ryker hadn't seen Minko for a few days. The boss had gone to Belarus where he was meeting with several highly influential businessmen and politicos from Ukraine and Russia in the hopes of gaining some favor for his cause from one side or another.

'You wish you were there?' Mackie asked as though sensing Ryker's downtrodden mood.

'I thought I was getting closer to him. Especially after how Crimea played out.'

'You mean how you killed one of his most trusted guys?'

'My point is, he sees me only as a tough guy, a fighter he can use to his advantage, but not someone he wants by his side to make decisions with.'

'Then maybe start acting with a bit more... sophistication.'

'Easy for you to say.'

'Perhaps you should take it as a compliment that he wants you protecting his family while he's gone.'

'You know what? I know the man and I'm pretty sure it's the opposite. He loves his son, but Natasha... she's little more than an inconvenience to him. And he's taken his most trusted guys to Belarus, I'm sure of that.'

'And yet he's told you all about this upcoming arms deal.'

'Yeah. And why do you think that is? Have you heard anything about it, other than from me? Do you have any idea where this supposed sheikh got these weapons?'

'No. But I've deliberately kept questions to a minimum, for the very reason that I don't want to stir anything.'

'Exactly. Because it's obvious it's a test. He thinks there's a mole—'

Mackie laughed. 'Yeah, I'm talking to him.'

'Right. And you sound really concerned for me.'

Mackie said nothing to that.

'You can't do anything to tip him off,' Ryker said. 'The arms deal has to go ahead as planned.'

'Which is when?'

'Two days' time. Northern Turkey.'

'You're going?'

'Everyone's going. Apart from Minko. He'll just watch from afar, like he always does.'

They both went silent. Ryker felt he was at a crossroads here. Even after all his hard work, all the bloodshed, he still wasn't sure exactly where he sat with Minko. And he still didn't even know if long-term Minko was going to be an ally or a foe for the JIA.

'Do you know who he's meeting in Belarus?' Ryker asked.

'Yes.'

'Are you going to fill me in?'

'You'll probably be able to read about it in the papers. There's no subterfuge to it.'

Ryker gripped the phone a little more tightly, channeling his frustration. Mackie was withholding.

'The Ukrainian election is in a few weeks,' Ryker said. 'If it doesn't go well for Minko, I need to know where I stand here.'

'Ryker, your objective remains the same whatever the result. Stay close to him. Relay everything you find out back to me.'

Which Ryker did, all the time, yet it always seemed as though Mackie was always several steps ahead. Had anything Ryker had uncovered so far made a difference for the JIA? Were any of the deaths worth it?

'I gotta go,' Ryker said when he heard the car engine the other side of the villa.

He moved back inside. Natasha and Gregor and Lina were back.

'That's me done,' Lina said as she dumped a hefty travel bag in the hall. 'I'm heading to the pool house to get wasted on my own. Don't party too hard, you three.'

'Party?' Gregor said. 'We're having a party?' He looked over each of the adults excitedly.

'No party tonight, Greggy,' Natasha said. 'It's getting late already.'

Lina headed out.

'Can I play in the pool though?' Gregor asked. 'Can James?'

Natasha looked really put out, but it'd been days since Ryker had been given the chance to cave to the boy's wishes.

'Half an hour. Then it's bath and bed.'

'Yes!'

The boy whizzed off.

'You OK?' Ryker asked her.

She really didn't look it. She pursed her lips and nodded her head in response.

'You want some company later?' he asked.

'I'm not sure that's a good idea. Do you?'

He shrugged. 'Sounds like a great idea to me.'

He pecked her cheek and she let a smile slip before he headed on out after Gregor.

* * *

Ryker lay back in the bed and sighed. A contented sigh. Very contended, actually. He'd waited too long for that. Even if her edginess had been obvious throughout.

Natasha came back out of the bathroom moments later, her silk robe now covering her. She lay down on the bed next to him.

'You should probably go,' she said.

'Because?'

'Because... I can't take this sneaking around. I... I hate having to face Gregor in the morning knowing you're still in my bed.'

'Sleeping next to you, holding you, is the part of this I look forward to the most.'

She slapped his arm playfully. 'Liar.'

'I'm serious.' And a little pissed off with her. 'So we're reducing this to just sex now?'

'This? I don't even know what this is.'

She held her head in her hands. He put his hand on her shoulder, but she shrugged him off.

'I care about you, Natasha, I want to—'

'What? Protect me?'

The question hung uncomfortably, and Ryker toyed with whether she wanted an answer or not.

'Yes,' he said.

She got up from the bed, her cheeks reddening with anger. 'Except you don't, do you? He beats the shit out of me. He forces himself on me whenever he wants. Have you ever stopped him?'

'You know I would if I could.'

'Ha! Have you seen him? You could stop him blindfolded and with your ankles tied together. You could stop him, if you really wanted to. But you choose not to.'

'You know it's not that simple.'

'Then when you see me with my face all bruised, swollen, cut, it's like... I'm not good enough for you. Until I'm pretty again.'

'That's bullshit and you know it.'

Ryker stood and went to take her hand, but she moved back from him, her face all twisted in disgust as though repulsed by him now.

'Why are you here with me?' she asked.

'Because I care about you.'

'But not enough to stop me being abused.'

'So what do you want from me?' Ryker asked, not bothering to hide his agitation now. 'You want me to put a bullet in his head? Then what, for me? For you? For Gregor?'

'You know what?' She picked up his clothes and tossed them at him. 'I'm not sure I want anything from you. Not this, or anything else.'

She averted her eyes as Ryker slung on his clothes.

He left without either of them saying another word.

27

TWO DAYS LATER

Ryker opened the rear door of the car and Gregor bounced out onto the gravel drive.

'Go find your mom,' Ryker said, and the boy raced to the villa.

Ryker sighed as he watched him go. He'd gone from body-guard to babysitter, apparently. Over the last few days Minko had been pulling Natasha further and further from her son to the point that she was more or less housebound, and every other poor devil had to fill in with parent duties – it wasn't like Minko actually wanted to do anything fatherly – and run Gregor here, there and everywhere. The toll on Natasha was evident in her weary look and downtrodden mood. She hadn't opened up to Ryker about the change, but something had happened. Something over and above Minko taking out his frustrations and anger on his wife every now and then.

'Gregor, wait!' Ryker shouted when the kid was about to open the front door. Even several steps behind he could already hear the shouting from beyond. And the look on Gregor's face showed he knew exactly who was on the receiving end, as usual. Gregor was as terrified of Minko as Natasha was, even if Ryker had never seen the man lay a finger on his son.

Yet.

But Minko was a natural bully. A narcissist who preyed on the weak to stroke his own sense of importance and power. Who knew what lay in store for Gregor over the next few years.

Ryker reached the door and moved in front of Gregor and opened up. The sounds of another angry tirade amplified. Kitchen.

'Go up to your room,' Ryker said, and Gregor nodded and rushed on tiptoes to the stairs, as though careful not to alert Minko and redirect his wrath toward him.

Ryker strode toward the kitchen, not as bothered as the boy about getting the boss's attention. No sign of anyone else here, Ryker noted. Most likely the other guys were all off hiding somewhere.

Ryker reached the doorway. Minko, rolling pin held aloft, stood over Natasha who cowered in the corner, hands up to her already bloodied face.

Both of them sensed his presence. Minko paused with the rolling pin midair before turning his head to Ryker.

'What the fuck do you want?'

'You really think that's going to make you feel better?' Ryker asked, his unbothered tone hiding his real feelings pretty damn well.

Minko roared and launched the rolling pin across the room at Ryker who ducked just in time before the wood smashed into the vase on the side table next to him. Glass shards and water and soggy flower stems flew all over him, the wall, the floor. He stood his ground as Minko marched forward and grabbed him by the neck. But Minko was a few inches shorter than Ryker, and even the boss man must have realized he was nowhere near as strong.

Ryker stretched up, straining the muscles of his neck to push against the pressure from Minko's flabby fingers and the guy seemed to get the message pretty quickly and he let go.

'I should have you skinned alive for walking into my home and talking to me like that!' Minko screamed as he jabbed a finger in Ryker's chest, spittle flying from his mouth.

'Yeah, you could,' Ryker said. 'Or you could calm the hell down and talk to me about what's got under your skin. Because I know whatever it is, it isn't her fault.'

'Oh, you know that, do you? You know a lot about my wife?' Minko glanced between the two of them as though not sure who he was more angry with in that moment.

When Minko faced Ryker again Natasha took her chance and scurried toward them and Ryker moved further from the doorway to give her space. Minko looked like he was about to step over and grab her but at the last moment he turned away from her instead and she rushed out, hunched down as though she still expected Minko to attack her from behind as she fled.

For a few seconds neither men said a word. But Ryker could at least tell that the adrenaline coursing through Minko's body was dissipating, his body relaxing, if only a little.

'You want to talk about it now?' Ryker asked.

'With you?' Minko said, a deep sneer as he spoke. 'No. Because whatever happens between me and my wife is none of your damn business.'

'I'm not talking about you and her. I'm talking about what's got you wound up.'

Minko sucked in air through his nose causing his nostrils to bulge. He held Ryker's eye the whole time, didn't blink.

'I'm starting to think Niko, Calhoun, the others are right,' Minko said.

'About what?'

'All the shit's that happening... it's all been since you came here.'

'Come on then. Spit it out. What are you accusing me of?'

Minko opened and closed his mouth a couple of times, clearly something on the tip of his tongue, but ended up saying nothing.

'I'm here because you asked me to be here,' Ryker said instead.

Before Minko could respond, the sound of footsteps from the hall caught their attention and Ryker glanced over his shoulder to see Lina approaching. From the living room? So she'd been inside the whole time, happy to leave Natasha to her fate. Not that Ryker's intervention had been anywhere near as strong as he wished it had been, but still.

'Are we all set?' Lina said, calm as anything, as though she hadn't just heard everything.

'Set for what?' Ryker asked.

'The deal,' Minko said. 'You're flying to Turkey tonight.'

Lina checked her watch. 'Driving out in less than an hour.'

'So you'd better go and get your things packed,' Minko said. 'Then you can leave me and my family in peace.'

Peace. One word Ryker definitely wouldn't use to describe the homelife here.

Minko sauntered off, walking tall as though he'd just delivered a knockout blow. He shoved open the patio doors to head out into the sunshine.

'Do you enjoy pushing people or are you just stupid?' Lina said to Ryker.

'Maybe both.'

Lina snorted. 'Seriously, whatever's going on in your brain, that was a dumb move.'

Ryker said nothing to that.

'I quite like you,' Lina continued. 'Sometimes. But if he asks me, or any of the others to end you... you know how that goes.'

'Yeah,' Ryker said. 'With me putting you and whoever else comes after me in a grave. In fact, I'll happily dig it for you.'

Lina laughed and smacked Ryker's shoulder. 'You're a hoot, Ryker. A real fucking hoot.'

'It doesn't make your blood boil, knowing how he treats her?' Ryker asked.

'What? Because I'm a woman?'

'Because you're a human. She doesn't deserve to be beaten just because he loses his temper.'

'Then you go right out and argue that one with him. It's none of my business, so I stay out of it.'

'Well aren't you full of warmth and empathy.'

'The fuck do you care so much, anyway?'

Ryker grumbled but decided against carrying on down that line.

'Don't get too close to her,' Lina added. 'It won't end well for either of you.'

'Now I'm not that stupid,' Ryker said with a wink, and the smile on Lina's face suggested she'd bought it. 'But what's got him all wired, again, that he's beating the crap out of Natasha? Again.'

'You didn't hear about Belarus?'

No. He hadn't. Because no one told him a damn thing around here, and Mackie and Winter had been holding back too, he sensed.

'It didn't go well?' Ryker suggested.

'The election is in two weeks. Minko wanted the buy-in of the president. Help him get re-elected in exchange for working toward a peaceful split. Except the Russians are already throwing their toys around about the idea.'

'Because Minko wants full independence, with him in charge. But the Russians want to bring Donbas back into the empire.'

Lina's eyes narrowed in suspicion. 'Thought you said you didn't know what had happened in Belarus?'

'Just working it through.'

'The point is, he played his hand to the Ukrainian side first, because that's where his heart is, and it's the only place a peaceful solution lies. And now he's stuck in the middle. Perhaps it doesn't even matter what happens in the Ukrainian election anymore. I think the Russian president is coming to take Donbas for himself, with or without Minko's assistance.'

'So the solution is what? Build his own army? But to take on who? Russia or Ukraine?'

'It's a good question, isn't it? For now, the solution is we go to Turkey.' Lina slapped Ryker's back. 'So I'll see you by the car on the hour.'

She headed off out of the house. Ryker didn't move for a few moments as he listened to the sounds around him. All quiet now. He moved slowly, cautiously up the stairs and peeped into Gregor's room. The boy sat on his floor playing with cars. He didn't sense Ryker there so Ryker backed off and went toward the guest room. He paused outside there, listening again. All quiet up here and down below. So he crept to the master bedroom instead and knocked lightly on the nearly closed door. He pushed it open. Natasha stood in front of the mirror, dabbing at the cut on her eye with a soggy, red-tinged washcloth. No tears now, she looked mad. With him?

'Are you OK?' he asked.

'Such a good protector,' she said. 'How can I ever thank you?'

He clenched his jaw rather than bite back. Hadn't he just saved her from a more severe beating? Although he knew what she meant. He hadn't exactly given Minko anything in return.

'Don't you have somewhere you need to be?' she added.

'I'll be gone a few days,' Ryker said.

'Lucky me. I have my husband all to myself. Wonder how that'll go next time something makes him angry.'

Ryker took a couple of steps inside, but she whipped around and the force of her glare caused him to stop.

'I can help you,' he said. 'I could get you out of here. Somewhere safe. You and Gregor.'

'You have no idea, do you? Even when you're so close to him, you can't see the monster.'

'I see it.'

'Then you know there's nothing you can do. Otherwise you would have.'

'Maybe you don't know me as well as you think.'

'Maybe not. But there's nowhere you could take me that he wouldn't find me.'

'You don't—'

'I do know it! The only way out of this is to kill him before he kills me. Except you won't do it for me, will you?'

Her words caused him to pause again. He hadn't expected her to blurt out talk of killing Minko just like that.

'See?' she said. 'You're terrified of the idea. So don't go giving me any more bullshit about how you want to protect me. Maybe I'll have to just do it myself.'

He still said nothing. He really didn't know how to reassure her, how to dissuade her if she was serious. And he didn't get the chance.

'You need to go pack,' she said moving to the en suite. 'Goodbye, James.'

She slammed and locked the door behind her.

28

PRESENT DAY

Voronezh Oblast, Russia

Ryker, Nadia and Gregor retreated back toward the border in the stolen car. Ryker sat alone in the front, behind the wheel while Gregor and Nadia had squeezed themselves in behind. Nadia seemed a little shell-shocked, not just by the fighting and the killing but by the overwhelming relief of having Gregor back by her side.

Gregor seemed... different to how Ryker had imagined. Physically his face looked more like his mom's than his dad's. Lucky for him, as Roman Minko was hardly what many people would have described as a handsome man. But perhaps he'd taken on other paternal traits. Certainly it seemed he was as ruthless as his father and Ryker was more than a little shocked – and perhaps saddened – by that.

Ryker glanced in the rearview mirror. Nadia had her head rested on Gregor's shoulder, her eyes closed. But Gregor was wide awake and staring at Ryker.

'I can't believe you came looking for me,' Gregor said.

'I heard you were in trouble.'

'My whole life has been trouble. You never came before.'

Ryker didn't respond this time. He knew Gregor was testing him, but he didn't know why.

'How did you hear?' Gregor asked.

Ryker thought before answering that.

'I was in the south of France. Two people tracked me down to tell me you were in trouble. Imprisoned in Siberia. Although they told me you'd escaped.'

'And who were the two people?'

'Their names were Irina Kakabadze and Giorgi Mekvabishvili. Do you know them?'

'No,' Gregor said after a moment's thought. 'I don't.'

'My initial thought was that maybe they were Russian SVR agents, given what they told me about the gulag and how you'd gone missing.'

'You think they thought you were helping me?'

'I don't know. And I never confirmed who they were working for, but it seems less likely now that they were SVR.'

'Why?'

'A few things don't add up. And Giorgi is now dead. Irina missing. So there's still plenty of parts to this story that don't make sense to me.'

'There's a lot that doesn't make sense to me too,' Gregor said. 'Like why is a man I haven't seen for twenty years suddenly back in my life. A man who I last saw on the night my parents were killed.'

'Like I said, those two tracked me down. Told me what happened. I wanted to find you to help you.'

'Yeah. And like I said, I've been in plenty of trouble before. You never came then.'

'Because I didn't know then.'

'Because you never bothered to find out what happened to me.'

Ryker decided not to say anything to that.

'I remember that night so well,' Gregor said. 'The night my parents were killed.'

'Me too,' Ryker said.

'You saved me that night.'

Ryker acknowledged the statement with a simple nod.

'If it wasn't for you, I'd be dead too.'

Ryker caught Gregor's eye again. He couldn't quite read the guy's tone, his mood.

'I always liked you,' Gregor said. 'More than all the other people who hung around my father, craving for his attention. You know why?'

'Why?'

'Because you were kind. To me. And you were kind to my mother.'

Ryker gripped the steering wheel a little more tightly as the thoughts of that time rumbled.

'I know how much you meant to her too,' Gregor added. 'It's why I was so mad at you after. Because when my life was ripped apart, I really hoped it'd be you that came to help me. You got me out of the house, alive, that night. But when I really needed someone like you to protect me... I never saw you again.'

'I'm sorry,' Ryker said.

'But I know a lot more about the world now than I did back then. As a boy, my father was just my father. And the guys like you who hung around him were just his guys. I didn't see the politics, the violence, the danger.'

'Probably for the best.'

'You think? But I see it now. I realized a long time ago who my father really was, and why so many other people wanted to be around him. But then... then there's people like you.'

'Like me?'

'Well, you're British, aren't you?'

'Yes.'

'You have any Ukrainian blood? Any Russian?'

'No.'

'So you never gave a crap about the politics. About my father's fight.'

'Not true. Just because it wasn't my personal fight, didn't mean I couldn't have an opinion. Or that I wouldn't want to help.'

'Then you agreed with my father's aim?'

'For an independent Donbas? If that's what the people there wanted, then yes. But I also know he never wanted what's happening now. A war sponsored by Russia, for Russia's gain.'

'No. He didn't want what we have now at all,' Gregor said with real bitterness on his tongue.

'Which I'm guessing is why you were working for the Panthers. Working against the separatist movement. Not because you wanted your homeland to stay within Ukraine, but because you don't want it to simply become part of the Russian empire either.'

Gregor didn't respond and when Ryker looked again in the mirror, Gregor's face was full of rage. Not directed at Ryker, he didn't think, but the situation.

'What do you know of the Panthers?' Gregor asked.

'Not a lot. That you were a rebel group. But it's been torn apart over the last few months. Particularly since you were locked up.'

Nadia stirred and opened her eyes and lifted her head from Gregor's shoulder. Perhaps she'd been awake the whole time and now the conversation was heating up to something close – and painful – to her, she couldn't fake it any longer.

Gregor looked at his girlfriend and she shook her head solemnly.

'He doesn't know,' she said to Ryker. 'He doesn't know what's happened.'

The two of them erupted in fast-talking Ukrainian, their voices too low and their words too quick for Ryker to decipher it all. Although he got the basics. She was telling him about the raids, the executions.

'There's nothing left,' Nadia said at the end.

The car fell silent for a few moments. A horribly tense silence as a new reality set in for Gregor.

'Yes, I was part of the Panthers,' he eventually said to Ryker. 'But I never did the things I was accused of. We only ever attacked military. Killed them before they killed us. We were never terrorists. We would never kill our own people like that.'

'I heard there were bombs inside Russia too,' Ryker said. 'A market?'

'Lies,' Gregor said, teethed bared in an angry scowl. 'All of it.'

'I believe you,' Ryker said. 'I've been in the same position plenty of times. I know how it works.'

Gregor scoffed. 'I'm sure you do. Because I know you're not just another grunt. Another mercenary. And I don't believe you're here now, or were with my family twenty years ago, for ideology, or even for money.'

Ryker kept his mouth shut.

'I don't know who you really work for,' Gregor added, 'but the list of who it could be isn't that long.'

Ryker shrugged.

'But what I see in you, James... is the type of man you are. I saw it then, and I still see it now.'

'What are you saying?'

'I'm saying thank you.'

A strange way of doing so, and Ryker was sure Gregor had more to say on the subject of his parents' death, and Ryker's allegiances then and now, but the next moment Nadia's phone rang.

'Papa,' she said, staring aghast at the screen before answering.

The conversation that followed didn't last long, and Nadia didn't say much, other than how much she loved her father and how sorry she was, over and over. When the call ended, she still looked a little shell-shocked, but in a different way to before. Now she was shocked by overwhelming, and perhaps unexpected relief.

'He's OK,' she said, turning to Gregor. 'They let him go and he's OK.'

She buried her head into his chest and Gregor held her tightly. The car fell silent again and not long after Ryker took the vehicle off tarmac and onto a dirt track, unmarked on his phone's GPS map. He carried on for more than twenty miles until they were back in the same dense woodland that he and Nadia had been in the night before. He eventually stopped the car and turned off the engine and looked around to his two passengers.

'The border's less than five miles from here,' he said. 'It's better on foot. But...'

'But what?'

'You really want to go back to Donetsk?'

'I have to see my dad,' Nadia said. Fair point, but his question hadn't really been directed at her.

'It's my home,' Gregor said.

'It's not the home it was. Probably never will be. And you're a wanted man now, on the run from the Russians. Plus, there's nothing left of the Panthers. So what's there for you?'

'It's. My. Home.'

'And mine too,' Nadia said.

The conversation would probably have been easier without her.

'You could go to any country in the West,' Ryker said. 'With who you are, what you've done, what you know, they'd take you in, give you asylum. I can ask around the right circles in the UK. We could be there in a day or two. A new life. For both of you.'

'The right circles,' Gregor said. 'Because you'd know all about such circles?'

'I'm offering you something good here.'

'Good for me, perhaps. Not good for anyone else. I can still make a difference in this fight.'

'How?'

Gregor shook his head and looked despondent, perhaps agitated that Ryker didn't immediately see his worth or power or influence.

'I don't know where you've been the last twenty years,' Gregor said, 'but I've been in one place, and one place only. My true home. I've lived through every minute of conflict since the first shots were fired in 2014. I've seen so many good people, good friends, not just hurt but murdered, executed, brutalized. So I'm sorry, but I'm not walking away now to save myself, just because the opportunity is there.'

'I understand,' Ryker said.

'You know what? I don't think you do. But I'd like to show you something that might help you, if you really are the man I think and hope that you are.'

'OK?'

Ryker waited, as though Gregor was about to perform a magic trick or something.

'Not here,' Gregor said with an eye roll. 'Back home. Come with us. I'll show you exactly what life has been like for people like me. It'll change your mind from why you think I'd be better off running and hiding. And it might even change your mind as to what you intend to do next.'

As cryptic as Gregor's words were, Ryker didn't have to think long.

'OK. Show me.'

29

DONETSK, UKRAINE

The next morning they traversed familiar territory, back in the same rental car that Ryker had left on the Ukrainian side of the border before their jaunt onto Russian soil. They'd slept little. All were tired, weary. But Gregor insisted that he needed to show Ryker whatever it was immediately. Before Nadia had even had a chance to reunite with her father.

Ryker had taken a call from Winter as they traveled. Had kept the conversation as brief as possible with Gregor and Nadia close by. It felt sneaky speaking to the government man with Gregor by his side, given everything that had happened in the past. Clearly the young man sensed... No, he knew Ryker was working with the British government back then. His veiled words had made that clear. Still, Ryker hadn't wanted to have a long, open conversation with Winter so had kept things to the point. He'd retrieved Gregor. Gregor was fine. They were headed back to Donbas. He'd call to update on his plans from there. He sensed Winter thought that meant Ryker would soon be heading west again, ready and waiting to offer his assistance.

Ryker wasn't so sure he was finished in Eastern Europe just yet.

'I went to the orphanage,' he said, breaking a drawn-out silence, a period during which the anxiety of his passengers had risen several notches. Even though this was their homeland, they weren't necessarily welcome here.

'Why?' Gregor asked.

'Because I knew nothing about your life. I was trying to find someone who did in the hope it'd help me find you.'

Gregor huffed. 'That wasn't the place to find someone like that.'

'It worked, in a roundabout way.' He momentarily caught Nadia's gaze in the mirror.

'I spent ten years in that place,' Gregor said. 'Ten years of abuse, of misery.'

'The matron I spoke to, Tetyana—'

'Is an evil witch. She's lucky I didn't bury her before I left that place.'

'Like Olek, you mean? I heard some of the boys called him their father.'

'You know about Olek?' Gregor asked. 'You really have been asking a lot of questions about me, haven't you?'

Ryker shrugged. 'I knew nothing about your life since you were six. So yeah, I asked a lot. I also got different stories. One boy you knew there, Vasily, told me about Olek. Told me you killed him.'

Gregor laughed. 'You went to see Vasily Dovbyk?'

'I did.'

'How is he? In a bad way, I heard.'

'Physically, maybe, but he seems to have cut a nice little life selling contraband.'

'Yeah, that's Vasily. A lowlife chancer. As kids, he was always bigger, tougher than me. And as kids that meant he and another brute, Sergei, ruled the roost inside the orphanage, especially as they were Fath— Olek's favorites. But in reality, Vasily was never destined for anything more than he's become.'

'But is it true about Olek? And you mentioned Sergei. I heard you killed him too.'

'Why do you care? You're bothered that I killed two despicable people who'd made my life a living hell?'

Ryker didn't answer.

'What about you, James Ryker? Have you ever killed someone before?'

Too many people, really.

'The last time I saw you, you were a little boy,' Ryker said. 'I'm only trying to get to know you, who you are, what you've been through.'

'But do I get to interrogate you about your life too? Ask for you to regurgitate all of your most painful memories from the last twenty years?'

Ryker didn't answer the question.

'Yeah,' Gregor said. 'That's what I thought. I spent way too long in that place. Don't forget I already knew a different life. A life that had wealth and had love, from my mother, at least. I was taken to that orphanage in my darkest moment. I never got out of that darkness until the day I left there.'

'You grew up to be your father's son.'

'Is that a question, or is that what you think?'

Ryker wasn't really sure.

'It'd destroy his soul to know how events spiraled here after his death,' Gregor said.

'But he'd be proud of you for what you're fighting for,' Nadia added, clutching his hand tightly. He didn't respond to the gesture at all, his eyes fixed on the road ahead as they neared the town. 'This is it. We're here. Why don't we walk the rest of the way.'

Ryker stopped the car and they all got out. Cold, as ever, and a recent heavy snowfall covered the ground. The pristine surface going into the town showed that no other vehicles or pedestrians had been this way recently.

'You know this place?' Ryker asked, looking ahead to the largely destroyed town, much like the one where the orphanage was located. Much like the one where Vasily Dovbyk now lived and carried out his business from.

'It's my hometown,' Nadia said. 'But nobody lives here now. You'll see why.'

And five minutes later, Ryker understood.

The three of them stood on a ridge of muck looking down to a dug-up, gaping hole below, ten feet wide, ten deep. The ridge carried on alongside them for another sixty feet.

'This is the only part that we excavated,' Gregor said. 'We didn't want to disturb it too much. But you can imagine how many bodies are buried here.'

Ryker could. And the cold had preserved the corpses well. Ghostly white flesh, hands, feet, hair, stuck out from the partially dug-up mass grave. Ryker had seen photos like this before. World War II. The Bosnian War. Cambodia. He'd never before stood on site seeing, smelling, sensing the death. The fear too of the poor people whose lives had been torn from them so brutally.

'More than five hundred people lived here,' Nadia said. 'I know of less than twenty who are still alive. My mom, my two brothers are somewhere underneath our feet.'

'What happened?' Ryker asked.

'Perhaps not what you're thinking,' Gregor said. 'But there's a good reason we didn't excavate the whole grave. It wasn't just for the dignity of the dead.'

'And that is?'

'Because we realized it was too dangerous. These people weren't killed by guns or explosives. They were poisoned.'

'A biochemical weapon,' Nadia said. 'Virus-based.'

Gregor must have sensed Ryker's dubiousness to that explanation.

'You haven't heard about any of this on the news in England, so you're automatically going to dismiss it,' Gregor said.

'I'm more open-minded than that.'

'But to you, your people, this is just one small town in the middle of nowhere. Nobody in America or England or France or Germany cares about these people.'

'But we do,' Nadia said.

'You're saying the Russian-backed forces are using chemical weapons in Ukraine?' Ryker asked.

'I'm saying more than that. I'm saying Russia is using our people to experiment with these chemical weapons.'

Ryker said nothing to that because he really was speechless.

'You don't believe me?' Gregor asked.

He didn't. Because small town in the middle of nowhere or not, he really hoped that news of this would have come out somehow before now if it were true.

'Ask yourself some key questions,' Gregor said. 'How did they die?'

Ryker stared at the corpses but didn't – couldn't – provide an answer.

'Do you see gunshot wounds?' Gregor asked. 'Stab wounds? Any major external damage at all?'

'No.'

'Starvation then?'

'No.'

'So we're narrowing down cause of death quite dramatically already. Disease?'

'It's possible.'

'But it's not the answer.'

'So you're saying the Russians used a virus-based weapon here?' Ryker said. 'How? How was it delivered? How did it affect only these people in this town? They all got sick and just stayed here until they died? It never spread outside the vicinity? And now we're just standing here on top of the corpses with this deadly pathogen right underneath us?'

'See, now you're asking the right questions,' Gregor said, looking more enthused despite the ghastliness around them.

'They barricaded the town for days,' Nadia said, who remained despondent. 'All roads were blocked by military patrols. They had men in the surrounding fields waiting to pick off anyone attempting to get in or out. I was in Donetsk that first morning when they arrived, taking my father to the hospital. He'd fallen in the shower and dislocated his shoulder. If it hadn't been for that... we would have been right here too.'

She tapped the ground with her foot.

'That explains some of it, but not all of it,' Ryker said.

'You think we're lying?' Nadia asked.

'I didn't say that. But... the people were infected? How?'

'We didn't know for sure then,' Nadia said, 'because they cut all communications.'

'But you know now?'

'Simple air release,' Gregor said. 'Pressurized canisters, most likely.'

'But it didn't spread from this town?'

'No. Like many airborne viruses it can't survive outside the body for long periods. Influenza, coronaviruses are all the same. They require close contact to spread. But this one... it has two big differences to previous viruses you've heard of that have caused widespread pandemics.'

'And those are?'

'It's even more deadly. By several factors. Mortality rate is over ninety percent, after three days of exposure. But on the flip side, it's even more fragile when it's airborne. It can survive for less than an hour outside a host. Most normally only a few minutes.'

'Although it can survive being frozen,' Nadia said. 'Which is why we still think the virus in the bodies could reactivate if disturbed.'

'It's been engineered specifically for its purpose,' Gregor continued. 'To kill people on a targeted level. This virus would likely never cause a global pandemic, because it's too sensitive. But it will kill a whole village, a town, a battalion.'

Ryker had nothing to say in response – he was too busy taking it all in, but also doubts and questions fired at warp speed in his mind. He didn't want to believe what he was hearing was true.

And yet he did believe it.

'How do you know so much about it?' Ryker asked.

Gregor looked a little offended by the question. 'Because I'm not just some young kid who got together a band of friends and a load of guns, who rode around in a truck looking to cause trouble.'

'So you're a biochemist now with world-leading pathogen-testing facilities?' Ryker asked.

Apparently, given his sneer, Gregor didn't appreciate that humor.

'No. But we do have people who've helped us uncover this much.'

'If you have evidence of this virus, this weapon... you need to turn it over.'

'To who?' Gregor said. 'Who exactly is on our side anymore?'

'Plenty of people will be when they know what's happened here.'

'And they will know,' Gregor said. 'But not yet. Because we don't have enough undeniable evidence.'

A slight smile rose on Gregor's face, but it didn't last long, the somberness of the situation quickly taking hold once more.

'We know where they first developed this virus,' he said. 'Where they've been testing it, cultivating it.'

'Where?'

'I won't tell you that yet. Because first I want to know you'll help.'

'Help what?'

'Help me get there. Help me get the evidence we really need, not just to uncover what the Russians did, but to stop them doing it again.'

'Why me?'

'Because I thought you said you came to help me. And there is no one else I can ask now. This is what I was working on before I was taken to the gulag. And except for Nadia, everyone who was helping me is already dead. I know you're more than capable.'

He stopped there as though he thought he'd already been convincing enough. Ryker wasn't so sure but continued to chew on the proposal.

'This is what will help me,' Gregor said. 'Help me get back at the people who destroyed my life, and the lives of so many thousands of innocent people.'

Ryker stared down at the partially exposed corpses again. A chill ran down his spine, the hairs prickling along his back. He looked away.

'OK,' Ryker said. 'I'll help you.'

30

TWENTY YEARS AGO

Trabzon, Turkey

Ryker sat in the car watching the group from afar through binoculars. Without the help of the lenses he could still see the small gathering – two hundred yards away across the sand – reasonably well, but he couldn't see the details. The facial expressions, the hand gestures.

There were seven men in total. Six vehicles. Four of the vehicles were articulated trucks, shipping containers already on the back. Hopefully full shipping containers. Once the exchange was complete, four of the men – all experienced truckers – would take the vehicles north into Georgia and onward around the edge of the Black Sea, eventually hitting Donbas in a few days. The route would require several customs stop-offs, but they were all in 'friendly' countries and a few sweeteners had already laid the path for them to cross borders without trouble.

Of the other three men, two were from the sheikh's entourage and had arrived in a dusty Mercedes G-Wagon. Calhoun was the sole official representative from Minko's team at the exchange.

Not that this was a particularly challenging trade. The money had already been transferred. This was simply the sheikh's guys showing Calhoun to the goods and confirming everything was as expected.

Little room for error. In theory.

And so Ryker and Lina were holding back, away from the exchange, to provide extra eyes on the area from an alternate angle, to further themselves from the exchange should police descend like last time, and to provide defense if needed. Hence the weapons they had. A handgun each. An upgraded AK-47. A bolt-action sniper rifle. Those two larger weapons remained on the back seat of the sedan and would hopefully stay there.

'All good?' Lina asked from the driver's seat.

'So far.'

'You think the weapons are really there?'

'We'll soon find out,' Ryker said.

'Paying in advance before we've even seen the goods? Bit risky.'

'There has to be some trust in these sorts of things.'

Lina chuckled. 'Yeah. People like us are so full of trust.'

Ryker didn't respond as he watched Calhoun walk along the backs of the trucks. He had one of the sheikh's guys open up the doors of the container on the left truck and he stepped up and inside and was out of sight.

'You think we'll have to do many more of these?' Lina asked.

'I've never been part of creating an armed rebellion before,' Ryker said. 'With the equipment he already has though, and enough capable manpower, he's enough to take a few towns probably, perhaps even one of the cities. Holding them if the Ukrainian army come back with force is another matter.'

'Which is looking the more likely path since Belarus.'

Ryker glanced at Lina, hoping she'd offer something more

about the failed negotiations in Belarus, because he'd still been told nothing other than the crap he'd read online, and the little she'd given in their previous conversation at the villa in Cyprus two days ago.

'You know, she's probably fine,' Lina said after a few moments of silence.

'Who is?'

'Natasha.'

'Why the hell are you bringing her up?'

'Why do you think?'

Ryker kept his eyes looking through the binoculars.

'You're into her. I get it. She's pretty. Most guys would want to screw her. I used to want to be like that.'

'Like what?'

'Nice body. Nice clothes. Nice house. Nice husband.'

'You think he's nice?'

'OK, rich husband then.'

'You still could be like that. I mean, you're not that ugly.'

She was actually quite attractive, but Ryker was only toying with her and her laugh suggested she got that.

'No, I'm talking about when I was a fourteen-year-old girl. Now I hate the idea. Just... look how she is. She's so damn needy.'

'Doesn't mean she deserves the abuse.'

'Whatever. My point is... you have to decide where your priorities lie because—'

'End of discussion.'

'But—'

'End of discussion. I think we're done.'

Calhoun jumped back down from the container. When the sheikh's guys turned away from him, he flashed a thumbs-up in Ryker and Lina's direction.

'Looks like we're good,' Ryker said.

He glanced up at the sky before he pulled the binoculars down. Firstly to look at the drone he knew Minko had up there, being controlled from distance. Secondly in case there was any sign of a helicopter about to burst onto the scene as had happened at the previous exchange.

'Wait, what was that?' Lina said. She nodded over to the east where one of the larger dunes rose up several feet above their position.

'What?'

'I saw a flash. The sun hitting glass or metal or something.'

Ryker stared there a few seconds. He saw nothing. Back at the exchange the G-Wagon was on its way out of there, dust billowing from its back end. Calhoun was waiting by his car as the trucks rumbled to life, the vibrations from their engines reaching all the way over to Ryker.

'Seriously, there's something there,' Lina said.

Ryker lifted the radio and called out to Calhoun.

'Hold on,' Ryker said.

'Hold on for what?' Calhoun responded. 'We're good here. We got what we came for.'

'Maybe. But off to your east. On the sand dune. We might have company.'

'Get the drone over there,' Calhoun said, looking at the sky.

Lina was already on it, speaking to Klaus, the drone operator, on the phone. But with the conversation mid-swing a flash of light in the air caused her to pause.

'Shit,' Ryker said as he watched the burning drone plummet downward.

Next, he spotted a flash of light from the sand dune and Calhoun collapsed to the ground clutching at his leg.

'Sniper!' Ryker shouted.

Not even a beat later and Lina had floored the gas pedal and the car shot forward, bouncing over the sandy ridges as they made their way toward the exchange site.

To the west the G-Wagon with the sheikh's guys had already disappeared. Ryker fumbled in the back for the AK. He got it. He opened his window and poked the barrel out but winced and ducked down when a spray of bullets smacked into the metalwork and the sand around them.

'Who the hell is shooting?' Lina shouted.

Ryker couldn't really tell because of the sand cloud enveloping them as they moved, but...

'There. To the west.'

The direction the G-Wagon had gone. Ryker thought the sand in the air there was only because of the departing SUV, but the cloud was moving closer to them.

'A raid?' Lina asked.

'No,' Ryker said.

A small explosion caused the car to jolt, and Lina wrestled to keep them heading straight. She managed it, but they lost speed in the process and Lina couldn't get it back.

'They shot out a tire!' Ryker shouted.

He again poked the AK out and this time let off several rounds toward where the sniper had been, although there was no sign of any gunfire coming from there now.

Lina swung on the wheel and the car glided to a ninety-degree stop by Calhoun who'd hunkered by his car.

Ryker dove out.

'Four vehicles, off to the west,' Calhoun said.

'We need to get out of here,' Ryker said, trying to drag the guy up.

'The trucks.'

Two of them had already started their departure, but had stopped along the sand, toward where the raiding party were making their advance. Smoke piled out of the front end of one. Another had several tires taken out. The last two remained right in front of Ryker but the engines were off and there were no signs of the drivers now. Hiding?

'For fuck's sake, come on!' Lina screamed as she fired off her handgun toward the line of attackers who'd now stopped fifty yards from them.

Ryker dragged Calhoun up and shoved him forward and in through the open back door of the car.

'Go!' Ryker said before he was properly in. The car raced away as he pulled himself into the seat and slammed the door shut behind him, just before a loud thunk as another bullet hit. In fact, the bullet came right through the door and lodged in the seat underneath him. A narrow miss.

'The sniper's still out there,' Ryker said, looking up at the dune again.

'Calhoun, you OK?' Lina asked.

He just growled in response.

'We can't just leave the trucks,' Lina said, although she didn't slow and she sounded dejected rather than up for the fight. Ryker glanced behind at Calhoun. The bullet had hit his thigh. It hadn't severed the femoral artery or he'd already be dead, but he was losing a lot of blood. He was in no shape to fight on.

'We have to,' Ryker said. 'If we want to live.'

'I'm not sure any of us live when Minko finds out about this,' Lina said.

She got no response, just kept on driving, her protest hollow.

'They're not following us,' Calhoun said as he strained to look out of the back window.

'No,' Ryker said. 'Because that wasn't the police. It was a heist. They were there for the weapons, not us. And now they have them.'

* * *

Ryker, Lina and Calhoun remained in the city after the ambush both as they strove for answers as to what had happened at the exchange, and as a delay in going back to Cyprus to face Minko in person. The day after the heist and Ryker finally found time on his own, away from the others, to speak to Peter Winter. In person.

The park sat adjacent to a weaving promenade on the Black Sea coast. Winter was already waiting for Ryker on a bench under leafy carob trees, the minarets of mosques behind the park poking up beyond the canopy. The spot was quiet enough. Trabzon wasn't a big or popular tourist city, but still Ryker felt nervy meeting outside where people roamed, his eyes rabbity as he walked toward Winter.

'Couldn't we have done this on the phone?' Ryker said as he sat down.

'No,' was all Winter said to that.

'You realize I'm suspect number one right now,' Ryker said.

'You think so?'

'I know it. I haven't spoken to Minko yet, but he was already dubious about me. Some of his guys even more so. That's two exchanges in a row now that have been sabotaged.'

Winter didn't say anything.

'Please, just tell me it wasn't us. It wasn't you or Mackie using the intel I gave you.'

'What does it matter to you?'

'You have to ask that?'

'Yeah. You do your job, we do ours.'

'Are you serious?'

'Deadly. It wasn't your money. It's not your weapons.'

'It matters because I'm risking my life so you can do your job.'

Ryker's hard tone seemed to cause Winter to pause for thought because he slouched a little, as though realizing he shouldn't poke the tiger in Ryker too far.

'I get you're doing a tough job, but don't forget your role is part of something much bigger.'

'Which is why it helps if I actually know what's going on around me.'

Winter sighed. 'It wasn't us. The simple fact is we don't know where the weapons are now.'

'And it wasn't the police or any other official authority either. It was too... messy. And they weren't there to apprehend us.'

'No.'

'The sheikh?'

'I don't think so. The weapons have disappeared. Two of the truck drivers were found dead in the desert. The other two have vanished along with the weapons. Most likely we think they're dead too.'

'So why don't you think it's the sheikh? He had them killed, stole the weapons and the trucks.'

'Like I said, we don't think that's the case.'

'But you're not going to tell me why.'

'I'm telling you what you need to know. We think, most likely, it was an outfit linked to Russia. Perhaps Chechans.'

Ryker worked that explanation over. 'So the Russians are making a move against Minko?'

'Officially? No.'

'How would they even know about the deal?'

'We don't know for sure.'

'There's another mole.'

'You suggested it yourself before.'

Ryker looked around himself again, checking for obvious eavesdroppers.

'We're meeting outside because you think my phone might be compromised,' Ryker said.

'We're ramping up protections. The truth is, we don't know exactly who is watching, listening, how or why.'

Ryker laughed.

'What?'

'And that's why it's you sitting next to me and not Mackie.'

Winter initially looked offended but then couldn't stop a slight smile, although he wiped it away pretty quickly. 'Yeah. It seems I'm expendable too. Although not as expendable as you.'

Perhaps he'd intended the last line as lighthearted, but it came out all wrong and he looked a little embarrassed by it.

'So what now?' Ryker asked.

'Keep on doing what you're doing.'

'Easy for you to say.' Ryker got to his feet. 'Anything else?'

'We know about Natasha.'

'Excuse me?'

'We know you two... you know.'

'How the fuck—'

'The point isn't how. The point is... it's you that'll suffer. Her too. Not us. So end it, before it's too late.'

Ryker said nothing but turned away, then stopped when Winter spoke again.

'You need to be ready. Your head in the game, one hundred percent.'

'Ready for what?'

'For whatever we tell you to do next.'

Ryker headed away, the true meaning of those words reverberating.

31

TWO DAYS LATER

Paphos, Cyprus

For all his advanced mental training, there was no doubt Ryker felt nervous as they approached Minko's Cypriot home. The crew had been called back. Minko didn't want to risk traveling to Turkey and Ryker, Lina, Klaus and the injured Calhoun had made no progress in finding out any information on the stolen weapons in the more than forty-eight hours since the failed exchange. Not that they'd tried too hard. Laying low and self-preservation was at the forefront of each of their minds, Ryker knew.

Except the nerves were wasted as Minko wasn't home when they arrived. A surprise. A welcome one, really.

No Minko, but Natasha was there, in the living room, looking lost.

'Where's Gregor?' Ryker asked her.

'They went to the beach.'

Ryker moved closer to her. She looked unexpectedly fresh, certainly compared to a few days ago. No obvious new injuries.

'I heard it didn't go too well in Turkey,' she said with a sly glint in her eye.

The fact she knew that likely meant Minko had flown into a rage again at some point. Except it didn't look like he'd lost it with her.

Interesting.

'You could say that.'

'Calhoun got shot?' she said.

'Yeah, I did,' the man himself said as he limped in. 'But I've had worse.'

'Of course you have.' Natasha got up from the sofa as Lina joined them. The two women shared a look. A strange look, really. Something knowing in it, but also both showing a certain distaste for the other. 'I'm going upstairs to rest.'

Natasha brushed past Lina and out.

'This is unexpected,' Lina said.

'What? You thought we'd get the Spanish Inquisition the moment we stepped inside?' Calhoun responded.

'Actually, yeah.'

'Maybe it's your guilt talking,' Calhoun said, and although he said it lightheartedly the flicker in Lina's eyes didn't go unnoticed by Ryker.

'You want to talk about guilt, you should be looking at this guy right here,' she said, pointing at Ryker. 'We lost Niko, we lost Zubarev, you've been shot. All since he turned up.'

Calhoun nodded and turned his glare on Ryker. 'Yeah, what do you have to say about that?'

'I saved you, didn't I?'

'You did,' Calhoun said. 'You also chose to do that rather than try to save the weapons.'

Ryker said nothing.

'You know I spoke to Roman right before we left. He told me

if things went wrong this time... he'd know he had a big problem. He kept this deal so quiet.'

'I know,' Ryker said. 'He told me the same thing. Probably you too, right?'

Lina nodded.

'So even if I was an informant or a mole or whatever you're suggesting, it'd be pretty damn stupid of me, of any of us, to let details slip and allow that ambush.'

'That's exactly what a rat would say,' Lina said, before she turned and walked out.

Ryker waited a few moments, making sure she'd gone.

'Everyone likes pointing the finger at me,' he said. 'But what about her?'

'Lina?'

'You know much about her past?'

'The basics.'

'Which is?'

'Are you asking me because you want to know or because you're testing me?'

'You decide.'

'She was Spetsnaz.'

'Right.'

'And your point is?'

'That last deal was derailed by the Ukrainians. It makes sense. The Ukrainian government see Minko as a threat. They don't want to lose Donbas. But this latest deal was different. I don't think it was the Ukrainians. What if it was the Russians?'

'Why the hell would the Russians want to sabotage us?'

'Because they can. Because they have the power to do so. Because of what happened in Belarus.'

Calhoun snarled, showing his growing distaste.

'You might think, being Irish, and my bloodline, my culture, having nothing to do with Minko's cause, that my heart isn't in this. But it is. I'm with him 100 percent. With everything I've got. Whereas you... you're a shit-stirrer. You were brought on board because you sold yourself as being able to solve problems. Except since you've been here, you've only brought them.' Calhoun hobbled over. He put his face right into Ryker's. 'And now you're deflecting onto Lina because... what? She's Russian? What do you say to her, to the boss, about me behind my back?'

Ryker didn't get the chance to answer because the next moment Lina went racing across the hallway behind him.

'Hey!' she shouted out. 'There's someone outside.'

Ryker ran after her, glancing out the front windows as he went. He spotted two black-clad figures out there, darting for the perimeter wall.

Lina slung open the front door and pelted out, gun in hand. She fired off before Ryker had even stepped outside. He didn't have a gun on him, but he was a faster runner. The door slammed shut behind him as he raced to overtake Lina who'd slowed to take aim. She fired off again but missed as the first of the intruders clambered up and over the wall.

'They have a vehicle!' Ryker shouted to her. He could hear the engine rumble to life the other side.

'Shit!' Lina said as she turned and went back to the house. Car key?

Both intruders had soon disappeared on the other side of the wall. Ryker heard the engine revving as the vehicle pulled away. He launched himself at the wall and scurried to the top.

The car was already fifty yards away. He tried his best to get a read of the plate. He got most of it. Perhaps enough for them to search for it, find it. But he had no chance of following.

He jumped back down from the wall on the inside and looked over to where Lina was heading out of the turning circle in a

BMW X5. He waved over to her, both arms aloft. She stopped the car and wound down the window.

'No point. They've gone,' he shouted out. 'But I got the plate.'

She thumped the steering wheel in frustration but then hit reverse. By the time he made it back to her by the front door he'd just about got his breathing back under control.

'What the hell was that?' she asked.

'Good question.'

'They didn't come to attack us otherwise they would have.'

'Let's get inside. We need to call Minko and make sure he's OK.'

Lina led the way in through the front door. Quiet inside.

'Calhoun?' Ryker shouted out.

'In here.'

Same place Ryker had left him. Except now he had Natasha with him.

'Protecting the boss's wife,' he said with a grin.

'Who were they?' Natasha asked.

'Don't know yet,' Ryker said, glaring at Calhoun.

'What? I was ready to move if I needed to.'

'Were they here to...' Natasha trailed off as she looked from Calhoun to Ryker and back. She was rattled.

Lina had her phone to her ear and a conversation started. Within seconds it was clear Minko was OK. Gregor too.

But she wasn't. Her skin had gone pale and glistened with sweat. She wobbled on her feet as she spoke, her hand shaking.

'We'll see you... in a... few...'

Lina collapsed to the floor and the phone spilled from her grip.

Natasha shot up from the sofa to go to her aid and Ryker was about to go to her too but then froze.

'Don't go any closer!' he shouted.

Lina lay there, her body violently convulsing, her panicked eyes locked on to Ryker's.

'Help her!' Natasha screamed.

'What the fuck!' Calhoun shouted.

Foam spilled from Lina's mouth, her eyes and nostrils dripped blood. The convulsions worsened, her whole body bucking back and forth uncontrollably.

'Please!' Natasha begged and Ryker had to throw his arm out to stop her getting too close. He wrapped her up as she begged and sobbed.

Then, just as suddenly as they'd arrived, the convulsions faded to just a few odd twitches, seconds apart.

Not long after that and Lina didn't move at all.

* * *

Ryker, Calhoun, Klaus and Minko stood around Lina's lifeless body. Natasha had taken Gregor upstairs. No one had moved or even touched Lina in the few minutes she'd lay sprawled there, although she'd at least been covered with a sheet to give her some sort of dignity in death. Or perhaps so that Gregor didn't accidentally see the ghastly features of the corpse.

'This was supposed to be me,' Minko said.

'I think so,' Ryker added. 'But it could just as easily have been Natasha, Gregor, any one of us.'

'You think it was the two people you saw?' Minko asked.

'It makes sense.'

'But... how? What are we even looking at here?'

'Poison,' Calhoun said. 'What did she eat and drink when we got back?' he asked Ryker.

'I'm not sure she had anything.'

'It must be something.'

Everyone looked around the room then as though searching for glasses or cups or plates as evidence of what Lina could have consumed. But there really was nothing.

'We weren't even back long,' Ryker said. 'We came in here. Natasha was alone. Then she went upstairs. Me and Calhoun and Lina were talking—'

'So where were you?' Minko asked Klaus, the accusation clear in his tone.

'I went to the pool house when we got back.'

'And you didn't even see these intruders?'

'I was in the shower. I had no idea.'

'Very convenient,' Minko said.

Klaus didn't answer. Probably the best response for him.

'So Klaus was... showering. Natasha had left the three of you in here,' Minko said, now turning his attention to Calhoun and Ryker.

'Yeah,' Calhoun said. 'But then Lina left too.'

'Left the house?'

'No. She left this room.'

'To where?'

Calhoun shrugged.

'Kitchen,' Ryker said.

All four of them piled out and off into the kitchen where they stood in a cluster again, examining all the surfaces. But the place was spotless.

'She didn't have anything,' Calhoun said.

'Doesn't look like it,' Klaus added.

'We're looking in the wrong place,' Ryker said.

'Yeah?'

'Those two intruders never came in here. Lina, from inside, spotted them and the first thing I knew she was racing to the front door. She chased them out there. I joined her... then...'

He turned and looked through the hallway to the front door.

Ryker picked up a tea towel and strode that way, the others followed. He stopped by the door and stared at the handle a few seconds.

'What the hell are you doing?' Calhoun said as he hobbled up behind the others.

Ryker tentatively reached forward with the towel in his hand and he quickly pulled open the door. He dropped the towel and everyone stepped back in anticipation, perhaps expecting an explosion or something given Ryker's hesitancy.

Except nothing happened apart from the open door letting in a swathe of warm sunny light.

'What are you on?' Calhoun said to Ryker, whose gaze was now fixed on the handle on the outside of the door. Evidently, he couldn't understand why Ryker was searching for answers there.

'You see it?' Ryker asked.

'See what?'

He pointed to the handle. To the ever so slight smudge where a liquid had dried.

'What are you telling us?' Minko said.

'I chased those intruders outside with Lina,' Ryker said. 'When we came back to the house... she opened the door. Then when you came home with Gregor—'

'You opened up from the inside,' Minko said to Ryker.

'So Lina was the only person to touch that handle after those two intruders ran off.'

'You're saying the poison was on the handle?' Klaus said.

'Not just a poison. It was a nerve agent,' Ryker said. 'Smeared onto the handle of the front door. Once ingested... Maybe she touched her lips or her nose or something... But it spread through her body in seconds, infecting every part of her nervous system. Every muscle went haywire, spasmed uncontrollably.

Same for her organs, her heart, her brain, until it all just shut down.'

'Nerve agent?' Klaus said. 'So you're saying—'

'I'm saying you were targeted for assassination,' Ryker said to Minko, whose face had gone pale. 'Not by a criminal gang or a rival or anything like that. This was the work of spooks.'

'The Russians,' Minko said, the color returning to his cheeks as anger took hold. 'The Russians tried to kill me.'

'You're suggesting we take her out of here and bury her?' Minko said to Calhoun as the four men gathered back around the corpse.

'It gets rid of the problem.'

'No it doesn't,' Klaus said. 'The problem isn't Lina's body, the problem is the Russians going to this length to try and assassinate Roman.'

Calhoun grumbled under his breath, but Minko nodded his head as though in agreement.

'Getting rid of the body keeps her death quiet,' Ryker said. 'You didn't do anything wrong here, but if you call the police and get them to investigate this then it all comes out in public. Russian involvement in trying to have you killed. Those responsible won't ever be punished or anyone reprimanded even. Most likely those two agents are already out of Cyprus and on their way back to the motherland for good.'

'They might be safe there from foreign governments, but not from me.'

'And you could go after them. But they're just doers. This came from higher up than the two who turned up on your doorstep.'

'So what's your suggestion?' Minko asked.

'Why did they want to kill you?' Ryker asked.

Minko glowered rather than answer.

'What happened in Belarus?'

The glower intensified.

'Fine,' Ryker said. 'You don't have to tell me, but—'

'How'd you even know about stuff like this?' Calhoun asked. 'Nerve agents and shit?'

Ryker shrugged. 'Why wouldn't I know about it? Google it. You'll see for yourself. It's an open secret and has been for years that the Russian government takes out its enemies however they want. Nerve agents are quick, clean. A lot of the time, if the bodies aren't found straight away, it looks like a simple heart attack. They get away with it over and over.'

'Yeah. That, or you're a lot closer to the world of spooks than the rest of us.'

Ryker rolled his eyes to show his disdain for that comment. 'What I'm saying is, you need to figure out why the Russians targeted you before we decide what to do with Lina. Which is why I was asking about Belarus. Because I'm sensing something happened there that's led to this. The ambush in Turkey, too.'

'You're right,' Minko said after a few moments of deliberation, and then he sighed as though building up to a reveal. 'The Russians took our weapons in Turkey. Now this. But it wasn't a bullet to the head. It was a message.'

'You don't think you were the target?' Calhoun asked.

'I think they probably didn't care, but it could have been me, Natasha, Gregor, any one of you.'

'What happened in Belarus?' Ryker asked again and this time the response from Minko wasn't anywhere near as angry.

'I was told, with finality and by all parties, that I can't have Donbas. If I go to war with the Ukrainian government on my own, the Russians will support them, not me. But I was told, and that's the key word here, told, because there was no negotiation, I was told the Russians would help me, militarily, diplomatically, however, if ultimately Donbas is annexed by Russia. We'd be independent of Ukraine. But we'd be dependent on Moscow. The Russian president would get to at least distance himself from the fighting in the eyes of foreign governments, but he'd be the one pulling the strings after.'

No one said anything to that. Ryker could see the turmoil in the man. His raison d'être was an independent Donbas, with him at the helm. Now it looked less likely than ever.

'What are you going to do?' Calhoun asked.

'The only thing I can do,' Minko said. 'They've already shown their hand. I'll never get us moving with Moscow trying to derail us, and knowing that I'm only ever moments away from them killing me or my family. I have to take what they're offering. We fight with Russia. Or we don't fight at all.'

He'd shrunk two inches saying those words. Normally formidably confident, the man looked forlorn.

'So what about the body?' Klaus asked.

'Bury her,' Minko confirmed. 'Cover up her death as best you can. And don't disturb me for the rest of the day.'

Minko walked out, tail well and truly between his legs.

32

Ryker had to await his moment, but despite the risk, he wanted to do this sooner rather than later. Calhoun and Klaus had taken Lina's body away nearly two hours ago now. Ryker didn't think they'd be gone much longer. In that time he'd not seen Natasha at all but knew she was somewhere upstairs. Minko, on the other hand, was now out by the pool with his son. A rare time for the father to spend some alone time with Gregor. Perhaps it was the close brush with death that had made him want to connect with the kid. And it certainly looked and sounded like they were having fun out there. Although Minko had also taken a bottle of bourbon outside with him. A bottle of bourbon that had started the afternoon pretty much full, and the last time Ryker had walked past the patio doors in the kitchen, that bottle now had little more than a third remaining.

Ryker did one final walk-by of the windows at the back of the villa. Minko was out of the pool and lazing on a lounger while Gregor splashed about on an inflatable.

All clear.

Ryker went upstairs. He found the master bedroom empty.

He carried on along the corridor to the sunroom at the far end – an oval room with large windows all around that contained little furniture other than a couple of chaise longues and a minibar in one corner. The room was hardly ever used although today he found Natasha there, on one of the chaises, staring outside.

'There you are,' Ryker said as he stopped in the doorway. She glanced over, her mood obviously pensive.

'What do you want?'

He moved over to her and perched on the adjacent chaise.

'You were lucky,' he said to her.

'Lucky?'

'It could easily have been you or Gregor rather than Lina.'

She turned away from him.

'I can't tell if you're cut up about her dying or not,' Ryker said.

'You think it doesn't bother me that someone died in my house?'

'I always sensed there was some tension between you two.'

She whipped back around to face him. 'Did you come up here to comfort me or to accuse me of something?'

'I didn't get it at first,' Ryker said. 'I thought maybe there'd been an incident between you two before I arrived here. Or maybe you were just polar opposites. But I figured it out eventually.'

'Please, James, just go.'

'The tension was because you suspected they'd planted her here. Right?'

'Who? Planted? This is—'

She went to move away, to get off the other side of the chaise but Ryker grabbed her wrist and squeezed hard as he pulled her back.

'You thought Moscow had put her here. To keep tabs on you.

But it wasn't true. She was just like all the others in here. A mercenary in it for the money.'

'Let go!' she said, squirming to try to release Ryker's grip.

'Perhaps you were even glad that she died today. Because for a moment, before the true realization set in, you thought it'd be a weight off you.'

'I said let go!'

Ryker didn't.

'You gave the Russians the intel for Turkey, didn't you?'

She growled and again tried to get away, but Ryker held firm.

'One question,' he said. 'Did you know what the Russians were planning today? I have to say, when I came back here earlier, you seemed… more confident than I expected. Now I get it. You thought today was the day.'

'James, you're hurting me!'

He only squeezed harder.

'I know it's you,' Ryker said. 'I know you're working with Moscow.'

She wrestled her hand free, but only because Ryker loosened his grip. She was left with rings of reddened flesh from his fingers. She nursed her wrist but didn't make any attempt to leave.

'How long?' Ryker asked.

'Too fucking long.'

'Since you met him?'

'Yes!' Her eyes welled but she somehow kept the tears from falling. 'But I'm not one of them!' she shouted.

Ryker looked to the doorway as though worried someone would have heard her, but everything remained quiet throughout the house.

'Not one of who?'

'A spy. A secret agent, whatever you want to call it. I'm just a normal woman but I've been forced to live this lie. I'm the mother of his child!'

'You're a sleeper agent. That's what they call it. A long play. In some cases very long. But it's the lengths the Russians go to.'

'I'm not an agent. I never was.'

'But you've been feeding information back to Moscow the whole time?'

She nodded.

'Today? Did you know that was happening?'

She nodded again. 'I thought it might be the end.' And now the tears did fall.

'It could have been Gregor. Anyone could have opened that door.'

'I didn't know how they were doing it! Otherwise I would never...'

She shook her head in frustration, unable to find the words, the justification.

He took her hand. Gently now. Comforting. And she didn't pull from his grip.

'I told you before, I can get you out of this,' he said.

'No. You can't.'

'Trust me, Natasha. We could even leave tonight. Get Gregor and go from here. There's a place we can stay the night while we make arrangements to get you out of the country. You don't have to live like this, to punish yourself anymore.'

Now she did pull from his grip.

'Why?' she asked.

'Why what?'

'Why do you want to take me from here? What do we do next? We go off and live a happy life on a white-sand beach somewhere. Paradise?'

He didn't respond as he figured the questions were more rhetorical.

'It's not going to happen, is it?' she said. 'And not just because it would never be safe for us, for my son, but because... I don't want it, James. I don't want you! Not like that. It was never supposed to be like that.'

He let go of her hand and took a moment before he got to his feet.

'So what now?' he asked.

'If you tell him he'll kill me,' she said.

'I have no doubt.'

'But you won't tell him, will you?'

Ryker didn't answer. At that moment, he really didn't know how to. He knew right then that he owed her no loyalty, even if he didn't think she deserved further punishment.

'No,' Natasha added. 'You won't tell him. Just like I won't tell him about you.'

He clenched his jaw. Balled his fists. He'd not heard her speak with that tone before. Hard-edged. Shrewd. A little bit vindictive.

'My handlers and your handlers work in the same circles,' she said. 'I don't even know if they all just sit around telling each other their secrets for kicks. But the Russians know about you. That you're here undercover, just like I am.'

'You told them?' Ryker said.

'No. They already knew. I don't know how.'

'That's why—'

'I stopped sleeping with you? Is that what this is about. You want us to be together? Oh, James... I thought you were more savvy than that.'

'You have no idea who I really am.'

'It doesn't even matter,' she said. 'They knew about you, and they told me to just let it play out. But now... maybe things have changed. Now that Roman is going to be working with Moscow from here.'

'To tell him about me you'd have to admit everything about your relationship is a lie. You'd do that just to get to me?'

'I might not have a choice. I do what I'm told to do. You want to get me out of here? To go somewhere safe? But perhaps it's better for you to leave, James. Save yourself while you still have a chance.'

He chewed over her statement. A threat, more than a friendly piece of advice, he decided. Downstairs he heard a door slam shut. He couldn't tell if it was the front or back, but someone had come in. The conversation was over. At least both of them knew where they stood with the other now.

Ryker turned and walked out without another word.

'What were you doing up there?' Calhoun asked from the hallway as Ryker made his way back down the stairs.

'Why?' Ryker asked.

'Answer the question,' Klaus said, coming up behind him. Ryker noted the dirt on his clothes, up his arms. He wondered where they'd buried Lina although he wouldn't ask.

'I was taking a shit,' Ryker said.

'Is Mrs. Minko up there?' Klaus asked.

'She definitely wasn't in the toilet with me.'

Both of them humphed, clearly not liking Ryker's answers although he didn't know why they'd grown so suspicious of him all of a sudden. It didn't make sense that Natasha would have told these two about him – there was simply no benefit to her.

'Roman's outside getting wasted on his own,' Ryker said.

'Actually, he's passed out already,' Klaus said. 'And Gregor was splashing around in the pool unsupervised. So good job looking out for him.'

'His father was outside with him. His mother's upstairs

staring out the window. But it's my problem that Gregor was
unsupervised in the pool?'

'Thought you said you didn't know where she was?' Calhoun
said.

'No. I said she wasn't watching me take a shit. I think she's in
the sunroom or the reading room or whatever it's called.'

'Whatever. I'm going to get cleaned up,' Klaus said. 'I've done
my job this afternoon. Make sure you're doing yours.'

'You got it, boss,' Ryker said with a salute.

Klaus growled before walking away. Calhoun shook his head
with disgruntlement but then limped off too. Ryker waited until
both men were out of sight before he bounded up the stairs and
rummaged in the bedside drawer of the guest room for his
phone. His other phone. Not the one he used for his business –
and subterfuge – with Minko. But he wouldn't make the call in
here. Knowing what he now knew for sure about Natasha... he
wouldn't be surprised if the whole inside of the villa was bugged
somehow.

But no time to waste for this. Whatever the risk, he couldn't
delay.

He paused on the landing and glanced back toward the open
doorway of the sunroom. He couldn't tell if Natasha was there or
not, but he saw no sign of her from his viewpoint.

He swallowed hard, pushing away the raw emotion he hadn't
expected, and certainly didn't want to feel in that moment. Ryker
headed down and outside. Minko snored on one of the loungers,
empty whisky bottle beside him. Ryker waved to Gregor in the
pool.

'You OK, kiddo?'

'Yeah!' Gregor shouted as he smashed an inflatable alligator
in the face with his fist, over and over and over. Father would
probably be proud. 'Can you play?'

'Maybe after.'

The alligator took an extra hard fist to the nose in response. Ryker carried on around the side of the house to the thicket of trees between the villa and the garage block – a quiet spot that he knew wasn't overlooked by the house.

Mackie didn't answer, so Ryker called Winter.

'We have a problem,' Ryker said.

'Yeah?'

'Natasha Minko is a Moscow stooge.'

Silence.

'Did you hear me?'

'She told you that?'

'She didn't have to. Did you know?'

'No,' Winter said. 'I didn't.'

Ryker didn't know the man well enough to decide if that was the truth or not. Although even if it was, Ryker still didn't know whether Mackie knew or not. Perhaps it didn't even make much difference now. Not to Ryker.

'Does she know you know?' Winter asked.

'Yes.'

'Shit. And... you?'

'Apparently she's known about me all along.'

Silence again.

'Winter, my cover, my life, is in her hands. And I've no idea who she's told or who she will tell. So... what do you want me to do?'

Another pause, then, 'I'll get back to you.'

The call clicked off.

33

PRESENT DAY

Gomel, Belarus

Another long, tiring, cold journey had seen Ryker, Gregor and Nadia traverse the Ukrainian-Belarus border on their way toward the southeastern Belarusian city of Gomel. Ryker had never been to this place before, but like many areas in the vicinity, Gomel had a past of varying occupation and allegiances, having at times been part of both Russia and Ukraine.

Most recently, the country as a whole had fallen back under the watchful eye of imperialist Russia, with a headstrong leader intent on proving his worth to the much larger and more powerful neighbor. An interesting corollary was that it was in Belarus too that Gregor's father's plans had first come unstuck.

'But what are you asking for exactly?' Winter asked, sounding more and more agitated at Ryker's lack of straight answers. Ryker, phone close to his ear, turned away from the car where Nadia and Gregor remained, huddling from the cold.

'I told you. We're near Gomel, Belarus. I need an extraction. A quick escape, helicopter would be best. Just give me a time, a location, but it needs to be soon.'

'You said that already. I'm asking why. What the hell are you doing in Belarus?'

'I can't tell you yet.' Largely because Ryker still didn't believe the whole story himself. 'But very soon we could have information that would drastically change the entire Ukraine war.'

'You said that already too. What information, Ryker? You went out there to find Gregor Rebrov, not to drastically change a war our country isn't officially involved in! Can you imagine—'

'Winter, please, just trust me? We only need a craft and a pilot. How hard can it be? Send me details of the extraction site when you can. We're southwest of the city. Make sure it's there.'

Ryker ended the call before Winter could respond, both because he was fed up with the back-and-forth conversation, and also because Gregor was glaring at him from the car.

He got back inside.

'That was your contact in SIS?' Gregor asked.

'Yes.'

'Is he your boss?'

'Not for a long time. I don't work for the British government or anyone else.'

'Not anymore. Not officially. But you did.'

Ryker looked out of the windscreen at the building a hundred yards away. The glitzy-looking office block, full glass facade, looked out of place inside the ugly barbed-wire-topped metal fence that surrounded it.

'Was he your boss back when you worked for my father?'

Ryker detected snideness in the question, but then his whole premise for knowing Gregor was built on lies, so perhaps the reaction was justified.

'No, actually. But I did know him then.'

'You've known him a long time.'

'And we've been through a lot together. He's got my back.'

'Explain to me, why did the UK government send you to spy on my father?'

Ryker turned around to face Gregor fully. 'Because Roman Minko was a hugely rich man who was using his power and influence to cook up a civil war in Donbas. You don't think that would be something other governments were interested in following?'

Gregor held his hands up in defense, perhaps because of Ryker's hard tone, though he looked a little smug knowing that he was getting under Ryker's skin.

'For a while it was nothing more than intelligence gathering,' Ryker said. 'But things changed quickly when the Russians forced your father's hand. In fact, it was after a meeting your father had here in Belarus that events spiraled. The Russians, knowing he didn't want their support, came after him. They sabotaged his plans, tried to assassinate him at his villa.'

'You're talking about that day Lina was poisoned,' Gregor said.

'You know about that?'

'I've had to put some of the pieces together since, but yeah, that day was a big turning point. For everyone. I also remember how destroyed my father was after the trip to Belarus you mentioned. As though years of planning, and his entire future, were shattered.'

'Yeah,' was all Ryker could say to that.

'Did you love my mother?'

Ryker clenched his jaw shut trying to think of a response to the unexpected question.

'I knew about the affair even back then,' Gregor said. 'I didn't know what it all meant, but I saw you two kissing once. And do you know what?'

'What?'

'I was actually pleased. She liked you. You treated her well. And... my father didn't. I know he beat her. He used to beat me too. More than once she put herself in harm's way to protect me.'

Ryker kept his jaw clenched again, channeling anger as those old memories surfaced. He hadn't realized Minko had beat his son too – he'd never seen marks or cuts – though it didn't surprise him really.

'He was my father, I loved him, but I'm not sure he was a good man. At least... he wasn't a good father or husband, even if what he was fighting for was worthy.'

Ryker kind of got the point, but didn't show his acknowledgment.

'Did you love my mother?' Gregor asked again.

'No,' Ryker said. 'I'm not sure that version of me was capable of love.'

'That version?'

'I'm not the same man I used to be. A lot's happened since then.'

'Not the same man?' Gregor said. 'That's a shame, because I'm kind of banking on you being exactly that man.'

Once more Ryker said nothing, although he thought Gregor probably meant he wanted Ryker to still be as tough and capable as he used to be, rather than anything else. Which he thought he was, age aside.

He checked his watch. 'Nearly time to go,' Ryker said. They'd move at midnight.

'Nearly,' Gregor said. 'But I have one more question for you first.'

Ryker sighed and he sensed his response offended Gregor somehow, as though he were belittling the man's attempt at catharsis. But in this moment, dredging up these memories was far from cathartic for Ryker, even if it was for Gregor.

'What really happened the night my parents were killed?'

Ryker glanced from Gregor to Nadia. Both of them looked at him intently. As usual, she'd said next to nothing in the conversation, as she so often did when Gregor talked of the past, of his parents, his father's plans. But Ryker sensed she knew a lot still. These two were seriously close, he knew, not just in terms of their affection for each other, but because of how little else now remained of their previous lives, friends, family.

'I don't know exactly what prompted it, but the Russians came that night,' Ryker said. 'Most likely because they realized that even after their threats, your father would never be satisfied working with them. It made more sense to them for him to be dead or in a gulag. Look what's happened in the years since. Russia has got exactly what it wanted. Your father would have done everything to stop events playing out like they have.'

Gregor nodded as though indicating that the explanation rang true.

'Do you know what I remember?' he asked.

'What?'

'I was woken by the sound of gunfire, but I was a sleepy six-year-old, and it really didn't make much sense to me at the time. I heard shouting. Vehicles. I thought maybe the police had come. Both my parents often told me how wary they were of the police. When I snuck to my bedroom door, I fully expected to see flashing blue lights and uniformed men darting about. Except when I poked my head out, what did I see instead?'

'I don't know.'

'I saw you. I saw your face and it immediately made me feel safer, even if I didn't understand what was happening. Then I saw the other men, men with guns coming for you, and when you called out to me, I did the only thing that made sense. I ran to you. And you took me out of there. You saved my life that night.'

Ryker simply nodded in acknowledgment.

'You know, I never got to see their bodies,' Gregor added. He chuckled. It didn't really fit the situation at all, and Nadia twitched uncomfortably. 'Not that it would have been a nice thing for a six-year-old to see. But I never went back to the villa either. I ended up in that orphanage, being told my parents were killed, but I didn't get to go to a funeral or anything like that.'

'I'm sorry,' Ryker responded. 'Like I said, I wasn't the same man back then. I should have done more to help you after. I really wish I had.'

'Over the years, as a boy, a young teenager, I even tried to convince myself that perhaps they weren't dead after all. That one day they'd arrive to take me away from there, to another life. I guess I still feel that way sometimes, even though I know deep down that it's not true.'

'No,' Ryker said. 'It's not true.'

'And you know that because... because you did see their bodies?'

'I did,' Ryker said, hanging his head. 'I saw them both. Believe me, they're both long dead, Gregor.'

'Well, I guess I can finally put that theory to bed once and for all,' he said, looking glum. But then a moment later he became more upbeat and he smacked Ryker's arm. 'It looks like it's time. Come on, let's go get this done.'

34

One minute past midnight. They walked side by side through the darkness toward the mesh fence, Ryker in the middle, Nadia to his left, Gregor to his right. Each of them wore all black clothing and they had balaclavas covering their faces. They hadn't had a lot of time to prep for this mission but had at least been able to get the clothes and some basic equipment, which included a handgun each from a stash that had belonged to the Panthers. A stash that consisted of a mishmash of weaponry – aging pieces largely from Russia, Germany and the UK, gathered by Gregor and his allies over years of rebellious but largely unfunded conflict.

Ryker hoped they wouldn't need the guns, but they had them for protection. Of the three of them, Nadia was the most nervous. She'd been fidgeting for hours now, unable to relax. Ryker could understand why. This was a risky mission. They were working largely off intel Gregor had got his hands on through a variety of means. Hacking, a whistleblower, bribes in the main. Like the Panthers' stash of weapons, the evidence Gregor had gathered was a mixed bag, virtually all of it circumstantial. Perhaps enough to get an intelligence agency like SIS interested and to look further, but what happened after that could take weeks, months, even years. This way sped up the process massively.

If they could pull it off.

But even if Gregor seemed to know a lot about what was happening at this place, they'd not had time to come up with a sophisticated, stealthy approach. Given Gregor's fugitive status and questions of how long they had before his enemies caught up, they would hit hard and fast tonight to get things over the line. As such they likely wouldn't be able to sneak in and sneak out undetected. Sooner or later their presence would be known. An alarm would blare. Guards and police would descend. The hardest part would be getting the three of them out and away unscathed.

He really hoped Winter would pull through with the helicopter. If not, they had a horribly long road ahead. He quickly checked his phone. No call or message since he'd last spoken to Winter.

'Are we good?' Gregor asked him when Ryker slipped the phone back away.

'Yeah. Everyone remember the plan?' Ryker asked.

'My plan,' Gregor said, as though the clarification was important. Except even if Gregor felt this was an operation of his doing, that didn't mean what came next was entirely of his making. Ryker had a lot more experience than these two of raids like this. A lot of those raids had gone exactly to plan, no problems whatsoever. Some hadn't. He just hoped if this one went awry that his two companions, in the heat of the moment, would follow his lead.

'Your plan,' Ryker said anyway, as there was no point entering a debate now. 'We go over the fence on the south side, because there are fewer cameras, fewer lights that side, away from the road. But there are no black spots, so we'll be visible. We need to move quickly for the building. If any guards spot us, take them down as quickly and quietly as possible. We have plenty of cable ties.'

'I see no guards this side,' Gregor said, peering into the darkness ahead of them. 'This isn't a fort.'

Which he was partly right about. The company that operated here, Avto-Bio, was a legitimate privately run business, that even had some of Europe's leading pharma companies as its key investors and sponsors. What wasn't so prominently mentioned on its website or anywhere else publicly accessible – as in, not mentioned at all – was that it had also entered into contracts with the Belarusian and Russian governments to carry out pathogen research. Such research was under the auspices of future pandemic management, from the sketchy documents that Gregor had shown Ryker, but the true story was potentially something far darker.

Still. The point was that this place was not a military barracks, even if it did have far more security than an average office.

'We breach from the southwest service entrance,' Ryker said, 'then up to the fourth floor.'

'We know all this,' Gregor said, sounding sullen now.

'Maybe, but it's good to keep each stage running through your mind. If you get separated, make your way back to the car. If you can't do that, communicate with the phones, but the devices stay off unless it's last resort time. We'll regroup on the outside. If you can't do that—'

'We understand,' Gregor said as the three of them came to a

top by the fence. 'But it won't come to that. We'll get in and out
together. OK?'

Nadia nodded.

'Yeah,' Ryker said. 'Then let's go.'

Gregor unraveled the thick blanket he'd been carrying and
tossed the end up and over the top of the eight-foot-high fence,
smothering the barbs there.

'Ladies first,' he said to Nadia, cupping his hands together to give
her a boost. She hesitated a moment, took in a big breath, then set to
it, scrambling up to the top. She moaned in pain, perhaps as a spike
caught her skin. The blanket provided some protection, but it wasn't
perfect. Within a few seconds she'd jumped down to the other side.

'Old men next,' Gregor said.

Ryker had been prepared to let Gregor go second, leaving
himself with the harder task of climbing the fence without a
boost. But if Gregor wanted that job, then fine.

Ryker bounced up from Gregor's hands, causing the younger
but by no means stronger or fitter guy to stumble. Ryker grasped
the blanket, now thoroughly wedged on the barbs, and dragged
himself to the top then swung his legs over and dropped down to
the ground next to Nadia.

'OK,' Gregor said. 'Old, but you've got some moves still.'

'Damn right I have.'

And Gregor definitely struggled more than Ryker believed he
would have as he attempted to scale the tall fence without
assistance.

'You OK?' Ryker asked Nadia who was busy inspecting a large
gash in the fabric of her trousers.

'I think so,' she said, although as she pulled her hand up
Ryker saw the fabric of her gloves glistening. Blood.

'Shit!' Gregor said and it looked like he was about to topple back down to the ground on the other side, but then he righted himself, clinging to the top one-handed like a monkey.

Ryker bounced back up, resting on the apex and helped Gregor to pull his body across before he rolled off and down to the inside, only just staying on his feet.

Ryker jumped down again.

'We good?' he asked as Gregor brushed himself down wincing as he touched a sore spot on his side.

'A few scratches, that's all,' Gregor said, a little out of breath from exertion.

'Come on, we don't have time.'

Ryker set off at pace toward the office. No sign of any guard here but they'd not moved five yards before a spotlight attached to the back of the building blared from their motion, casting them all in bright white light.

'Move!' Gregor hissed and the three of them strode with even more purpose for the building. They hadn't quite reached there when a security guard came around the corner of the building ten yards away. No weapon in his hand, only a flashlight, his sidearm still holstered.

A bad move for him.

Gregor diverted and reached him before he could pull his gun free, and Gregor pistol-whipped him in the head to send him to the floor. He hit him a second time, even more forcibly than the first, and Nadia flinched in shock before the guy's head lolled.

Brutal, but effective.

'Help me pull him out of the light,' Gregor whispered as he hog-tied the guy.

Ryker and Gregor dragged the guard into a dark spot by a large propane tank. They quickly checked his pockets, took a phone, radio, the gun and a keycard.

Gregor held the keycard up victoriously. 'Looks like we go in the easy way.'

'Let's go,' Ryker said.

They were soon clustered together at the service door. They each held their breath as Gregor pushed the card against the keypad. A momentary hush before a green light flicked on and the magnetic locks released.

Ryker pulled the door open and they all filed in then stopped dead to look and listen. The corridor was dimly lit, quiet.

'Elevator there,' Gregor said, indicating the cluster of lights about twenty yards ahead.

'Take it easy,' Ryker said as they all set off in tow. He glanced up at the ceiling as they moved. A camera up there. Nothing they could do about that. But a place like this likely had tens of cameras, too many for someone to be eyeballing every single feed every moment of every day. For now they were simply riding their luck. No other way to do it from here.

They reached the elevator without incident. Gregor once again used the keycard and they were on their way up.

'Do you think they're watching us right now?' Nadia said.

Ryker glanced at the camera in the corner.

'Maybe they'll be ready to shoot us as soon as the doors open,' she added, her nerves obviously getting the better of her.

Neither Gregor nor Ryker got to say anything in response before the elevator reached the fourth floor and the doors opened.

No one there.

Nadia let out a long sigh.

They stepped out into a much nicer corridor than down in the service area. A little clinical, but almost space-age with sleek lines and glossy finishes to the floor, walls and ceiling, and ambient, hidden strip lighting that spread outward down the corridor as they moved forward. They walked past closed doors and windows, laboratories beyond that were crammed with elaborate-looking equipment.

'There's no one here,' Gregor said.

'Which one are we looking for?' Nadia asked.

'This one,' Gregor said, almost aghast, as he stopped outside the door to 4F.

He tried the handle. Locked, of course. And this door didn't have simple keypad security, but a PIN-pad attached to a small camera.

'Retina scan,' Gregor said.

A ping caught their attention. From further along the corridor, by the main elevator bank.

'No!' Nadia shouted as the doors slid open. Ryker and Gregor had a different response, and both darted forward to tackle the at first unsuspecting guard. He whipped his gun out with one hand as he stepped back into the elevator and slammed the buttons to close the doors. Then he fired off a hurried shot at his onrushing adversaries that smacked into the floor by Gregor's feet. Ryker fired back. He hit the hand that held the gun and the guard's weapon dropped free as the doors whirred closed.

Gregor lunged forward and shoved his hand between the nearly closed doors which smacked off him before returning open again.

Ryker held back on the outside and pointed the barrel of his gun to the guard's head.

'Hands where I can see them,' he shouted.

The guard did as he was told then cowered as Gregor launched himself for him. Gregor thumped him in the side, smacked him in the face before yanking off his utility belt. He emptied the guard's pockets then went to hit him again, but Ryker grabbed Gregor's shoulder to hold him back.

'That's enough.'

Gregor shrugged him off.

'Are you cool?'

Gregor said nothing, but Ryker knew he wasn't just running on adrenaline but anger too. Understandable, given what he and his friends had been through, and right now he was in his enemy's lair. But still, the guy needed to control himself before he made a mistake.

'We need him for the door,' Ryker said, trying to sound as unfazed as possible.

Gregor huffed. 'Get up,' he said to the man.

The guard again complied and with Ryker's gun at his back they marched him toward Nadia.

'Open the door,' Gregor said to him.

'Please...'

Gregor pushed the barrel of his gun to the guard's skull.

'Open the door or you're dead. We only need your eye for the retina scan. It doesn't matter much if you have a hole in your head.'

'No. But we do need him to tell us the code too,' Ryker said.

'We can hack the code,' Nadia said, which was true.

'But we don't need to,' Ryker said. 'Because he's going to open the door for us. Aren't you?'

The guard shook with fear, his hand trembling as he nodded then reached forward to the keypad. He clumsily pressed out six digits, although Ryker really didn't know if his fingertip had hit home in the right places or not given his tremors. But a green light blinked before the camera lens rolled open with a whir, the security system awaiting the next input.

Gregor shoved the guard's face toward the camera. 'Open your eyes!'

Although the guard's eyes were already wide-open, and the

next moment Ryker heard a click as the lock on the door released.

'That's it!' Nadia said. She reached forward and pushed the door open and had taken a single step forward when the lights across the entire floor flicked off.

Dim red lights came on in their place.

A second later a pulsing siren blared.

35

Gregor roared with anger and grabbed the guard by the scruff of his neck and swiped his gun across the man's cheek.

'What did you do!'

'Gregor!' Ryker shouted back. 'It wasn't him.'

Gregor grumbled but let go of the guard. 'We need to be quick.'

'Go!' Nadia shouted to them both.

'Watch the corridor,' Ryker said to her. 'And don't let that door close. We could be on lockdown here.' He turned to Gregor. 'Come on, let's find what we came here for.'

They rushed off into the lab.

'You go to the cold storage,' Ryker said to Gregor. 'I'll get the data.'

Although he really didn't know if they had time now. The intention had been to 'acquire' not only the virus itself, but as much electronic data as they could from the Avto-Bio computer systems, because just having the virus on its own proved little without the paper trail of what it was, and what it was being used for. Ryker had a bunch of USB thumb drives that he could plug

into anything with a port, and which would automatically take
mirror images of the hard drive contents. But that process wasn't
instantaneous, and he'd much rather have gone for the servers
that ran the company's computer systems than individual
machines.

Still, within sixty seconds he'd plugged five of his devices in
to desktops and laptops and met up with Gregor in the far corner
of the lab where two large horizontal freezers lay against one
wall.

Ryker opened the lid of the first unit and icy vapor wafted out.
He pulled up individual glass vials and larger metal canisters,
scanning the labels.

'The code for the virus is FAR21-B.'

Ryker nodded in response.

'It must be here,' Gregor said, sounding hurried, desperate.

'Guys, come on!' Nadia shouted. 'We don't have much time!'

Probably not, but they'd only been looking for seconds.

They continued to rummage, Ryker intermittently looking
behind him, both to the door and to his thumb drives, each of
which still had a red light glowing to show the copying process
was progressing but not complete.

'This is it!' Gregor shouted out, holding up one of the canis
ters – a metal tube, a foot long, a couple of inches in diameter.
Then his face turned to something much more contemplative.
'This is it.'

'How many are there?' Ryker said, moving over.

'A dozen. Maybe more.'

Ryker looked around the room. 'There.'

He headed across and picked up a Styrofoam box that had
several pre-formed holes in it to fit the containers.

'Guys!' Nadia shouted. 'I hear them!'

Neither Gregor nor Ryker had even looked over to her before

gunshots blasted out, the sound cutting above the din of the siren. Nadia screamed and threw herself to the floor inside the lab.

The door locked shut behind her...

'No!' Gregor shouted, and at first it wasn't clear if he was shouting because of the door or because Nadia had been shot. She was clutching her leg, writhing in pain as Gregor rushed to her. 'She's hit.'

'We'll get her out of here.'

Gregor tried the door. No good.

'We're trapped!' Nadia yelled.

Ryker finished packing the box. He lifted it up and was about to move to the others but then hesitated as his eyes caught on the glass screen in front of him. A small incinerator sat behind it.

Perhaps it'd be the best thing for the deadly concoction in his hands.

'Fucking hurry up!' Gregor shouted.

Ryker rushed to the other two at the door. He slipped the Styrofoam box into the empty holdall they'd brought as Gregor helped Nadia to her feet.

Gregor tried the door again as though he'd get a better result a second time.

'We're trapped,' Nadia repeated.

'No,' Ryker said. 'We're not.'

'What the hell do we do now?' Gregor asked.

'For now, they can't get us in here,' Ryker said.

'No, but within minutes we could have an army waiting out there for us.'

Ryker again glanced across the room. Five red lights from his thumb drives looked back.

'Shit,' he said. He didn't want to leave yet, but...

'Aaarghh!' Gregor roared as he launched a swivel chair at the window by the door. Ryker and Nadia both ducked as the pane shattered and thousands of pieces of neat safety glass tumbled to the floor around them.

Gregor poked his head out into the corridor and bullets pinged toward him from the main elevator bank.

He yelled in surprise as he reeled back inside.

'There's a stairwell by the service elevator,' Ryker said. 'Get Nadia down there. I'll cover you from here.'

'And then what?'

'I'll be fine. I need to wait for the downloads.'

'Screw the data! We have what we need.'

'No. We don't. I'll only be a few minutes. If I hold out here, keep them at the far end, it'll give you more time to get out.'

Gregor looked uncertain, but then got to his feet and made a move for the holdall.

'You worry about Nadia,' Ryker said, pulling the bag to him. 'You can't manage both this and her.'

'Gregor, come on!' Nadia said, using him to pull herself up, barely able to put any weight on her bleeding leg.

Ryker moved forward and poked the gun out into the corridor and let off several shots. He had no idea if he hit anyone, but in retaliation a small metal canister was sent cascading along the corridor.

'Tear gas!' Ryker shouted. 'Get out of here!'

He covered his nose and mouth with his sleeve as noxious smoke billowed all around them. He fired off more shots as Nadia and Gregor hurried out, Nadia clutching to Gregor to hold herself up. Soon they were out of sight behind the wall of fog.

Ryker let off the remaining shots in his magazine then ducked back inside where the smoke was still rapidly building. He took a couple of deep breaths, coughing and spluttering as he did so.

He grabbed the guard from the floor and hauled him and the

holdall to the very back corner of the lab, hoping for some fresher air for a few seconds at least.

Two of the thumb drives now blinked green. They were done. Ryker would have to make do. He heard tentative footsteps along the corridor and grabbed the guard by the scruff of his neck.

'How do I get out of here?'

The guard said nothing, not in defiance but because he was in a panic, barely able to breathe, his eyes streaming from the tear gas, as were Ryker's now as the smoke built around the room.

'Tell me how I get out or we both die in here!'

'The connecting doors,' he said, pointing to the near corner. 'Go through the labs to the south side. They... lead to a roof.'

'We're in lockdown.'

He shook his head. 'Not for the connecting doors. Or the fire escapes.'

A roof? Three floors up? Perhaps better than any other option he had right now.

Ryker raced across the room, pulling out his thumb drives. He used the guard's gun to send more warning shots toward the corridor where he knew men were now clustered, waiting to attack.

He picked up the holdall. Looked once more at the incinerator.

He shook his head in frustration and darted for the door.

* * *

Gregor pulled up to the fire exit door on the ground floor, his arm around Nadia's shoulder still to pull her along. Getting down the stairs hadn't been easy. More than once one of them had lost their balance, nearly sending them both tumbling. Each time they'd reached the next floor down they'd taken pause, both to recuperate and to wait and see if there was anyone coming to attack them, either from above or below.

There wasn't. And they'd nearly made it to the outside now. Although they still had the security fence to scale to reach their car, which wouldn't be the easiest task given Nadia's leg.

They'd heard shooting, banging from above. Ryker under attack. Nothing Gregor or Nadia could do about that now. He really wished he'd just taken the holdall with him too but in the moment some other sense had won out – the need to get Nadia to safety.

'Ready?' he asked her, gun in hand, the heel of his palm on the bar release in the middle of the door.

She looked anything but ready, yet she still nodded. Gregor pressed down on the bar and pushed the door open but no sooner had he done so than a bright spotlight from somewhere across the grounds shone into his eyes and he squinted and retreated as bullets zinged into the metal door.

'What do we do?' Nadia asked, the fear clear both on her face and in her words.

Gregor knew exactly what to do. He pushed open the door once more, only a few inches, aimed the handgun and fired.

The explosion as the bullet hit the propane tank was huge. Far larger and more severe than Gregor had anticipated and both he and Nadia were flung to the floor from the power of the blast. The fact they were right by the door, which wildly slammed shut behind them, was probably the only thing that saved their lives.

It took several seconds for them to both recover and get to their feet.

'You OK?' Gregor asked, his voice drowned out not just by the ongoing siren but by the chaos outside too.

No nod or anything from Nadia this time but they couldn't dwell. Gregor pushed open the door once more and heated air blasted in and he had to pull back a few seconds. Flames engulfed the outside of the building and spread out across the grounds where liquid gas had spilled.

He spotted two, three bodies lying unmoving, ablaze.

'Come on.'

He dragged Nadia out, ignoring the heat, pointing the gun his way and that. In the distance, off to the north side, he saw strobes of blue lighting up the night sky. Police. Soon this place would be heaving with them. But for now, he saw no more guards on the outside at all. At least not any that were still alive.

They reached the fence and Gregor allowed himself a small smile. No need to worry about scaling the structure now. The force of the blast had taken a row of three posts right out of the ground, the fence hanging on its side, only a couple of feet above the ground at the barbed-wire end.

They took a tentative walk across the metal, it holding their weight right to the end. Gregor jumped off then held his arms out to Nadia who more or less fell onto him.

Gunfire back at the building. But not aimed at them. Ryker shooting or being shot at. Gregor and Nadia shared a look but neither said a word before they set off. Nadia's adrenaline, with them so close to safety now, saw her nearly forget about her injury and she jogged almost unaided alongside Gregor as they moved into the darkness and for the getaway car.

Gregor sank down into the driver's seat, Nadia in the passenger side next to him.

He didn't start the engine.

'What should we do?' Nadia asked.

Gregor didn't answer.

He gazed across at the burning building. At the adjacent blue lights getting closer all the time.

'We have to go!' Nadia said. 'This could be our only chance.'

Gregor still said nothing. The police were approaching from the north. From the direction of the city. The getaway car he and Nadia sat in was to the southwest of the building. They probably didn't have much time sitting here, but at least they were away from the initial cavalry arriving.

'Babe, we have to go! Ryker's probably dead already!'

'It's not Ryker I'm worried about.'

'Please? I'm... scared.'

'No,' he said, absolute defiance. 'We came all this way for a reason. Something that's far bigger than me or you. So we wait for him. We see this through.'

36

Ryker pushed open the door and stumbled out onto the bitumen roof. He'd made it through three laboratories to get here, doing his best to barricade the doors behind him each time, but the chasing pack was still close. He could hear their shouts and more than once they'd taken potshots at him as he moved from room to room. He'd fired back too and was now out of ammo.

He rushed to the edge of the roof, the cumbersome holdall banging against his legs. Probably less cumbersome than having to drag Nadia, but it certainly hampered him still.

He peered down. Not three stories as he'd expected but one, because there was another flat roof below him.

He bent at the knees and flung himself over the edge, grasping hold of the top to let his body swing down. He let go and fell the few feet to the roof below. Heated air greeted him there. He'd heard the explosion a few moments ago. So big it had rocked the whole building. He saw the flames now, licking up the side of the building right by him. He'd no doubt the explosion, the fire, was down to Gregor and Nadia one way or another.

Whether they'd survived the blast was a very different question.

Ryker moved toward the next edge and looked down. Two floors this time. Grass below. The shouting behind him grew louder, closer. He glanced up to see three figures rush up to the end of the roof above him.

He really didn't have much choice.

A shot was fired his way, the bullet missing him by inches. He swung over the edge again, his legs dangling. Another bullet came his way, smacking into the rooftop right by his fingertips. A downspout sat a couple of feet to his left. Just within reach. He swung toward it, let go of the roof and grasped the metal pipe as tightly as he could, trying to wrap his ankles around it too. But he misjudged. Or just couldn't get a firm enough grip, and he plummeted, trying his hardest to keep hold and stop his momentum.

No luck. His body peeled away from the pipe, and he did as much as he could to turn himself over and roll into the impact. The holdall bounced away across the grass as his right shoulder and hip smacked into the ground. A heavy, painful fall. But he couldn't stop now. Within seconds those men would be at the edge, their guns trained on him.

Ryker grasped the holdall and ignored the pain shooting through him, the heat of the nearby fire too, and rushed for the fence.

He clambered over a broken section, taken out by the blast, he assumed. He heard shouting behind him. But he was in the darkness now. No potshots came his way but the guards, the police would fan out in this direction within seconds.

Ryker rushed for the car. At least, where the car had been. Would Gregor and Nadia have waited for him?

Doubts grew, as there was no sign of it in the dark.

At least not until he was only a few steps from it.

They'd waited for him after all.

'Get in!' Gregor shouted, firing up the engine, though leaving the headlights off.

He released the brake and got them moving, although took it steady rather than blasting off at speed. No one said a word until they'd reached the main road taking them further south and west from the Avto-Bio inferno.

'You took your time, old man,' Gregor said, catching Ryker's eye in the mirror.

Ryker huffed in agreement. He patted the holdall sitting next to him which was where Gregor's gaze fell next.

'So we really got it?' Gregor asked.

'We got everything we came for,' Ryker said, fanning out a couple of thumb drives in his hand.

Gregor yelled in delight, pounded the steering wheel a couple of times. Ryker beamed too. Nadia remained a whole lot more subdued.

'How's your leg?' Ryker asked her.

'Like someone drove a hundred nails into it.'

'We'll see to it as soon as we stop.'

'We will,' Gregor said. 'But first priority is to get out of Belarus.'

Ryker took his phone out.

'Has he come through?' Gregor asked.

Ryker stared at the message. A simple message. A time, and GPS co-ordinates.

'Yeah. He's come through.'

Winter always did.

* * *

It only took them a half hour to reach the rural location. They'd seen next to no traffic on the nighttime roads. No sign of police. Almost too good to be true, as though something bigger and badder was on the horizon for them.

They dumped the car in thick woodland and made their way on foot to the edge of the clearing where the helicopter was due in under an hour.

Not a long time to wait really, though for the three of them the minutes ticked by like days.

Ryker tended to Nadia's leg as best he could with the basic first aid kit they had. The bullet wound really wasn't that bad, only a graze. In fact, the nasty gash she had from the barbed wire was almost as bad. He treated both with antiseptic wipes and a gauze dressing while Gregor looked on, clutching at the holdall with his big prize inside.

'I got a lot of data too,' Ryker said to him. 'It'll take time to sift through, but we should have everything we need to blow open what the Russians have been doing. The whole world will know.'

'But will they?' Gregor asked.

Ryker didn't answer, as he didn't really understand the question.

'In a few minutes we're being picked up by people associated with the UK intelligence services,' Gregor added. 'You really think the likes of SIS are going to let us do this the way we want?'

'Peter Winter has a lot of influence. And he's a good man. He'll do the right thing here.'

'Or maybe they'll take everything from us and it'll all be buried. Maybe the intel, the evidence, will even just be used against Moscow behind closed doors for political points.'

'It won't happen like that,' Ryker said, even if he knew from experience that what Gregor said rang true. Sometimes, but certainly not always.

'But you don't know that do you?' Gregor said.

'I trust Winter.'

'That's not the same thing.'

Gregor finally let go of the holdall, pushing it to the ground as he got to his feet to look out across the clearing.

'Then what do you want to happen?' Ryker asked. 'We need his ride out of here.'

'Maybe we do. But that really is all I need.'

Ryker didn't like the way he said that. He liked even less the way he turned around and looked over Ryker's shoulder the next moment. To where Nadia was.

'Do it!' Gregor shouted out.

Ryker pulled his head down to his chest, a basic defensive move as he knew a blow was coming, but the crack of the gun against the back of his skull was still punishing. The second sent his head spinning. Then came a stab to his neck. A dull prick that was followed by a surge of cold liquid through his veins.

Gregor lunged on top of him, knocking Ryker to the ground, the younger man on top as he pummeled Ryker's face with his fists.

'Get the ties!' Gregor shouted.

Ryker roared with effort to throw Gregor off him. He managed it, tossing Gregor to the side who rolled and bounced back to his feet as Ryker took another hit to the head that sent his brain swimming.

He tried to get to his feet but ended slumped on his knees. He felt pressure on his wrists. A sharp tug as plastic dug deep into his skin, pulling his hands together.

The next moment Gregor kicked him in the shoulder and Ryker crumpled back down to the ground, his face smacking on the cold, wet grass. Two sets of ties for his wrists. Four sets of ties to his ankles.

'You... piece of shit,' Ryker slurred, unable to move as the tranquilizer took effect.

Gregor crouched down by his side, his confident grin, caught in the dim moonlight, making him look ghoulish. He searched through Ryker's pockets, taking the thumb drives.

'Thank you for your assistance,' he said, holding the device up. 'But I think I've got things from here.'

He patted the holdall. In the distance Ryker heard the whoop-whoop of the approaching chopper.

'You know your problem, Ryker?' Gregor asked. Ryker didn't even attempt an answer. 'You have an over-inflated opinion of yourself. It clouds your judgment. For example... you really probably thought you knew my parents better than I did, just because I was a young boy back then. But don't forget who they both were.'

He moved his face closer to Ryker's now. So close Ryker could smell the guy's coffee breath.

'I know who my mother was. She told me. She had to because she had to do everything to protect me if things went wrong.'

He pushed his nose right onto Ryker's and grabbed the back of Ryker's head to force their faces right together.

'I know what you did,' he hissed. 'I know what you did to them. I've always known.'

He let go, got to his feet and grabbed the holdall which he slung over his shoulder. Across the clearing the helicopter made its careful descent.

'We should kill him,' Nadia said, sounding all cool and calm now. Clearly she'd known all along. Perhaps her earlier nerve had been more about this part of the plan than the heist.

'No,' Gregor said. 'He doesn't need to die. Because I want him to see what comes next.' He found Ryker's eye once more, though it was becoming more and more of a struggle for Ryker to stay awake now. 'I told you before, Ryker. I'll make sure the people who destroyed my life are punished. And that's exactly what you're going to watch me do.'

Gregor and Nadia made their way over to the helicopter as Ryker's eyelids slid closed.

37

TWENTY YEARS AGO

Paphos, Cyprus

Clean the whole house. Everything.

Gun at the ready, he stepped inside.

With absolute silence he tiptoed across the carpet, moving around the edge of the bed, his eyes focused there, now accustomed to the dark. He could make out the two forms under the covers. He moved closer to the right-hand side, to Minko, the raspy sound of his breathing drawing Ryker in.

Ryker's shin touched the edge of the bed. He pulled the pistol up, pointed to the center mass of the man beneath the sheets. A simple plan: Two quick taps where he now aimed, then one final to the head, barrel to skull to make absolutely sure. After that, two quick taps to the other side of the bed.

Then a third there too to make absolutely sure...

Except he knew, despite everything he'd trained for, those second three pulls on the trigger would be much harder than the first set.

His finger pressed against the trigger. He felt resistance.

Bang. Bang.

But no sooner had he delivered the shots than the lights burst on and an alarm blared and he spotted Natasha across the room, darting toward him, rage spilling from her lips. He fired off toward her a moment before she clattered into him, but he'd been ready and she bounced off his steely frame and to the floor while he only had to take a knee as he backstepped.

Ryker pointed the gun toward her but he didn't get another shot off before Minko dove off the bed on top of him, roaring as a primal survival instinct surged. He knocked Ryker onto his back. Minko grabbed Ryker by the throat and tried to choke him, even as the two holes in his chest pumped out blood.

Ryker lifted the gun, the barrel a few inches from Minko's ear. Not the barrel to skin contact he had planned, but a lethal shot still.

He pulled the trigger and blood and brain splatted out the other side and onto the wall. Ryker heaved Minko off and saw Natasha there, standing over him, gun in hand now.

He quickly adjusted his aim as he rolled away and fired a rushed shot. She did the same. Both of them missed. Ryker bounced back up and launched himself forward. He took Natasha around the waist and they both flew through the air. Her back hit off the corner edge of the bed causing them to flip and she landed on top of him, momentarily knocking the wind from his lungs. He lost his gun in the process. She didn't.

She brought the barrel up toward his face.

But she didn't fire. And her hand was trembling. There was fight in her. But she hadn't lied earlier. She wasn't like Ryker.

'It doesn't have to end like this,' Ryker said.

Natasha said nothing but she looked terrified.

'This isn't you,' he said.

'You didn't just come to kill him, did you?' she said.

Ryker didn't answer.

'And Gregor?'

'He's fine.'

Thinking about her son, his fate, it looked like she was about to have a full breakdown, but then from nowhere her body, her grip on the gun, stiffened.

'You deserve this,' she said.

Ryker reached up and smashed his forearm into hers and when she pulled the trigger – a shot that would otherwise have ended him – the bullet headed wayward, into the wall behind him. Panic swept across her face as Ryker grabbed her hand and twisted her wrist, twisted her wrist as far and as fast as he could, and she pulled the trigger again just before the pain became too much for her. The shot went off. Ryker let go of her and the gun fell from her now loose grip and bounced off his shoulder and to the floor.

Natasha fell off him backward, gargling for breath as blood pulsed out of the hole in her chest.

Ryker got to his knees by her side and took hold of her hand.

'I'm sorry,' he said. An empty gesture, he knew. But he meant it. If there'd been another way...

He didn't wait for her to take her final breaths because he could hear the shouting below. The response to the alarm. And the response wouldn't just be from those in the house.

Feet bounded up the stairs.

Ryker took both guns and rushed for the door. He peeked out. No sign of Klaus or Calhoun or anyone else but Gregor stood in the doorway to his room, rubbing at his eyes.

'Gregor, come here,' Ryker whispered, beckoning him over.

The boy didn't move and the next second a head bobbed up t the top of the stairs before a spray of bullets swept Ryker's way. He reeled back inside. Stuck his head back out a moment later when the shooting paused.

'Gregor! Come here!' Ryker shouted.

This time he did move, racing toward Ryker who waited until he boy was only a few yards away before he swept out of the oom and scooped Gregor up in one arm. As he did so Klaus evealed his position, AK-47 in his hands. But he didn't fire. Not with Gregor's little body in the way.

But Ryker fired. Two shots. Both of them hit home. Leg, houlder. Not kill shots. So Ryker rushed forward with Gregor ouncing in his grip and he delivered one final bullet to the head nd Klaus's body flopped to the floor. Ryker knelt down to prize way the AK-47 but Gregor tried to worm free.

'No,' Ryker said, redoubling his grip. 'You stay with me. I'll eep you safe.'

'Mommy!' he shouted out as tears rolled.

'She's OK. We need to get you out of here. I'll take you to her. ou trust me, right?'

No answer either way. Ryker spotted movement downstairs.)nly Calhoun remained here tonight, but Ryker knew the ackup would be here within seconds.

'Calhoun!' Ryker shouted out. 'I've got the boy.'

No response.

Ryker edged to the top of the stairs.

No signs or sounds from Calhoun down below.

Ryker started down, taking the first three steps with care. `hen decided to go for it instead because he heard the furor of ehicles approaching.

He was on the second to last step when Calhoun poked out

from the kitchen doorway. He hesitated, just like Klaus had, th
human shield enough to cause a moment of doubt. That momen
cost him his life. The single bullet from Ryker's gun tore throug
his neck and he went down clutching the gushing wound a
though he thought he could somehow stem the flow.

Ryker dropped Gregor by the door.

'Don't move.'

He really didn't know if the boy would listen or not. Ryke
rushed to the kitchen and opened up every gas ring on the multi
burner cooker. He ran to the fireplace in the dining area an
yanked the cord behind the fitting and gas hissed out.

When he emerged in the hallway Gregor was nowhere to b
seen.

'Gregor!' Ryker shouted out.

Nothing. He didn't have time to dwell. He'd tried.

Headlights swept around outside as the vehicles made thei
final approach. Ryker was about to head toward the back bu
then saw Gregor reappear from the closet under the stairs, coa
and shoes now on, the little dinosaurs on his PJs sticking ou
beneath the thick coat that dropped down to his knees.

A horrible feeling tore in Ryker's gut.

He ignored it and scooped Gregor back up. 'Good boy. I'll ge
you to your mom. But we have to get out of the house.'

His phone vibrated in his pocket.

'Yeah?'

'Get out the back,' Winter said. 'Thirty seconds.'

The call ended. Ryker had no time to deliberate the meanin
of Winter's words before he heard the whoop-whoop of th
helicopter.

He rushed back through the kitchen. The smell of gas wa
almost overwhelming.

'Wait by the pool,' he shouted to Gregor as he opened up th

door. The boy rushed off. Ryker took aim at the cooker and fired. The blast wave from the gas igniting sent him flying back. He pulled himself up on the stone slabs outside then stepped forward toward the heat to kick the patio door closed to keep the flames concentrated inside. With any luck the fire would take hold soon enough. The house would be a shell before anyone was able to put it out.

'Gregor!' he shouted, and as he turned Ryker saw him cowering under a parasol, hands over his head to protect him from the swirling wind created by the helicopter's rotors.

The craft descended down onto the lawn a few yards away. A gunman sat at the open back, the meaty weapon pointed to the side of the house. Ryker didn't look there but as he ran forward to take Gregor once more the gunner opened fire.

'Hurry up!' came an almost entirely muffled voice from the helicopter. Winter, beckoning Ryker forward.

But then as Winter appeared at the back the look of urgency wavered.

'Ryker, no! You were told to clean everything!'

'He's coming with us.'

Ryker reached the helicopter; Gregor clung to him like a koala.

'We can't take him!' Winter shouted a moment before the gunner let rip again, causing everyone else to hunker.

'Look him in the eyes and tell him you're leaving him here!' Ryker screamed.

He glanced over his shoulder. The house was ablaze already.

'You take both of us or neither of us.'

As the words left his lips the new arrivals finally fired back, and bullets thwacked into the grass and one clanked into the front of the helicopter.

It was enough to cause Winter to relent and he shuffled

further inside giving Ryker space to haul himself and Gregor up and in.

As his foot left the grass the pilot was already taking the chopper back into the sky.

Within a few seconds they were airborne and heading away from the burning mansion.

38

PRESENT DAY

Northern Ukraine

Old demons – painful memories of his own brutal actions in the past – tormented him as Ryker took the quickest route south to the border. Whatever his next move, he first wanted to be out of Belarus where he'd be hunted as a fugitive. Ukraine was, for now, a safe place, even if he was damn sure it wasn't where he needed to be.

He arrived back in Ukraine on foot in the middle of the night, having dumped the stolen car he'd traveled in close to the border the other side. He took another car in Ukraine – along with a cell phone – from an unsuspecting customer at a gas station. Yes, he felt terrible about that, but was consoled by the fact that he really had little other option. Time was not on his side now.

He called Winter again. He'd tried several times already but perhaps the time of night or the fact he was calling from an unknown number meant his old ally hadn't yet answered.

But this time he did.

'It's me,' Ryker said.

A short pause before, 'Is it done?'

'Not exactly to plan.'

'Go on,' Winter said, not sounding in the least worried or surprised, as though he'd fully expected hiccups.

'Gregor tricked me. He knew about his parents. That I killed them.'

Another pause. Perhaps Winter was reliving that time too, like Ryker had so much over the years, but particularly recently. Except Winter had the easy job both then and now. He'd given the order, but it was Ryker who'd pulled the trigger. Then, and on many other occasions.

I'm not the same man now that I was then.

How he wished he believed his own words more.

'He was using me,' Ryker added.

Winter sighed. 'I did wonder. Those people sent after you in Antibes—'

Ryker clenched the phone a little more tightly. 'Weren't agents at all. Which is why you found nothing on them. They were probably acquaintances of Gregor's. Nothing to do with the Russians. He sent them looking for me because he needed help getting out of prison.'

'Except he got lucky on that. He was already out when those two found you.'

The two of them were trading thoughts as much as anything else. But it seemed like they were on the same page at least. For now. Because Ryker had to tell Winter what had happened at Avto-Bio, even if he knew Winter would explode.

'The Russians are circling in on him now,' Ryker said. 'Which explains why those two are dead or missing, and nearly everyone he associated with in Donetsk is the same.'

'OK. I get it, Ryker. But now it's probably a good time to tell me what the hell happened in Belarus. And what's about to happen next. Because I know you didn't call me in the middle of the night for a friendly chat. And I know I'm not going to like it.'

'No. You won't like it. Not one bit.'

* * *

You fucking idiot!' Winter screamed down the phone. Not for the first time. Ryker had known the man for many years, had pissed him off plenty of times, but had never heard the man shout like that. 'You've let a madman get away with a deadly virus! You decided not to tell me that you were in Belarus to steal evidence of Russia using biochemical weapons! You—'

'Winter. We don't have time for blame game.'

'This isn't blame—'

'He's going to use that virus. And he's going to kill thousands.'

'So where the hell did he go, Ryker? Where the hell is he?'

'He wants to punish the people who ruined his life. That's what he said to me. More than once.'

'Russia. You're telling me he's going to attack Russia. The Kremlin?'

Ryker said nothing, but it made sense. Gregor's mother had been a Russian spy, sent to steal secrets from Roman Minko about his plans for Ukraine. But other than that Gregor had no allegiance to that country or the regime, and he'd fought against them in Donbas and was now a wanted fugitive in Russia.

Back in the day, when the Russians gave Gregor's father their 'proposition' of assistance... Minko had had no choice but to concede. Ryker had been ordered to kill Minko largely because of that, but it hadn't stopped Russia. Bit by bit the president had gained proxy control of Eastern Ukraine until finally launching a full-scale invasion. He'd taken what he'd always wanted any way, destroying towns, cities and killing thousands of people on all sides.

Gregor's life, his family's lives, and the lives of all the people closest to him had been destroyed by Russia's aggression.

'What happened to the helicopter?' Ryker asked. 'Where did it land?'

'How the hell should I know! Maybe you didn't realize but I wasn't sitting at home at the ready watching live feeds of your botched mission, nor tracking live data of the helicopter I organized for your—'

'Find out where it went. As soon as you can. And... I need you to organize another transport. For me. To follow wherever Gregor went.'

'You're actually serious about that, aren't you?'

'I know you'll do the right thing.'

Ryker ended the call.

He didn't have to wait long for a response. Eight minutes. With his mind turning over thoughts at warp speed, it'd felt like eight seconds.

'I found the helicopter,' Winter said. 'The pilot too, who thankfully is still alive.'

'Where?'

'Poland. So they didn't go far.'

'Because they already had the next stage of their journey planned.'

Which only made Ryker all the more mad. He'd been well and truly played.

'Possibly,' Winter said. 'But why travel west into Poland if Moscow is the aim?'

Ryker already had the answer to that. It was the main thought that had churned as he waited for the call back. Winter's reveal of the helicopter's location had only confirmed it.

'Because he's not going to Russia.'

'But you said—'

'I know what I said, but I was wrong. Russia isn't his target.'

'You said he's going after the people who destroyed his life?'

'Yes. He is. It's us, Winter. He's going to England. So you need to get me there as soon as you can.'

* * *

It was still dark as the helicopter touched down at RAF Northolt, a few miles west of Central London. Winter greeted Ryker there and they rushed into a shiny black Range Rover before speeding off toward the motorway. They weren't alone in the back. A woman, thirties, with black hair pulled into a tight bun and angular glasses on an angular nose, sat the other side of Ryker.

'This is Susan Fairbourne,' Winter said. 'She's my biochem adviser. Susan, this is James Ryker, he's... Yeah.'

Ryker and Fairbourne briefly acknowledged each other.

'Have you found him?' Ryker asked Winter.

'No.'

Nothing more to the answer than that.

'And the lockdown?'

'We can't shut down the whole city,' Winter said. 'You must realize that. Even if there were absolutely no doubts here as to us dealing with an imminent attack, it's just too vast an area to cover with the resources we have.'

'Doubts?'

'We're working here on your say so, Ryker, and little else tangible.'

'You don't believe the threat is real?'

'Honestly, I have no goddamn idea. I'm not saying you're lying, but... do you know what's really happening?'

'Tell us more about the virus?' Fairbourne said. Biochem adviser. Although that really gave little information about who she worked for or exactly what her job entailed.

'I don't know much,' Ryker said. He briefly explained about the destroyed town in Ukraine, the mass grave. The comparisons Gregor had made to coronavirus, flu. Its apparent mortality rate, but also its delicateness. 'Does that all make sense to you?'

'One hundred percent,' Fairbourne said. 'It's no different to countless examples of lab-bred viruses that many countries have been researching, us included. It's likely the coronavirus that causes Covid-19 came about the same way, before it leaked either accidentally or deliberately.'

'But this virus has been specifically designed for use as a weapon,' Ryker said. 'To act over a small area, its sensitivity meaning it's unlikely to spread far.'

'It's plausible, if you have sufficient containment,' Fairbourne said.

'Containment? In a city of nearly nine million people,' Winter responded. 'So we're fucked?'

'It could cause a big problem if he has sufficient quantity of the virus,' Fairbourne said. 'And if he can find a way to release it over a large area.'

'So you're saying we're not fucked?' Winter asked.

'I'm saying it's highly unlikely that nine million people could be infected just like that,' she said with a click of her fingers. 'But this could still do some serious damage, if it's anything like what Ryker has described.'

Except she sounded doubtful. Ryker didn't know whether he felt positive about that or not.

'How is it weaponized?' she asked.

'I'm not sure it is. It's in canisters. A dozen. This big.' He showed with his hands.

'That means little without knowing the concentration.'

'I'm sorry. That's all I know.'

'But assuming each one contains the virus suspended in pressurized gas... all he needs to do is open those canisters in an enclosed environment and... we could have a big problem.'

'Enclosed environment,' Ryker said. 'That has to be it. He's not looking to infect the whole city. Based on what we know about the virus, I don't think he could anyway. He'd have to release it over hundreds of different sites. This is a targeted attack.'

'Then we need to shut down key sites,' Winter said. 'Parliament. Embassies. The royal palaces.'

'The underground,' Ryker said.

'It's seven in the morning. We'll hit peak rush hour soon enough. Do you have any idea how much police it would take to close off every underground station and manage the crowds?'

No one answered.

'Shit. Let me see what I can do.'

* * *

They arrived in Central London not long after, on the banks of the Thames outside a gloomy-looking office building, several stories tall. Not the more glamorous and well-known SIS headquarters at Vauxhall Cross a few miles down the river. This place was deliberately nondescript, used for clandestine meetings between people who lived and breathed the clandestine world. Ryker had been here once before, though not to the war room that they ended up in on the fourth floor which already had fifteen people hurriedly working on phones and computers. Ryker didn't know if this room was always occupied by these people, ready and waiting for an emergency assignment, or whether the crew had been hastily assembled in the small hours of the night as Ryker had traveled west.

Winter got everyone's attention. Clearly he was the most senior in the room and every eye turned to him as he laid out what he knew. A basic regurgitation of the conversation in the car.

'So we need to find Gregor Rebrov and Nadia Kozlova now. I want every airport, train station, bus station, every CCTV tower in the entire city under watch for them.'

Which Ryker knew was an impossibility in real time. There were likely tens of thousands of cameras across London, and only fifteen people in this room. But he got the point, and was sure everyone in the room did too. They'd work on the obvious first, major train routes into the city and the like, and narrow down from there.

'Could they have changed their appearances?' a young woman piped up, sticking her hand in the air like a kid would in school.

'Of course they could,' Winter said. 'But we can only work off what we know.'

'Kozlova was shot in the leg,' Ryker added. 'She'll be limping pretty badly. It might help identity her.'

'What about other accomplices?' another man called out. 'Are we sure we're only dealing with two people?'

'No,' Ryker said, jumping in before Winter could. 'I know for a fact that Rebrov has connections, followers perhaps. So it wouldn't surprise me at all if he has others working for him on this. But there were only twelve canisters, so the number of people actually carrying the virus can't be large.'

'But we're to make no assumptions,' Winter said a moment before a young suited man scuttled up to him and whispered something in his ear. Winter's face reddened in anger.

'OK. We currently have no agreement from the director general of MI5 or from the Met commissioner for a wholesale shutdown or evacuation of the underground, or of any key sites in the city. We need more evidence. We need it now. Where the hell is Rebrov?'

The question seemed rhetorical to Ryker, but three hands shot up in response. Winter pointed at the blonde woman on the right who had a headset lopsidedly hanging from her ear.

'I think we found how they arrived,' she said, looking somewhere between bewildered and ecstatic. 'A helicopter landed in Surrey this morning. It wasn't scheduled, they called in en route. Using tracking data I see that... the flight path is partially missing, but it came from Europe, and although it's a UK-registered—'

'OK, Hannah! Just tell me where it landed,' Winter said.

'About two miles from Redhill.'

'Brighton mainline,' Ryker said.

'Which would take him to where?' Winter asked.

'London Bridge or Victoria are the two end points here.'

'Someone get me a damn Tube map, now!' Winter shouted. 'And get hold of the CCTV towers from Redhill station. I want confirmation immediately if Rebrov and Kozlova have passed through there. Then we might just get the lockdown we need.'

Everyone rushed back to their positions and clicks of keyboards and hurried phone conversations filled the room. An A3-printed map of the London Underground was thrust in front of Winter who laid the paper out on a desk.

'Victoria and London Bridge,' he said, pointing to each station on the map. 'Both are right in the heart of the city.'

'The stations themselves could be the targets,' Fairbourne said. 'How many thousands of people pass through them on a typical weekday morning?'

'No,' Ryker said. 'He wants revenge. This won't be an indis
criminate attack on everyday people going to work.'

'Then what, Ryker?' Winter asked, sounding frustrated, bu
with Ryker more than the situation.

'Westminster is right by Victoria,' Ryker said, putting hi
finger on the map.

'Buckingham Palace isn't even a mile from there either,' Fair
bourne said.

'And there's at least Rebrov and Kozlova working togethe
Both places could be targets.'

'You think one of them is just going to walk right past th
guards at the palace and go find the king and let off this virus i
his face?' Winter asked.

Ryker didn't get a chance to answer the obviously facetiou
question because one of the guys in the room shot up from hi
desk and yelled out for attention. Ryker, Winter and Fairbourn
rushed over and were soon staring at CCTV footage from Redhi
station. The time stamp was a little over an hour ago.

'Is that them?' Winter said to Ryker.

He stared a few seconds longer at the screen. Not an old
school grainy CCTV image, this one was full color and high i
detail. Both Gregor and Nadia had changed clothes. Both ha
caps covering their heads. No big, bulky holdall now to carry th
virus but they each had a backpack over their shoulders. Even
he could see little of their faces, everything about their appear
ance told him who he was looking at.

'That's them,' Ryker said.

'It's not all,' said a woman across the room, the same woma
who'd earlier spoken up about appearances. A smile sprea
across her face, but she quickly wiped it away as though realizin
this wasn't the place. 'I think I have them at Victoria. Not eve
fifteen minutes ago.'

'We have to lock down what we can,' Fairbourne said. 'The station. Parliament. The palace.'

'Lock down?' Winter said, now sounding dubious even though that was what he'd been asking MI5 and the police for already. 'You want to trap some of the most important people in this country inside buildings that might soon have a deadly pathogen free-flowing through the air?'

'Based on my scenario modeling and the little else we know, it's the safest course of action,' Fairbourne said. 'And it's what I'll strongly recommend to the director, to MI5, to the Met. Take your emotion out of the situation, you must see it makes sense. If we evacuate those buildings after the virus is already released... the damage could be much worse.'

Winter looked to Ryker as though hoping he'd help him out.

'I agree,' Ryker said. 'Even if you evacuate now, you'd have to keep all the people quarantined somehow on the outside, to reduce any risk of spread. You'd have MPs, members of the royal family out in the open. It could create an even bigger target for a secondary attack.'

'Are you saying you think that's Gregor's plan? An outside attack? Bomb? Sniper?'

'No. I'm saying I think you should trust the advice.'

All eyes turned to Winter. 'Get me the director on the line,' he demanded. 'Now!'

39

The drive across London was typically slow, even with the police escort to help them weave through the clogged rush hour streets. Ryker, Winter and Fairbourne again traveled together in the back of the Range Rover. Winter spent most of the time on the phone, battling through various layers of bureaucracy. The biggest problem for him was that, in working for SIS, even as senior as he was, he had no official jurisdiction for operations on UK soil. Internal security was dictated by MI5 and police forces – the Metropolitan Police, within Central London. Ryker had no doubt both MI5 and the Met already had their own task forces rapidly working through the response here, but given how events had played out, Winter still found himself in an instructing role, sitting in the middle of the agencies who actually had the authority to make things happen.

'Tell me again what MI5 agreed to,' Ryker said as Fairbourne typed away on her laptop.

'The director general gave the go ahead to shut down the underground and clear Victoria station,' Winter said. 'Because we don't believe it was the main target so we don't think those people will be infected. Westminster and the palace are on lock-down. No one in, no one out.'

Fairbourne shook her head.

'What?'

'As long as it goes on record that I asked for Victoria to be locked down too. If Rebrov already released the virus in the station, then clearing everyone out of there only increases the chances of the virus spreading uncontrolled. Right now I'm working on a series of scenarios, but letting thousands of poten-tially already infected people out into the open is potentially a huge mistake.'

'Except we don't think the station is the target,' Winter said. 'Plus the police aren't letting anyone go yet.'

'No, Ryker doesn't think the station is the target. We're putting an awful lot of faith in his word.'

Winter stared at Ryker a moment, as though trying to decide whether that faith was well-placed or not.

'I agree with Ryker's assessment,' Winter said.

'Too damn late if you didn't,' Fairbourne responded.

'The priority now is to find Rebrov and Kozlova,' Winter added.

'Although we need to make sure they didn't simply surf out of the station in the crowd,' Ryker added. A fair point, he felt, although he only received a disgruntled grumble from Winter in response.

The outside of Victoria station was awash with yellow-jacketed police and throngs of confused pedestrians being ushered away from the entrances. Fairbourne remained in the car, crunching whatever data she was crunching, while Ryker and Winter pushed their way against the tide. Winter showed his credentials to a uniformed officer and eventually they found themselves on the much quieter and eerily calm inside of the

station where armed officers and highly trained sniffer dogs
roamed.

'Everyone's out, and no more trains can come in this way,' said
a man who'd introduced himself as Forsyth, a thickset man
decked out in tactical gear and carrying an M4 carbine loosely in
his grip.

'OK, I need to see the most recent security footage,' Winter
said to him.

'And we also need to know of every possible way out of this
place,' Ryker said. 'Not just pedestrian routes but commuter train
lines, service lines, maintenance tunnels, whatever.'

'I'm on it,' Forsyth said. 'Security's that way. I'll get you the
rest right now.'

He set off at a jog as Ryker and Winter were ushered into a
windowless security room by another armed officer. Two station
staff members sat in chairs inside, their faces ashen.

'You two control the security footage?' Winter asked.

Nods from both.

'Then let's get to work.'

They already had the time of Rebrov's initial appearance at
Victoria, but the team back at the SIS war room didn't have full
access to every feed under Transport for London's control, so they
hadn't so far any idea where Rebrov had gone after getting off his
train.

'He could be anywhere on the underground network by now,'
Winter said, not yet ready to put his doubts aside. But it was only
his nerves showing. Ryker trusted the process.

'That's him there,' Ryker said, pointing to the screen. 'Where
is that?'

'He's heading from the mainline station to the underground.'

'So he didn't go up onto the street?' Ryker said.

'At least not straight away.'

'She's not with him,' Winter added. Which was another ood point, because there was no sight of Kozlova on the creen.

'Did he get on another train?' Winter asked.

'The station serves the Victoria line, but also Circle and District, we have multiple platforms.'

'Then follow him, and see which platform he ends up on,' yker said.

'And do it quickly,' Winter said. 'Like, ten minutes ago uickly.'

'I am, but...'

'But what?'

'Going down on that south staircase, he should have ppeared on one of the other platform feeds by now,' the man aid.

'What are you saying?' Winter asked.

'That he... didn't. It doesn't make sense.'

'What else is down there?' Winter said. 'Service tunnels, nything like that.'

'Shit,' Ryker said, a horrible feeling creeping over him. 'Guy awkes.'

'Excuse me?' Winter said.

'You said before he's hardly going to walk straight past the uards into Buckingham Palace, up to the King. Same for arliament.'

The reality dawned on Winter. 'He's going in from nderneath.'

'And we just locked those places down. If the virus is ispersed, we—'

'Are there tunnels connecting Victoria to Westminster?' Winter asked.

'N... no... not that I know of?'

But the next moment Forsyth strode into the room wit reams of paper in his hands.

'Here we go,' he said, hurriedly unfolding the papers – map blueprints.

'We're looking for the south side,' Winter said.

Ryker had already found it. He placed his finger on the spo and traced it down.

'Where are the next cameras after that staircase?' he aske the security guy.

'Here. And here,' the guy responded, pointing to th locations.

'So we have a black spot here,' Ryker said, using his finger t circle the small area where Gregor had disappeared.

'And there's a service entrance to the train line right there Forsyth said.

Ryker followed the route onto the train line, then north, the east. A couple of hundred yards.

'There. What is that?'

He got no answer.

'Because it looks to me like it might be a direct link to Wes minster. That's where Gregor went.'

'Then you'd better damn well get after him,' Winter said.

* * *

Ryker had no weapon, but he had a gaggle of armed Met office: with him, Forsyth leading them. He also had an earpiece t communicate directly with Winter who'd stayed behind a Victoria to continue scouring for any sign of Gregor or Nadi and to continue his role of overseer.

Nadia's disappearance continued to worry Ryker as the traipsed along the quiet and dark tramline.

'We're coming up on the tunnel entrance now,' Ryker said for Winter's benefit.

Ryker stepped forward and tried the door. Unlocked. Because who the hell would come down here on a normal basis when the trains were running?

A thought struck Ryker. He didn't say it out loud because he didn't like the implication, but had Gregor lain in wait at the edge of the train line, waiting for the station to be locked down before he headed across it? Perhaps Ryker and Winter had handed him the opportunity to continue to his target safely.

'What the hell is this place?' one of the officers asked as the group entered the cold, dark and damp space, barely three feet wide, not quite six feet tall which meant Ryker and a couple of the others had to stoop to walk.

'Did you know tunnels have existed under London for hundreds of years?' someone else piped up. 'Since the fifteenth century, at least. For shelter from war. For storage. For moving contraband. Monks used them to store wine in. Then the Victorians used what was already there to build out their sewer network. There's hundreds of miles of the things, carrying all our shit away. But some of those original hundreds of years old tunnels still remain. Some are even unmapped because who the hell wants to cross over a river of sewage to go exploring?'

'Thanks for that, Brains,' Forsyth said.

'No worries, boss.'

'Next river of shit we get to, you go first.'

'Appreciate it, boss.'

'We're heading east now, right?' Forsyth said, tapping Ryker on the shoulder.

'Yeah,' Ryker said.

'Can't be far off Westminster.'

'No.' But then Ryker stopped because they'd come to a junction. No doors, but as well as the path ahead, another tunnel lay both to the left and the right.

'Winter, we're at a junction. About a hundred fifty yards into the tunnel.'

No response.

'Winter? Do you hear me?'

'Signal's no good with all this Victorian brick around you,' said Brains. Ryker had no idea if that was his actual nickname or not.

'We carry on east,' Ryker said, moving off, but unable to escape doubts. Torchlight from the officers' weapons continued to light the space ahead, giving perhaps fifty yards of clear sight before it all ended in a gloomy haze. Except as Ryker continued forward, that haze disappeared and the arcs of light got shorter and shorter. Ryker slowed up his pace a little.

'What is that?' Forsyth said.

Then Ryker realized. 'It's blocked.'

He continued forward, the rubble becoming clearer with each step he took. He came to a stop at the blockage. Not recent, he didn't think, judging by the slimy dampness dripping down some of the debris.

'Shit,' Forsyth said. He moved forward and poked the pile of bricks with his gun, as though testing whether he could knock through the barricade or not.

'I wouldn't push too hard,' Brains said. 'The whole structure this side could be weakened. We should backtrack.'

'You think Rebrov did this?' Forsyth asked.

Ryker said nothing, but turned and walked past the policemen, picking up his pace, his frustration growing too.

'Winter, do you hear me yet?'

Still no response.

They soon reached the junction again.

'Why are we stopping?' Forsyth said. 'You think there's another way around?'

'South will only take you under the river,' Brains said. 'If Westminster is his aim, no way he went that way.'

'We're not all rushing off north on a whim,' Forsyth said. 'You two...' He pointed to two of his men. 'Check it out. But the rest of us are going back to the station. We have to approach from above ground.'

'No,' Ryker said.

Forsyth shot him a glare.

'No, what?'

'I think I made a big mistake.'

Forsyth's face turned gloomy, angry.

'Westminster isn't his target.' He looked to the south tunnel. 'Where do you think that tunnel leads? Bearing in mind where we started?' He turned to Brains, sensing – hoping – perhaps he was the one who would know.

'I already told you. South. Under the river,' Brains said.

'Yeah. And what's the other side of the river?'

Brains shrugged, shook his head, but then his face dropped and he whispered an expletive.

'He's gone to Vauxhall Cross,' Ryker said. 'He's going to attack SIS headquarters.'

40

Vauxhall Cross was certainly not as prominent a target as Westminster or Buckingham Palace, if this were a simple terrorist plot. But for Gregor the situation was deeply personal. He didn't blame Russia for his parents' death, for the war. He didn't blame the British royals. Perhaps he didn't even blame the government. He blamed Ryker, Winter, SIS. He wanted them to suffer personally.

'Winter, do you hear me yet?' Ryker said for the umpteenth time. No response still.

'There's no point,' Forsyth said. 'It's not going to work now.'

Ryker would continue to try anyway. Only the two of them had carried on this way. Some others had gone to check the northern route, the rest had rushed back to Victoria station to update Winter, who'd have to make a call now that could potentially subject his boss, his many colleagues to their deaths. Would he instead change his tactic now and insist on an evacuation of SIS headquarters? Or lock everything down still and wait to see if Ryker – anyone – could stop Gregor in time?

'They probably don't even know yet,' Ryker said. 'So don't expect much help when we go up there. It's me and you.'

'Sounds fine to me.'

They reached a closed door. Ryker tried it. This one was locked. Interesting. But it wasn't a particularly good lock and two kicks saw the door splinter around the metal and Forsyth heaved it open.

'Where do you think we are right now?' he asked Ryker.

'I think we're right underneath.'

'Yep. That's what I thought too.'

They moved with a little more trepidation into the taller, wider corridor. Concrete here, rather than Victorian bricks.

'Up there, do you think?' Forsyth said, indicating to the metal ladder, attached to a shaft that rose up fifty feet above them. 'Ladies first.'

Ryker ignored the jibe and started off. Soon he stepped off the top of the ladder onto a small landing, another closed and locked door in front of them.

Forsyth joined him at the top.

'What are you waiting for?'

'I'm not sure my dainty little feet can handle it. But a big boy like you?'

Forsyth cackled before smashing his foot into the door. Nothing. He did it again. A creak, but nothing more. He hit it a third, fourth and fifth time. He put more venom into each strike, but with each one the smirk on his face fell further away, leaving an embarrassed scowl.

A sixth hit finally sent the door crashing inward.

'My. How strong you are,' Ryker said.

'Whatever.'

Forsyth pulled his gun to the ready now as they moved into a

concrete corridor. Much like the one below, except here there wa
lighting to guide them. They came to a junction.

'Winter, do you hear me yet?' Ryker said.

Still no response.

'How far below ground do you think we are now?' Forsy
asked.

'A couple of stories at most.'

'OK. We split up here,' Forsyth said.

'Agreed. We're looking for the air-conditioning maintenan
room. It's the obvious way for him to disperse the virus.'

'One way or another, I'll see you there,' Forsyth said. H
reached to his side and pulled out his Glock handgun an
pushed it out to Ryker.

'No,' Ryker said. 'You keep it. I'm not planning on shootir
anyone.'

'Whatever you say.'

Forsyth rushed off. Ryker moved away at pace too. He wei
through an unlocked door, up a set of metal stairs. Into y
another concrete corridor. Finally through another door and in
the bowels of Vauxhall Cross. Ryker knew the building well. He
never been to this spot but something about the place still fe
familiar, perhaps the smell, although he couldn't help but thir
about the airborne virus with every inhale he took.

This corridor was lit too, the concrete walls painted off-whit
the several doors he passed were green.

He followed the noise as much as anything else. A building
big as Vauxhall Cross required a substantial amount of HVA
equipment, and it was far from silent.

'Winter, do you hear me?'

'R... er... where... you?'

'SIS. Are they locked down?'

'SIS? What are... talking about?'

'Did the others not get back to you?'

As he took a few more steps the static cleared.

'Winter?'

'Ryker, what do you mean, SIS?'

'That's where I am. It's where I think Gregor is.'

'SIS, but—'

Just then Ryker heard thudding footsteps through the earbud, hurried voices. The police had only just made it back to Victoria. The people in SIS had no clue yet.

A bang further ahead stole Ryker's attention. He crouched low as he moved forward now. The bang came again. From behind a closed door. He tried the handle and slowly pushed the door open. A small storage room. Dark. Though with the light from the corridor Ryker spotted the bound and gagged figure on the floor straight away.

He rushed over and knelt down and pulled the cloth gag out of the security guard's mouth. He gasped for air.

'Where'd he go?' Ryker asked.

'No fucking idea!' He was mad rather than scared. 'I was right by the service elevator when he jumped me.'

'Is he alone?'

'Yeah. He's alone. And if you take these ties off, I'll tear him to pieces!'

Ryker didn't. He backtracked and closed the door behind him, though could still hear the guy beyond yelling expletives. Extra help would have been welcome if the guy wasn't so wound up.

Ryker ventured further forward, the whir of the HVAC system getting louder still. He pulled up against a corner. Thought he could hear faint footsteps the other side. Someone approaching stealthily.

At least until they pounced. But the moving shadow across

the concrete floor gave Ryker the warning he needed, and he crouched down and rushed out across the corridor and grabbed the lunging figure around the neck, wrestling them off the ground. He was about to slam them down onto their back when he realized who he had hold of.

'Ryker, get the hell off me!' Forsyth yelled.

Ryker let go and Forsyth splatted down but quickly jumped back to his feet.

'I nearly damn well shot you,' he said, retaking hold of his M4.

Ryker didn't bother to say anything to that. He looked along the corridor to the double doors only five yards away.

'You think that's where he is?' Forsyth asked.

'We're about to find out.'

They pulled up by the doors. Ryker gave the nod and in a quick motion he turned the handle and shoved open the door as Forsyth darted in, M4 held up to his face as he quickly scoped out the room. Not quickly enough as Gregor pounced from the side. He took hold of Forsyth and slammed him into the open door and then went to prize the gun free. Ryker grabbed hold of Gregor by the neck and tried to lever him off. The M4 blasted. Gregor let go of the weapon but kicked out at Forsyth to send him crashing backward and to the ground. At the same time Ryker twisted around and tossed Gregor to the floor in the other direction.

Both of the fallen men rose up to their feet, Forsyth intent on recovering his aim with his gun, Gregor intent on...

Pulling out a remote control. He held it aloft, his thumb hovering over the button.

No one said a word for a few moments as Ryker's eyes glanced at the mega-sized HVAC units in the room. Three in total, each the same make and model. Identical in every aspect, even down to the two metal canisters taped to the side of each, tubing connecting their outlets into the air system.

'You don't have to do that,' Ryker said.

But Gregor was focused on Forsyth and the gun now pointed at his head.

'You think you can cut me down before I press this switch?' Gregor said.

'He's not going to shoot you, Gregor,' Ryker said, before giving a 'calm' signal to Forsyth with his hand.

'Where's Nadia?' Ryker asked.

'We found her,' came Winter's voice in Ryker's ear. He'd forgotten all about that. Hadn't intended the question to be directed at him. 'On foot. Near Westminster. We got there just in time. But... she's dead Ryker. There was no other way.'

Ryker said nothing but Forsyth laughed.

'Your girlfriend's been taken down,' he said. 'Just like I'm gonna take you down whether you press that button or not.'

'No!' Ryker shouted at him. 'You're not going to shoot him.'

But Gregor looked mad now. 'Is that true?' he asked Ryker. 'She's dead?'

'It's what we just heard. I'm sorry.'

Gregor scoffed. 'No, Ryker. You're not. Not yet.'

'Gregor, please. We're not your enemy.'

'You always have been. I just didn't know it back then.'

'You're wrong. I didn't want it to end like that. Please believe me.'

'You murdered her! Both of them. You executed them! Because of the say-so of the people above us right now!'

'Yes, I killed your father. But... your mother attacked me. I had no choice.'

'And what about me?' Gregor said. 'You were supposed to kill me too? I remember the argument you had with your boss when he saw I was with you.'

'I was told to kill you all. I couldn't do it.'

'You destroyed my life.'

'No. The Russians did.'

'But they were always going to attack. You, your people, had the chance to stop them, but instead chose to kill my family. Then the uprising, then the war. Nothing. You even have the chance to stop the Russians still today. But no one up there ever has. They never will. Because we don't matter.'

His thumb twitched and Ryker flinched. 'Please! Gregor, listen.'

Gregor paused, flicking his gaze back and forth between Ryker and Forsyth.

'With the evidence you have of the virus, we can make a difference. Where'd you put the thumb drives? There's enough data on there for us to expose the truth to the whole world.'

'You know as well as I do that'll never happen.'

'Forsyth, do you have a shot?' Winter asked. 'Take him out as soon as you can. We don't have time for drama.'

'No!' Ryker shouted, to Gregor's surprise. 'We're not shooting him down. Gregor, you can still change this. Do the right thing. What would your father think of this? Your mother? Is this what they would have wanted? For you?'

Gregor snarled as his thumb moved once more.

'Ryker!' Forsyth shouted.

'No! Wait. Just... wait. Gregor. Listen to me carefully.' He had the kid's attention, but not for long. He was running out of hope, patience. 'Don't push the button. Your life ends if you do that.'

'You think I'm scared of being infected?' he scoffed.

'I'm not talking about the virus. I'm talking about what comes next.'

'I'm prepared to die for this.'

'No,' Ryker said. 'I don't think you are. Because you'd die for absolutely nothing.'

'Not nothing. I'd—'

'You wouldn't kill a single person up there.'

Gregor looked confused.

'There is no virus.'

Dubious. He didn't want to believe the words, but Ryker saw the doubt in his eyes.

'When you and Nadia left me... I made sure you left the virus with me.'

He shook his head but didn't respond.

'I already doubted you then,' Ryker said. 'It just didn't make sense. Those two people coming to find me in Antibes. Them disappearing soon after. Nadia, and how she so quickly went along by my side to find you. I'm sorry, but I never fully trusted you. And I couldn't risk that virus getting out for the wrong reasons.'

'You're lying.'

'I'm not lying. I put the real canisters in the incinerator. The ones you have are empty. Nothing but air.'

'Ryker, what the hell kind of bullshit is this?' Winter shouted. 'Are you actually egging him on to push the button?'

'Put the remote down. This might not end as badly as you think for you.'

But he didn't put it down. The next moment his thumb hit the red plastic.

Forsyth fired. Three shots. Each one hit Gregor's Kevlar vest. The power of the hits was enough to send him to the floor and the remote flew from his grip.

But he'd already pushed the button. A green light on the small circuit board next to each pair of canisters blinked and

then the sound of pressurized gas releasing rose above the din
the HVAC units.

'Fuck,' Forsyth said, covering his mouth and nose with h
arm. 'We're all dead.'

'Ryker. What the hell is happening?'

Ryker didn't bother to cover his face. Or to respond to Winte
He knelt down next to Gregor whose face was twisted in pain. H
clutched his chest as he sat up.

'You were... lying?' Gregor said. 'Please tell me you we
lying.'

Ryker slowly shook his head.

'No,' he said. 'I wasn't.'

Gregor roared in despair as his head slumped to the ground.

41

———

A benefit of already being at SIS headquarters was that Ryker didn't need to go anywhere else for the initial debrief. Within moments of Gregor accepting his fate, swarms of police had arrived on the scene, and he'd been taken away in cuffs. Winter had arrived not long after, in a foul-tempered mood, and pretty soon Ryker was on the top floor of Vauxhall Cross in a small ante-room outside the closed door of the director's office. Winter had gone inside five minutes earlier, and when the door next opened Ryker thought he was about to be beckoned in too, but instead Winter closed the door behind him and took a seat by Ryker.

'He's on the phone to the prime minister and some of the key cabinet members.' Winter said. 'After that he needs to debrief the Met, MI5. Then it's your turn. So you've got a while to come up with a damn good explanation for that shit you've pulled.'

'Excuse me?'

'What were you thinking?'

'Isn't it obvious? I didn't want a live and deadly virus out in the open.'

'But you could have told me about the bloody plan! We've

thousands of police officers out there thinking this was a real threat, thousands of innocent people too who—'

'Who won't be dying anytime soon because of that one decision I made.'

'Gregor never needed to have made it to the UK at all. If you'd just told me about Avto-Bio I could have done this properly.'

'But would that really have happened?'

Winter glared at him but said nothing.

'I know you're high up now in this organization,' Ryker said, 'but you still answer to the man behind that door. Who still answers to a group of politicians who know nothing about our world. And despite what they all say they only really care about clinging on to their own positions of power.'

'Now you're twisting things. Even for you, this was just ridiculously... reckless.'

'Reckless? Other than Nadia Kozlova, not a single person died today.'

'That's not the point! As far as everyone knew, we were up against a live threat here.'

'Exactly. And that's the way it had to be. Because honestly? I didn't know Gregor's full plan. I didn't know his exact targets. I didn't know how many other people he had helping him. By letting it all play out, knowing the virus was never a threat... we got to see exactly what he intended. Plus you, MI5, the Met, got to see exactly where your pitfalls are for this sort of thing. I mean... Gregor literally walked into SIS and very nearly wreaked havoc.'

'Oh, so now we're supposed to be thanking you for highlighting the failures in our security measures.'

'You know what? I really think you should be.'

Winter thought about saying something else but then only huffed and shook his head and looked away.

'The point is, the virus is real,' Ryker said. 'And we can still find the evidence to blow open what Russia did in Ukraine. And what happened today in London happened in broad view of the public. It'll be reported around the world. There's no hiding from it. It'll help to tell the story, to convince people that this was real and that it's the Kremlin that caused this.'

Winter still said nothing, but Ryker could tell he didn't agree at all. The door to the director's office opened and his assistant stared out.

'He's ready for you now.'

Ryker got to his feet. Winter stayed where he was.

'You're not coming too?' Ryker asked.

'You don't need me in there. You have all the answers, after all.'

Ryker said nothing to that and moved for the door.

* * *

Two weeks later

There was no doubt Winter's frostiness had mellowed as the story of the day London was nearly paralyzed by a deadly biochemical weapon played out across the world's news. No mention was made of Ryker, or the fact the virus had never made it to British shores. Only that the threat had been quickly neutralized by the joint efforts of the police and the UK's security services. Heroes.

Fine by Ryker.

He met Winter outside the visitor section of Belmarsh Prison on a frosty gray morning. The first time they'd met face to face since the big day.

'Good morning,' Ryker said, not sounding as cheery as he'd wanted to, but he still felt little happiness about the situation.

Still felt immense guilt too about how his hand had started the events twenty years ago.

'Better than some I've had,' Winter responded.

'Thanks for agreeing to this.'

Winter humphed but said nothing.

'Any news on the virus?' Ryker asked. He really wished he already knew the answer to that, but he'd been well and truly sidelined over the last two weeks and as tempting as it was to find answers himself, he knew that'd only further sour Winter's impression of him.

'No,' Winter said. 'Just one of the many pitfalls to your ill thought-out plan. Apparently, Avto-Bio's labs were destroyed in an explosion. The night you were there, surprise, surprise. There's nothing left. No virus, no records about any development or use of viruses as weapons for the Russian government.'

The whole facility destroyed? Certainly not from that one explosion in the south corner. So that was either a lie from the Russians or the facility had been levelled at some point after as a cover-up.

'What about the town in Ukraine?' Ryker asked. 'The mass grave? The virus is likely still frozen in those bodies.'

'There are no bodies. We had an SAS team fly in there three days ago. The town's been razed. There's evidence of trenches or... something, but no bodies.'

Ryker closed his eyes a moment, trying not to let the feeling of despair take over.

'You're dealing with something far more powerful here than just you or I,' Winter said. 'The Russian government aren't just going to let a secret like this come out. Leave evidence of it lying around. Of course they're denying it all. The attack in London was by a pro-Ukrainian terrorist, and everything else is conspir

cy, propaganda. They've come out of this looking pretty damn
sy.'

'Except I got the evidence out,' Ryker said. 'Gregor stole it
om me. I know it's still out there somewhere.'

'Then you'd better go in and find out where the hell he put it.'

* * *

ot a normal interview room at all, but Gregor was no ordinary
risoner. He sat on a chair in a huge glass box in the middle of a
ig black room. No other prisoners in here, no guards either, just
 lot of cameras keeping watch from several different angles.
yker sat in a chair in front of Gregor, the other side of the glass.

'Nice place you got here,' Ryker said.

Gregor smiled. 'I quite like it,' he said, his voice muffled
rough the glass which only had a small square with a series of
r holes drilled through it to aid their conversation. 'You've been
 a gulag, haven't you? This place is real luxury in comparison.'

'I'm sorry about Nadia,' Ryker said.

Gregor's smile faded.

'I mean that,' Ryker added. 'She didn't have to die. For you.'

'You played a dangerous game.'

'I only went along with your game.'

'You're lucky I didn't walk around London spraying bullets
om an AR15.'

'But I knew you wouldn't do that,' Ryker said.

'You don't know anything about me.'

'I knew a lot about your parents. And, in different ways, I see
em both in you.'

Gregor clenched his cuffed hands together, anger no doubt
ubbling away inside at Ryker's mention of them.

'I really did care for her,' Ryker said.

'You can stop talking about my mother now.'

'But you have to think about who she was. She would hav
betrayed your father eventually. And who knows how that woul
have turned out. For them. For you.'

'I said I don't want to talk about her. About either of them.'

'But I do. I'm sorry for what I did. I wish I'd had the strengt
then to say no.'

'It wasn't about strength. It was about morals, decency. Yo
have none.'

'Maybe you're right. Back then, at least. But I know I'd neve
follow through with an order like that anymore.'

'Because you're this new man now? Bullshit. You're just th
same.'

'I know I won't change your opinion on me. But you can sti
help your father's cause.'

Gregor's eyes pinched, his jaw clenched. He was gettir
madder and madder.

'I'm serious,' Ryker said. 'I know you hate me—'

'You have no idea.'

'I followed the order and killed your parents. But it was th
Russians who forced our hand. Think about the bigger pictur
We were trying to stop a war.'

'Your actions probably made everything even worse.'

And that thought stung Ryker, because he had no way c
disproving it, even if he didn't believe it.

'The Russians are the aggressors,' Ryker said. 'Whatever I di
then to try and stop it, they're the ones who've destroyed you
homeland, your father's legacy. They're the ones who killed you
friends, who let that virus run amok through an entire village.'

'You need to go,' Gregor said through gritted teeth.

'I will. And I see your anger. But you know what I'm saying
right. While you're sitting here, those atrocities will go unpur

ished. More could occur too. Because we don't have enough leverage to stop them.'

'It's not true. Your government could send the army in tomorrow if they wanted.'

'But we both know that will never happen, rightly or wrongly. You can still make a difference here though. Tell me where you hid the thumb drives.'

No response.

'I know you didn't destroy the data.'

'You really think I'll help you after everything you did to my family.'

'I told you before, I'm not that man anymore.'

'And I told you before, you're exactly that man.'

'I can still make a difference outside these walls. You can too. Do it for your mother and father. For Nadia.'

Gregor tried to stay strong, tried to stay angry, but as his body trembled from rage and other conflicting emotions, his eyes welled with tears.

'Please,' Ryker said. 'Help stop what happened in Nadia's village from ever happening again.'

Gregor said nothing but nodded in response.

* * *

One month later
Antibes, France

It may only have been early spring, but together with the bright sunshine on the Côte d'Azur, it felt a world away from the dreary weather in England, the frigidness of Ukraine and Russia. He had no plans to go back to any of those places anytime soon.

He walked along the promenade, checking his watch. He'd

arrived a little early so stretching his legs wouldn't do any harm. His phone vibrated and he hesitated a moment before answering.

'Winter, how are you?'

'You've been watching the news, haven't you?'

Actually, he'd watched it closely. Hours a day watching TV broadcasts, scouring news articles, social media, message boards. The leaked data from Avto-Bio had caused an international storm for Russia. Sanctions that Western countries had imposed at the start of the war in 2022 had been ramped up several fold. The immediate impact was a near destruction of the Russian economy and a crippling of their frontline efforts in Ukraine. But the president and all of his powerful cronies remained defiant, belligerent, claiming all of the leaks, all of the evidence of biochemical weapons were fabrications. That in fact, they had evidence that Ukraine had used such weapons.

And so the war rumbled on, propaganda and lies covering the truth and at times making it impossible for independent eyes to determine which was which.

But the truth was out there at least, and in the long run it would help.

'I've been catching it here and there,' Ryker said.

'Ha, yeah, good try. Anyway, where are you?'

'Just taking a break in the sun.'

'Antibes?'

How'd he know? Ryker looked around him as though expecting to see his old friend, or maybe just someone Winter had sent to follow him.

'Yeah,' Ryker said.

He saw no one.

'I sensed you might have some unfinished business there.'

Ryker didn't respond.

'But I'm not calling to talk about that. I'm calling to talk about what's next.'

'What is next?'

'Plenty more where we left off. That's what.'

'I thought I'd be off your list after... you know.'

Winter sighed. 'Yeah. Me too. But... you remain a unique talent, Ryker. And a good friend.'

Goose bumps ran along Ryker's spine at that. In a good way.

'One question for you, though,' Ryker said.

'Yeah?'

'Back in Cyprus. When you gave me the order—'

'Ryker, we really don't have to talk about this anymore.'

'But I want to. You gave me the order and—'

'I've regretted it ever since. Even at that time I regretted it, but it came from above me.'

'Mackie.'

'Yes. And believe me, we fell out big-time. It's why you didn't see me for several months after that. I was cast out for a while until I built his trust up again.'

'But you still gave me the order. To kill the Minkos. Gregor included.'

'I did. I wish I hadn't. And I know I wouldn't give that order now. It didn't have to end like that. But just like you think you're different now... so am I.'

And Ryker really did take comfort in that.

'I'll let you know when I'm ready,' he said.

'But Ryker—'

He didn't wait to hear what Winter had to say next because he ended the call when he spotted her parking her car outside the police station across the other side of the main road. He jogged over and she noticed him coming just as she reached the revolving doors.

'James?'

'Charlotte.'

'You're... back.'

'I am.'

She looked around, a little embarrassed.

'I'm surprised,' she said.

'Why?'

'You got what you wanted here, didn't you? Put down the bad guys.'

'I did my part. I heard what happened.'

'Pichon?'

'Yeah. Stabbed to death in jail.'

'Why would Litvinov ever let him stand trial? It's what powerful men like him do.'

'But he is still behind bars.'

'For now. Awaiting trial. But I don't hold my breath. What I do is check over my shoulder every time I get out of my car, every time I leave my apartment.'

'You think you're a target?'

'Of course I do.'

'Sounds like you could do with an extra pair of eyes around here for a while then?'

She scoffed. 'You really think I want you around?'

'You have to say the result last time I was here wasn't so bad.. really.'

'The outcome may have been good, but not the deceit.'

'I'm sorry.'

'Don't tell me, you're a changed man or some other bullshit.'

He cringed at that. She wouldn't understand.

'I'm here to see you. Not for any kind of work,' he said. 'Honestly? I need a break.'

Silence from her now but he sensed she was mellowing a little.

'So I'll take you to dinner after work?' he suggested.

'How do you know I'm not seeing someone else now?'

'I don't... Are you?'

'With my work life? Of course not.' She sighed. 'But I'm not sure I've forgiven you yet either or forgotten that I told you I wanted to see you behind bars.'

He decided it best not to say anything about that.

'But... maybe... maybe if you stick around here a while... I won't lock you up after all.'

'I'll pick you up later then?' Ryker said. 'Say seven?'

She said nothing but couldn't hold back a smile before she spun on her heel and headed inside.

Ryker watched her until she was out of sight, then turned and headed back toward the ocean.

* * *

MORE FROM ROB SINCLAIR

Another thriller from Rob Sinclair, *Dance with the Enemy*, is available to order now here:

www.mybook.to/Dance_EnemyBackAd

ABOUT THE AUTHOR

Rob Sinclair is the million copy bestseller of over twenty thrillers, including the James Ryker series. Rob previously studied Biochemistry at Nottingham University. He also worked for a global accounting firm for 13 years, specialising in global fraud investigations.

Sign up to Rob Sinclair's mailing list for news, competitions and updates on future books.

Visit Rob's website: www.robsinclairauthor.com

Follow Rob on social media here:

facebook.com/robsinclairauthor

x.com/rsinclairauthor

bookbub.com/authors/rob-sinclair

goodreads.com/robsinclair

THE
Murder
LIST

**THE MURDER LIST IS A NEWSLETTER
DEDICATED TO SPINE-CHILLING FICTION
AND GRIPPING PAGE-TURNERS!**

**SIGN UP TO MAKE SURE YOU'RE ON OUR
HIT LIST FOR EXCLUSIVE DEALS, AUTHOR
CONTENT, AND COMPETITIONS.**

SIGN UP TO OUR
NEWSLETTER

BIT.LY/THEMURDERLISTNEWS

Boldwood

Boldwood Books is an award-winning fiction publishing company seeking out the best stories from around the world.

Find out more at www.boldwoodbooks.com

Join our reader community for brilliant books, competitions and offers!

Follow us
@BoldwoodBooks
@TheBoldBookClub

Sign up to our weekly deals newsletter

https://bit.ly/BoldwoodBNewsletter

Printed in Great Britain
by Amazon

58236195R00218